LOST AND BOUND

Lost and Bound

Book One of the Displaced Series

BRYAN SCHARF

Reliably Chaotic

I want to give special thanks to my wonderful players and great friends: Andrew, Nicole, Matt, Matthew, and J.J. for lending me their skills and storytelling abilities, their wonderful characters and creativity, and time spent exploring this world together. Without their contributions, this story would have been nothing more than an empty shell, a dusty folder on my desktop, a forgotten idea in the back of my mind. They are the real heroes of this story and a light in dark places.

AUTHOR'S NOTE

This book concept came to me when discussing the idea of running a campaign with friends where we were regular people from all across time who were ripped from our homes and dragged into a magical world filled with wonder and creatures we in our small existences had never considered to be possible. A young man, raised on a southern plantation in early America, a samurai warrior practiced and honorable in battle, a young woman seeking to hunt down Jack the Ripper and stop his reign of terror, all suddenly facing down dragons and monsters. Sounded like a really fun campaign to be a part of.

Well, all you tabletop role players out there know how that one went. We talked about our characters, loved the idea, and it went nowhere. It went in the bin and dissolved into memory, until one day when I was putzing around with what could possibly be done with my group now that we were coming to the close of a nearly three year long campaign. This displacement idea seemed like a good one, seemed like something they'd all have fun with, but there was something about it that wasn't quite right. The light bulb went on and I realized I needed to flip the script.

I gave my players the guidelines, told them they had to make human characters, whatever they wanted except for a particular class, but they had to be human. I gave them no insight as to what they were about to be facing save for one of them. They needed an inside man, and so I let one of them in on the secret. Game day finally came, and they were ready for their next foray into the magical realms. Except this time, that's not what they got. What they got was magical player characters in the very much non-magical world of modern day America. The script fully flipped, my players went out into a fully sandboxed world that I had created out of my few trips to Boston, beginning their battle for survival and search for a way home.

There was a post online recently where a writer said they just watched their characters make poor decisions and they wrote up the incident report. I found it amusing since it came out right after session fourteen of the campaign as I was settling in to knowing these characters well enough to put their story to 'paper.' That is literally all I am doing. I am writing up the incident report in the best way possible to depict what my players are doing in this world. I warn you now, some decisions may not make sense to you (as they don't make much sense to me), there may be plot holes that come from players fully forgetting things that happen in game as the weeks go on, and character death may come before storylines are resolved. I am changing nothing of the story; I am on this ride with you, dear readers, as much as you are with me.

Now sit back, relax, and get ready to shake your head along with me as we go into the tale of the Displaced Campaign.

~ 1 ~

LUIS

As Luis L'hopital opened his eyes they were assaulted with the flaring brightness of pure white. Above him were squares of white flecked with imperfections banded into perfect rows with white lines. The walls of the room he found himself in were smooth white, illuminated by bars of white light that hummed above his head. For a brief moment, he thought he was adrift in a void of white nothingness.

A rhythmic noise, shrill and irritating pulsed in time with the blood that rushed through his aching head. He tried to move, but his arms felt heavier than they ever had through any of his battles or training he'd undergone. Looking down at himself, he found that he was covered in an itchy white blanket, his arms lying placidly on top where he could clearly see a white bracelet latched to his right wrist. Peering closer, Luis saw there was writing on the bracelet: J. Doe 26964.

Something was wrong, the world was in chaos and Luis knew what to do at any time when he needed order restored to his life. Closing his pale blue eyes, Luis calmed his mind and reached out to his goddess, to Nike, herald of Victory, the name he invoked when charging into battle, whose strength was lent to him in times of need, whose calming touch allowed him to face down the beasts of hell without flinching.

Whose presence he could no longer feel.

Panic gripped his chest. Throughout the past decade he had never had his ties with Nike severed. She had always been there, proclaiming that victory would soon be at hand so long as his faith held. The irritating tone intensified and his head began to ache further. The air he sucked in was harsh and burned his throat with every breath. What evil had brought him here? He tried again to reach out with his senses, to breach the veil of what might be hidden with the power of the divine, but again the power eluded him, and again his breathing intensified along with the shrill noise.

"Easy there!" A voice pierced through his panic. Luis looked up to see a woman enter the room, pulling back a white curtain that had hidden the door she entered through from his sight. She was wearing strange clothing, a white tunic and loose fitting pants that seem to be decorated with three strange monkeys repeating in different positions, but her green eyes were calm and offered reassurance. Luis found himself relaxing slightly as the woman came into view.

She checked a couple of the strange devices Luis had barely taken notice of in his panic, brushing away one errant lock of blonde hair that had escaped the tail she had pulled it into. Luis tried to address the woman, but his voice came out in a harsh croak rather than actual words.

"You shouldn't try to talk yet," the woman said, turning to a strange pink pitcher and cup that were sitting on a white table across the room. She poured what looked like water into the cup before putting a strange white stick into it.

"Here," she said, pressing the stick to Luis' cracked and dry lips. "Drink slowly, you don't want to throw up."

After a few sputtering attempts, Luis realized the stick was hollow like a reed and drank readily from the cup. The water was cold, and amazingly had chunks of ice floating in it. He was curious as to how such a thing was possible, but the refreshment that came along with the drink soon drove such curiosities from his mind. After a moment he pulled back and the woman took the cup away.

After clearing his throat, Luis attempted to speak again.

"Where the fuck are we?"

There was a flicker of surprise on the woman's face, but she returned to her calming demeanor a moment later. Luis was beginning to feel his strength return and guarded himself against her disarming persona. He wanted to be ready in case she were a foe.

"You are at St. Augustine's," was the only answer she gave him, as if it should answer his question. Luis felt irritation rise in the back of his mind.

"Who the fuck is St. Augustine?" Luis asked, his voice getting stronger. The woman looked at him strangely, but decided to answer as she started unhooking frail looking cords and pressing her foot against his bed, which made several loud clicking noises. The shrill noise stopped.

"He was a great religious figure, focused on spirituality and the Holy Trinity, though to be honest theology was not my area of study." Luis felt the bed beneath him begin to move and gripped the rails on either side of him tightly as he began to move.

"Where are we going?" He asked, unable to keep a slight tinge of panic from his voice.

"You are scheduled for therapy with Dr. Courser," the woman said without answering anything.

A large man stood in the doorway of Luis' room. He was wide and strong looking, wearing clothing very similar to the woman's, though without the monkey creatures on it. His dark hair was cropped short, much like Luis' own light brown hair, and instantly Luis recognized the man as a member of one military or another. He felt his body tense, but saw the same comforting look in this man's eyes as he'd seen in the woman, though there was a sense of apprehension hidden in the look as well.

"Need help getting this one into the chair, Emily?" the man asked the woman Luis now assumed was named Emily.

"Thank you, *Nurse Sanchez*," Emily stated, emphasizing the title. "And I'll remind you in a professional setting, you need to refer to me as Nurse Corbit."

"Right, I'll remember that," Sanchez said in a voice that Luis believed that the man had no such intention.

Sanchez flipped the blankets off of Luis' lap and lowered one of the rails he was gripping. Slowly, Luis relaxed his grip, though he realized that he would not have had the strength to stop Sanchez from removing him if need be. The man quickly and easily lifted Luis bodily out of the bed and set him into a chair that had a large pair of wheels on either side of it.

Nurse Emily Corbit began walking down the hallway in one direction as Sanchez began pushing Luis down the other way, the wheels silently carrying him through a blur of more white walls and ceilings only occasionally passing a brown wooden door. Finally, after a dizzying journey through maze-like passages, they stopped outside a white door with a long pane of glass set vertically above the handle. A small black box rested on the left-hand side of the door. Sanchez reached over with a small white square in his hand. The box beeped and Sanchez opened the door, wheeling Luis inside.

Several other people were sitting within. Each, like him, was sitting in a chair with wheels and wearing the same paper-like clothing. All except for one woman who sat at the head of the room. She was wearing a long white coat over strange but seemingly formal attire. Her skin and hair were both dark, contrasting her sharp, light eyes. She held a bit of wood in her hand and seemed to be writing on it with a plume-less quill. A pair of spectacles rested on the bridge of her nose.

"Thank you, orderly," she said, gesturing at Sanchez, barely taking the time to look away from what she was doing. "If you would, put him in the circle. And then you are dismissed."

Sanchez nodded to her and pushed Luis to join in with the others. He looked around at those around him.

Sitting closest to the dark skinned woman was an older man with a short grizzled beard of grey and black hairs. He sat placidly, his eyes half closed as if on the verge of taking a nap. Luis wasn't fooled. The old man was more dangerous than he let on, clearly to those who knew what to look for that he was taking in information and processing it. For what purposes, Luis did not know.

To his left was a young woman with short brown hair and a band of freckles under her darting green eyes. She was fidgeting absent-mindedly with the sleeve of her tunic, revealing hints of a tribal tattoo banding around her bicep. As he watched her, Luis got the impression of a captured animal seeking any means of escape.

Beside her was a young man, about Luis' age, sitting peacefully as if in meditation and with such stillness that Luis questioned if the man were still alive. Though the scars that cut white marks into the deep tan skin along his knuckles, wrists, and arms proved that death would have a hard time taking such a man.

Finally, he met the grey eyes of the last one sitting in the circle. Long platinum hair spilled over this man's tunic, though even with all that covered his skin, the number of twisting tattoos that crept from beneath would have been impossible to hide, even if he had any intention of doing so. There was a flicker of devotion in this man's eyes that Luis felt a kinship with, but could not explain why.

Luis turned his attention to the woman sitting at the front of the room. She sat with posture that indicated she was in complete control of her surroundings, and considering he had barely any control over his body currently, she must be the one behind his weakness. Staring at her, his eyes burning like embers, he decidedly broke the silence.

"If you are a witch, I will find out." His voice was strong, far stronger than it was when he first spoke to Emily in the white room. It drew the attention of everyone in the room and caused the woman to stop writing.

She lowered her quill and turned to address Luis.

"I am not a witch. I am a medical professional," she said in a calm voice that further raised Luis' irritation rather than abated it. "My name is Dr. Mercedes Courser. I am the head psychologist here at St. Augustine. You are all here because each of you is suffering from delusions. We here just want to help you overcome these delusions, become well, and reenter society as fully functioning members. Why don't we all go around and introduce ourselves and why we are here, like I did?"

Dr. Courser's eyes burned into Luis', but he did not flinch.

"My name is Luis L'hopital," Luis stated proudly. "And I have been sent out on a mission by my master. Beyond that, you need not know."

"Master," Dr. Courser said cautiously. "That is a strange word to use when depicting another person in your life. You do not need to ever refer to any one as your master, because in this world no one has mastery over you. You do understand that, don't you?"

"It seems you are the one lacking understanding of what it is to have a master willing to take you in," Luis retorted.

"Perhaps, but we'll get into that later on in our sessions." She turned her attention to the tan skinned man covered in scars sitting next to Luis. "What about you?"

Without opening his eyes, the man spoke, his voice carrying a hint of a brogue. "My name is Thola Igerk Mue Moonflayer."

Dr. Courser, who had been writing when the man started his response, paused. "Uh... Excuse me?"

"Thola Igerk Mue Moonflayer," the man repeated.

"Could you spell that?" Dr. Courser asked.

The man sighed, opening his dark green eyes to look pointedly at the doctor. "Just call me Timm."

"Timm," Dr. Courser repeated with more confidence in her voice. "We can work with that. And why are you here, Timm?"

"Damned if I know," Timm said, shrugging. "Woke up here with this lot, didn't I? Figured you'd be the one to tell me."

"I suppose that's to be expected. You all suffered from a bit of trauma that left your memories a bit... incomplete."

"I remember just fine," piped up the older man, opening one eye. "Ma damned kids are obnoxious little brats who ain't got no respect for their elders. Stuck me in here saying I'm seeing things."

"Seeing things? What do you mean by that Franson?" Dr. Courser asked.

"I told you not to call me that!" The man barked. "Call me Smithers or don't call me at all."

"My apologies Mr. Smithers..."

"Just Smithers!"

"My apologies, Smithers," Dr. Courser said, her smile appearing forced and tired. "What kind of things did you see?"

"I ain't telling you," Smithers snorted. "Last time I talked about it, they locked me in here with the crazies."

Dr. Courser clicked her tongue, "Now Smithers, we don't like to use that word here. Crazy is a very insensitive and over simplistic way of describing the plight of others."

"The boot fits, don't it?"

With a sigh, Dr. Courser turned her attention to the young woman. "And what about you, dear?"

"Uh... Morgan. Betony." The woman stuttered slightly. "My name is Morgan Betony. And... I'm kind of a medical person as well. I was out collecting herbs last I remember, then I was here."

"Collecting herbs?" Dr. Courser asked, a hint of skepticism in her voice.

"Oh yes," Morgan's voice lost some of its apprehension. "There are many wonderful herbs for healing by my home. I was out collecting to create a salve for..."

"You know, modern medicine has come a long way," Dr. Courser cut her off. "Those old world methods are dangerous and could actually cause more harm than good. You'd be better off allowing actual medical professionals, doctors such as myself, handle tending to the sick."

Luis watched as Morgan deflated slightly under the words of Dr. Courser and felt hot words fleck at the end of his tongue before the final person in the room cut him off. The man with platinum hair turned to Dr. Courser and spoke in a calm, clear voice.

"I'd never heard of doctors before, but I am a healer and found that herbs work quite well to aid in the process. I have healed the wounds of many in my time."

"And where did you study in order to gain the skill to heal?" Dr. Courser asked him.

"The temple," the man replied plainly. "My name is Lee Eraple, cleric and priest of Goibniu, God of the forge and hospitality. Perhaps you should study his teachings as well."

Luis could not help but smile at the remark. It both brought this Dr. Courser down a peg or two, but also explained why Luis felt such kinship with Lee. It was good to see another holy man in these trying times, and if his order had taught him anything, it was that there was strength in numbers.

Dr. Courser put on that strained smile again while facing Lee. "Yes, it seems that we have been less that hospitable with some of you..."

"We were drugged," Timm replied, for the first time letting irritation slip into his voice. "I do not like when someone takes away my ability to use my body properly."

"You'll find that it was necessary," Dr. Courser explained. "With the trauma, confusion, and memory loss, some of you were more... violent... than others."

She turned her attention fully to Timm, "It seems you left Orderly Sanchez with a black eye for weeks upon your admission to the hospital."

Timm cowed slightly at the remark, but before he was given another chance to speak, Dr. Courser changed the subject.

"Since we now all know a little more about one another, why don't we get into today's therapy session? Group therapy is a great way for us to understand how other people think and how we should best respond to different, and sometimes conflicting, ideas. I am going to ask you a series of questions, and I want each of you to respond with the answer you feel best reflects your point of view, do you all understand?"

Luis understood, but he was feeling particularly contrary, so he merely folded his arms and nodded while the others murmured in the affirmative.

"Very good," Dr. Courser said. She shuffled through pages attached to the wood she was writing on and began. "Under what circumstances do you feel it is acceptable to hurt another person?"

Luis felt the answer leave his mouth before his mind could even formulate the answer. His time training at the temple had taught him the answer, "If they are evil."

Lee nodded and answered as well, "If they are trying to harm you."

"Or someone else," Morgan piped up, but pulled back again a moment later. "Or an animal, or something..."

"When your life is in danger," Timm stated plainly.

"I'm with them," Smithers agreed. "When you got to defend yourself."

"Very good," Dr. Courser said, Luis sensing only a slight bit of condescension in her voice. "Let's move on to question number two: Would you help someone whose life was in danger, regardless of who they were?"

"Yes," Luis answered with the same resolve as the last question, but locked eyes with Dr. Courser and added, "then ask questions later."

"Yes." Lee nodded again, but offered no further explanation.

"Depends on the situation," Timm shrugged. "Were they harming others first? Were they put into this situation because of evil actions? It all depends."

"Of course," Morgan stated, giving Timm a quick look. "Lives should not be cut short unnecessarily."

"Yeah, I suppose so," Smithers answered.

"Some conflicting opinions, but all in all seems like the consensus is still to help others, very good." Dr. Courser nodded as she continued making notes. "Question three: What would you name a boat if you had one?"

Luis felt his eyebrow creep up slightly. He did not have an immediate answer to this one, but his memory flashed back to a gentler time before the soldier's life had taken him completely and heard his voice say, "The Pink Corsage."

"An interesting choice," Dr. Courser said, making note.

"Edwards," Lee responded, solemnly. "After someone who died."

"Nicolisa," Timm said, wincing slightly before looking at Lee. "After... a relative."

"Gotta be a boat?" Smithers asked, a wicked grin under his graying beard. "Had a tractor once named John."

"The Tempest," Morgan said.

"Ah, a Shakespeare fan, I see," Dr. Courser said, making note on her papers.

Morgan looked at her in confusion, "Who's Shakespeare?"

"Someone who shook a spear," Luis chimed in with a shrug.

"Ah," Morgan replied.

Dr. Courser looked at them with confusion, but apparently decided this course of conversation was not worth pursuing. "Next question then: What was the most foolish thing you've ever done that has caused yourself harm?"

"These questions," Timm said, leaning back in his chair slightly. Luis smiled at this and looked to Dr. Courser before she could fire back at Timm.

"Jousting with no armor," he said plainly. He knew that he had done this before, though as he tried to recount the memory, a sharp pain went through the back of his skull.

Dr. Courser, who had been looking at Timm in aggravation, quickly turned her attention to Luis. "Ah, I see, so you were a reenactor?"

"No," Luis replied. "I am not an actor."

Confusion crept across Dr. Courser's face, and Luis found himself reveling in it. As confusing as the world he found himself in, it seems that his own life confused this obnoxious woman just as much. However, before she could press further, Lee spoke up thoughtfully.

"I never really did anything to cause myself harm out of foolishness," he pondered. "I suppose you could count the times I stood between another and harm. I did nothing in that instance, though I suppose doing nothing is as much an action as doing something."

Dr. Courser turned her attention from Luis to Lee, "That's a noble way to come to harm, though it's never shameful to defend one's self."

"Nor is it shameful not to," Lee responded.

The room was silent for a moment, as tension seemed to grow between Lee and Dr. Courser. Morgan then broke the silence as she suddenly seemed to think of her own answer.

"Oh! Well there was this one time when I was talking to this bear..." she started to explain.

All eyes in the room turned to look at her with a mix of confusion and surprise.

"What?" she asked, "We were having a nice chat, and then my niece and nephew burst out of the hut, and the poor thing got spooked. Wasn't the bear's fault I got slashed."

"Uh," Smithers said, drawing out the sound. "On that note, ya know how guns have safeties on them?"

"Moving on to question five," Dr. Courser said, cutting him off. "What quality do you value most in another person?"

"Loyalty," Luis said, again without hesitation.

"Determination," Lee said with the same conviction as Luis.

"Kindness," Morgan said, folding her hands in her lap.

"Compassion," Timm responded, his voice dropped so low Luis could barely hear him. As he looked at the man, Luis noted that Timm lowered his eyes, hiding his own expression.

"They on my lawn?" Smithers asked.

"Let's assume not," Dr. Courser, smiled at Smithers.

"Then we good," he responded, leaning back and cupping his hands behind his head, eyes closing again.

"Well," Dr. Courser said, placing her quill down. "I think that has given me a good place to start with your files and how we should move forward with therapy. I believe I have asked you quite enough questions. Do you have any for me?"

"Where are we?" Morgan asked.

"You are in St. Augustine's Hospital," Dr. Courser answered.

"No," Morgan shook her head. "We've been told that plenty of times. But where is St. Augustine?"

"Well, St. Augustine was renovated from an older mental hospital here in the city of Boston, Massachusetts," Dr. Courser explained. "I assure you that you are perfectly safe here and have not been sent far at all from where you were discovered after your traumatic incident."

"When will we be allowed to leave?" Luis asked, bluntly.

Dr. Courser smiled at him. "When we deem you fit to reenter society."

"And when will that be?" Luis pressed.

"After our evaluations are complete," Dr. Courser answered just as vaguely as before.

"Is there any way we can speed that process along?" Luis asked. "I have gold."

Dr. Courser shook her head. "It is not a matter of money or bribery. It is my job to make sure you are not a danger to yourself or others, in that instance..."

The lights above them began to flicker before settling again. Dr. Courser let out a despondent sigh.

"It seems that's all the time we have for today. I need to go check on a few things, so in the meantime you may talk amongst your-selves." She stood and walked across the room to the door, pressing another square to a black panel on the inside of the door. It made a beeping sound and she pulled the door open by the handle. "The orderlies will be along to collect you all and return you to your rooms shortly."

With that, Dr. Courser left the room and Luis looked around at the strangers who sat before him. He flexed his fingers, feeling the drugs in his system wearing off. He looked over at Timm and Lee. Both of them nodded to him and a silent pact was made. Wherever this Boston was, they were soon going to be seeing a lot more of it.

~ 2 ~

TIMM

Timm saw the determination in both Lee and Luis' eyes, and felt a similar flame of conviction flicker to life in him that he had not felt since the last time he was in his master's presence. These, he determined, were men of similar quality. While trying to gather his thoughts he noted the older man, Smithers, open his eyes and look in his direction.

"So, now that the doc's gone, where are y'all from?" The man's wavering voice seemed to direct to the room in spite of holding eye contact with Timm.

Timm started to answer, but felt the names of his homeland escape him. The world around him was alien to him, but he did not think that it was responsible for his lapse in memory. For a moment he clawed at the fleeting wisps of memory before Luis broke the silence.

"Another world, it seems, from this one," the man's strong voice came out, bringing Timm back to the present. This was a skill he remembered his master once told him would be one of his greatest challenges. And at the very least, that memory was intact.

"Right," Smithers said, drawing the word out and casting a quick glance at the door.

"Right now we need to take stock of our assets," Luis continued. "I don't have my weapons or armor with me. Are any of you magic users?"

Lee and Morgan both raised their hands in response.

"I am a healer," Lee responded, concisely.

"I have some magic," Morgan said, her voice more timid. "Some healing, but I can do... other things too. Um... of a more... natural persuasion."

"Very well," Luis nodded, seeming to find their answers satisfactory. He then turned to Smithers. "I'm assuming you're from this world... Massachusetts."

"Well, actually I'm from much further south, but been staying here in Boston lately," Smithers answered.

"So Boston is a city in the country of Massachusetts?" Morgan asked.

"Uh... no," Smithers said, giving her a confused look. "Boston is a city in the state of Massachusetts. One of the fifty states."

"I see," Luis said. "Your world is made up of fifty provinces called states?"

"Our country is," Smithers said. "There are lots of other ones across the planet."

"Massachusetts is a state within your country then?" Morgan asked, and Smithers nodded to her. "Then what country is that?"

"Murica," Smithers answered plainly.

"This must be a different kingdom then. Do you have a strong king?" Luis asked.

"The guy's a complete dumbass," Smithers said with a wave of his hand.

"Then would you like to come with us to our world, once we find a way back?" Morgan asked him. "Considering you have such an incompetent leader?"

"Nah," Smithers said. "I'll just wait for them to vote for the lesser evil next time we get the chance."

Timm, getting bored with the conversation and not seeing how it was helping them in the present, stood up and began walking on unsteady feet. Slowly he felt himself regaining his balance and strength. With every step he grew more confident and after a moment found himself at the door that Doctor Courser had exited out of. He tried the handle, and strangely felt it move under his grasp, however when he tried to open the door it seemed the latch had not disengaged after all.

"You need the card," Timm heard Smithers call from behind him. He turned to face the old man.

"What do you mean, card?" Morgan asked Smithers, walking over to the door next to Timm.

"Didja see that square plastic thing she had in her hand?" Smithers asked. Morgan shrugged slightly, but Timm nodded his head though he was unsure of what the word 'plastic' meant. Smithers continued, "Well you take that, and the RFID chip in it activates the door when you press it against that box there."

Smithers pointed to the wall next to the door. Timm turned to look and saw a black box mounted to the wall with a red light blinking in one corner.

"Is this some kind of magic?" Morgan asked, examining the box closely.

"Magic?" Smithers laughed. "Of course not."

"Well then," Morgan said, "Perhaps we can find a way to—"

Timm drew back his fist and slammed it into the black box, which burst into shards and fell to the floor. Satisfaction swelled in his chest as Timm watched the little red light fade to dark.

"Try it now," Timm said, proudly. He turned to see Morgan's shocked expression at the abrupt action flicker away to a more composed look before she nodded at him and tried the door.

It was still locked.

Timm felt his cheeks grow warm as his head drooped slightly. He was unsure of why he felt embarrassed, however he found it difficult to look at Morgan. Keeping his head low he mumbled out,

"Well... could you maybe turn into something small and go under the door? You're a druid, right?"

Morgan smiled at him and said, "Yes, but I'm not that powerful yet. I still have to learn more before I am able to unlock that ability in myself."

"Oh," Timm said timidly.

The sound of heavy footfalls echoed down the hallway, causing Timm and Luis to snap to attention. Two men in white shirts and tan colored pants approached the doorway. One held a card in his hand like the one Smithers had described while the other carried a small black box with him.

"Sir," said the one with the card. "I need you to back away from the door."

Timm shot a quick look to Luis, who nodded at him. Giving the knight a nod back, Timm turned to face the men, held his hands up, and took a long step back from the door. The man with the card stepped forward and his hand moved out of view through the window. There was a beep and a click and the door opened before the two men stepped inside.

"Okay," the one with the card said, "now I just need you to go back to your wheelchair and sit down. We're going to take you back to your rooms for your medicine."

In response, Timm moved forward, channeling all the speed his training had given him and threw an upward punch into the man's stomach, forcing him to double over and heave. Before he had a chance to recover, Timm threw his opposite elbow across the man's jaw. His jaw cracked audibly, and as he hit the ground, Timm was confident the man would stay there for quite a while.

Before the other man, the one with the black box, could react, Timm pivoted around him in an attempt to block his path through the open door while simultaneously keeping the door from swinging shut and locking them inside. Confusion flickered clearly across the man's face before it was set into an expression of fury at Timm.

Which is why he didn't see it coming when Luis hit him from behind with the folding chair that Doctor Courser had been sitting on during their session. The man staggered forward but did not fall. Turning, he saw Luis, chair in hand.

"Come at me, bitch!" Luis taunted him.

Timm saw the anger in the man's eyes flash as he gripped the little black box tighter in his hand. It began to hum and then flashed with a crackle of blue light as he lunged at Luis.

"Oh crap," Timm looked up to see Smithers, who hadn't gotten up from his seat, looking at the box in the man's hand. "Taser!"

Luis jerked his head back, narrowly missing having what Smithers called a taser get stabbed into his neck. Looking at the weapon and the worry it caused the native Smithers, Timm lunged forward again, narrowly dodging Morgan as she pulled the body of the unconscious man out of the way of the fighting. He felt a surge of pride in the girl's actions, putting herself in harm's way to keep others out of the path of danger. He did not get the chance to think too much on that, however, as he saw the man preparing another strike against Luis.

Arms moving with the fluid speed of a serpent, Timm wrapped them around the man's neck in a constricting lock. Tightening his grip, Timm felt his blood choke take hold and the man began to struggle against his attacker in what little time he had left before blacking out.

Timm's master had trained him many ways that someone would try to get out of this kind of hold. Some would writhe and twist until they slipped free, others would attempt to rely on brute strength to break the hold, while still others would attempt to drive a weapon blade first into a vital point, breaking his concentration on the lock. However, it was only the body hardening and pain tolerance training his master had put him through that allowed him to retain his hold on the man as he lifted the taser and simply touched Timm's exposed skin.

Pain flooded Timm's body, as if lightning had been called down upon him. He twitched and spasmed against the small weapon's powerful assault, and screamed out for someone to land the finishing blow.

Luis obliged as he swung the chair again. However, it seemed that in an attempt to avoid hitting Timm with the chair, the knight's attack came up a little short. As luck would have it, though the chair missed its target, it clipped the taser in the man's hand and ended its effect on Timm. Seizing the moment, Timm tightened his grip on the man's throat, and after a brief struggle he felt the man slump to unconsciousness in his arms.

"Thanks for the help," Timm said to Luis, as the knight helped him to his feet.

"No problem," Luis said, looking around the room. "No one else seemed to be of much use."

Timm followed his gaze and took stock of what the rest of the group was doing. Smithers, only just getting out of his chair, wandered over to the taser laying on the ground and picked it up to inspect. Timm shuddered at the thought of the device and thought if the old man wanted it, he could have it.

Turning to look behind him, he saw Lee and Morgan tending to the man that he had first knocked out. Though once they were sure he was stable, they began rifling through his pockets for anything useful. Timm walked over to see what they had found.

"Anything useful?" Timm asked.

Lee held up a folded pouch of leather. "This seems to have some kind of importance to it."

"There's a... card?" Morgan said, searching for the right words. "There's a card in there with a picture of his face on it. And a name, Vasquez Juan."

"It's his wallet and ID," Smithers said, walking over. "See if there's any money in there."

"Like gold?" Lee asked.

Smithers sighed, and Timm noted some irritation in the fringes of the man's voice. "Green paper. Look for any green paper in his wallet."

Morgan flipped through it and pulled a few pieces of paper out. "One of these says five and the other says ten, oh! And this one says... fro-yo." She turned and looked up at Smithers. "What is fro-yo?"

"An abomination to ice cream," Smithers said, taking the papers that didn't say fro-yo on them from her. "Let's take this, his key card, and get the hell out of here."

"I'm taking his clothes," Timm said hurriedly and he began to strip the man down.

"Why in the hell are you doing that?" Smithers asked.

"Could be a good disguise," Timm responded, stripping his own clothing off in order to exchange it for the man's. As he did, he noticed Morgan turn away quickly, her cheeks slightly red. Quickly, Timm flipped the man's pants over to cover himself, and something tumbled across the floor with a metallic clatter. Luis bent over and picked it up.

"What is this?" he asked, holding up the metallic tube.

"Ah, now we're talking," Smithers said. "A friction lock."

"A what?" Luis asked.

"See that button on the side?" Smithers asked, pointing to the device. Luis examined it and nodded. "Push it and flick your wrist."

Luis did as Smithers instructed and the small metal tube expanded out into a short club about the length of Timm's forearm.

"A weapon," Luis said, satisfaction in his voice. "This will do until I get my sword back."

"Sword, right..." Smithers said. "Do y'all work for one of them Renaissance Faires or something?"

Timm finished pulling on the man's shoes, a size just under his own, but would do for now, and looked up at Smithers. "A what kind of faire?"

"Never mind," Smithers sighed. "So, what do we do now?"

"We get out of here," Lee said, peering out the door and down the hallway. "The path seems to be clear for now. We should move quickly."

"I like this plan," Smithers said, "Lead the way."

Lee nodded and began to skulk down the hallway. Timm waited until everyone else had left the room and took up the rear position as they made their way deeper into the heart of St. Augustine in hopes of finding their way out.

~ 3 ~

LEE

Lee continued down the hallway, not bothering to check and see if the people who had been with him during that Courser woman's interrogation were following him. While he appreciated their zeal and determination, the violence with which Timm and Luis acted was a bit much for him. Lee had hoped that there would have been some discourse and attempt at reason before jumping forth into full-blown assault, but it seemed Timm had other plans. He could hardly blame Luis for jumping in as he did, since violence was upon them, however he was disturbed with the apparent thrill the man got from it. Thankfully no one had been killed, but without skilled healing Lee believed the men they had felled would have a long recovery ahead of them.

That was, however, not his current predicament. Lee found himself surrounded by strange folk in a world he did not know and could not hope to understand without further information. He determined, then, that the only way to navigate this world would be to find that information and filter through it until he learned enough to get by, and then learned enough to get home. Where Timm used his fists as his first defense against this world, Lee would use his mind.

The long hallway Lee found himself in was peppered with several more doorways. As he passed, he took quick glances in them

~ 24 ~

and found that they were for the most part dark inside. Unlike the room they were kept in, the doors did not seem to be sealed with what the man Smithers called a key card, but rather were locked with typical, albeit rather small, locks in their handles. Lee tried several of these doors, but found them all to be locked.

Halfway down the hallway he came to a room with a placard bolted to the door. The placard read 'Human Resources,' and had a light on inside. Peering in, Lee found the room to be empty, and tried the door. With barely any sound, the door swung inward. Quickly, he shot a look over his shoulder to see that the others he had been with were indeed following them. He nodded at the open door and slipped inside.

The room was furnished with a large metal desk covered in stacks of paper, a strange chair that seemed to have been built with very small wheels on its legs, and rows of metal squares piled on top of one another. Between a pair of these metal boxes on the opposite wall to the one he entered from was another door that opened onto another hallway. Lee found it strange that this room had two entrances, but continued his investigation. Stranger still, there was a glowing box sitting on the desk that had images flashing across it of places that Lee had never seen before, but had heard some tales of by sailors and other travelers who would tell in the markets of...

Lee shook his head. For some reason his mind couldn't grasp the name of his home. Try as he might to recall, it eluded him as though he were trying to grasp smoke in his hands. Returning his mind to his work, Lee began going through the papers on the desk.

"What are you looking for?" Lee looked up to see Morgan peering at the papers as well, though seemingly unsure of what the task could accomplish.

"They've had us here for a while," Lee responded, continuing to pour over the paperwork. The filing system seemed familiar to him, lending some credit to the claim the 'doctor' made about working with medicine. "And they seemed to know quite a bit about us. They must have some kind of file on us, or something, here. If we find it, we may know why they took us. Or at least, what they intended to do with us."

"How does that help us get out?" Luis asked, his eyes scanning up and down the hallway they had come from through the open door, keeping watch for any approaching danger.

"It doesn't," Lee answered, returning to his search. "But if they come after us again once we're out, I'd rather know why and what we're facing. Ah-ha!"

Lee had found something at last. The image of a wheel, its spokes drawn to create a horizontal hammer flashed out at him. It was the image of the holy symbol of Goibniu he wore around his neck. Either he had found their file on him, or another follower of Goibniu who they had captured. He began reading through the file.

D.I.A.R.D. Case File: 57076

Contents: Medieval style weaponry and armor. Shipped to facility for storage.

Jewelry as pictured above. Kept in a secure location on site for transport.

Lee read the file over again and again, but was unable to make any more sense of what D.I.A.R.D. was or where his belongings could be kept. He noticed Luis taking note of his discovery and walking over.

"The holy symbol of my god," Lee explained before Luis could ask. "But there isn't much more use than this."

"Allow me to take a look," Luis said before turning to Timm. "Keep watch."

Timm nodded and went to the door as Luis began digging through the papers on the desk. It was not long before Luis found a similar paper with a large, black check drawn across the top.

"What is that?" Lee asked.

"The holy symbol of my goddess," Luis explained. "Nike."

"You worship Nike?" Smithers asked, unable to keep a note of amusement from his voice. Lee noted that Luis didn't seem to notice it.

"Yes," Luis replied. "My goddess will bring me to victory, and I shall praise her name in glory."

He began to read the paper and didn't see Smithers shake a bit as he laughed silently to himself. Lee was unsure of what amused the old man enough to bring him to this level of mockery, but he did not feel now was the time to broach the subject.

"It just says 26964 and lists my belongings," Luis said, snapping Lee out of his thoughts. "Some are in a facility, whatever that means, and some are on site."

"Seems like not all our stuff is gone from here," Smithers said, recovering from his laughter. "If we can find where they're keeping it, we won't have to wander around on the streets in medical gowns. Might be a good first step."

"That would be good," Luis nodded. "But what are these numbers? How are they associated with us?"

Lee pondered this also, but had not come to any conclusion. He was ready to dismiss it when Morgan bounded up in excitement and grabbed him by the wrist, examining the little bracelet he had found on his wrist upon awakening. She then went over and did the same to Luis, who was far more prepared for the sudden breach of personal space.

"They're the same!" she cried out. Lee looked at her in confusion, then down at the bracelet. Printed in blocky grey letters, Lee saw the numbers 57076.

"The numbers on the bracelet, they match the numbers on our files," Lee said, understanding.

Making quick work of the filing system, now that the code had been broken, Lee managed to find each of their files in turn as they called out their numbers. Each seemed to state the same information about larger belongings being sent to the facility, while smaller items were kept on site for the time being. There was one that differed from the others. As Lee read through Smithers' file, he found some confusing information.

"Smithers, your name is on your file," Lee said, looking up. "It says 'F. Smithers.' And it says you refused to leave your... truck?"

He paused over the word, confused. Then he looked up.

"Just F? Do you really dislike your name that much?"

"Don't ask," Smithers said, clearly annoyed. "But if ma truck's still here, means we got a way out. Hopefully my keys are in that storage unit. Otherwise we're hotwiring her to get out of here, and I don't want to do that to my baby."

Lee, still unsure of what a truck was or why the F was an issue for Smithers, decided that his answer was sufficient enough to prove they had a means of escape were they able to find it. This was acceptable and he decided to leave it at that.

Smithers walked over to a plaque on the wall by the door. "According to the fire escape map, we just have to get downstairs and there's a nurses station in front of the doors, but it looks like two hallways that have rooms large enough to be storage rooms on either side of it. If we can just get past the nurse on duty, we should be able to find our stuff and get the hell out of here."

Smithers mapped the escape out, showing them the path he intended to take, and Lee found it pretty straightforward. Finally, he felt that they had a solid plan and a means of escape. Which meant that of course something had to come along and shatter his confidence.

"Then let's go," Timm said, opening the door and beginning to head the direction Smithers had indicated.

With more strength and speed than Lee had given the older man credit for, Smithers reached forward and grabbed Timm by the back of his newly acquired shirt and pulled him back into the room.

"What is wrong with you dumbasses?" Smithers snarled. "There is a camera right above this door! It can see you the second you walk out."

"What?" Morgan exclaimed in astonishment. "Like a scrying spell?"

"I can't even begin to deal with you right now..." Smithers said, placing his face in one hand for a moment, taking a deep breath before opening his eyes and continuing. "Think of it more like magic viewing boxes. Whatever it's looking at, people in another location can watch."

As Smithers explained this to the group, Lee began to formulate ways of getting around these boxes, looking for blind spots and holes they could use to their advantage to move through and...

And Timm jumped up and broke it.

"There," Timm said, beaming with pride. "Now they can't see us."

Lee watched in amazement as Smithers' body began to shake and his face turned red. It was a typical reaction to something that angers you, but what was particularly fascinating was the way he spoke to Timm afterwards. His voice was eerily calm.

"Why did you do that?" Smithers asked, only a slight quiver to his voice.

"This way they can't see us," Timm said proudly.

"But now they know where we are," Smithers responded.

"How could they?" Timm said with a smirk, "I blinded them."

It was at that moment that Lee came to the same conclusion as Smithers.

"You knocked out one eye," Lee said. "Which means they just need to check the location where that eye was."

Timm's face dropped as the information hit him. All he mustered up to say was a simple, dejected, "Oh."

The sharp sound of boots stomping towards them filled the air. Lee and Smithers exchanged a look, unsure of how the aggressive members of their group would react to this. Thankfully, Luis went with a different approach this time.

"Hide, now!" Luis called out, darting forward to a door across the hall from them. Luckily, it was unlocked, and though Lee questioned

the wisdom of jumping into another unknown door without knowing what's behind it, the idea of being caught and drugged again
was far less appealing. He followed quickly and without question.

Surrounding them in the quasi-darkness were walls of strange
metal boxes with large glass windows. Looking inside, Lee saw
some were empty, some filled with cloth, and others swirling with
water, making a loud humming noise. Before he could examine
them closer, someone grabbed him and pulled him into a large cart
sitting in the middle of the floor. Luis threw some of the fabric
over them both before the door slammed open and light flooded
the room.

"The laundry, really?" a voice sounded in the darkness. Lee
heard irritation in his voice, but could not determine why, other
than being unable to find his quarry hidden so close at hand.

"We were told to check everywhere," another voice responded.

"So we have to check the greatest cliché in cinema history?" the
first voice asked, his footsteps getting closer. Lee, beginning to feel
his heart beating harder against his chest, started to worry that
these men would soon be able to hear it as well.

"It works in those movies," the second voice said, seemingly
going the opposite direction of his companion. "All the time."

"They're movies. That's just stupid."

A dull thud sounded from nearby.

"You don't know."

A similar thud sounded further off.

"Seriously? This is the hill you're going to die on?"

Lee suddenly understood what the thudding noise was as a sharp
blow cracked him in the head. Stars burst across his vision as tears
welled up in his eyes. It took all his might to not cry out in pain;
rather he clamped his jaw down and clenched his fists.

"There, see?" the closer voice called out, directly above him.
"Can we go now?"

"Yeah, fine," the other voice said, obviously disappointed. We'll
meet up with the rest of the team to finish sweeping the floor."

When the sound of their footfalls finally faded away, Lee pulled himself out of the laundry cart, rubbing the knot on his head that he was sure would be sore for days unless he saw to it. But without his holy symbol, he feared his powers may not even be accessible to him. The fear he was trying to ignore, the idea that his god's power might not reach this world, began to rise again. Lee quashed it down and looked around. Timm walked over to him from a side room, dripping with water.

"What... uh..." Lee looked him over. "What happened to you?"

Timm gave him a dark look that cowed him to silence.

"He got into a fight with a shower head," Smithers said, obvious glee on his face as he ignored the same dark look from Timm. "He lost."

Luis came over and tossed Timm a dry towel. The man nodded his thanks and began drying off.

"We should go now," Luis said. "While they are sweeping this floor, they won't be at the stairwells thinking them already clear. We have a small window, and we should not miss it."

"Agreed," Lee said, heading for the door and trying to ignore the throbbing in his skull. "And let's try to avoid the cameras by moving in their blind spots while we can."

"Not a bad idea for an off-worlder," Smithers said. "How'd you know about blind spots?"

"Anything with eyes, has blind spots," Lee answered, without looking at the old man. He was too busy calculating their next move. After a moment, the path was clear to him. "Follow me."

And once again, Lee led the way through the hallways of St. Augustine toward what he hoped was eventual escape.

$$\sim 4 \sim$$

SMITHERS

Smithers felt his joints ache a little as they made their way down the stairs. It was just one among many other little annoyances to his day. First those damn kids locked him up in this loony bin, but now he was stuck trying to get out of here with actual loonies. To be fair, he thought to himself, it served him right for telling them damn yuppies about what he saw while he was out hunting, he should never have told them anything about anything ever. The only time they listened was when they could interfere and 'do what was best for him.' Now he was stuck with people who thought they were from another world.

For a moment, he remembered that blue light and the forms of strange people coming out it, only to be beaten down by men in strange suits. Looked almost like those government people from that alien movie Spielburg did that was so popular. A shudder went through him. Aliens? Was that what these people were? Or did they just think they were? And what was worse?

What was worse was getting stuck in this hellhole with them for another damned therapy session with a woman asking stupid questions that didn't mean nothing to anyone. Smithers shook his head and got it back in the game. These orderlies were not messing around and he did not want to be the person who was off his guard when these idiots got them caught.

He looked around at the people he found himself with. Lee was leading the way, and seemed to have a good head on his shoulders, had a knack for reading people and the environment. Luis was more of a military man and a bit uptight for Smithers' taste, but wasn't afraid to get his hands dirty, and that was something to be respected. Morgan was hard to figure, a young girl like her mixed up in all of this, Smithers didn't know what to make of that, but he was determined to keep an eye on her and keep her out of harm's way. Seemed like a bad place for a defenseless young girl to find herself, but she was in it with them now, might as well make the best of it for her sake.

And then there was Timm. There was no doubt that the boy had skill, but he never seemed to think before he acted. The first time it worked out okay for them, getting away from the orderlies and all, but you can only skate on talent for so long before it catches up with you, and never in a pretty way. Smithers didn't want the boy to get killed, and wanted to get caught in that crossfire himself even less.

As they got to the bottom of the stairs he whispered sharply to Lee, "Hold up!"

Lee stopped and turned to look at him. Smithers pointed and Lee followed his gaze to where a large reception desk stood blocking the path to the exit doors. On either side were the hallways that they assumed lead to where their belongings must be stored. Standing at the desk was what Smithers wanted to warn Lee about.

Standing at the reception desk was the familiar form of Nurse Corbit who had escorted both Luis and himself to the meeting room earlier. She was a sweet thing and while cynical about many things, Smithers wanted to believe that she wasn't involved in the worst of what was going on here. Or at the very least, not be noticed by her or hurt her to find out for sure.

Lee seemed to understand and quietly motioned for the others to follow him as he turned down one of the hallways they determined were the way to go. Smithers ushered the others when he was sure

Nurse Corbit wasn't looking their way, but had to be quick about it. He saw the pink earbuds were in and she probably couldn't hear them, but he didn't want to take chances. A moment later, they passed her and were making their way down the hall.

Lee tried the first door they found down the hall, which seemed like a bad idea to Smithers. Opening every door without knowing what was behind it could lead to more trouble than they were prepared to deal with, but since he didn't have a better idea, he didn't say anything. He was a firm believer in keeping one's mouth shut about a problem if you weren't offering or asking for a solution.

Once Lee got the door open, the others quickly filed inside. Smithers, being last to do so, watched as they began raiding the maintenance closet they found themselves in.

"Ah-ha!" Timm exclaimed, a little louder than Smithers was comfortable with. "A bag of holding!"

Smithers turned to see him struggling to open the duffle bag he found sitting on a shelf. He watched dumbfounded, as the boy was just about to tear open the bag as the zipper flapped lazily around, locking the bag firmly closed.

"Yes, it's a bag for holding," Smithers said, rolling his eyes, and walked over to help the boy. With one swift motion he unzipped the bag. Looking up, Smithers saw the amazement in Timm's eyes.

"Are you a wizard?" Timm asked.

Smithers looked at him for a moment before saying, "I honestly don't know where to go with that."

As he walked away from the boy, he heard him say to the others, "Look at what Wizard Smithers showed me!"

Smithers felt a twitch in his eye and turned to say something about his new nickname, but then saw Morgan moving the zipper back and forth in amazement. His irritation vanished when he saw the girl's wonder. With a sigh he felt he could be Wizard Smithers for a while if need be.

With the help of Luis and Lee, they managed to find some useful items, including some duct tape and a multitool.

"Alright, we ready to head out?" Smithers asked.

"Yes," Luis nodded. "We shall try the next door."

"Oh, I'll lead the way!" Timm said excitedly, his enthusiasm returning quickly after the last fiasco. And before Smithers could stop him, Timm was already moving down the hall. He had just about caught up with him before the boy opened the door far wider than he should.

Smithers froze and pressed himself against the wall. Through the door jam he could see into the room and felt his blood run cold. Inside was a man, lying on a cot, an issue of some dirty magazine or another propped up. As the door opened, the magazine drooped down as the man looked up at Timm.

"Hey there, can I help you?" the man said.

Smithers turned to see Morgan directly behind him, but Luis and Lee standing in the doorway to the maintenance room. He waved them off, trying to communicate that they should back up and hide. Luis gave him a strange look, but Lee seemed to understand, pulling the larger man back a few steps and out of view of the hall. Smithers breathed a sigh of relief and just had to hope that the door would be enough to hide himself and Morgan.

"Uh..." Timm stammered out. Smithers saw the man get up and tuck the magazine into the tool belt that was slung over the corner of the cot. Must be the maintenance man then. Smithers felt a twinge of guilt. This must be the man they just robbed in hopes of making their escape. It was one thing to take from a company, but another thing entirely to take a man's tools.

The man walked up to Timm and Smithers felt himself start instinctively holding his breath and tried not to close his eyes in an attempt to hide better. Honestly, he had no idea why people did that.

"Relax boy," the man said, his voice right on the other side of the wall. "I'm not one of them big wigs you gotta impress around here. I just fix what gets broke. You new here? I don't ever remember seeing you."

"Uh... yeah," Timm said. "It's my first day."

Smithers got a better look at the man now that he was so close. He wore a set of coveralls that was stained with a variety of possible jobs the man worked in a place like this. His baldpate was crowned by long silver hair along the sides of his head pulled back into a ponytail. He was on the larger side, but not obese, just a man who has decided comfort was more important to him than looks. Smithers found himself liking the cut of this man's jib, and felt that guilty twinge grow a bit more in the back of his mind.

"Nice to meet you," the man said, offering his hand to Timm. "My name is Hershel Hawkins. I'm the handy man around here. What's your name?"

"Uh... Norman Homan," Timm responded, quickly reaching out to shake the man's outstretched hand.

It was all Smithers could do not to slap himself in the face before reaching up to slap the stupid out of this boy.

"So, Norman, did you end up getting turned around or something?" Hershel asked, apparently not realizing the stupidity of Timm's name, or at the very least being too polite to say anything about it.

"I... uh..." Timm said, and then looked down at the bag in his hand. "I needed to bring this to the patient storage... room. Which way was that?"

Smithers stared at the boy for a moment, marveling at the brilliance of the play he just made. For a moment he couldn't believe that this was the same person. Hershel looked down at the bag as well.

"Huh, is that an Ed Hardy?" Hershel asked.

It was then Smithers remembered that he was also asking the owner of the bag where to bring it and felt his heart drop into his stomach.

"No?" Timm responded, and Smithers felt he too sensed that the jig was up.

"Ah, that's alright," Hershel said. "I get the knockoffs myself. No sense paying all that money for a name. Just go past the reception desk in the main lobby, the hall will be right down from there, turn right, second door on the left next to the emergency exit door. Can't miss it."

"Th... thanks," Timm nodded to him.

"Oh, and one more thing," Hershel said to him, "That Nurse Corbit up there, she's a real sweetheart, and single if you get my drift."

From the look on Timm's face, Smithers was sure he did not get the drift.

"Just some food for thought," Hershel said, giving Timm a hearty clap on the shoulder. "Now if there's nothing else, I'm going to get back to my reading."

"Oh, just one more question," Timm said to Smithers' dismay. He wanted to scream at Timm to just end the conversation so they can get out of here. "These are just the small things they had. What happens to the bigger stuff? I saw one guy come in with armor and a quarterstaff."

Hershel scratched at the stubble that was growing in around his chin, "Well, the metal stuff gets loaded into a truck. Sent off somewhere, dunno exactly where that somewhere is. As for the wooden stuff, they just had me throw it in the chipper."

"The... chipper?" Timm asked.

"Yeah, the wood chipper," Hershel responded. "Turned 'em to mulch and spread them on the plants. Not sure how good it is for them, but I just do as I'm told."

"Thanks, Hershel," Timm said, obviously crestfallen.

"No problem," the handyman responded, holding out his hand again. "And remember what I said about Nurse Corbit."

"I will," Timm responded and shook Hershel's hand again before he went back into the room, closing the door behind him. Smithers finally felt like he could breathe again, but decided it would be best to take two large steps backwards first.

"I can't believe that worked," Timm said, excitedly and still louder than Smithers felt comfortable with.

"Neither can I," Smithers said, feeling his heart rate begin to slow down. "Come on, we've got to sneak past Corbit again, then we can get to the storage room. Lets get the others and go."

"Right," Timm nodded, and they began to backtrack the way they'd come.

Smithers was nervous about passing Corbit again, but felt that after the show of brilliance that seemed to come out of nowhere from Timm that the boy would be a little more forward thinking and things would go smoothly. And so as the group formed up and started to attempt slipping by her desk again, Smithers did so with far more confidence than last time.

"Hey!" Nurse Corbit's voice called out from behind the desk, causing all of them to freeze in place with terror as they turned to see her bobbing her head back and forth, her back still towards them.

"I just met you, and this is crazy!" Nurse Corbit continued singing in a halfway decent singing voice, all things considered.

"God bless terrible pop music," Smithers uttered to himself before urging the others forward. "Go! Go!"

Without stopping to question him, thankfully, the others began powering forward and they made it past the reception desk before they had any further trouble. Following Hershel's directions, they managed to find the storage room. Using the multitool and some skills he hadn't since his twenties, Smithers managed to get the door open and they all piled inside.

Inside the walls were lined with plastic storage containers that looked like they were right off the shelves of some cheap retail store. Odds were that they probably were, though he found it odd that they were using plastic bins instead of cardboard. Looking at the numbering system and reading his off his bracelet again, he noted that there was probably a high turnover rate for the bins, and being able to reuse them was a beneficial quality.

Opening the box, Smithers found his real clothes and quickly changed into them, throwing his leather jacket on and quickly checking the pocket for his car keys. They were still in the right hand pocket where he had left them. Breathing a sigh of relief, he turned to see what the rest were doing.

"I swear," he said with a sigh. "It's like you all are right out of a damned Renaissance Faire."

Each of the others had donned some form of clothing that would have made them fit right in with any production of some Shakespearean play. Tunics, boots that buckled up to the knee, and two of them were even wearing robes. Timm was busying himself tying a literal piece of rope around his waist as a belt.

"I still do not know what kind of faire you are referring to," Luis said, dropping a silver Nike logo around his neck, grasping it in his hand, and began muttering to himself. Smithers decided it was in his best interest not to say anything about it.

"Well, now that we've got our stuff back, we need to get out of here, get to my truck, and get away," Smithers said, bringing the conversation back around. "It isn't going to be easy."

"It will be a lot easier now," Lee said, placing his own medallion around his neck. "Now that we have our magic back."

"Right," Smithers said, skepticism dripping from the word. "There ya go with that magic stuff again."

"You don't believe in magic?" Morgan asked him. The question wasn't condescending exactly, it sounded more to Smithers that she was just as surprised at his disbelief as he was at their belief.

"Don't know how things work where y'all are from," he told her. "But round here, there ain't no such thing as magic."

Lee walked over to him and placed his hand on Smithers' shoulder.

"There is always magic in our worlds," he said before closing his eyes.

Smithers stood there awkwardly. For just a moment, he could have sworn he'd seen a slight glow appear around Lee's hand, but he shook it off, chalking the hallucination to stress mixed with good hospital drugs.

"Anyway, we gotta get going, unless there are any other weird old gods y'all need to tell me about," Smithers said.

"Well," Timm said tentatively. "My master and I were followers of Belenus."

Smithers stared at him for a moment. "Of course you are. Okay, everyone, get your coats, time to go."

"Coats?" Morgan asked.

"Yeah," Smithers said, looking at her. "You ain't going out in Boston during the dead of winter dressed like that."

Morgan looked down at her clothing, clearly not seeing what was wrong with wearing a mere tunic and pants with a pair of sandals. Smithers sighed again and turned back to the plastic tubs, pulling several off of the shelves and kicking them open.

"Grab something warm and put it on," Smithers said.

"We're just going to take these people's things?" Lee asked.

"I mean," Smithers shrugged. "They ain't using them. And you guys need them."

Luis stepped forward and dug out a biker jacket, looked it over, then nodded with approval.

"Wizard Smithers makes a good point," he said, drawing a cringe from Smithers. "We need to make our escape and then determine what we're doing here. Freezing to death would make that difficult."

Lee pursed his lips, obviously debating the point in his mind, but soon conceded the point and dug out a denim jacket lined with fur. Morgan found another leather jacket that resembled Smithers' and Timm pulled out a pea coat, donned it, and suddenly resembled the kind of person Smithers would avoid talking to in public at all costs.

"Alright," Smithers said, walking over to the exit. "Lets go."

He held his arm up to stop Timm from walking forward through the door, then pointed up. "Read that sign for me."

"Emergency Exit," Timm said, looking back at Smithers who gestured back at the sign. "Alarm will sound... oh."

"Yup," Smithers said, pulling out the multitool from their stolen duffle bag. "Thankfully, I know what to do about that."

A moment later, Smithers had the Emergency Exit alarm disabled and pressed on the bar to open the door to the frigid Boston air. The cold howled in, chilling them to the bone with their first breath of free air in far too long.

"Now, let's get the hell out of here," Smithers said, stepping outside.

$$\sim 5 \sim$$

MORGAN

The frigid air rushed around Morgan as they exited the building and something primal surged through her. It hadn't occurred to her what those stone walls were doing to her all this time, but as soon as she reentered nature's embrace, a forgotten vigor awoke in her.

Or at least it would have, but she could feel that something was wrong. The ground beneath her feet still felt like that inside the building. It was perfectly smooth stone, black and painted with strange colors barely visible beneath the snow. Metal fences stood between them and the stunted trees that reached like the boney arms of the malnourished for a starless sky. Nature was here, but only barely, and it caused her to shudder.

"C'mon," Smithers said, breaking Morgan out of her thoughts, "My truck has to be parked over here somewhere. Stay close to the wall and keep quiet."

They moved as silently as they could, and the dread Morgan felt creeping into her mind as they exited the building was quieted slightly by the light crunching of snow beneath her feet. Though the cold was cutting through her clothing and her sandaled feet were growing numb, she silently thanked the wisdom of Wizard Smithers on grabbing these coats before leaving. She also took a moment to thank the animal who'd given its skin so she could avoid frostbite on hers.

The group stopped and looked out over what Smithers called a 'parking lot' at the collection of strange enclosed carriages with shiny bodies and black wheels. Morgan had never seen their like before, and wondered where the horses that would be pulling them were stabled.

"Damnit," Smithers muttered. "I have no idea where they put her."

Morgan watched as Smithers fumbled with the keys in his hand for a moment before settling a black square with several colorful buttons into his hand.

"Here's what's going to happen," Smithers said, looking each one of them in the eye to be sure they were all paying attention to him. "I'm going to push the unlock button, that will tell us where she is. It's going to be loud, so we need to run to my truck as soon as we hear it. We get there, we get in, we get gone, got it?"

Morgan wasn't sure she understood all of what he was saying, but she nodded along with the others. The plan seemed simple enough, follow Smithers and do it quickly. The rest of what was going on she could figure out later.

"Good," Smithers nodded. "Because if you decide to go off doing something stupid and get caught, we're sticking to the plan and getting gone. Best of luck to you."

Morgan felt his eyes lingered on Timm a bit longer than any of the rest of them, noticing the younger man squirm slightly with discomfort, but the moment passed as Smithers turned to face the lot.

"Alright," Smithers said, gritting his teeth. "Here we go."

Smithers pressed a button and there was a flashing of light and the honk of some strange horn. With speed of reaction and body that Morgan would not have expected from the older man, Smithers was off and running across the parking lot. His gait seemed strange to her, but she did not dwell to think on it as she began to run alongside him. She soon worried the others would surpass them, but soon realized why Smithers was running the way he was.

Ice had crept along the surface of this strange stone, making it slick and dangerous to cross at high speeds. She looked back and saw the others adjusting their own running to keep from sliding along its surface.

They reached the truck and Smithers flung open the door gesturing to the other side and shouting, "I can fit three in the cabin at most, two of you gotta jump in the back!"

Without hesitation, both Lee and Luis jumped into the back of the truck, clinging to the short walls that encompassed the open area. Timm pulled the door on the other side in, pausing to allow Morgan to climb inside. Upon entering, Timm and Smithers slammed their doors shut and Smithers began fumbling with the keys again.

"Where are the horses?" Timm shouted, the panic in his voice echoed that which rose up in Morgan's mind.

"Horses?" Smithers asked, confused. "Boy, we ain't got time for your nonsense."

Morgan looked back at the doors of St. Augustine and saw the forms of several orderlies running towards them, skidding slightly in the snow and ice, but not being slowed enough to persuade her that they could make good on their escape. Her heart sank and she could not help but agree with Smithers: they were out of time.

"A-ha!" Smithers said, a note of victory in his voice as he twisted the key near the wheel in front of him.

The roar of a mighty beast springing to life made Morgan's chest swell as light flooded out of the front of the truck. With the jerk of a lever and the stamping of his foot, the truck lurched forward at Smithers' command. Morgan felt a shriek come from her throat as they headed for another truck sitting in front of them, but Smithers twisted the wheel and broke off towards the exit. There was a barrier of yellow and black wood barring their path, but Smithers never slowed and soon the sound of shattering splinters and Smithers' laughter filled the night air as they tore away from St. Augustine.

Smithers reached across Morgan and Timm's laps and pulled open a panel Morgan had not noticed before. It seemed to be filled with an assortment of papers, but Smithers pushed them out of the way to grab a long metal tube with a wooden handle.

"Ah Sebastian!" Smithers cried out with joy. "I am so glad they didn't find you."

He kissed the metal tube and slipped Sebastian into the left side of his coat with his right hand, patting it as he made sure everything was secure. Timm leaned in and whispered softly to Morgan.

"I don't know what that is, but there's something about it I don't like."

Morgan nodded, but felt now was a bad time to ask any further questions. Her heart was still pounding at their escape and her head was beginning to spin with all the strangeness that this new world seemed to offer.

The next half hour or so was a blur for Morgan. The lights surged past them, bathing the world in a strange fairy light that upset her night vision as they were plunged into darkness again, as though skipping from pool to pool. Colors swirled as they passed and other vehicles Smithers told her were not trucks, but called cars, rushed past them. She was told to speak up if she saw flashing red and blue lights, but soon was too overwhelmed to offer any such information to anyone.

Eventually, Smithers pulled up to the edge of a more natural looking area he called a park and then put the car into something else he called park, leading Morgan to become quite confused about how language worked in this world, before turning around and sliding open a small window looking out at Lee and Luis. Morgan felt the chill of the night's air enter the cabin and only just realized that the warmth she felt coming from the truck did not extend to where the two men were huddled in the back of the truck bed. They were shivering violently, but trying hard to hide that from the others.

"Well," Smithers said. "How you boys holding up back there?"

"Fine," Luis said, his burning eyes did nothing to keep the shiver and chill from his voice.

"It is rather cold back here," Lee replied, offering honesty to counter Luis' pride. "Is there any place of note we may be able to go to for sanctuary? A local temple of sorts? Or maybe a mercenary guild?"

"Uh..." Smithers seemed confused by the question. "Well there are places we can stay, though I'm guessing you lot don't have any money on you?"

Morgan shuffled through her pockets and excitedly took out the green paper they had taken from the orderly in St. Augustine's. "You mean this?"

"Yeah," Smithers nodded. "But fifteen bucks isn't going to get us far. We're going to need some means of making money if we're going to be able to get by around here. Especially if we've got people looking for us. We need to deal in cash."

Morgan felt a bit deflated, but this had not been the first time she'd felt embarrassment over not knowing how currency worked. Back in the forests of her home, money was not a thing. People helped each other, or traded in goods. Animal skins, meat, and tools were far more useful than some shiny metal or rocks. The people from the nearby town of... of...

Shaking her head in frustration, Morgan felt the memory of that town's name and in fact even her own home disappear from her mind. Trying to claw at these memories felt more like trying to grab smoke from the air. Timm's voice managed to pull her back into the moment and help her ignore the lingering concern of her faulty memory.

"I have an instrument," he said, patting his pack. "Perhaps I can perform and collect some money for us. If anyone else is able to help we may be able to make what we need to find lodging."

"Oh!" Morgan piped up. "I have an instrument as well!"

"There," Luis' voice came shakily from the back. "We have a means of procuring money. But performing on the street isn't exactly lucrative. Perhaps a tavern or similar establishment?"

"A bar?" Smithers asked, quickly looking at a glowing panel inside the truck. "We've got time before closing. Luis, my boy, you look like I could use a drink."

Before Luis could comprehend the odd statement, Smithers closed the window again and set the truck in motion to the bar. Less than a quarter of an hour later, they were walking into an establishment Smithers simply called O'Malley's.

For the first time since waking up in this world, Morgan felt something familiar and untouched. The wooden floors and paneled walls were warm and inviting, though the stench of stale beer and strong alcohol was a bit more pronounced than she would have liked. Strange lights hung from the ceiling, though they were covered with beautiful stained glass domes that cast warm colors and cut the lights' harshness against her eyes. A long bar with several stools had been built into the far wall. Standing behind it was a plain looking man in a black apron. His expression was stone, but cracked with a smile as soon as Smithers walked in.

"Smithers! It's been a while. What can I get for you?" The man asked.

"Hey there, Tom." Smithers nodded his greeting. "If you could, whiskey and a quiet place to talk."

The man named Tom nodded. "You can have the back room. No one is in there now. I'll send Jess in to take your orders, but remember we stop serving at two, so you'll have to get them in quick. Want me to put it on your tab?"

"That would be great, Tom. Thanks." Smithers said, making his way to a pair of double doors adjacent to the bar. Morgan followed with the rest, but trailed behind to watch the man work as he pulled strange metal cups and glass bottles down from shelves to begin mixing. She noted that his hands were lined with white scars, similar to how Timm's were. For a moment she entertained the thought of him throwing punches in brutal fights, but as she caught his eyes watching her, she quickly followed the others into the back room.

Much like the front, the floor and walls were wood, but here a long table bisected the room. Matching chairs sat at either head of the table, then lined three on either of the longer sides. Another door led off to a side room. Everyone was seated, so Morgan quickly slipped into a chair between Smithers and Lee.

"Alright, so it seems we're in a bit of a bind," Timm started the conversation. He turned his attention to Smithers. "You seem to know the most about this world, but nothing about magic. You know a lot we need to know, but first you gotta know, magic is real."

Smithers nodded. "Sure it is, buddy. Maybe we should have left you in that loony bin."

Morgan shook her head. "No, Smithers. It really is. Here, watch this."

Shakily, and for a moment doubting her own power, Morgan reached out to the primal spirits of the world, the magic that existed within nature. She felt the leather of her bracelet grow warm and smiled, knowing for sure now that her connection to the nature of this world was not severed. The heat grew until a small flame began to dance in her palm. She opened her eyes and looked at Smithers, expecting amazement or awe.

What she got was an unimpressed sound and pursed lips. The old man reached into his pocket and pulled out a little green tube with a metal top and wheel. He flicked the wheel, causing it to spark and a small flame danced on the end of it.

"Neat trick," Smithers said, releasing the flame and sticking the device back in his pocket. Morgan huffed, clenching her fist and extinguishing her own flame and the side door opened and a young woman entered.

She was probably only a few years older than Morgan with light brown skin and dark, curly hair cut short to frame her face. She had a warm smile and light grey almond shaped eyes that seemed to radiate warmth and kindness. Immediately, her frustrations with Smithers were banished and she felt at ease.

"Hello everyone, my name is Jess. Can I get any of you anything to drink?" She asked, taking a single glass of deep amber liquid off a tray she carried and placed it on a napkin in front of Smithers.

"I'll have what he's having," Luis said, pointing at Smithers' drink. Jess nodded and took their orders. Morgan and Lee both seemed to think water was the way to go for now, which Jess accepted, however she was a bit confused by Timm's order for ale, and instead offered him the winter lager. Once she was satisfied with the order, she gave them all a nod and left the room the way she had come.

As soon as she was gone, Luis turned to Smithers. "It seems you need further convincing. I will show you something that in no way could be confused with a trick."

Luis reached into his own pack and pulled out a small knife. Before anyone could say something to stop him, he pressed it into his own flesh and sliced, drawing blood in a quick and brutal display.

"What the fuck is wrong with you?" Smithers cried out, nearly jumping from his seat in an attempt to get away from the knight.

"Nothing," Luis responded, holding his hand over the wound. A light glow appeared from underneath, and instantly the bleeding stopped. "My goddess allows for me to remove the pains of battle to carry me on towards victory."

Smithers looked at Luis, skepticism in his eyes, and then looked down at the blood dripping from his arm. "You one of them crazy fanatics, boy? Cuz there's something wrong with you."

Before Luis could respond, the side door opened and Jess reentered the room with a tray of drinks.

"Alright, everyone. I have your... oh god!" Jess stopped short in what she was saying as soon as she saw the blood on Luis' arm. Quickly she set the tray down on the table and moved to his side, pulling a cloth napkin from her apron pocket as she went. Before he could protest, Jess was wiping the blood from Luis' arm, but a second later she stopped.

"Wait... was that ketchup or something?" She looked at Luis in confusion. "I could have sworn that was blood, but there's no wound."

"Oh, I get it!" Smithers said with a laugh. "It was one of those trick knives, with the blood pack in it! I've seen magicians use those all the time."

"Magicians?" Jess asked, looking around the table. "I suppose that would explain the clothes. Sorry to interrupt your trick, sir."

She moved back to her tray and dispensed the drinks. "I'll leave you all to it, if you need anything else from me, just holler."

Before another word on the matter could be spoken, Jess was gone. Luis watched her leave, looked over at Smithers, and just picked up his drink, conceding the point in lieu of alcohol.

"In spite of the faith or understanding of our current situation, we can all at least agree on a few facts," Lee said, breaking the silence. "We are in dire straits for a place to stay that is warm, safe, and not likely to be raided by those who wish us ill."

"We could always camp out," Morgan offered up. "That park Smithers took us too had some pretty good tree cover."

"That does kind of take away 'warm' from the equation," Lee said with a soft smile. "And any fire we built to keep warm would likely attract attention."

"Oh," Morgan said, sheepishly. Though she appreciated the gentle tone Lee used. He was not shooting down her idea with the harshness others had before, but rather offering up a good reason to reject the idea with kindness. Morgan felt she could appreciate this quality in the holy man.

"What about the temple idea?" Timm asked, sipping at his drink. His eyebrows furrowed, and he turned to look at the dark brown liquid. He studied it for a moment, then shrugged before continuing to drink.

Lee nodded. "Temples are a good place to find sanctuary, though that is dependent on the god the temple serves." He turned his attention to Smithers again. "What kinds of gods are worshipped here in your world?"

"Well," Smithers said, thoughtfully scratching his beard. Morgan felt he was choosing his words carefully rather than compiling a list. It seemed that in order to communicate with one another, they would have to attempt to speak to each other's experiences rather than being blunt. The magic lesson fiasco was proof enough of that.

"Honestly, there are a bunch, and even more sects that worship the same gods in a lot of different ways. If we're talking popularity though, we're probably looking at some kind of Christian church," he explained. "Honestly, I'm not much of a religious man, but I know of one nearby. Have to pass it now and then to get here. It's a Catholic place, think it's called the Cathedral of the Holy Cross. Big brick building, has a place where they let the homeless sleep now and then, so might have a spot for us."

"Then we shall go there," Luis said, slamming his now empty glass down.

Morgan winced slightly, but took his zeal in stride. "Before we go, Timm and I were talking about performing for some money..."

"Right," Timm said. "Should we speak with this Tom on the way out?"

Smithers shrugged. "Couldn't hurt. Lets finish our drinks and go check out the church. Probably better to wake someone up there earlier rather than later."

Morgan sipped at her water as Smithers and Timm finished their drinks. Lee and Luis had finished their own and were sitting at odds with their patience. Lee seemed calm and relaxed, while Luis seemed to be feeling the need for action. She marveled for a moment the vast difference between the two holy men and their approach to religion. Just looking at them, she could envision them as a pair, like a sword and a shield, ready to work at odds, but also as one.

"Alright, let's head out," Smithers said, once again pulling Morgan from her thoughts. They made their way out of the back room, and Smithers walked over to Tom at the bar.

"Hey Tom, any chance a few of my friends can do some live performing here, make a little extra cash?" Smithers asked him.

Tom pondered for a moment, looking the group over. "I suppose they can use the stage on Tuesdays. I'm not able to pay them anything, but they can set up a tip jar and see how generous the patrons are feeling that day. Maybe if they pull in enough of a crowd I can see about compensating a bit."

"Sounds like a fair deal," Smithers said, shaking Tom's hand. "We will see you Tuesday then."

With that, they left O'Malley's and headed back into the cold. Lee and Luis hunkered down in the bed of the truck again, and Morgan felt a little pang of guilt as she climbed into the warmth of the cab. Smithers set the truck in motion and they began their journey to the Cathedral of the Holy Cross.

~ 6 ~

LUIS

For the second time that night, Luis huddled against the bitter wind that whipped around the bed of Smithers' truck. At least this time he had the alcohol in his system to numb himself against the cold, but even that was wearing off as the others had taken their sweet time to finish their drinks and discuss performing music for money like street performers. Luis felt even more bitterly that the ones who took their time were currently sitting in the warmth of the cabin up front.

He turned his eyes to Lee, who sat calmly as seemed to be his custom. They had found blankets in the back, but they did little to cut against the cold. Even still, Lee barely shivered with either cold or anger, as Luis found himself doing. For a moment, Luis just watched the man, content with the world, and soon found the same energy rushing into him. Even the chill of the air did not permeate him the way it had at the beginning of their journey.

Reaching up, he placed the tips of his fingers against the cool metal of his holy symbol. The warmth of Nike flooded him, barring the cold of the evening away, and Luis smiled. He supposed every now and then even a man of devotion needed a reminder of the power of faith. For the rest of the journey, Luis attempted to emulate Lee in his faithful piety.

Whether the rest of the trip was not long or it just seemed that way in his meditative state, Luis soon felt the truck slowing down as they circled around the exterior of an old brick building capped with a white wooden sigil. Luis assumed this was the holy symbol of the faith, the cross for which the church itself was named, but the more he observed it, the more it reminded him of a sword plunged tip first into the ground.

The sound of glass scraping turned his attention to the cab of the truck as Morgan pulled the window open.

"Smithers said we need to go to the back lot where we can be less conspicuous," she said, and Luis noted an apologetic tone to her voice. The anger he felt earlier shifted slightly to guilt, but he just nodded.

Soon Smithers was pulling the truck into a spot behind the church, a bit of a ways off from the building. Luis questioned the wisdom of keeping their means of escape so far from the building they were planning to hide in, but noted that the truck would be obscured from easy view of the street by the foliage surrounding it. He felt a smile pull at the corner of his lips. It seemed this Smithers had more than just a passing knowledge of strategy in spite of his pigheaded denial of magic.

The roar of the truck quieted into silence, and Luis quickly leapt from the back of the truck. Lee moved with more caution and care, but it would be impossible for Luis to emulate everything the other man did. He felt his muscles ache with the need to move as Smithers, Timm, and Morgan clambered out of the truck and they all began their cautious walk toward an old looking wooden door.

While Luis felt the need for action, he was able to temper it with the need for caution. It seemed to him that Timm felt no such need as the group had barely ascended the stone steps before he banged heartily on the door. Smithers opened his mouth to say something, but closed it with a sigh and shook his head. Luis realized they had no idea whom they'd be addressing, or even what story they would be telling them, but it seemed that this thought was too little too late, as just a moment later the door was opened.

Standing before them was a man in his early thirties. Luis could tell there was muscle on the man, but he did not carry himself like a warrior. His garb seemed rather relaxed as well. He wore blue trousers that seemed to match the material of Lee's jacket, minus the fur, a thin cotton tunic with the letters VBS emblazoned black on the tunics left breast against the stark white of the rest of the material, and a strange pair of shoes made in a style that Luis could not determine. On his face was a pair of spectacles made of brass colored wire that framed his light brown eyes. His mussed hair was not that of a man roused from sleep, but rather one who was burning the candle at both ends.

While the man's expression was tired, he still managed a warm smile at the group who had appeared strangely at his doorstep in the middle of the night.

"Good evening, or rather, I should say good morning," the man said. "How can I be of service to you all?"

"Evening, padre," Smithers said. "Any chance you still have beds available? Seems we're in a bit of trouble and find ourselves in need of sanctuary."

"Ah," the man said. "Of course. Come in, please. It's quite cold out tonight. Would you care to join me in my office for a moment? I fear we do need some documentation of who stays with us."

"Uh, sure," Smithers said, then gave the rest of the group a look that told Luis to be on his guard before walking inside. Luis put his hand in his pocket, firmly gripping the friction lock club before following Smithers inside.

The man led them all through the halls of the Cathedral, and Luis could not help feeling the warm sense of home. This most definitely was not the kind of temple he was used to, but the familiar sense of faith that permeated these walls was like a comforting blanket wrapped around his shoulders. The man opened a door and stepped through, moving to a chair behind a simple and neatly kept wooden desk. Luis looked around at their surroundings: a pair of chairs faced the desk next to a set of bookshelves that appeared filled to capacity, a plush carpet of burgundy sank under his weight, and a clear view of the parking lot was visible through the windows behind the man who had granted them access.

"Well then," the man said. "I apologize for the mess, but I was busy working on my sermon for the week when I heard your knock. My name is Father Franklin Mitchell."

They each introduced themselves in turn, earning a warm, but firm handshake from Father Mitchell.

"If you could just sign your names here on this clip board, it just helps us know how many beds we need and how often. We just passed our busiest season, but still, helps to be prepared," Mitchell said as he handed a wooden square to Smithers.

Luis recognized it as the same square device that Courser woman used, though it seemed to not carry such nefarious connotations here, as Smithers took it willingly. Luis noted that he simply wrote 'Smithers' on the line and did not offer further information. As it was passed to him, he did the same as Smithers, offering little extra information.

"So what sort of trouble are you all in that you came for sanctuary?" Mitchell asked.

"Oh, we're not looking for that kind of sanctuary, padre," Smithers said quickly. "It's just we're not from around these parts, and we're a bit hurt up for money. Put that together with being a bit lost, and we found ourselves needing a bit of help."

Father Mitchell, whether he believed this story or not, nodded sympathetically and smiled. "Well you can always find a place here with God in times of trouble. What kind of neighbor would I be to allow you to go cold? Or hungry?"

"Which god?" Luis asked, earning a sharp look from Smithers, which he promptly ignored.

"Excuse me?" Father Mitchell asked, genuine confusion on his face.

"Which god do you worship here?" Luis asked the question again. "While we appreciate your offer for help, we would not want to seek shelter in the temple to an evil god."

The look Smithers was giving Luis reminded him of the looks he would give Timm throughout their escape from St. Augustine. However, Luis felt the answer to this question was more important than keeping up the ruse Smithers seemed so desperate to secure. Luis refused to parley with evil, even in times of strife.

"Ah, I see," Father Mitchell said, seeming to understand. "You wish to know about Christ, and how we worship?"

"Exactly," Luis nodded.

"How familiar are you with the Christian religion?" Father Mitchell asked.

"We don't know anything," Timm answered.

Father Mitchell gave Timm a strange look. "Really? I find that rather surprising. However since it is late and I'm sure you don't all want me to bore you with the full details of our religion, how about I give you the information as concisely as possible, then you can determine if you feel comfortable staying here or not."

"That would be acceptable, yes," Luis nodded.

"Well, I suppose in short, we here worship God and his son, Jesus, who offered up the greatest sacrifice for all of us in order for those of good and kind spirits to move on to heaven when they die," Mitchell explained, though Luis could sense that he was dissatisfied with his own explanation given the amount of time he had to give it in. "In order to get to heaven, one must lead a good life in the eyes of Jesus, giving to the needy, not allowing hate to drive them, and to spread the word of peace and forgiveness through their actions in their daily lives."

Luis nodded as Mitchell spoke. It certainly seemed to him that Mitchell believed in a good and just course of action in life, and that through his own actions he tried to live such a life. He turned to Smithers and nodded to communicate his approval of the situation. Smithers, however, seemed less than impressed with Luis' approval.

"Thanks padre," he said, and Luis sensed the faintest note of irritation in his voice, though was unsure what had earned it. "Now about those beds..."

"Of course," Father Mitchell said, getting up, but Timm interrupted him.

"Wait a second, Father," Timm said, drawing yet more irritation from Smithers. "That sounds pretty interesting to me, how can I learn more about it?"

"Well, you are welcome to talk to me as much as you like on the subject," he turned and looked to a device on the wall. "But seeing as it's nearly three in the morning, I would greatly appreciate some sleep. How about I give you a copy of our holy book? You can read it at your leisure and then come to me with any questions that you have."

Timm nodded, "That would be great, thank you."

Father Mitchell went over to one of his shelves and pulled a book from it. He turned and passed it to Timm.

"You can keep it," he said with a smile. "Don't worry, I have plenty more where that came from."

He then turned and addressed the group. "Now then, you all look quite tired. Let me take you to your room for the night."

Father Mitchell led them down a flight of stairs into a large subterranean room. There were no windows, however light shone through those odd rectangles Luis had woken up to on his ceiling in St. Augustine. Several beds were set up around the room, though only a few were occupied. Father Mitchell turned to them and gestured at the beds.

"Fall in where you'd like. We do have some food available for breakfast if you need," he gave them all a nod. "Good night."

"Good night, father," Luis said, and made his way to the bed nearest the door. He lay down on top of the blankets, allowing himself freedom of movement should they be attacked in the night. The others fell into their beds, and he watched as Smithers patted the left side of his jacket before kicking off his shoes and getting into bed. Luis wondered what the old man had there, but figured it could wait until morning.

Easing back into his cot, Luis felt the gentleness of sleep take him, reflecting how he had woken up that day a prisoner, and now was going to bed a fugitive. All in all, he felt this was a step in the right direction.

$$\sim 7 \sim$$

TIMM

Timm lay awake a while longer than everyone else, the small leather book propped open in his hands. He read stories about magical gardens, the flooding of the earth, and then a lot of really old and disturbing laws that Timm hoped were no longer in effect. Some laws required cracking a bird's ribcage open and letting its blood flow across the altar. If this were the case of how the religion worked, he would not want to stay here another night. However, once he completed the first half of the book, the second got a bit more light hearted, and as his eyes began to itch and burn with exhaustion, he drifted off to more peaceful thoughts.

The next morning, Timm awoke, assuming he'd be the last out of bed having gone to sleep the latest, but found himself waking up before anyone else.

Smithers slept with his right hand under the left side of his jacket, causing Timm to shudder as he remembered the metal tube he'd pulled out of the truck the night before. Trying not to think of the ominous tube, he shifted his attention to Lee, who seemed to sleep peacefully with the same demeanor of a body laid out at its own funeral. Only his chest rising and falling could persuade Timm that the man was not, in fact, dead.

Luis had opted to sleep closest to the door, probably something to do with rank or protection, a military thing Timm didn't understand, nor did he particularly want to. Luis was good in a fight, and that's all that mattered to Timm when it came to someone watching his back.

Finally, his eyes turned to Morgan. The girl had carried herself well through the night, showing compassion to their enemies while protecting her newfound allies. And the power she wielded, while she did not claim it to be much, was still more than he had. She had conjured flame in the palm of her hand, a feat that was wasted on Smithers, a man who could not understand what he was looking at. The girl was impressive, he was sure about that.

Timm felt his face grow warm, and pulled his eyes away, suddenly aware of the hole in his stomach chewing away at his attention. He set off in an attempt to take Father Mitchell up on that offer of breakfast.

He found Father Mitchell in a large room near the top of the stairs he'd led them down the night before. There were a few tables set up sporadically through the room and a long counter framed by cabinets above and below it. Father Mitchell stood at the counter eating from a bowl and dressed very differently than the night before. He wore all black, except for around his neck where Timm could see a small square of white fabric. His hair was neatly combed and when he looked up to meet Timm's gaze, his eyes were bright and alert.

"Good morning, Timm was it?" He asked before gesturing to a bowl on the counter. "Care for some off brand cereal?"

"Yes," Timm answered, then reached for a bowl. "And yes, thank you."

"You're quite welcome," Father Mitchell said, passing a box with a drawing of some ridiculous looking animal on it that Timm did not recognize. "So how did you sleep?"

"Well enough, I suppose," Timm answered. "Though I've got to say, your holy book paints one hell of a bloody image."

Father Mitchell nodded knowingly, "You started from the very beginning, I suppose?"

Timm shot the man a quizzical look, "How else d'ya read a book? I'd be a right lump for starting in the middle of it, don't you think?"

Father Mitchell snorted as he laughed at the comment. "I suppose you would be, though if I'm being honest with you, that's actually the place to start."

"What d'ya mean?" Timm asked, feeling confusion mix with embarrassment, hoping desperately that he neither offended the man nor made a fool of himself. "Why would you start in the middle?"

"Well you see, the first part is the holy book of the Jewish people, or the Old Testament," the father explained. "The second half is where Jesus came in to fix the problems with the Old by replacing it with the New Testament. But in order to understand how he fixed the Old in the New, you need to know what was going on in the Old."

Timm stood in silence for a moment, chewing on the cereal thoughtfully. There was a lot of old and new being thrown around, but if the bloody things that so concerned him in the book were seen as problems needing to be fixed by this Jesus guy, then Timm felt that the two of them must think rather similarly. And in that case, he and the father probably stood on fairly common ground.

"Yeh don't go round cracking birds open on yer altars anymore, right?" Timm asked, cautiously.

Father Mitchell laughed heartily, "Oh no, that practice stopped thousands of years ago. Now its candles and incense only on our altars."

Timm nodded, satisfied with the answer. He resolved to finish reading the book, get to know their story a bit more, but he was going to finish it in order. Timm didn't think he was ready to start asking the father the right order to read things yet.

Soon, the others began to filter upstairs as well and Father Mitchell went to talk to the other two men who had been sleeping there last night. The rest approached Timm who handed out bowls and the cereal to them. Smithers walked over to a white chest on the wall, opened it, and brought out a cold pitcher of milk, pouring it on the cereal and offering it to others. Timm was fine with his cereal the way it was, but others braved the new concoction.

"So what's the plan?" Luis asked after they had gotten something to eat.

"What do you mean?" Timm asked. "We have a plan, get money so we can secure lodging. I mean, we have secure lodging here I suppose, but we really can't rely on charity forever."

"Well, that's just the first part of the plan," Lee said. "We're here for a reason, and we need to figure out what that reason is."

Luis nodded, "And we were being held by an unknown enemy. We need to make that enemy known, and make them suffer."

"Okay, cool your jets, boy," Smithers said, interjecting. "First of all, you're not going to make some shadowy group pay with a friction lock while dressed like a Renaissance Faire reject."

"I don't know if they look like rejects," Father Mitchell said as he approached the group, eyeing each of them. "They look rather authentic if I do say so myself."

"People keep saying that," Morgan said, a bit of milk dribbling down her chin. She awkwardly wiped at it in a way Timm found endearing. "What does that mean?"

Father Mitchell eyed her closely, "This just raises further questions. But on the matter of finding yourselves some more modern clothing, you could always go down to our thrift store. We usually sell donated clothes for nominal fees. Normally so folks don't think of it so much as charity, but as a great deal. Head down there and let Ethel know I sent you."

"Thank you, padre," Smithers said. "For everything, the beds, the food, you've been a real help."

"That's what I'm here for," Father Mitchell smiled. "Now, I hope you don't mind repaying that favor. I would be happy to see you all for service on Sunday."

"Not to be discourteous, father," Lee interjected. "But some of us serve other gods."

"Well, maybe think of it as a chance to study how another culture worships," Father Mitchell suggested before excusing himself. Timm pondered this for a moment, thinking how his master taught him to seek out knowledge from all places.

"Maybe we should go," Timm said to the group. "I mean, he's been really kind, and a service is nothing in repayment."

"We'll cross that bridge when we get there," Smithers said, but his nod to Timm shared a level of agreement. "For right now, let's get you looking a bit more... normal."

As they walked through the hallways following the signs to the thrift store, Morgan turned to Smithers.

"No one answered my question," she said. "What are Renaissance Faires?"

"Ah," Smithers said thoughtfully, "it's just a place where nerds go."

"What are nerds?" Luis asked.

"You guys," Smithers responded.

"So if we're nerds, what does that make you?" Timm asked.

"A victim of society," Smithers smiled cryptically.

A short while later Smithers led them through a door and Timm's senses were immediately overwhelmed by the scent of must. Piles of clothing and odd knick-knacks were strewn about in a way Timm assumed somebody considered order. An older woman stood on the opposite side of a glass counter and adjusted her spectacles as they came in. She wore all purple, though her sweater had a strange green design that looked similarly to a tree knit into the front of it. Her grey hair was cut short and curly. As she walked over to them, Timm noted that she was bent over slightly and took very small steps as she walked, almost as though she were afraid she'd fall over if she moved too quickly.

"Oh hello, I'm Ethel," she introduced herself. "Father Mitchell said you were looking to find new outfits and that you might be needing some help."

"Yeah," Smithers answered for them. "See, they're a bit too dedicated to their roles and it seems the circus crew lost their luggage."

The older woman laughed, "Oh you are a witty one, aren't you? Well, if you know what you're looking for I'll let you browse, but if you need help I will do what I can."

"Uh, actually..." Morgan started, though her voice trailed off.

"Yes dear?" Ethel asked.

"I could use some help," Morgan said shyly. "I've never really shopped for clothes before and..."

"Oh not to worry dear," Ethel said, taking Morgan's arm and leading her to a different part of the shop. "I can help you find some things that will look good on you. You do remind me of my granddaughter after all. Now lets see... it's too cold for sundresses..."

Timm watched as the two of them disappeared behind racks of clothing. His curiosity at what Morgan was going to find played in his imagination for a moment before he turned his attention to finding what he needed to fit in. Something similar to what Father Mitchell had been wearing the night before, maybe?

Quickly he found a pair of what Smithers called jeans and slipped them on. They were a bit loose compared to how Father Mitchell had worn them, but he tested their flexibility and found them lacking. If he wanted to be able to move freely, then he'd have to make the sacrifice and wear them a bit loosely. With that thought in mind, he scooped up a belt and looped it around his waist as well. Remembering how cold the snow was on his feet the night before, he also found a pair of hearty boots that laced up to about his ankle. Finally, he pulled off his older tunic and grabbed a black tee shirt and threw it on. Satisfied, he turned to Smithers, who took one look at him and started laughing.

"What?" Timm asked, his cheeks flushing. "Didn't I get it right?"

"Oh, you did," Smithers said, still snickering. "But did you read that shirt before putting it on?"

Timm looked down at the shirt he was wearing. It took him a second to read since it was upside down, however eventually he managed to make out the words 'I would bottom you so hard.' He looked up at Smithers.

"What does that even mean?"

"Boy, if you don't know, I'm not having this conversation," Smithers shook his head and walked away.

Timm pursed his lips, but before he could ask any questions, Lee and Luis came from behind a rack of clothing. Luis was dressed similarly to Timm, a pair of dark jeans, boots, and a tee shirt, only his had the image of a knight's helm in profile and a pair of swords in an x-shape behind it. Around the image were the words "Waterbury Knights Football." Timm didn't know who these Waterbury Knights were, but it seemed they were fond of blue and silver.

Lee was dressed in what seemed like more formal attire. In fact, much like how Timm had tried to emulate Father Mitchell's clothing from last night, Lee had donned an outfit much like what the Father was wearing this morning. He was wearing black pants and a black shirt that buttoned down the front. The only thing missing was the white collar that the father had been wearing, though Timm supposed that was a difference in clergy and how they would present themselves.

"Seems we're all just about ready to go," Lee said. "The only one we're missing is... Oh, here she is."

Timm turned around to see Morgan approaching. She was wearing baggy, tan pants that seemed to have a multitude of pouches sewn into every reachable location. Her sandals were gone, replaced with more functional boots. And it seemed she also wore a tee shirt like Luis and Timm did, but she had pulled some sort of sweater over top of it so he couldn't see if anything decorated hers. But Timm did notice that this sweater had a hood sewn into the back of it, cleverly making it function as both a sweater and a cloak.

"All I'm saying, dear, is that you may want to consider it," Ethel was saying to her. "I know we don't really carry any, but it would do wonders for support. Especially for your back."

"Thank you," Morgan said, turning a bit red. "I'll consider it."

Smithers went up to Ethel as she rang up their total, so Timm took the opportunity to walk over to Morgan.

"Looks good," Timm said, not really knowing what else to say.

"Thank you," Morgan smiled.

"So..." Timm said, looking around the room. "What was that she was talking about? Some kind of support?"

Morgan immediately turned bright red. "Nothing! Nothing. Don't worry about it. Um... why don't we all go talk to Father Mitchell? Thank him for his help. See if there's anything we can do for him. Something like that?"

Before he could answer her, Morgan was already going through the door. Timm looked over to Luis and Lee, who both shrugged at him and followed after her. Looking back, he saw Smithers shaking slightly and it took him a moment before he realized the old man was laughing again. Pursing his lips in irritation, Timm stormed off after the others, wondering just exactly what Smithers found so funny, and what he had said wrong to Morgan.

~ 8 ~

LEE

Lee followed a flustered Morgan through the hallways leading back to Father Mitchell's office, but did not lend much of his attention to the girl's frustrations. He was rather lost within his own thoughts. This strange new world seemed to work on very different rules than his own, and though he knew that there was still some wall blocking him from pulling up any specific memories of his home. He could remember his god, he could remember his family, but he could not pull any specifics of where he was from to mind. It was quite a conundrum.

What was worse, however, was the immediate problem. Their gold gone, and the currency here being vastly different, he was concerned with just how long they could survive on the charity of others before there was some kind of repercussions. Father Mitchell seemed like a decent enough man, however there would always be a catch to someone's kindness and generosity and it would not do to be indebted to the wrong people of this world, especially when they may have a difficult time identifying who those people are. Smithers was a good guide, but there was no guarantee the man would always be there to help them; Morgan and Timm were good kids, but the emphasis there was that they were kids; Luis had a good head on his shoulders, though that head could oftentimes get a bit hot.

Lee had come to his conclusion: they would need to find some form of employment and become financially independent before they could make any further plans on how to proceed. He resolved to be sure and ask Father Mitchell about how this could be accomplished and set to work on it right away.

His train of thought was broken as the sound of shouting echoed through the halls. He looked up just in time to see Morgan rushing forward towards Father Mitchell's office, and even Luis' pace increased substantially. Quickening his own, Lee moved into position behind the other two and caught a glimpse of what was conspiring within.

A tall man with gangly features stood before Father Mitchell. Thin wisps of grey hair were smoothed back across his balding skull. His hooked nose and skinny neck gave Lee the immediate impression of a chicken. The man was dressed very similarly to Father Mitchell, though with far more extravagance than the younger man donned. The holy symbol around his neck was made from gold rather than the much more humble wooden one Mitchell wore, and his gnarled fingers each had a gold ring adorning them, some even set with precious stones. He was in midsentence as they approached.

"We have had thefts!" he was saying to Mitchell in an authoritative tone. "You cannot leave them unsupervised!"

"I understand your position," Father Mitchell said, attempting to placate the older man. "However it is our duty..."

Luis gave the door a sharp knock, bringing the attention of both men upon him. The older man's eyes burned with irritation. Lee sensed none of the warmth and kindness that came from Father Mitchell's faith coming from this man. He was cold, calculating, and would obviously be unsympathetic to their plight. Avoidance would be their best means of handling this man in the future.

"Excuse us," Luis said, his own stare matching the older man's firmly. "Are we interrupting anything?"

The older man ignored Luis and turned back to Father Mitchell, iron in his voice.

"This conversation is not over." He said.

"I am aware," Father Mitchell said, his voice tired but resolved, as a man who has had the same argument many times would say. "However, some of my flock have come to visit, so we'll have to put it off to another time."

With a sneer, the older man turned and walked past them, and Lee was sure to give him space. While Luis stood his ground and kept his eyes firmly set on this man's, Lee felt it was best to allow him passage without creating further tension. He did not fear the single man, but there was something of the sense of authority he wielded that made Lee uneasy. Not only that, but it reaffirmed his thoughts from earlier: they would need to become independent soon. Lee had no desire to become indebted to this kind of man.

Father Mitchell sighed and took a seat as Timm and Smithers caught up to them. He waved his hand at the pair of chairs in front of his desk. Morgan took one and, seeing as no one else was taking the other, Smithers slipped himself into the other.

"What was that all about?" Morgan asked in a quiet tone, as if she worried the old man may still be listening in on them.

"That was Father Pearson," Mitchell explained. "He is the head priest here. And seeing as I'm the newest and youngest priest at the church, he feels it is in my best interest to remind me who's in charge."

"Your best interest," Lee asked. "Or his?"

"Tale as old as time, I suppose. The older generation doesn't like how the younger generation does things, so they try to extend their will over them. Though it's hard to think of myself as the younger anything, as it were." Father Mitchell's smile grew tired. "To be fair, this argument comes up every year. I open our doors to those in the community who need aid, he argues that my actions open us up to harm, and I argue that is Christ's way."

Father Mitchell paused to think on this for a moment. Lee recognized a man in crisis, but did not feel it was his place to intervene. This was between the man and his god.

A moment later, Father Mitchell shook himself out of his own thoughts, turned to them, and smiled brightly again, "Now, what can I do for you all?"

"We are going to need money," Luis said, with his usual directness. "How would we go about procuring it?"

"Uh, well..." Father Mitchell seemed taken off guard by Luis' line of questioning. "There are several unemployment offices I can put you in touch with. I assume you all have valid forms of ID?"

Luis reached into his bag and pulled out a scroll tube, handing it over to Father Mitchell. "I assume this will suffice?"

"Uh..." Father Mitchell took the tube, confusion in his eyes. He slowly opened it and pulled out the rolls of parchment that were inside. Sifting through them, he looked up at Luis. "What are these, exactly?"

"Scrolls of Pedigree," Luis said, with pride.

"Like for a dog?" Mitchell asked, confused.

Luis looked back at him, indignation in his eyes. Quickly, Lee intervened.

"These are what we would use as identification where we come from," he explained to Mitchell. "Your confusion leads me to believe that this is not sufficient for here?"

"No," Mitchell said, replacing the scrolls and handing them back to Luis. "You'd need a photo ID, like a license or student ID."

He reached into his back pocket and pulled out a piece of folded leather, pulling out a small card like the one Morgan had found in the orderly's pocket the night previously. It had Father Mitchell's name and picture, as well as other information that Lee noted was not available for any of the rest of them such as address and date of birth. For a moment he wondered how similar this world's calendar was to his own before readjusting his thinking.

"Thank you, Father Mitchell," he said, returning the card to him.

"Let me know if I can do anything else," Father Mitchell said, before turning his attention to the clock on his desk. He became visibly agitated. "Oh no, I'm running late. I hope you don't mind me cutting our meeting short."

"Got somewhere you need to be, padre?" Smithers asked.

"Yes," Father Mitchell said, gathering his coat and putting several items in his pockets. "I'm afraid one of our parishioner's children is in the hospital. She's sick and sad to say, probably not long for this world. I make sure I go visit her every day to pray and see if there is anything I can do for them."

Lee contemplated this for a moment. How powerful must this sickness be that a man of the church was unable to cure her? To take such a special interest in the child must mean that there was definitely something worth knowing about this sickness. Lee met Luis' eyes and understanding passed between them. Whatever this hospital was, it was definitely worth looking into.

"Would you mind if we joined you, Father?" Luis asked.

"Uh, sure," Father Mitchell said, confusion on his face. "Though I'm unsure why you would want to."

"We don't know much of this city," Lee said. "It would do us good to know where this hospital is, and learn about things on the way. Besides, we may be of some assistance to the girl or your parishioner."

Not seeming to fully understand, but not finding any flaw in the logic, Father Mitchell agreed. A few moments later they were down in the cold again, piling into what the Father referred to as the church's 'van.' After explaining the importance of a 'seat belt' and teaching them how to buckle in, the van was moving and they were underway.

Lee still felt some discomfort in these strange vehicles, though this ride was made far superior as he was now riding on the inside. In an attempt to occupy his mind with anything other than the rolling of his stomach, Lee studied how Father Mitchell operated the van. The stop and go seemed to be controlled by his feet, which Lee was unable to see, but the turning was controlled by a wheel that sat right above his lap. While unable to really grasp the operations of the van, Lee turned his attention to how Father Mitchell inter-acted with the rest of the road.

With so many other vehicles to contend with, Lee noted that without a system of trust there was no way they could function. It seemed that a system of lights and signs, which were fairly easy to comprehend, littered the roadways and directed operators on how they should be moving and when. By the end of the trip, Lee felt that he had developed a pretty firm grasp on how to navigate the roadways.

As they approached the hospital, Lee noted several large, box shaped vehicles with flashing lights emitting loud alarms as they drove past. He saw Luis grow tense and put his hand on the pocket Lee knew contained his collapsible weapon. Quickly, he put his hand on the knight's arm and pointed at Father Mitchell and Smith-ers. Luis looked and saw what Lee did: neither of them was reacting with anything other than casual acknowledgement of these vehi-cles. Luis nodded, understanding that if this were a threat, then they would have reacted to it somehow.

Eventually, Father Mitchell positioned the van into a grid with many other vehicles and twisted the key, silencing the van.

"Alright," he said, opening his door. "We're here."

It took a few moments more for everyone to understand how to remove the seatbelts, but soon enough they were walking through the familiar halls of the hospital. Morgan was marveling at the doors that would open at their approach, as if by magic, but Lee could tell that Timm and Luis were on edge. Considering the similarities this building had with St. Augustine, he did not fault them on that. How-ever, much like in the car, Lee took his cues from Father Mitchell and Smithers, who walked calmly through the bustling hallways.

After speaking with a bored looking woman at what Smithers called a "nurses' station" and being given name tags that stuck to their fingers and clothing, Father Mitchell led them to a pair of doors that opened at the touch of a button. As they opened, Lee noted that the room they were going into was barely big enough to hold all of them.

"This is the room we're looking for?" he asked, confused.

"No, this is just the elevator," Smithers said, ushering them all inside. "Come on, people are waiting."

Confused, but not wanting to cause a scene, Lee assumed that Father Mitchell and Smithers knew something he didn't and stepped on board, trusting in their knowledge of the world. The others were a bit more hesitant, but Lee hoped that his own leap of faith would inspire the others to follow on. They did shortly, and a moment later, the doors closed.

A sense of claustrophobia began to settle on Lee for a moment before a whirring noise filled the air and a sense in the pit of his stomach like being lurched upwards made him feel slightly ill. In an attempt to keep his mind off this new, unpleasant feeling, Lee looked around for something else to focus on.

There was a panel of buttons on one wall by the door, each one numbered, but only one was illuminated: button sixteen. Above the panel was a small black square with an ever-changing number illuminated in red. It currently said nine, but was steadily increasing. He watched as the number grew higher and higher, until finally it hit sixteen and the horrible lurching feeling stopped. A moment later, the doors opened again and Smithers stepped out allowing for the others to follow.

Lee walked out of the small room and found himself in a completely different place than when he had stepped on. He looked at Smithers, who was grinning at Lee's confusion, he was sure, but then turned to a window and looked out. A sense of vertigo washed over Lee as he saw that he was now hundreds of feet above the ground. It took a moment for his addled senses to quell down before something clicked in his mind. Lee turned to Smithers.

"Elevator," he said, his voice steadying as he spoke. "We've been elevated."

"Does what it says on the tin," Smithers nodded, and Lee was unsure if the man used the colloquialism unknowing that Lee did not understand what it meant, or uncaring. Either way, the two men followed Father Mitchell as he went down the hallway, the others in tow.

Father Mitchell led them through the brightly painted corridors past several stations, some filled with nurses and others filled with strange toys and sad looking people. They passed multiple rooms with beds where official looking people moved in and out on regular intervals. Lee took a glance into a few as they passed, noting that the person in each bed was in fact a child. A strange sick feeling washed over him. This entire area was filled with sick and dying children. He said a small prayer as Father Mitchell stopped at a particular door.

"There are too many people for you to all come in," Father Mitchell said.

"No problem," Timm said, turning to Morgan, "Want to take a walk?"

"Uh, sure," she answered, and the two began to circle the floor again.

"I suppose that will work," Father Mitchell said, looking at the three who remained. "Just be quiet as we go in, they may be asleep."

The room looked just like all the others they had passed along the way. Sterile white walls and floors, a curtain pushed back to reveal a bed containing one very small person whose eyes were locked onto a strange box on the wall showing a living sponge running around with a pink star shaped creature. Beneath the box was a woman sleeping in a chair, her dark hair as rumpled as her clothing. It seemed to Lee that she must have spent the night in that chair. Lines formed on her face even in rest, portraying just how stressful and difficult this time in her life must be. Lee felt pity for the woman, but admired her strength.

The little girl turned her head as the sponge changed to a man talking about needing something called a lawyer and repeatedly yelling a number at them. She smiled when she saw Father Mitchell and attempted to roll over to greet him.

"Father Mitchell," she said, weakly.

Father Mitchell quickly made his way to her bedside, helping her roll so that she did not injure herself. Lee saw quite clearly the effects the disease was having on her. Her dark skin was gaunt, paling to a color it should not be, and stretched thin across her frame. Too much of her skeleton was visible, though the untouched food on the table near her told him it was not due to neglect. She was malnourished, weak, and quite clearly dying. He doubted that she would last more than a few days.

Turning to Luis, he saw the knight could tell the same thing from looking at her. However unlike Father Mitchell, Luis had not accepted the girl's inevitable end. The fire Lee had seen in his eyes so many times before ignited as he set his jaw. Lee felt a small smile pull at the corners of his lips. It was the admiral trait of ones like Luis, the inability to accept defeat as any form of inevitability.

"You should be resting, Patrice," Father Mitchell was saying to the young girl. "Look at your mother, she's getting more sleep than you. How is that possible?"

"Mama works all day," Patrice said, weakly. She then turned her attention to the three of them standing in the doorway. "Are these friends of yours?"

"Yes," Father Mitchell said, turning his attention to them. "Why don't you come in and introduce yourselves?"

Luis stepped forward first, speaking out with more strength and volume than Lee thought appropriate for the room. "I am Luis L'hopital! It is a pleasure to meet you."

The little girl giggled a bit, and though weak, it was a pleasing sound to hear. Lee stepped forward next, introducing himself with a bow of his head. "My name is Lee Eraple."

They both turned to Smithers in the doorway, who looked a bit uneasy about coming inside. He looked back at both of them and sighed before stepping fully into the room and addressing the girl.

"I'm Smithers," he said, with a smile. "But you can call me Old Man Smithers."

His introduction got another giggle out of her, and even drew a smile from Father Mitchell, which given the circumstance seemed a lot more impressive.

"Are you guys priests too?" Patrice asked.

"I am," Lee answered, noting the confused look on Father Mitchell's face. "However, from a different religion than Father Mitchell here."

"I'm not a priest, exactly," Luis said, kneeling down besides the little girl's bed. "But would you like to pray with us?"

"Sure," the little girl said, smiling weakly. "Father Mitchell comes to pray with us every day, I'm sure you're welcome to do it too."

"Then take my hand," Luis said, reaching out and taking the small child's frail hand gently in his own.

Lee saw Father Mitchell about to interject and held up a hand. Father Mitchell paused in confusion. Lee just smiled and pointed at Luis, whose eyes were closed and a soft radiant light glowed in his palm. It was common practice back home for holy knights of his sort to perform this kind of healing on the battlefield, however Lee found it fascinating to watch when his life was not on the line. With a quick flash of light, the entire sense of the room just changed, and Lee felt an enormous weight dissipate.

"There," Luis said. "It is done."

"What's done?" Father Mitchell asked.

"The healing," Lee answered, smiling. "She's healed."

"She... she can't just be healed," Father Mitchell said, turning to a device on the wall. Lee had barely noticed its low, rhythmic sound, but now it was quicker, and somehow seemed stronger. "It's been months of treatments..."

"Father Mitchell?" Patrice asked, her voice stronger than it had been moments before. "Could you please pass me my tray? Suddenly I'm really hungry."

Father Mitchell stared at her for a moment. He wore an expression mixed somewhere between shock and joy, eyes welling with tears and color draining from his face. For a moment, Lee thought he may too be in need of some healing, but then he darted towards the door, calling out.

"Nurse!" he cried. "Nurse!"

Panic flashed across Luis' face as he looked at Lee. Lee looked to Smithers who just stood in the room, color drained from his face as well, though he did not look as elated as Father Mitchell did. Unable to read the situation, Lee turned inward and focused on his own god, in hopes that he may gain some clarity on how to approach this reaction. Before he got an answer, a woman dressed all in green rushed into the room.

"Vitals look fine," the woman said, looking at the machines. She began doing an assortment of other things that Lee did not fully understand, but assumed were how medicine in this world must function. She looked at papers, machines, rattled off numbers that were associated with different bodily functions. Finally, she seemed to exhaust all of her resources and turned to Father Mitchell, who was standing next to the woman in the chair, now sitting awake, her face strained. "She's fine, Father. I told you not to call us without need."

"What did you say?" The father asked.

"I said she's fine," the woman responded, then paused for a moment and looked down at the papers in her hand again. "She's fine..."

The woman quickly ran through all the numbers again, this time with a different goal in mind. Lee watched as she scurried to check once, twice, even thrice before coming to the same conclusion.

"She's fine," the woman said, wonder in her voice. "We need to run some tests to be sure but..."

"But what?" Patrice's mother asked, tears streaming silently down her face.

"I'm hesitant to say, Ms. Garret," the woman said. "But it's like your daughter never even had cancer."

Ms. Garret dissolved into tears of joy in Father Mitchell's arms. Lee walked over to Luis, touched him on the arm and nodded at the door. The knight nodded to Lee and escorted a still stunned looking Smithers to the door. As Lee stepped out of the room, he felt a hand on his shoulder. Turning around, he saw Father Mitchell, wide eyed and sputtering.

"He... he healed her," Father Mitchell said, looking as Luis walked down the hallway with Smithers. "I'm a man of God, I've seen a lot of things in my time, but that is the first genuine miracle I've ever seen."

"Are you not capable of that kind of healing?" Lee asked him, feeling he knew the answer, but wanting to be sure.

"No one is," Father Mitchell responded, his voice shaking. "Only con-men claim they could do such a thing. But I saw it, with my own eyes. He touched her hand and she was cured..."

"To be honest with you," Lee said with a shrug, "that kind of healing is common where we're from."

Father Mitchell's eyes grew wider as he turned to look at Lee. "Where are you from that such miracles are an everyday occurrence?"

"A world other than yours," Lee said plainly, feeling no need to beat around the bush with the father. He was a good man, and had helped them in a time of need. There was no reason to lie about their basic existence to him. "We come from a place very different from your world, but we are the same as you in one very important facet. We seek to do good."

Father Mitchell nodded at Lee, still seemingly lost in himself. Lee did not begrudge the man this, for he had just witnessed something that shook his view of reality. This was a feeling Lee could more than empathize with.

"When we get back to the church, I would ask you to speak with Donovan Hughes, our caretaker," Father Mitchell finally was able to say. "He has concerns that I am unable to do anything about. But you all... you might just be the miracle we're looking for."

Lee nodded and put his arm around Father Mitchell's shoulder, guiding the man back to the elevator and down to the van. Smithers took the keys from Father Mitchell and they all piled back in to return to the church.

SMITHERS

Smithers drove with his hands and ten and two. The radio was on, playing a good selection for the first time in forever. Creedence was on, and as soon as someone attempted to talk to him, he reached over and turned up Fortunate Son loud enough to get the point across that he did not want to speak at that moment.

His mind was in a bit of a spiral at the moment. He managed to keep his eyes on the road, follow traffic laws, and keep from hitting anything, so basically driving better than the average person, but his mind was still in the hospital. These people he'd been with since the night before sitting in that shrink's therapy group had seemed insane the whole way. They were insisting on magic being real, they were claiming to be from another world, but none of that made a lick of sense. Magic wasn't real, gods weren't real, and nothing they claimed to be true could possibly be true.

Then they went into that hospital room.

Smithers had seen cancer before, and it was a fucking shit show. Seeing it again, but in a pediatric ward, that was the hardest thing he'd ever done in his life. He was worried when they went in there, that Lee or Luis would try sharing their religion and giving that poor woman false hope. The boys wouldn't have meant anything by it. They were true believers, like a lot of folk who traded in faith, but the number of snake oil salesmen Smithers had scared off with a shotgun taught him that even the best of intentions could leave the wounded bleeding more. He stayed to watch and be sure they didn't say or do anything stupid.

He hadn't bargained for what he had seen. The little girl, Patrice, she looked better after Luis laid his hands on her. Brighter, cheerier, like one who was touched by faith and had just prayed are wont to be, but the hunger, the energy, that wasn't normal. The nurse checked everything and acted as if this sick child who was nearing her end had never been sick in the first place. Smithers wasn't sure about the people around him anymore. They could bring with them the answer to every problem the planet was facing if they were telling the truth. Hell, they could bring the end of it if they're telling the truth too. All a lie would mean is that they were crazy and he was crazy for ever thinking they were telling the truth.

He wasn't sure which one he was hoping for.

The van was back at the church and in park before Smithers even realized he was doing it. La Grange was ending and Smithers couldn't think of a reason to stay in the van, so he killed the engine and unbuckled his seatbelt. Getting out of the van, he saw Father Mitchell walking towards the back door in and his eyes scanned over to where his truck sat. Reaching into his pocket he could feel the keys pressed against his stomach. He could just get in, take the gas money, and head south. Out of the cold and out of the crazy. It was a decent plan. He turned and saw Lee coming over to him.

"Father Mitchell asked us to talk to Donovan, the maintenance man," Lee said to him. "You coming?"

Smithers wasn't sure if Lee knew the weight of the question he had just asked. He considered everything that had happened in the past twenty-four hours. His gaze turned to follow Father Mitchell as he walked into the church, his thousand-yard stare even more obvious than Smithers' own.

"Alright," Smithers said with a reserved sigh. "Let's go."

Not ten minutes later, Smithers found himself standing in a garage big enough for two cars had it been empty, but the sheer amount of stuff that was piled against the walls and scattered on work tables left very little room for the garage to perform its primary function. There was a sense of chaotic order here that made Smithers feel right at home, except for the old radio in the corner warbling out some kind of Chinese music he didn't recognize, but caught a phrase here or there he'd picked up somewhere along the line.

Donovan came up and introduced himself to the group. He was probably about mid-forties, of Asian descent, and covered in grime and grease from his day's work, even though it was barely noon at this point. He wiped his hands on an old rag and shook hands at each introduction.

Lee offered his hand last and asked, "Father Mitchell said you had an issue we might be able to help with. What can we do for you?"

"Well, it's less for me and more for someone we both know," Donovan explained. "You see, we have AA meetings down in the basement from time to time."

"AA?" Morgan asked, her face quizzical.

"Alcoholics Anonymous," Smithers explained. "For people who drink too much and make it other peoples' problems."

"One way of putting it," Donovan said. "One of our regulars, Richard, hasn't shown up in a couple weeks."

"Fell off the wagon?" Smithers asked.

Donovan shook his head. "I don't know, I just know he was in a bad way before the meetings. He was getting a bit better, but he was in one hell of a dark place before them. Father Pearson hasn't let anyone from the church act in an official manner considering Richard isn't a parishioner, so basically he's not the church's problem."

"That's a shitty way of thinking," Luis said, gritting his teeth.

"The thought reflects the man," Donovan said, solemnly. "I'm not able to get away and Father Mitchell has his hands tied on the matter. If I gave you the man's address, you think you could look in on him?"

"Sure," Smithers said, stepping forward before throwing his thumb over his shoulder at the group behind him. "Any chance we could borrow the van? My truck ain't big enough to load all these guys."

"You'd have to ask Father Mitchell about that," Donovan said. "But here's what you need."

Smithers took down the address and told the others to wait by the car while he went to speak to Father Mitchell. There was no point dragging the whole motley crew in there to deal with picking up keys. He knocked on the door and waited for the father to give him the okay to enter. A moment later he stepped in.

Father Mitchell looked the way Smithers felt. His glasses were sitting on the desk in front of him, a distant look in his eyes.

"How can I help you, Mr. Smithers?" The scent of whiskey was on his breath as he spoke. Smithers did not feel like correcting the usage of mister and his name at this moment would do anything to correct the action, so he just decided to take the direct approach.

"Any chance we can borrow the van?" Smithers asked. "We're going to go check in on that Richard guy, and I don't really feel like shoving two of them in the bed of my truck is going to scream 'low profile' if you get what I mean."

"Right," Father Mitchell said, not taking his eyes off the wall. He reached into his desk and pulled out a set of keys, holding them out to Smithers. Smithers reached for them, but when he took them, Father Mitchell didn't let go. He turned to look at Smithers, something nearing madness in the depths of his eyes.

"I've believed in God my whole life, Mr. Smithers. I've believed that we are the instruments of his will. His hands upon the earth with which he does all his work," he said, calmer than his look suggested to Smithers. "And now I have seen divine intervention. It is real and it is active in this world. For two thousand years we've yet to see a genuine miracle beyond that which is written in the bible. But today, I saw a man who worships another god cure cancer with a touch."

"Technically, Nike is a goddess," Smithers said, before thinking.

"Nike," Father Mitchell said, releasing his grip on the keys. "Because why wouldn't it be Nike. Good luck, Smithers. I have a bit of soul searching to do. Please take care of Richard. He's not in a very secure place right now. Be gentle with him."

"I'll do my best, padre," Smithers said, pocketing the keys. "You just try to get some rest."

"Right, rest." And with that, Father Mitchell closed his eyes and leaned back in his chair. Smithers closed the door as he left, hoping that it would encourage others to come and speak with him another time. Smithers walked out to the parking lot where the others were waiting, unlocked the van, and clambered inside.

"How's Father Mitchell doing?" Morgan asked, her voice concerned.

Smithers found it hard to be angry with Morgan. She was a caring soul, and reminded him of what he'd want in a granddaughter, if his had been worth talking to. He could hear the sincerity in her voice and decided to break his current oath to ignore these people as much as possible.

"He'll be alright," Smithers said. "He just took a little medicine to help him sleep and is getting some rest."

"Oh," Morgan said, apparently satisfied with the answer. "Well that's good then."

Smithers put the van in gear and began driving to the address Donovan had given him. As they drove, Smithers noted that the neighborhood was going from bad to worse. Drug deals done in broad daylight, prostitutes standing by the side of the road presenting their wares, and not a single cop car in sight. Seems they didn't even bother with trying to improve the lives of the people who lived here. It wasn't hard to believe that a man like Richard, in a bad place and making it worse with hooch, would find himself in this part of town.

Smithers sighed and shook his head. Best to keep his mind on what they were here to do. They were here to check on him. No need to worry about saving the guy. Let whatever gods that were out there sort that mess out themselves.

Having to circle the block a couple times before finding a spot to park in, Smithers was already irritated by the time the rest were all piling out of the van. His hand was on the door handle when he stopped to look at the duffle bag thrown in the back seat. Taking a quick look around, Smithers zipped it open and slipped his shotgun into his jacket pocket. It may not be exactly legal, but all that did was make him fit in better in these parts.

Making sure the van was locked, Smithers joined the others outside the door. They seemed to be discussing something important as he walked up.

"We could just break the glass," Luis was saying. "Open the door from the inside."

"We should be a bit more careful," Morgan said. "Does anyone know a spell that could open the door?"

Smithers just sighed, "Alright, you guys, clear a space."

He walked over to the panel of buzzers on the wall by the door and pressed the first one he saw.

"Hello?" A voice crackled from the other side.

"Pizza delivery!" Smithers said, cheerfully.

He had to try this about six or seven times before one of the voices on the other side chimed back.

"Awesome! I don't even remember ordering one! I'll buzz you up!"

The door buzzed and Smithers pulled it open, holding it and gesturing for the others to go inside.

Timm stared at him once they were inside. "You really are a great wizard."

"Boy," Smithers said. "I told you not to call me that."

The elevator in this building was broken, forcing them to go up the dimly lit concrete stairs. How this building wasn't already condemned was beyond Smithers' understanding, but after a few nervous minutes they found themselves outside of Richard's doorway. The sound of soft sobbing came through from the other side of the door.

"Alright," Smithers said softly. "Now we're going to want to do this gently and carefully, as he's probably not in his right..."

Timm pounded on the door and the sobbing sound stopped.

"Mind." Smithers finished, staring daggers at Timm, who merely looked back at him with a wide grin on his face. "Seems he ain't the only one, is he?"

"Who is it?" A shaky voice called from inside, though the sound of footsteps told Smithers he was coming closer.

"Lookin' for a Richard," Smithers called back, before anyone else could say anything that might spook him. "Is that you?"

The door opened a crack, but was stopped by a thin brass chain that Smithers knew people only bought to make themselves feel more secure, not that it actually did anything. The bleary red eye of a man in his mid-forties who'd seen more mileage than one would expect stared back at Smithers, darting quickly around at the rest of the group.

"Yeah," he said, his speech slurring slightly. Smithers was unsure if it came from the man being drunk or his voice being strained from crying. "I'm Richard. What do you all want?"

"Father Mitchell sent us," Luis said. "He wanted us to check on you and see if you were okay."

The door was slammed in their faces before Luis managed to finish the sentence. The sound of locks clicking into place echoed through the hallway.

"Well," Smithers said, no longer surprised at their luck at interacting with people. "That seems to have gone as well as could be expected."

Morgan stepped forward and pressed her ear to the door. Furrowing her brow, she closed her eyes and listened intently.

"That's strange," she said, her voice barely above a whisper. "It sounds like wood grinding against wood... And clanging metal."

Smithers looked at her for a moment, impressed by her hearing. But what was he doing? Opening a drawer and grabbing a knife? Moving a table and picking up some pans to fight them off? Didn't make sense. This guy had gone full fight or flight mode, and he ran from them immediately. That meant...

"Shit!" Smithers snarled, "He's going down the fire escape! Quick, downstairs and after him!"

~ 10 ~

MORGAN

Morgan was surprised to see the agility Smithers had when flying down several flights of stairs. While Timm still managed to get out front ahead of them all, the rest of them managed to keep pace until they hit the street. Bursting through the door before the rest of them, Timm looked around wildly before seeming to notice something. Morgan's feet had barely hit the landing before she saw Timm take off down the street shouting back to them.

"He's going this way! Hurry up!"

The cold air hit Morgan's lungs like a knife, but she couldn't let up and leave the others to deal with Richard alone. The poor man was scared, running like a rabbit from wolves. They weren't here to hurt the man, but there was no way for him to know that. Besides, Luis and Timm were both men of action, they would try to subdue the man, she was sure. And while Smithers and Lee were gentler in their approaches, she didn't see a way out for this man that didn't end in violence currently.

So on she ran, her face stinging from the cold and eyes watering from the wind, she ran. After about fifteen minutes or so, the grey, blocky stone that made up her understanding of this city began to turn to warmer, red brick. Vines, shriveled and brown and waiting for spring crawled up the sides of them, giving way to more of a natural surrounding. Trees became more plentiful, and soon sprouted on either side of the road. They passed a sign and Morgan managed to read the words *Paul Revere Park* fading against the green wood.

As they came around the corner, Timm burst forward and blocked their path, his finger to his lips while his other hand waved at them to stop. Morgan felt her footing almost slide out from under her as the icy concrete beneath her feet refused to give purchase. Her hand reached out and she grabbed Timm's elbow in order to keep herself upright.

"What's going on?" Smithers asked in a harsh whisper. "Where'd the guy go?"

"He's on a bridge ahead," Timm said, his breathing barely heavy, but his voice ragged. "He's standing on the edge of it, looking like he's trying to make a pretty big decision."

"That's not a good sign," Luis muttered darkly. "I can only think of one decision he'd be making there."

"We must approach this with caution," Lee said, nodding. "If we run up, we'll startle him and maybe make his decision easier to make. We should try to sneak forward. Talk him down if we can, grab him and pull him back if we must."

With their plan set, they started moving forward. Morgan felt the smooth surface of the stone beneath her feet. It was quieter to move across than the concrete, and seemed to be in better condition too. With fewer cracks it was easier for her to move silently alongside Timm and Smithers. However, it seemed that it was also easier for ice to form, as a yelp from behind her drew their attention. Lee had stumbled, slipped on the ice, and fell directly into Luis' arms. Morgan turned to see the knight supporting the priest in an awkward half hug that barely kept them both on their feet.

Realizing they've been given away, Morgan turned to see Richard's eyes on all of them, a look of horror plastered over the man's pale face.

"I can't. I can't. I can't..." he muttered, repeating the phrase. As he repeated himself, his voice grew until he was practically shouting. "I can't!"

The boys lurched forward, reacting quicker than Morgan was able. Luis, Smithers and Timm circled around Richard, all hoping to be able to rush in and grab him should he attempt to jump, while also cutting off his escape route should he try to rabbit again. Lee moved forward and waved his hands while muttering. A light radiant glow appeared first on him, then flickered to life on the others besides her and Richard.

"I CAN'T!" Richard screamed even louder, though this time, Morgan noticed another face, almost superimposed over his own. It twisted and screamed, mirroring Richard's, but clearly was not the same. Another person, perhaps, trapped within the man.

The face, almost pulling itself free from Richard's body, twisted to look at Smithers and let out a ghostly wail. Morgan felt a chilling cold rush over her that required all of her resolve to keep from succumbing to. She looked up in fear at Smithers, hoping he had not fallen to this... thing's... attack.

The old man shook his head and sneered, "Don't talk back to me, boy."

Morgan saw an opening. As it was distracted, she rushed forward and wrapped her arms around Richard's middle and pulled with all of her might to get him away from the edge, and hopefully the being that was afflicting him.

To her surprise, he moved easily, and she practically stumbled back as they went. But rather than falling to the ground in her arms, Richard's body floated three feet off the ground. She looked up in shock as the horrid face looked down at her, eyes burning with hatred. Morgan felt herself wilt a little inside, but managed to keep her grip on Richard.

"Boy! Don't you float at me!" Smithers cried out, pulling out the stun gun, which crackled to life in his hand. He looked at Morgan, and she saw apprehension in his expression. He didn't want to attack while she was still within range. So instead he seemed to be goading the being. "Hey! I'm talking to you!"

Timm seemed to have fewer inhibitions about it, running forward and unleashing a whirlwind of attacks on Richard. He leapt forward, spring boarding off the stone edge of the bridge, and swung three times in quick succession, hook to the left cheek, hook to the right, and finally an elbow under the chin, snapping Richard's head back. Timm landed and turned with a grin to see the damage he had done.

Richard's head slowly rose, turning his pitch black eyes directly on Timm. Morgan watched in horror as Timm's grin faded into a grimace. He had unleashed a full barrage and it seemed to have done nothing.

"Timm! Stop attacking him!" Lee called out, the symbol around his neck glowing with a fierce white light, like that of metal left to soften in a forge. "He's possessed! We need to attack the root of the problem!"

Chanting more words in a language Morgan did not recognize, a burst of radiant light erupted from Lee. As it washed over Morgan, she felt a light tug at her body before the full and sudden weight of Richard collapsed into her arms. They both fell to the ground together, and Morgan looked up to see the entity that had been causing the man so much grief.

A spectral form of a heavy-set man, donning just a pair of overalls hovered in the air. In one hand he held a bottle, while in the other he brandished a knife. His heavy, ruddy cheeks would have made him seem comical if they hadn't been framed by a pair of black, empty sockets. His eyes like the void, empty and cold, scanned across the battlefield before he reared back and screeched.

"Man," Smithers said, breaking the spell of this thing's arrival. "They told us who to call, but they could have at least given us a number."

Luis, now with a target, charged forward and waved his hand. A bracelet of radiant thorns appeared around the specter's wrist, causing it to shriek in sudden shock and pain as Luis flicked his wrist, unleashing the baton and swinging it in a wide arc at the ghost. The baton itself did little to upset their enemy, but the explosion of white-hot light that followed caused the creature to shriek in agony.

In retaliation, the ghost swung with its knife, the spectral blade passing through Luis' armor. Luis cried out in pain and Morgan could see the skin where the blade touched turn black as it dug into his flesh, not drawing a drop of blood.

Seeing the danger Luis was in, Morgan moved forward to help, but paused, realizing there was nothing she could do against this kind of threat. She shook her head and forced herself forward. Even if she couldn't aid in the battle, she was going to do something at the very least to help. She reached forward, grabbing onto Richard's limp form and began to drag him as far away from the fray as she could. The whole while watching as Smithers moved in with the stun gun, sweeping it through the creature, eliciting little reaction as Timm moved in, his fists doing nothing as they passed harmlessly through the creature.

She felt small. She felt weak. There was nothing she could do to protect them. All she wanted to do was protect them all. But what could she do? The pain in her head grew worse as the ringing sound of battle echoed in her mind. Her magic was paltry compared to the holy spells Lee and Luis were wielding. A little flame? Cause a bud to bloom? How was her so-called power supposed to help?

Her stomach began to churn with the anxiety of it all. She wrapped her arms around her guts and fell to her knees. Pain began to ripple over her body, but why wouldn't it now? Why wouldn't she be falling apart when they needed her most? It only made sense.

No it doesn't. Another voice said to her.

She gripped the cold stone beneath her, nails scraping against it, creating a sharp, grinding sound in her ears. Of course it does. Seasoned warriors, all of them. And she was just a little girl.

Little girl? The voice said, curiously. *Not so little I would think.*

Morgan felt her bones grinding, her skin burning with pain as it stretched and ripped, making way for something new, something else that she was not prepared for. She tried to cry out in pain, but the cry became a bellow of fury and rage. Moran shook her shaggy form and viewed the world, for the first time, through new eyes.

The night crystallized before her, the cold of the frost nothing against her hide. The scents of a thousand humans wafted in the breeze, but still wasn't strong enough to hide the nocturnal world that thrived beyond the sight of those who didn't know how to look. But the bear knew. And now that Morgan had become the bear, she knew too.

Power rippled through her muscles and her eyes turned to Timm as his fists feebly passed through the ghost. She had power now, but to be a beast was more than power. She had to use the human mind to know when to use it. Charging in now would be foolish. Morgan looked back at the lump behind her. Richard lay open and exposed. Should the fight turn too far against them, it would be up to her superior strength and speed to get him to safety.

Wisdom and power, the voice whispered as it slowly drifted away as though on the wind. *No mere girl indeed.*

Lee came running over, breaking the spell the voice had kept Morgan under. The frenzy of battle had returned as he slid into place beside her, barely even noting her change in form. He began checking Richard for vital signs, finally leaning down and sniffing at his breath. He sat up and cried out to Luis.

"He's been poisoned!" Lee yelled. "That thing must have been possessing him for weeks, forcing him to do nothing but drink! I cannot heal this, he needs you!"

"I'm a little busy!" Luis snarled back, parrying another blow from the knife with his baton, though the spectral blade only slowed to the radiant energy Luis had imbued it with. With a startlingly quick repost, Luis spun until he had come around the back of his attacker and drove the weapon down with two hands.

Another explosion of white light erupted on the bridge, illuminating the surrounding area as the ghost let loose a final wail, its body dissolving into a spray of ectoplasm coating all who stood nearby it. Luis stood calmly, wiping the quickly evaporating ectoplasm away from his eyes and began walking over towards where Lee and Morgan stood over Richard.

"There," Luis said, upon reaching them. "Now what did you need?"

Lee pointed down at Richard, unimpressed with Luis' demeanor. "Heal the poison from him. Please."

"Very well," Luis responded, collapsing the baton before kneeling down and pressing his hand against Richard's chest. The man released a small groan of discomfort before settling back into unconsciousness.

Morgan turned her attention to Smithers, who in spite of being in decent shape, was currently breathing heavily. They locked eyes and Morgan smugly dropped the form of the bear, feeling no pain or even discomfort in this transformation. One moment she was a bear, the next she was Morgan.

"Believe me now?" she asked, smirking.

"I believe I need a drink," Smithers said, dismissing her statement and starting to shuffle over.

Rolling her eyes at his stubbornness, Morgan turned her attention to the view from the bridge. The little stone bridge spanned high above a large pond that sat in the middle of the park. It would have been beautiful had the circumstances been different. As she stared out and the ambient glow of the snow across the water, a fog began to roll across the surface of the water, too quickly to be natural. From within the fog a sickly green light began to glow. A strange form took shape within the fog, and stepping out from it came the shape of a massive elk. It stood, seven feet at the shoulder, antlers longer and wider than any other she'd seen of its kind.

However, its size was not the thing that struck Morgan the most. The glow itself seemed to be emanating from this beast as its skin sloughed off, its matted fur dry and brittle like grass left to bake in the sun, and exposed bone lay bleached and bare before her. Empty sockets turned to face her and a chill ran down her spine.

A hand clapped her on her shoulder and Morgan jumped, ready to swing at whatever was attacking her. But when she turned, to her surprise it was only Timm, who quickly stepped back and out of her reach.

"Whoa," Timm said. "Are you okay?"

Morgan whirled around to point out the creature on the lake, only to find that it had disappeared without a trace. The soft, ambient glow of the pristine white snow was all that reflected back at her.

"I... uh..." she said, confused at what she had just seen. Had she just been seeing things? Maybe it was only the stress of the fight and her new ability to shape shift that had caused her to imagine another threat? Or what if she was going crazy just when she had become useful?

"Yeah, I guess I am," she lied. It was all she could do. There was too much for her to sort out.

"Alright, then. Come on," Timm gestured over his shoulder. "Smithers said we need to drop Richard off at the hospital. Seems we're spending a lot of time there, doesn't it? Hope that's not some kind of sign or anything."

He started to walk off towards the others. Lee and Luis were lifting Richard and beginning to carry him down the path as Smithers directed them. Timm caught up leaving Morgan standing alone on the cold stone bridge.

"Hopefully not," Morgan said, beginning to shiver as she stared out over the lake where the strange green creature had been watching her. "I really hope not."

~ 11 ~

LUIS

For the second time that day, Luis saw the hospital come into view. It seemed to him like such a building was of greater import than any other in the city with the frequency people went there and the work done within. Though rather than feel pride for the respect given to the healing arts, Luis felt a bitter sadness fill his chest. This world must be very sick indeed if such a building was his destination so often. Children wasting away, a man poisoning himself even before the malicious spirit took him over, these events were mere symptoms of the disease that ran much deeper in this city. It needed rooting out, but there were no clues as to where the source may lie.

Smithers pulled the van up to a parking area away from where the boxy ambulances were coming and going. He hopped out of the van and Luis took this as a cue to do the same, but the older man held up a hand.

"Hold on," he said. "I'm going to go grab someone with a stretcher, no sense carrying the man as he is. We may do more harm than good."

Already out of the van, and feeling anxious energy tingling in his muscles, Luis nodded but did not return to his seat. He and the others wandered closer to the doors as a pair of men in blue uniforms wheeled what Smithers called a stretcher to their van and loaded Richard onto it. Luis watched their precision with admiration, seeing an almost militaristic cantor to their movements. If left in this world, perhaps theirs would be an occupation worth pursuing.

"Can you believe it?" A nasally voice caught Luis' attention as the glass doors slid open to admit Richard on the stretcher.

Luis turned and saw a woman with her reddish hair pulled into a bun talking excitedly to a man in a cap carrying a large black box on his shoulder. Before the doors shut, Luis slipped inside in order to hear what she was saying clearer.

"That little miracle is amazing! A girl, on the brink of death, just recovering! Out of nowhere!" The woman continued while taking notes on a small pad of paper. Her hands were shaking with such excitement that Luis thought she might end up dropping her pen.

He thought for a moment about what they were saying. It stands to reason they were probably talking about Patrice and his actions earlier that day. The excitement over the recovery of the child made him smile. Perhaps he should talk to this woman, tell her of his deeds and how the mercy of Nike sped her course to victory over the disease. He felt himself stepping forward with this plan for a moment before her next words stopped him in his tracks.

"Thought we'd be coming here for another 'angel going back home' story," the woman said, a note of disgust in her voice. "I freaking hate those. But this! This could really do something. Maybe get me on a real network! Or even, imagine! A Pulitzer Prize! That miracle baby is a real miracle for my career."

The bitter sadness that had been welling up in Luis' chest began to burn into anger. This woman cared nothing for Patrice, or her recovery, just what it could mean to her own career. It was in that moment that Luis believed he found the source of sickness that plagued this world.

"I don't know," Luis heard Smithers say. "We were just walking through the park, saw him collapsed, and got him to the hospital as quick as we could."

Luis saw Smithers talking to one of the men in the blue uniforms, who was nodding and taking notes as the old man talked.

"Okay," the man said. "But if you don't mind waiting around a bit, we'd like for you to give a statement to the police."

"Uh, sure," Smithers said, a little nervousness to the smile on his face. "Lemme just grab my grandkids out of the van. No point in them freezing out there."

"Sure thing," the man said, before nodding and getting back to work.

Smithers turned and quickly made his way towards Luis and the door. As the older man reached Luis, he grabbed the knight's elbow and leaned in to whisper.

"Grab the others, get in the van, and let's get out of here."

"Shouldn't we wait to give the statement?" Luis asked as Smithers dragged him to the door.

"Not unless you want to spend a night in a cell," Smithers replied.

A few moments later, they had all piled back into the van and were making their way back to the church, the hospital vanishing from the rearview mirror. Luis sat and contemplated for a moment all that he had just witnessed. The church had needed those outside it to save a member of the congregation because the leaders were disinterested in helping. The police, supposed protectors of the realm, would arrest them for doing good deeds while people like that woman could openly profit from the suffering of children without any retribution. Corruption was poisoning this world, turning its protectors and guides into the enemy. How anyone could live with hope in such a world baffled him. However, this was not a defeat, it was a challenge. And challenges were meant to be met, and overcome. Luis resolved himself to meet all the challenges this world would throw at him and defeat them, one by one.

"Hang on a sec," Smithers said, breaking the spell of Luis' thoughts. "I'm starving, anyone else with me?"

"Oh yeah," Timm said from the back seat with a grin.

"Okay then," Smithers responded, looking around. "I think I know a place we can afford around here somewhere. Just gimme a minute."

A few minutes later, Smithers pulled the van into a parking lot where a large, luminous bell glowed in yellow and purple lights. Turning into a small lane, Smithers put the van in park behind a row of other slow moving cars and began counting change from his pocket.

"It's not a lot," Smithers said, "But Taco Bell is cheap enough that we can all at least get something in our stomachs before we starve."

"What's Taco Bell?" Morgan asked, her normally quiet voice a little huskier, and Luis turned around in his set to see her eyes, dilated and obviously hungry.

Smithers answered without looking up or noticing the difference in Morgan's demeanor. "Just fast food. Not as good as a real Mexican place, but good enough for our needs at the moment."

Smithers ordered a few of what he called tacos and a couple drinks for them all to share. Luis opened his and was met by a glob of brown mixed with yellow, white, and what passed for vegetables mixed in.

"What is this filth?" He asked.

"What passes for a taco to corporate America," Smithers answered without answering as he often did. Luis grimaced as he turned to see the others.

Morgan was wolfing hers down with abandon, probably not even tasting the food as it passed. Timm took a bite and chewed for a moment, but then his face paled and turned slightly green, meeting Luis' eyes and his expectations for the so-called food. Lee took a bite, chewed, then swallowed, smiling before taking a sip of his drink.

"Food is food," Lee said to the others. "And we who have had so little should at least be grateful for what we have. Thank you,

Smithers, for the meal you've provided us with. I'm sure without you, and it, we would be in a much worse place right now."

"No problem," Smithers said, somehow managing to eat and drive the van at the same time.

Luis looked down at the 'meal' in front of him, but contemplated Lee's words. Corruption comes from being unsatisfied and feeling entitled to more than you are due. Luis recognized that arrogance and pride in his own actions and shook his head, smiling. The priest was right; they needed to be grateful and pious. He said a silent prayer of thanks to Nike and, quickly as he could, ate the taco. Truth be told, he preferred the Mountain's dew better than the food, at least.

The group ate in silence as Smithers made their way back to the church. Upon reaching their destination, Luis' feet met the pavement with a stronger stride, refreshed and rejuvenated having bested an enemy in combat and somewhat filling his stomach. They made their way to Donovan's workshop as quickly as they could, hoping the man would still be in even at this late hour.

The warbling radio signaled that he was in fact still in, and Luis led the group into the room, finding Donovan at his work table packing up tools.

"Donovan!" Luis exclaimed. The man turned with a start, but relaxed when he saw them approach.

"Ah, you're back," he said, slight relief to his voice. "Any luck with Richard?"

"Yes," Luis confirmed. "It seems he was possessed by a vengeful spirit, but we banished it from his body and destroyed it. He is now resting and getting help at the hospital."

Donovan stood, stunned for a moment, before shaking his head and smiling. "You know what? I'll take it. So long as Richard is getting the help he needs, I don't really need to ask many more questions. Thank you."

"You are welcome," Luis nodded to him.

"Is there anything else we can do?" Morgan asked, coming up next to Luis. The knight looked at her, noting that her voice was back to its normal, timid tone and her eyes had returned to their soft green color, no longer dilated in hunger. It seems the Taco Bell had served its purpose after all.

"Why yes, in fact," Donovan said. "If you have the time, the AA meeting should have just finished up. There are a lot of chairs for me to put away, and it goes a lot quicker with some extra hands."

"Then hands you shall have," Luis said, and followed Donovan up the stairs to a large room filled with odd chairs.

Donovan walked over to one, grabbed the back and the seat and pulled so that the chair collapsed into a flat sheet before their eyes, then lifted it and hung it on a rack on one wall.

Luis stared in amazement along with Morgan, Timm, and Lee. Smithers walked up and looked at them.

"They're just folding chairs," he said with a sigh. "Is everything going to be like this with you guys?"

Lee shook his own head and joined Smithers and Donovan in folding up the chairs. Luis and Timm stepped forward and did the same, but Luis looked back and noticed Morgan folding and unfolding a singular chair over and over again. For a moment he chastised himself, thinking that such a young girl could hold within her danger worth worrying too much about. As feral as a hungry bear may be, she was also as filled with wonder as a raccoon with a fork.

Once the work was finished, Donovan turned to all of them.

"Thank you again," he smiled. "Please, help yourselves to the coffee if you'd like. I know it's a bit cold out there."

"Oh, no thanks," Smithers said, holding up his hand. "It's a bit late for me. I think it's about time I turn in."

Turning to the rest of them, Smithers added, "It's probably best if we all do the same. Who knows what we're going to have to deal with tomorrow."

Smithers began walking down the stairs to the cots. Luis sighed in agreement and began to follow. There was a lot he had to think on, and he believed that it would be best to do so while well rested. Their first day free to roam this world was far more exciting than he thought it would be and exposed far more depth than he anticipated. Perhaps a good night's sleep was exactly what he needed right now.

TIMM

Timm waited for the others to go to bed, feinting sleep until he was sure they were all asleep themselves. Once he was certain, he quietly slipped out of bed and made his way towards the stairs. Morgan stirred and Timm froze. His eyes locked on her for a moment, sure that she could sense him moving. That thing with the bear was impressive, but he wasn't sure just how linked she was with these new animal forms. Could she smell him moving? Hear his footfalls even in sleep?

A moment later she settled back into her covers and lay still again. Timm held his sigh of relief until he reached the top of the stairs. Quickly, he made his way towards Father Mitchell's office. Streams of light still poured from the crack under the door, so Timm took a chance and lightly knocked.

"Come in," the Father's voice called from within. Timm steeled himself and entered the room.

Father Mitchell sat, no longer in his priestly garments, but rather a pair of jeans and a light cotton shirt. He was flipping through a book at his desk, making notes on a pad, but looked up from his work as Timm entered. He closed the book and smiled.

"Timm! Good to see you, though it is a bit late," Father Mitchell gestured to the chair across from his desk. "Please, sit. I hear things went well with Richard."

"Yeah," Timm said, lowering himself into the chair. "He's at the hospital now, recovering."

Father Mitchell nodded. "Yes, there are far worse places to be than in the hospital, I suppose. At least there he can get the help he needs."

"Not sure if the hospital can do much about ghosts, but we took care of that at least," Timm said.

The father paused. "Normally, I would assume you meant he was dealing with the ghosts of his past and that was a struggle that we all need to go through on our own, but considering what has been going on I'm going to assume you mean real ghosts."

"Yeah," Timm nodded. "It was an angry spirit who..."

Father Mitchell held up a hand. "This is one of those things I'm just going to trust you on and hope for the best with. Are you hungry?"

"No," Timm shook his head and pressed a hand to his stomach. It hadn't felt quite right since dinner, but he didn't want to complain about the meal Smithers had provided, especially after what Lee had said about it. "We stopped at Taco Bell on the way back."

"Taco Bell?" Father Mitchell said, furrowing his brow. "Not the best thing for you to be eating that late at night. Though I must admit, I'm far happier you got that than McDonalds. The van smells for weeks if we get McDonalds in it."

Timm didn't really understand what the father was saying, but smiled and nodded anyway. His eyes swept over the desk until they finally landed on the book Mitchell had been reading.

"So," he asked. "What is that you were reading when I walked in?"

"Ah," Father Mitchell said, picking up the book. "This is the scripture, my religion's holy book. Currently I'm reading the story of Lazarus, I don't suppose you've heard that one in your time here yet?"

Timm shook his head.

"Well it is indeed one of my favorite stories," Father Mitchell continued. "What I love most about it is how it flies in the face of everything, going against the established order. I decided to revisit it today since you and your friends do the same. You fly in the face of every established order that I have set my entire life upon."

"I'm sorry," Timm said, feeling a slight panic in his chest, hoping that the father wasn't saying the worst. Saying that he was sending them away. "We didn't mean to…"

Father Mitchell again silenced him with a hand. The motion wasn't dismissive, but very similar to that his master would use to calm an excited apprentice who was getting ahead of the lesson.

"The way I see it, such a power to upset the natural order can have one of two sources; either it is a power of heaven or a power of hell," Father Mitchell explained. "Those who work for heaven or God spread his power and message through their actions. And from what I've seen, I believe that you and your friends are indeed doing God's work."

"But we believe in different gods," Timm said. "Even among our group, the three of us who are religious follow different gods from one another, much less your god."

"I never believed that there was only one path to God," Father Mitchell said. "If you do not believe in my God, nor I in yours, does that mean we are enemies? No, especially if the gods we believe in both work towards the same ends. Both our gods ask us to perform good in their name. Should I condemn you for doing good but not in my god's name? What kind of person would that make me?"

"I suppose not a great one," Timm smiled, though the smile cracked and faded quickly. "What if I'm starting to doubt the gods in general? Doubt the teachings I had as a child. Someone… someone close to me died. And my god… he wasn't there. How do I know I'm doing the right thing?"

"Faith is never supported by knowledge," Father Mitchell said, standing up and making his way over to a bookshelf. He perused the titles for a moment before finding what he was looking for and returning to Timm. "Here is what I wanted. Kierkegaard."

"What?" Timm asked.

"Soren Kierkegaard," Father Mitchell repeated. "He was a German philosopher who talked of, among many things, the earliest views of nihilism. Without going into too much detail, he believed that life was suffering, and that we have to find the things in life that were worth suffering for. So that is your quest in life, learning what pain is worth it, and what pain you need to let go from your life. God does not abandon his people, and I would dare say that your god would not either. Perhaps the pain of loss was something you needed to feel in order to be ready for what was to come."

Timm tried to keep the tears from falling, but a few escaped his hold. "I was lost before, but at least I knew where I was. Now, I'm still lost, but I don't even know where I can begin to look."

"Look to those around you," Father Mitchell said, placing his hand on Timm's shoulder. "Those you help."

Timm smiled faintly. "That's funny. My master used to say the same thing."

"Different gods, same message," Father Mitchell stepped back and offered Timm his hand. Timm rose, grasping the priest's forearm, seemingly taking the man by surprise, but Mitchell clasped Timm's as well and they shook heartily.

"You are a blessing to this place," Father Mitchell said. "Thanks to you many will suffer far less than life had planned for them. I hope you will continue to do good works."

"We will do our best," Timm nodded, though a gurgling in his stomach made him quickly clutch it.

"Ah," Father Mitchell said, seeing Timm's reaction. "It seems the downside to the inexpensive Taco Bell is rearing its ugly head."

"Is all food like this here?" Timm asked, feeling the cramping in his stomach settle a bit.

"Fast food tends to be," Father Mitchell nodded. "We have a food pantry open on Tuesdays and Thursdays if you need something, though we don't really have a lot of places for you to actually sit down and cook. Though it may treat you a lot better than fast food will. I doubt your bodies have built up the tolerance necessary to eat it regularly without problems."

"I'll suggest it to the others in the morning," Timm nodded.

"Until then," Father Mitchell said, walking over to the door and opening it. "Might I suggest the restroom? Down the hall and on the left."

Timm nodded his thanks and left the room, making a mental note to shoot down the next time Smithers suggests any form of fast food. He'd much rather wait for something that was more agreeable to his system.

~ 13 ~

LEE

Lee woke up the following morning to the sounds of Luis getting dressed in his workout attire. He crinkled his nose a little, thinking just how pungent the smell of those clothes was getting, and decided to broach the matter later that day. Timm was stretching and seemed to be intent on joining Luis for his run. Figuring there was no sense lounging in bed while the others were already up and about, he got up as well and began his morning prayers.

By the time he had finished and made his way upstairs, he found Morgan and Smithers at one of the tables the church made available. Morgan was eating some kind of cold oatmeal out of a bowl while Smithers drank a cup of what he referred to as coffee. Picking up his own bowl, Lee sat and joined Morgan in her meal.

"The others are out on a run, but should be back soon," she informed him. Lee nodded and began eating while she talked. "And since we have that performance tonight, we have the whole day to go exploring."

"Information gathering may be a bit more helpful," Lee stated, not wanting to shoot down Morgan's spirit, but feeling a bit antsy about the world he currently found himself in.

"Agreed," Smithers said, wiping a bit of coffee from his mustache with the sleeve of his shirt. "We need to find out about the people who took us and see if they know anything about how you lot got here... What was their name again?"

"DIARD," Morgan answered with conviction and without hesitation. Lee noted the hard look in her eyes, but brushed it off as none of his business. He was no fan of these DIARD people either, and supposed her personal feelings were her own.

"Where might we be able to find information on these DIARD people?" Lee asked Smithers, assuming he would be the best source for information in this world outside of Father Mitchell. The Father was knowledgeable, however Lee did not want to become a burden on the holy man, nor did he want to leak too much information to him. It wasn't that he didn't trust the man, but Lee worried that their involvement with such dangerous fellows may spill over and harm the priest and his so-called flock. It was not a risk worth taking while Smithers was already in the heat of it with them.

"Hmm..." the older man pondered for a moment, taking another sip of his coffee. "We might be able to find some information at the college library. I doubt we'll find anything specific on a shadow government agency in the stacks, but we can use their internet to do some private snooping, and who knows, their periodicals may offer a bit more insight than we'd find online, depending on how far back these jackasses have been operating."

Lee nodded, understanding most of what Smithers was talking about. "So we go to this library and piece together as much disassociated knowledge as we can to start forming the picture of what we're up against."

Smithers turned his eyes towards Lee, "Uh... yeah. That about sums it up."

Lee nodded and returned to his breakfast. While the meal was cold and wet, the tiger did not lie. It was indeed great.

"Then we wait for the others to return, and head over to this library," Lee said. "We all agree?"

The other two did, and so once Timm and Luis returned and cleaned up, they all loaded up into the van after bidding the father a good day.

"We'll have the van back by this evening, dad," Luis said to Father Mitchell.

"Its... its father, actually," Father Mitchell corrected the knight with a weary sigh.

"The two are synonymous," Luis said, a puzzled expression on his face. Lee just smiled as Smithers pulled away and the morning sun shone off of the piles of packed snow that had been pushed off the road by large vehicles Smithers had called plows.

The ride was smooth and pleasant, in spite of the bitterly cold air. It seemed many others had a similar notion as he, since they were all out and about wandering the streets, bundled up against the chill, though the heat of the sun did bring many to unbutton their large coats and allow the air to cool them.

It seemed a delicate balance to Lee, trying to keep the warmth of the body in without allowing it to consume you entirely. How much to keep in versus how much to let in? Many of the people out in the streets could not seem to make up their minds, zipping and unzipping, buttoning and unbuttoning, freezing or burning alive... Lee wondered which was worse.

"Are you alright, Lee?" he heard Morgan's voice cut through his own thoughts.

"Yes," he answered. "I'm fine."

"You're sweating a bit," Morgan said, worry in her voice. "Are you sure?"

Lee touched his fingers to his brow and felt the beads of sweat cling to his fingers. Only then did he realize that he was uncomfortably warm as well. He lowered his fingers to brush against the top button of his coat, but did not undo it. Instead, he smiled at her and nodded.

"I'm fine, this is nothing compared to the heat of the forge," he said, his tone hopefully pleasant and neutral. "I didn't even notice."

"Well, okay," she smiled back. "Just be sure to tell us if you're getting too warm, we can always have Smithers turn down the heat."

"Thank you, but I'm sure we'll be arriving soon." Lee responded.

And he found that he was not wrong. Just fifteen minutes later they arrived at Boston University's Mugar Memorial Library. Approximately fifteen minutes after that, they found a parking spot in a garage Smithers muttered about being over priced and a far walk from the library. On the walk over to the library from the garage, which Lee suspected may also run them about fifteen minutes if their current luck held the same, they passed a few shops filled with strange technologies, obscure books, and coffee that Smithers described as 'overpriced milk that barely counts as coffee.'

"Why is it so expensive?" Timm asked, his eyes lingering on the line of people walking away with their green and white cups. "Is it like a brothel or something?"

"What?" Smithers sputtered. "Boy, stop asking nonsense questions! Or at least stop asking them in public where people can over hear you."

"But it's a whole new world!" Timm argued. "I want to learn everything I can."

"It hasn't been the new world in centuries," Smithers muttered a dark reply. "And I can tell you the less you know about it the better off you'll be."

Lee pondered on this plea for ignorance over knowledge for the rest of their travel to the library. He barely noticed as a woman stepped into his path as he passed through the doors of the library.

"Here you are sir," she said as she pressed something into his hands. Lee barely got a look at the blue, rubbery tab as she continued barraging him with unsolicited information. "If you're looking for a place to work, there's no better place to start than with our bank. You'll learn the ins and outs of the economic system while helping others build their financial future. As you build theirs, you build yours!"

"Uh," Lee desperately tried to piece together his thoughts as he was pressed with more information about his current employment status and education level. "What is going on?"

A hand gripped his arm and tugged him away from the woman. Smithers moved him towards the others who had apparently not gotten the abrasive woman's attention as they passed.

"It's a recruitment fair," Smithers said, pushing Lee along. "They're all trying to get the students here to apply to work for them. Figure they can nab them while they're young and inexperienced enough to work extra hard for not nearly enough."

Lee noticed the sour expression on the woman recruiter's face as Smithers spoke, but she painted on a phony smile and directed her attention to another pair of people walking in, pressing the same blue rubber thing into their hands as she did.

"What's with this thing?" Lee held up his own blue rubber thing to Smithers, who had let go of him, allowing Lee to walk under his own power again.

"It's a cheap little key chain," Smithers answered. "They give those away for free to try and lure you in. Works well to get you interested in hearing more because you feel you owe it to these people to hear them out now that you've accepted something from them."

Lee pondered this for a moment, but couldn't figure out who would be so interested in something they didn't need that they'd listen to someone's pitch for something they didn't want.

"Ooh! Free things?" Timm said excitedly and started making his way back towards the recruitment fair.

Ahh.

Smithers grabbed Timm by the collar of his pea coat. "Nope! We've got work to do. You want to explore the fair, fine, but they're here until six. Work first, free stuff later."

Timm reluctantly rejoined the group as they made their way into the library proper and away from the bustle of the fair. Lee felt a bit of relief as his eyes scanned over the books that lined the walls of the massive room they found themselves in.

Lee watched as Smithers pulled himself in front of a boxy device he called a computer while Luis watched on in fascination. Timm almost immediately became bored with the situation and wandered off. Morgan watched a bit longer, but soon followed suit and went off into the stacks. Feeling that he could not contribute more to the search without knowing more about the world they were in, Lee decided to thumb through a few books on the nearby shelves.

Most of what he found was based around this world's history and cultures. Reading through, Lee found that except for the absence of magic, history did not seem all that different in this world than what he could remember from his own. Wars, famine, plague... all of it was present and accounted for. It seemed like there was not much that could prevent these horrors from rearing their ugly heads. Lee read deeper on until he heard a yelp and looked up.

Timm was lying on the ground, his chair tipped over beneath him and a pair of heavy books next to his face. Morgan stood over him, hands clapped over her mouth in what looked like a mixture of embarrassment and worry. A pair of female students walked by, giggling as they saw the scene. Timm got up, gave them a little bow, and set to cleaning up the mess he'd made while Morgan quickly made her exit, seemingly to Lee, in an attempt to compose herself. Lee sighed inwardly a bit, feeling that the boredom of these two would eventually cause them further issues, but turned to see Smithers coming back from the desk where a woman seemed a bit annoyed after having spoken to him. Lee could sympathize with her.

Feeling progress may have been made, Lee stood up, returned his book to the shelves, and walked over.

"What have you found out?" he asked Luis and Smithers as the older man's fingers flew across the keyboard.

"She said there's not much here about odd happenings or government involvement, seemed to think I was some kind of paranoid kook asking about it," Smithers said, causing Lee to bite his tongue slightly. "But she said that there's some faculty here who focus on paranormal studies due to a lot of ghost stories and hauntings in the New England area. A-ha!"

Smithers leaned away from the computer screen to show what he had found. Lee leaned in slightly to make out the blurry words.

"Faculty member Norman Arbuckle, expert in paranormal studies. Office location, Math/Science building, top floor." Lee read aloud. "Does this really help us that much?"

"No idea," Smithers admitted. "But considering what you guys are would be considered 'paranormal' in our world, he's probably our best bet. Plus if that's what DIARD is involved in, he may know something. Best lead we could hope for here."

"That is correct," Luis nodded. "We are operating with little to no understanding of what we're facing, and any chance at information should be hunted down."

"A little information can be a dangerous thing," Lee said solemnly.

"Then let us get more than just a little." Luis stood firm on his convictions, but Lee should have anticipated as much.

"Alright," Smithers said, standing up. "Let's get the kids and take a look at that fair. Might be a few useful items floating about, though I doubt anything too sophisticated. Usually just pens and those weird triangular highlighters. I have no idea why they think anybody uses those damned things."

Lee was unsure what he meant by that, but he figured this would be a good opportunity to learn a little more about this strange culture he was being exposed to.

* * *

Lee was correct, he was indeed learning a lot about the strange culture he found himself in. Specifically how he felt very uncomfortable in it. As he looked around the so-called "job fair," he made sure to appear as unapproachable as possible for these people. They were quite aggressive at making their pitches towards anyone and everyone who got close, expressing why their company would be the best to work for. He was reminded of the snake oil salesmen that would come into town, claiming the magic and wonder of their concoctions that would cure all ails and help you build a perfect life. There was something in their smiles that boasted their ingenuine nature.

His gaze rolled over the crowd, seeking out each of his companions as he went. Morgan was off talking to some man in a suit under a large white and blue banner, though on closer inspection he realized she wasn't even paying attention to the man as he spoke. Her attention was completely on a tank filled with small green lizards. Lee read the sign again and assumed it was probably for the best. Who would want to work for a company that misspelled 'gecko?'

Continuing his search, he found Timm talking to a man at a booth simply labeled 'army.' Lee found this to be quite insufficient as a banner as it did not tell you the name of the army he represented. This army-man seemed to be looking at Timm with a great degree of skepticism until Timm rolled himself back into a handstand, proceeding to do push ups from that position. Now the army-man was amazed. Lee understood that well himself; the first time he'd seen Timm do that he was also amazed the boy didn't break his neck.

Out of the corner of his eye, Lee noticed some people approaching him, the crocodile smile of a con artist on their faces. Since they did not have a booth specifically for their pitch, Lee assumed that whatever they were about to approach him with was not condoned by the establishment and moved off towards Luis, who he spied approaching a banner that stated "Law, Order, and Enforcement."

With a quick glance over his shoulder, he saw those toothy grins fade and his pursuers peel off. Seemed he was right to assume they were not completely on the up and up. Lee felt a small grin creep across his face, but quickly quashed it. It was a victory, yes, but no reason to get cocky about it.

Approaching Luis, Lee found he was in deep conversation with a pair of individuals wearing black shirts with the letters FBI printed on their right breast. The pair, a man and a woman, seemed to have starkly different personalities.

The woman was standing in a powerful stance, feet spread in a way that Lee recognized as one that anyone trained in martial combat would have. It would not be easy to knock her down, but she held the stance with a relaxed confidence that he was unsure if she even realized she was standing in such a way. She was of average height though it was clear she was built with far more toned muscle than the average person of this world. Short reddish-brown hair was beginning to gain the appearance of unruliness as tight curls were forming. On her waist, she had a small leather fold hanging next to what Lee was confident to be a gun, though smaller than the one Smithers carried around with him, and far more prominently displayed. Her grey eyes were sharp, and while she maintained eye contact with Luis, Lee sensed her measuring him up as he came alongside the knight.

The man on the other hand was lounging back in his seat, balancing his girth on the back two legs of the chair with his booted feet propped up on the booth. Though his shirt was tucked in the back, his prominent gut had forced the front of the shirt to break free from its restraint and expose his navel. It seemed to Lee that a good portion of his hair must have migrated from his head to his stomach, as he was balding up top, and not gracefully. He styled it in such a way that he seemed desperate to hide the fact and was doing a poor job of it. His watery brown eyes were not quite as sharp as the woman's, though he blearily opened one to acknowledge the two seemingly new recruits standing at his booth.

"You got this one, Fulmer?" he said in a gravelly voice that fully expressed his disinterest in the situation.

"Yeah, I got them, Charlie," the woman, apparently named Fulmer, replied. "Just like the rest of them today." Then, under her breath, just loud enough for Lee to hear she added, "Cept the co-eds."

"I told you not to call me that," growled Charlie. "It's Charles or Special Agent Brown. You know I hate being called the same thing as that cancer kid."

Lee caught a snarl appear on Fulmer's face for just a second before she turned her attention away from the man and changed her expression to one of polite discourse to address him and Luis, though Lee could still see the smolder of anger in her eyes.

"So, are you gentlemen interested in a career of crime fighting and solving mysteries like all the other procedural crime junkies out there, or are you looking to do some real good in the world?" she asked them.

"A little of both," Luis responded. "Though I like the crime fighting more than the mystery thing. That's more his speed."

Luis gestured to Lee who responded with a polite nod.

The woman cocked an eyebrow at the two of them for a moment then softly laughed. "Well, at least you two have a sense of humor about it. My name is Special Agent Temperance Fulmer with the FBI. And this is my partner, Charlie."

"I told you not to call me that," growled Charlie, picking his head up to glower at her. "Special Agent Brown."

"Do your job, or it's Charlie Brown," Fulmer said without looking at him or losing the diplomatic smile on her face. Then, addressing the two of them again, "What kind of career would you be looking for here with us at the FBI?"

"What does FBI stand for?" Luis asked.

"What do we got?" Special Agent Brown rolled his watery eyes. "Clowns?"

Fulmer shot him a look, but Lee could tell she was wondering about the same thing. "It's an acronym, stands for Federal Bureau of Investigation. We look into crimes committed on a federal level, determine who the culprit or culprits are, and take them into custody to stand trial."

"Ah, you're a contingent of your king's army!" Luis said, feeling he understood more clearly.

Fulmer looked at him quizzically and Lee decided to take this moment to intervene on Luis' behalf.

"I do apologize, we're not from around here and we are trying to get our bearings on how things work," Lee explained.

"I see," Fulmer said. "Are you here on a Visa or are you American citizens? Because unless you are citizens you are not able to apply to work for the FBI."

"Understood, ma'am," Lee nodded respectfully again. "However, are we still able to ask you questions about the FBI?"

Fulmer looked up and down the aisle they were standing in. Very few people were stopping at this booth, either to talk or even look. She turned back to them and smiled.

"As I don't currently have a mad rush, I don't see why not," she said. "Ask away."

"The FBI is an organization that combats crime here," Lee started. "Are there others?"

"Well yes, there are local police forces, the CIA, Homeland Security, and several others included in the military branches." Fulmer explained, though Lee could tell she was very confused about having to explain it.

"Many of them seem to be acronyms," Lee noted, eliciting a nod from Fulmer. "And what makes them all different from one another if they all have the same job?"

"Well, we all have the same general job overall, but each organization focuses on different specifics. The FBI focuses on dealing with federal criminals specifically, though we do help and get help from other organizations to do so."

"What about from an organization called DIARD?" Luis asked, taking Lee off guard. He had been hoping to fish for that information a little more delicately, though it seemed the knight had no qualms about tackling the topic head on.

Quickly, Lee looked at Fulmer, her puzzled expression seemed quite genuine to him. He did not believe that she knew what Luis was talking about. Shifting his gaze to Brown, Lee did not expect to get anything from the lazy lout, but he figured it would be best to cover his bases.

Lee's blood ran cold. Brown hadn't seemed to move much, but Lee could tell that his watery eyes were clear and presently focused on Luis. Small beads of sweat percolated under what was left of his hairline. The muscles in his legs and arms had tensed up, making his leisurely stance all the more out of place. There was no doubt in Lee's mind, Special Agent Brown recognized the word DIARD.

"Sorry, I've never heard of that agency," Fulmer shook her head, bringing Lee's focus back to her. "Are you sure they're real, or that you have the correct name?"

"Yes I am," Luis answered, "It was the name of the organization that put us in the..."

"Hey boys!" Smithers appeared from the crowd, clapping his surprisingly strong hands on to both Lee and Luis' shoulders. "Glad you got a chance to look around, but it's time to get going."

Lee felt Smithers tugging on his shoulder, desperately trying to lead him away. He didn't fight the old man, figuring he knew of a danger they were in that he didn't, but Luis seemed to resent being led around like a sheep.

"We were asking these FBI agents about DIARD..." Luis started to say before Smithers interrupted him.

"Oh, no need to waste their time with that," Smithers said jovially, but there was a look in his eyes that clearly screamed at Luis that they all needed to get out of there. Luis seemed to pick up on the cue and begrudgingly began to walk through the crowd.

Smithers continued to lead Lee away, though something caused the priest to look back. He saw Agent Fulmer lift a small black box the size of her palm up to eye level, point it at him, and tapped it. Even across the crowded room, Lee heard a faint clicking sound. Then, she simply placed the box into her pocket. She locked eyes with him for a moment, but soon too many people blocked them from one another.

Lee followed Smithers through the crowd, curious about what Fulmer had done with that strange box, but after a moment shrugged the thoughts away. If it were important, he'd learn about it more later. If not, it was nothing worth worrying about.

~ 14 ~

SMITHERS

Smithers dragged Luis into the hall, feeling his heart pounding in his chest the whole way. With a shove, Luis broke the grip, and Smithers spun on his heel to face the delusional knight.

"What the hell do you think you were doing, boy?" Smithers snarled, trying to keep his voice as quiet as possible.

"What the hell do you think you're doing?" Luis shouted back, not bothering to keep his voice down. Smithers winced and tried to get the boy to lower his voice, but he would not have it. "I was talking to those people trying to get the information we need! What is the point of sneaking around and gathering useless information to try and piece answers together when we can just go to a source that may know?"

"Keeping ourselves alive!" Smithers hissed. "Now keep your damn voice down before you get everybody staring at us!"

Luis glowered at Smithers, but stood quietly as the others approached. Timm was laden down with an assortment of lanyards, keys, pens, and other worthless accoutrements from the booths. Morgan seemed a bit pouty, though Smithers had seen her looking at that car insurance place's geckos. He was just glad that she hadn't set them all free. Thankfully, Lee seemed to be able to follow directions and got his ass out of trouble before it really began.

"Listen, I get it, where you're from you can just go up and gather information, but here we have to be a little more subtle about how we go about things," Smithers tried to explain to Luis. "Most people don't take kindly to the fact that a group of people broke out of a mental hospital the government put them in. They in fact think those people are dangerous and crazy and will get people... killed..."

Smithers began to reflect on the words he was saying to them and realized that they were in fact dangerous, crazy, and so long as they're running around free there is a good chance that people would die. Specifically himself.

However there were a lot of things that forced Smithers to keep his lot in with them. While they were all dangerous and crazy, this world was getting doubly so at every turn, and Smithers was convinced his best chance at staying alive, at least for now, was to keep himself around them.

"So we have to be subtle," Lee said, looking at Luis, who was fuming but seemed to have collected himself.

The knight was still glaring at Smithers, who felt a brief flicker of nerves, remembering the heavy blows that this young man was capable of. Smithers was unsure if Luis ever lost his temper, that he'd be able to take him on. Maybe if he had a damned good head start, then he could take pot shots as he ran, but he's seen the power of the knight's strike in action... it was like the fury of a god.

"Very well," Luis' voice was hard as steel and his eyes never left Smithers', but there was a slight shift in his shoulders that told Smithers the immediate danger had passed. "Smithers, you're the expert on this world, so tell us. What is our next step?"

Smithers breathed a sigh of relief and composed himself. Best not to let the kid know he'd gotten to him. After making sure that he'd be able to speak clearly and with the proper confidence, Smithers began to outline his plan for the group.

"There's a guy that works here, a professor. His name is Norman Arbuckle," Smithers explained. "He's the guy we need to talk to."

"Why him?" Morgan asked, taking the array of lanyards off of Timm's neck in an attempt to untangle him from the Gordian knot he'd gotten himself into.

"An expert on paranormal studies, according to the records on the college," Lee answered before turning to Smithers. "Though I'm still not sure what that means. What exactly are paranormal studies?"

"It's a branch of 'science' that researches things that are outside of the realm of the natural or possible," Smithers explained. "Like ghosts and monsters, and other things that can't possibly exist."

"But you fought a ghost," Luis said. "Alongside us."

"Yeah, see, still not sold on that bit," Smithers said. "But if for no other reason, Arbuckle would be good to visit in order to set the record straight on that."

That answer seemed to appease the group and they all started off, following Smithers to the Math and Science building where Arbuckle's office was located. Smithers understood that they fully believed in this paranormal nonsense, and that a lot of very strange things had happened along the way to this point around them, but he was still not prepared to accept their explanation for what was going on. If what they said was true, that opened vistas of such terrifying possibilities for his reality that Smithers most definitely did not want to start pulling on those threads. And here he was, on his way to get more tangled than a kitten with a yarn ball.

Smithers walked through the doors of the Math and Science building and over to the elevator. The thing was old, but he was not keen on taking his older bones up to the top floor by stairs alone. Pressing the button, Smithers began to wait. The rest of the group, however, began trudging up the flight of stairs on his left.

"Uh," Smithers called out. "Where do you think you're going?"

"You said his office was on the top floor," Luis answered curtly. "We're going to the top floor."

"Yeah, I got that," Smithers said, trying to keep his tone from getting too sarcastic. "But why are you all planning to climb up like a thousand steps when we've got an elevator right here?"

"Um, Smithers? Do you remember the last elevator ride we were all on?" Morgan asked, leaning over the rail. Smithers felt a twinge in the back of his brain and had to resist the urge to yell at her not to lean too far out.

"I remember, you were all fine as I recall," Smithers responded. "It elevates a hell of a lot easier than an old man like me. And a lot faster than all of you."

"Can't be faster than me," Timm said, almost indignantly.

As if on cue, there was a ding as the elevator arrived and the doors opened. Smithers stepped inside, calling out to them all as he went.

"Feel free to climb if you want, but I'll be waiting for you at the top."

A moment later the rest of the group clambered into the elevator, looking around with a mixture of worry and hesitation.

"How long could it possibly take to get to the top?" Timm asked, though Smithers was fairly certain he caught a note of concern in the boy's voice hidden behind that mask of pride. "I could be up there in less than a minute. Maybe we should have a race, Smithers?"

Without answering, Smithers leaned over and pressed the button for the top floor and leaned back with his hands on the rail as the doors closed. A moment later, the familiar lurch of the elevator rising announced that they were moving.

He could have probably prepared the rest of the group better for the difference between that newer model in the hospital and this old hunk of junk the University will probably wait to replace until after every cable snapped, but a wave of petty victory swelled in his chest as he watched them all try to regain their balance like dogs in a moving car. That sense of victory reached its head as Timm reached out and grabbed Smithers by the arm to catch his balance as the rattling old box jerked slightly in transit.

That victory soured a bit as Morgan did the same to Timm, adding even more weight to Smithers' arm. He had not expected the slight girl to weigh as much as she did, though with what he saw of her abilities, there's a good chance she was packing quite a bit of muscle. Thankfully, Lee seemed to mimic his own plan and gripped the railing encircling them with a death grip that rivaled that of a man clinging to a rope bridge over a gorge.

Only Luis appeared unaffected, standing perfectly still, his feet planted wide and arms crossed. Smithers noticed the knight was stiff as a board and beginning to perspire. Petty revenge was fun, but the old man really hoped that the kid wouldn't blow chunks everywhere because of stubborn pride.

A moment later, the elevator rang again, announcing the end of the ride, and as the doors slid open, each of them evacuated the elevator around Smithers so quickly, he was reminded of a Looney Tunes cartoon. Smithers stepped out calmly to find them all panting and leaning against walls.

"Oh come on," Smithers said. "It wasn't that bad."

"That was horrible and I never wish to do it again," Lee said calmly, but with steel in his voice.

"But look," Smithers said, pointing out the window. "We're elevated."

The rest of them looked out the window in amazement at the city skyline before them. Smithers was reminded of grade school children on a field trip going into a tall building for the first time. Even Luis seemed to marvel at the sight before them. Smithers let them enjoy it for a moment before breaking the spell on them.

"Come on, top floor," he said. "Arbuckle's office has got to be somewhere around here."

After about fifteen minutes of searching the floor, Smithers finally found what he believed was Arbuckle's office. It was a plain wooden door with no window and no sign. Only by sheer luck did he notice the faded numbers barely visible on the wood that designated it an office rather than a storage closet. Frustration mounting, Smithers rapped his knuckles on it a little harder than intended.

"Go away!" A voice called from inside. "Office hours are next week!"

"He's in," Smithers said to the group. With a twist of the handle he pushed his way into the room.

Smithers felt like he had been transported into a movie set of what they thought an academic's office looked like. It was dark inside, as only a single desk lamp surrounded by piles of dusty books stood to illuminate the room. Several bookshelves were jammed into every corner of space the room could afford to lose, and each of them was stuffed to capacity. Odd trinkets and totems were scattered around the room, adding an element of the macabre to the scene. Alone, next to a window smaller than a porthole, stood a pot of dirt with aspirations of a plant growing out of it.

"Who are you?" the same nasally voice called out. "How dare you barge into my office?"

The man, Smithers could only assume was Norman Arbuckle, fit his stereotypical room with a stereotypical appearance. Looking much like a parody of the nineteen-eighties, Arbuckle seemed to only be lacking a lazy orange cat. His brown, curly hair was a bit wild and unkempt as though he didn't particularly care about his appearance. He was dressed in a cheap looking three-piece suit, though the tweed jacket meant to top off the outfit was draped over the back of an overstuffed chair. His glasses were made of thick plastic and for a moment Smithers thought they might have been one of those joke pairs of horn rims that are sold at cheap toy stores before recognizing the thick coke bottle bottom lenses.

"You call this an office?" Smithers asked, gesturing around. "Looks like a rejected set piece from Raiders of the Lost Ark."

"Hrmph," Arbuckle huffed. "At least you didn't say Temple of Doom."

"Hey, I have some taste," Smithers responded.

A small smile betrayed Arbuckle before he smothered it and took on a professional demeanor once again.

"Be that as it may, I told you once already that office hours are next week," he said, making a shooing motion with his hand.

"We don't know what these office hours are, but we need to talk to you now," Timm said, stepping into the room. "About DIARD."

It took all of Smithers' strength not to turn around and whoop the boy's ass. As soon as the word DIARD left his lips, Arbuckle's demeanor went from that of an attempted authoritative instructor to a terrified child. His eyes went wide and his body began to tremble. Smithers wouldn't have been surprised if the man pissed himself.

"You're one of them!" the professor cried, his voice abnormally high pitched compared to a moment ago. Suddenly, Arbuckle darted forward much quicker than Smithers would have given the man credit for.

Smithers thought he was going to rabbit and charge the door, however instead of moving forward, Arbuckle dodged to the side and ripped open a desk drawer. Before he could react, Smithers saw the barrel of a very large revolver pointing directly at him.

"No we ain't," Smithers said as calmly as he could with the cannon of a gun bearing down on him. "We're no friend to them I can assure you..."

Timm blurred into his vision from the side, darting in on Arbuckle before he could react. With his left hand, Timm batted the gun to one side and twisted it from his grip, sending the weapon clattering to the floor. Using the forward momentum, Timm's arm shot up as though to strike Arbuckle under the chin, but instead slid his forearm against the outside of the professor's neck and whipped it around into a grapple, forcing Arbuckle's head into the side of his body. A choking noise escaped the professor as Timm's grip tightened, securing the man in a guillotine style headlock.

"Damn," Smithers said, looking at Arbuckle's reddening face. "Now he'll let you go in a second, but we ain't with DIARD, we're actually on the run from 'em. So we just need a little help from someone who knows a little something about them. And it sounds to me like you do."

Smithers walked around to where Timm was facing. The young man was panting heavily, but Smithers knew that it wasn't because of any exertion. This was a man focused on holding back. It would have been all too easy for the boy to snap this man's neck with ease. Another one Smithers knew it would be best to look out for.

"Gonna have to let him go now, son," Smithers said gently. "We need him awake to talk to us."

There was a wildness to the young man's eyes that made Smithers uncomfortable, and for half a second he thought that the rush of battle may take the boy a step too far, but gently, Timm shifted his grasp on Arbuckle to where Smithers could hear the deep, panicked breaths. Morgan stepped up, gently placing a hand on Timm's shoulder, but addressed Arbuckle.

"Maybe this will help," she said, reaching out her hand to the dying plant on his windowsill. The scent of fresh plant growth and warm earth filled Smithers' nose, months too early, and oddly pleasant given the cold winter. He breathed deep to enjoy it, then sucked the air in harshly, forgetting to breathe out in surprise, as the browned fern flooded with green new life.

Morgan pulled her fingers away from the now reinvigorated plant and turned to face Arbuckle, whom Smithers just noticed was just as shocked as he was.

"Um," she said, "Ta-da?"

"You're one of them!" Arbuckle said, this time his voice stricken with awe rather than terror.

A deep sigh came from the doorway.

"We're getting nowhere with this," Luis commented, his voice gruff with irritation. "He still isn't convinced. Are all people of this world so pig-headed?"

"No, no, no," Arbuckle said, wriggling against Timm's grasp. "A different 'them' in this case. You're one of the..."

He paused and looked up at Timm. "Do you mind?"

"Are you going to try to hurt any of us again?" Timm asked him, his voice hard.

"Unless you're planning on breaking my neck from this position, it seems that I have little choice but to speak peaceably," Arbuckle answered. "Besides that, I get the feeling you're not working with the organization as I had originally assumed."

Timm looked pensively at the man for a moment. Smithers couldn't decide if it was because he was trying to read the motives of the professor and doubted his intentions, or if it was because he was trying to work out exactly what was just said to him. After a few seconds, however, Timm must have decided that it was safe to release him. As he did, Timm made sure to impress upon Arbuckle that he would be staying close at hand, a message that the professor did not miss.

Arbuckle quickly walked over to the windowsill where Morgan was standing. Timm made a move to step forward, however Smithers held his hand out. Giving the boy a stern look, he shook his head, hoping that Timm would get the message and stand down. Begrudgingly, the boy did, and Smithers turned his attention back to the professor who was studying the plant in amazement and chattering with Morgan.

"You managed to completely reverse the ill-effects of my neglect on this dead plant," he was saying. "How marvelous."

"Oh, it wasn't dead," Morgan shook her head. "If it was dead, I wouldn't have been able to do anything to help the poor dear. It was dying, but still had some life in it. So I just reached out and used my power to nurture it back to health."

"Druidic magic," Arbuckle said, now staring at Morgan in the same manner in which he observed the plant. It made Smithers uncomfortable, but Morgan didn't really seem to notice. "Astounding to think that it actually still exists in the world."

"Wait," Smithers said. "Are you telling me that they're actually magical? I thought they were just crazy."

"How are you still unable to believe this?" Lee piped up from where he stood in the doorway near Luis. He gestured at the knight. "You saw him cure that girl's cancer. You've seen Morgan turn into a bear. And you've seen a ghost trying to kill all of us. What more evidence do you need?"

"I'm sorry, cured cancer and became a bear?" Arbuckle said, cutting through the tension that was building. "You're capable of such things?"

"Well," Morgan said, shifting uncomfortably, "Not in here. There's not enough room."

"Yes, yes," Arbuckle said. "Of course. Though that's a far cry from the typical claims I see and have disproved. But yours is the first actual evidence I've seen of real, true claims of power. Usually I just get faith healers and mediums who do nothing but run scams and do cold reads on people to manipulate them into giving money. Though I find this bit about the ghost strange. Mediums to tell of talking to lost loved ones."

"This one was not all that interesting in talking," Lee said.

"So we had to put it down," Luis finished.

"Ah," Arbuckle nodded. "I see. And how did you do that?"

"Well, bullets weren't working, so I used my taser," Smithers said, enjoying seeing Arbuckle's eyebrows creep up slowly in disbelief.

"And then I invoked my god's wrath and smote it down," Luis said firmly and with pride. Arbuckle's eyebrows crawled higher.

"Your, god, you say?" Arbuckle asked. "And who is that?"

"Nike, goddess of victory!" Luis' voice cried out with pride.

"I see..." Arbuckle looked a bit disquieted, but only muttered quietly as he went back to his desk. "The difference between a cult and a religion."

"Government funding," Smithers answered, drawing a wry grin from the professor. "So Prof, think you can help us?"

"Perhaps, though I'm not sure how much use I can be. Honestly, the power they're claiming to have, which I'm more inclined to believe based off of the display I just witnessed, has me wondering where people like them could have been hiding." Arbuckle began flipping through some papers and books on his desk.

"We're not from here," Timm said, firmly. "We're from... uh..."

Smithers noticed a pained expression cross Timm's face. It looked like he was clawing at the edges of his memory, but couldn't quite grasp at what he was reaching for. The image of a man swimming into deep water to retrieve treasure while trying to ignore his burning lungs manifested in Smithers' mind. He wondered, briefly, if all of them had such a difficult time dredging up the memories of their home. Was it too painful to remember, or could they just not?

"That would explain it, then," Arbuckle said, his voice annoyingly tainted by that smug tone that came from someone who knew something that the rest of the room didn't. Irritation grew in the back of Smithers' mind, but he fought it down, reminding himself that he needed this man to help him be rid of these nut jobs.

"Explains what?" Morgan asked, far more politely that Smithers would have managed.

"Why DIARD is interested in you." Arbuckle explained. "Do you know anything at all about them?"

"We know they run St. Augustine," Lee explained. "And that they're for some reason interested in people like us."

"Yes, that's because people like you are very special," Arbuckle said.

"Us?" Morgan asked. "How are we special?"

"Says the girl that says she can turn into bears and bring plants back to life," Arbuckle said with a smile. "First of all, DIARD is not just a name. It is an acronym. A word who's letters represent other words."

"Like the FBI!" Luis called out excitedly. "The Federal Bureau of Investigation, like that woman at the job fair told us."

"Precisely," Arbuckle answered, very much in his praising teacher voice, Smithers noticed. "Only this one stands for the Department of Immigration Applied Research Division. To the outside, any average person would believe that it was dedicated to researching new ways to secure borders between countries, specifically ours and Mexico's, given the current climate. However, I've been looking into some of their more... unusual projects."

"But if it's a government agency, how can you be looking into that stuff?" Smithers asked. "Isn't that classified?"

"Oh yes," Arbuckle nodded. "However, the paranormal investigation community is not a large one. And when you can't get your orders filled because someone else with a lot of capital is buying what you need to do your personal projects in bulk... well you start getting curious and working your way down a set of very interesting rabbit holes. It's not that I know what their projects are based on their plans, but based on their manifests."

"Look at what's missing and see what they can make when put together," Lee said, nodding.

Arbuckle and Smithers both turned to look at him in amazement. The priest just shrugged.

"Your technology and our magic aren't all that different," Lee explained. "Material components are needed to derive a particular effect. Those that study these effects are far more likely to be able to create them on a larger scale given the proper components, time, and energy."

"Right," Arbuckle said, "If you're ever looking for a TA position, let me know."

Turning his attention back to the group, he continued. "Well, I noticed that a lot of the materials missing were those used in contact rituals, like those to speak to ones who have moved off our plane."

"Summoning demons?" Luis asked, anger present in his voice.

"Or loved ones who've died, which is far more common in our circles," Arbuckle explained, appeasing the knight. "However when I looked at the rest of the materials being bought in that amount, it seemed more archaic than what you would find in a book at the mall."

"What's a mall?" Timm asked.

"We'll burn that bridge when we come to it," Smithers said, holding up a hand. Turning back to Arbuckle, he asked. "What did these components make to go along with the summoning?"

"It made something that wasn't a summoning at all!" Arbuckle said, excitedly. "It made a doorway! Originally, I thought that they were just trying to cross over to wherever we go when we die, which I found rather stupid. I mean, what value to a military war machine like America would that be? But now, meeting all of you, I think the doorway was to go to your worlds and bring you here!"

"We were kidnapped?" Luis asked, incredulously.

"Wait, their worlds?" Smithers asked. "You mean these fuckers are from another universe?"

"No," Arbuckle said. "Uni means one. We're talking more along the multiverse theory here. Many different worlds, moving around one another at different frequencies, overlapping but never touching. The work that DIARD is doing may very well be taking people like you and bringing you to our world."

"For what purpose?" Lee asked, quizzically.

"That..." Arbuckle sighed, "That I do not know, but yes, I do feel that it would mean that you were in fact kidnapped by this agency and brought to our world against your will."

"Why is it that we can't remember anything outside of our own lives there?" Timm asked. "I remember the people I care about, but I can't remember the names of places, countries, or even the mountain I lived on."

"Again, I do not know," Arbuckle said. "I have been doing my research. It's been slow, but I can continue looking into it for you if you would like. In exchange, I'd need to get information from you on your abilities, your worlds to the best of your memory, and anything else that may help speed this research along."

"What kinds of things would you need to know?" Luis asked, suspicion painted plainly on his face.

"Well, for one thing," Arbuckle explained. "What makes your worlds so different from ours? I mean, we lack the magic of your worlds, but I know of some historical reasons that may be. But there has to be something other than our technological differences that makes your world as enticing as it has been for DIARD. Assuming you're all from the same world, that is."

"You mean like how there are no elves or dwarves here?" Morgan asked.

Arbuckle turned to look at her, shock in his eyes.

"Yeah," Luis nodded, scratching at the stubble of a beard beginning to grow in on his chin. "I had noticed that as well."

"You have such creatures where you're from?" Arbuckle asked.

"Well yes," Lee said. "As well as an assortment of other sentient races like Orcs, Halflings, and Gnomes. None of whom I've seen around here."

"That's because here those are fantastical creatures that do not exist outside of stories and games," Arbuckle explained. "Fascinating. I wonder if your world is the same as those stories and only exists because of the minds of those in our world that breathed life into them through their imaginations... or if they think they're imagining these worlds in their dreams but are really mentally linked with real worlds that run parallel to them... or maybe..."

"Professor," Smithers interrupted him, seeing the glazed looks on the rest of the groups' faces. "As interesting as the quantum physical ramifications of this information are, I think you're losing them here."

"Oh," Arbuckle said, looking at the group of very far travelers. "It seems you are correct. Perhaps I should delve more into that on my own time. But for now, this is the first real lead I have on what DIARD may be up to. I will be taking a deeper look into my notes and into the histories and mythologies that may somehow be related to all of this, and get back to you on what I have come up with. Thank you for your help in my research, and hopefully I can be some help to you in your journey, wherever that may lead you."

"I believe many of us hope that it will lead us home," Luis said, reaching out to shake Arbuckle's hand. "Though I believe a pit stop at DIARD to pay them back for their injustices would also be greatly appreciated."

Smithers had to hold back a smile as Arbuckle's face switched between amusement and fearful realization that the expression of determination on Luis' face was not in fact a joke. This man fully expected to be able to take the fight to DIARD, and Arbuckle had jumped right on into the fray. Smithers shook the professor's hand as well and mulled over the consequences of what just happened.

These people were not crazy, or at least were not as crazy as he first had thought. Even this professor, nutty though he might be, believed that they were from another world. And as much as Smithers would like to try, he could not ignore the fact that they were very much fish out of water in this world. The facts were lining up, and Smithers did not like the picture being painted around him. He had been dragged into some kind of government conspiracy, all because he decided to take a walk in the woods one night and stumbled across something he shouldn't have seen.

The images of that night flooded back to him. The pale glowing blue light in the middle of the forest. Bodies falling from it, crumpling on the ground in confused panic. Figures in hazmat suits swarming around them, clamping on bindings and shouting orders. The one that turned and saw him hiding among the trees. The running, attempt to escape, and finally...

DING!

Smithers jolted back to the present. The elevator had finally reached the ground floor and the doors slid open. Smithers stepped out alone and leaned against one of the walls of the Math and Science building, watching as kids went waltzing about their business, going to class, complaining about work loads, and leading normal lives. Smithers scoffed a little as he watched the rest of them, led by Timm, coming down the stairs. Young, strong, and whole lives ahead of them. Isn't that what this kind of movie was supposed to be about? All these young adult books with bow wielding heroines and broom flying chosen ones, they're supposed to be about young kids, coming of age. Old geezers like him weren't supposed to be stuck on these kinds of adventures. But here he was, and it seemed here he would stay, at least until the old bones gave out.

"Alright," he said, once they'd finally gotten off the damned stairs. "What's the plan now?"

~ 15 ~

MORGAN

Morgan sat on the streets, her fingers flicking across the strings of the small, compact dulcimer she had kept in her pack. She was pleased that DIARD had not thought enough of it to put it in a chipper like they had done with Timm's staff, or so much of it that it had been shipped away. The calming melody flowed from the box and filled her soul with a freshness that drowned out the bustling city streets around her and made her half believe she was in the glades of her forest back home. The odd occasional clink of coin or rustle of dollar broke her meditation as passerby after passerby put money into the lid she had left sitting next to her as she played, but she paid them no mind. As much as this was a means of helping the group take care of the financial burdens they now found themselves in, it was also a way for her to depart from the other problems she had discovered.

DIARD was hunting them, and though he remained calm through the rest of their conversation, Morgan could not forget the fear and hate Norman Arbuckle reacted with when they first mentioned the organization. He had been so scared that he pulled a weapon on them before inquiring into the reason they had been there. Even if they had been members, why would he assume that they meant him harm? His story and his actions did not add up. However, she had not thought of what this insight could possibly mean, and decided to keep quiet on the matter. All necessary knowledge would divulge itself through time.

By now a small crowd had gathered around her, and she wondered if Timm were having similar luck. They had decided that in preparation for their performance at O'Malley's tonight, they would practice as street performers. Smithers had told them to be careful, but thought it might not be a bad way to pull in some extra money as well. Lee decided to go off and preach the word of his god, which Smithers had seemed somewhat amused by, but encouraged just the same. With any luck, they would be able to bring in enough income to lessen the financial burden on themselves, and the burden they were placing on Father Mitchell as well.

The priest had been quite kind to take them in, and even more so to help them understand the world they had found themselves in without mockery. So many times she knew that Smithers was trying not to tease or belittle, but his intentions betrayed him. Father Mitchell on the other hand, was far more patient with them as they learned, and Morgan wished desperately they could repay that kindness. As unfortunate as it seemed to her, the best way to show their appreciation would be with their absence.

What could have been moments, or what could have been hours, passed. Morgan felt a hand on her shoulder and broke her meditative stance. She looked up to see Timm standing over her, his violin in hand. It seemed to her that DIARD had not had an interest in their instruments, and so she did not question further their safekeeping.

"It's getting to be time," Timm said, as he offered her a hand up.

Feeling that her legs had gone numb from the time spent cross-legged on the cold ground, she gratefully accepted the help, though only so far that she could kneel and pack up her instrument and collect the assorted bills and coins that had been placed in her case. It was not an impressive amount by her understanding of this world's currency, though she never really did have a strong grasp on the concept of currency to begin with. Everything she had ever needed the earth had provided, but to survive she knew that it was necessary.

"How did you do?" Morgan asked, slipping her dulcimer into her pack.

"About the same as you," Timm responded, gesturing for her to follow him as he began walking down the street towards O'Malley's. "Though I got chased off by two or three other people who claimed I was 'working their corner,' whatever that means."

"They were probably just territorial," Morgan commented, her eyes roving around the tall, unsettling buildings that sprouted above her. "Wanted to make sure you weren't taking resources that were theirs."

"This many people, you'd think there'd be enough money to go around," Timm commented. "Especially with how much everything seems to cost. Smithers was talking about something called 'supply and demand,' but I started to lose interest in that pretty fast. Never really liked the idea of money."

"Oh, that's right," Morgan said. "You trained in a monastery. I suppose you and the other monks didn't really have much use for money there."

Timm got oddly silent and for a moment Morgan thought that she might have upset him. She was about to ask him as much, before he picked up his pace to a light jog.

"Tavern's up here," he called back. "We're almost there."

Morgan was unsure if he knew just how quickly he moved, or if that running was his way of dealing with these problems, but they had a job to do, and if it would help their situation Morgan was fine with letting Timm keep his secrets private. It was always best to tackle one problem at a time.

While livelier than the night they first arrived at O'Malley's, the place still was not all that crowded. Beside themselves Tim, and Jess, there were only three other people milling about the bar. There was one other woman, probably twice Morgan's age, but she was wearing clothing that felt even a bit too wild for her. The tightness and cut left very little to the imagination, and Morgan found herself idly straightening her own clothing just to be sure everything was covered.

Down the bar from her sat a man wearing brightly colored garments, an odd set of tinted glasses, and sported a glint of gold as part of the sleazy smile he shot her way as she and Timm entered the bar. The man turned back to his drink, as though afraid someone may take it away if left unattended too long, and slid his hand over his oily hair in an attempt to make it even flatter than it already was.

There was a tired looking man sitting next to Smithers. They were chatting cheerfully, and Morgan found herself feeling drawn more to their conversation than allowing herself to be drawn in towards the others. So while Timm excused himself to the restroom, Morgan made her way over to the bar and had a seat.

"This is the only place I can get any peace," the man was saying to Smithers. His shirt was stained with sweat and his tie hung loosely around his neck. The redness of his bleary eyes almost matched the ruddiness of his face. Morgan was unsure, but it seemed a little early for him to already be this drunk.

"Wife running you ragged?" Smithers asked, sipping much slower from a glass filled with ice and whiskey.

"Work, wife, and two daughters," the man laughed back. "Teenage years too. Love them to death, but sometimes I feel like they're going to be the cause of it."

"I hear ya," Smithers responded with a grin and a quick look to Morgan. She wasn't sure what the look meant, but it seemed somewhat poignant.

"So is this one yours?" the man asked, using his nearly empty glass to gesture to Morgan. "You look like you could be her father, or grandfather."

"Not one of mine, thankfully," Smithers said, and Morgan wondered if he disliked her so much he didn't want her to be family, or disliked his family so that he wouldn't want to be spending time with them. "No, I'm just babysitting her and the rest of her ilk."

"Interesting way to say it," the man said, then turned and nodded at Morgan. "Well not to be rude, my name is Carl Newman, pleasure to meet you, young lady."

"Morgan," she said, nodding politely back. "And we're going to be performing here tonight if you'd like to stick around."

"Believe me, I'm not going anywhere," Carl said, waving down Tom behind the bar with his glass, signaling he'd like another. "But hey, music will definitely make the night go better."

Morgan looked over to the door and saw Luis and Lee entering among a crowd of what Tom referred to as more regulars and over the course of the next quarter hour, the bar began feeling more like the lively taverns that she was used to. It seemed to her that this was as good a time as any to get started and see if their tip jar plan would yield any fruit. As she scanned the bar for Timm, she found him practically petrified against the wall as that woman she had seen upon walking in stood uncomfortably close to him. She appeared to be very interested in getting close to Timm, and Morgan felt bad for having to interrupt them, but with time running short, she approached anyway.

"Uh, hey Timm? It's time to go on," Morgan said, walking up to them.

"Oh, you're a performer?" The woman asked, not turning her attention away from Timm. "Well, I'm very excited to see you play. Maybe I'll even become your groupie."

"Sure, uh, Delilah," Timm said, a nervous edge to his voice. "I'm sure that would be great, whatever that means."

As Timm scurried to the stage and began to set up his violin, Morgan looked over at Delilah with a smile. Surprisingly, that smile was met with fierce eyes, like those of a predator staking a claim. Morgan blinked in shock. She was unsure what challenge she had issued, but knew better than to turn her back to that look. She slowly backed to the stage, shooting a quick glance over to Smithers, who seemed quite distracted by his conversation with Carl.

When she got to the stage, she began to set up her dulcimer and tried to catch Timm's eye. He was either ignoring these attempts or was too distracted by his strings that eventually she just gave up and began plucking a soft tune that drew her mind away from the thick, hazy air of the bar to the clear open skies of a mountain top. The high, lofty sounds of Timm's violin joined hers like a songbird taking flight over the snowy peaks, and the rumbling sound of voices smoothed out into the bubbling of a lazy riverbed.

Song after song passed, shifting tone and tune to fit the mood of the bar around them, however Morgan failed to notice the drunkards or darkness of the enclosed space. The music transported her and soon time had slipped away. It seemed like mere moments to her before she felt Timm's hand brush her shoulder. She let the last note ring out from her strings and looked up at him.

"Time for a break," he told her. "Get a drink, and sooth your throat a bit."

"Why?" Morgan asked, but choked the word a little, feeling her throat go dry.

"Well, if I'd been singing like that for the past hour, I'd need one too," Timm said with a smile. "Pretty language, by the way. Never heard it before."

"I was singing?" Morgan asked, gently placing down the dulcimer and following Timm off the stage. "I hadn't even noticed."

Stepping up to the bar, Tom offered them both a drink on the house. Timm got a glass of water, but Morgan felt a bit of hot tea was in order. Tom nodded at her.

"That will take a couple minutes to steep," he told her. "Have a seat and Jess will bring it over when it's ready."

"Thank you," Morgan said with a smile.

Her instincts kicked in as she felt a pair of eyes burning into her from the other side of the bar. Shifting her field of vision, Morgan saw Delilah staring back at her. As their eyes met, the older woman slipped her hand around the shoulders of the man she was pretending to listen too and let out a loud, forced laugh that reminded Morgan of the calls of a large cat. Her teeth gleamed in the dim bar light, highlighted by the dark red lipstick she wore.

Morgan shuttered. "There's something wrong about that woman."

Timm looked over and nodded his agreement. Morgan turned in shock to see a mug of tea being set down in front of her. Jess stood there, a slight grin on her face, though it was hard for Morgan to tell considering how she had styled her hair that evening. It wasn't held back as it had been when they first met her, rather hung loosely, hiding her soft, kind features.

"Nothing too wrong with her," Jess said, though Morgan noticed her voice was a bit raspier than it had been before. "Delilah Cook is just your typical cougar."

Timm looked at her in confusion. "Is she some type of were-beast?"

Jess laughed a little at that, but winced slightly and pressed her left elbow a bit closer to her side, as if holding her rib. Morgan narrowed her eyes and took the girl in a bit more closely as she spoke.

"No," Jess said. "More like she likes her men about half her age and fit. I'd watch out if I were you, boy-o. Especially with that brogue of yours."

She was favoring her left side a little, and the way she positioned her arm Morgan could tell that at least one of her ribs had been cracked, if not broken. Her gate had changed as well. No longer the graceful strides of a young woman in her prime, but staggered, as if affected by a limp of some kind. While it was cold outside, it was quite warm in the bar, and Morgan had needed to strip away her sweatshirt just to tolerate the sweltering, stale air. Jess however was wearing a sweater that came up to cover her neck, but could not hide the beads of perspiration that formed around her temple.

"Tom," Morgan said, more authoritatively than she had originally anticipated. The bartender snapped to attention and walked over to her. "When is Jess staying until tonight?"

"Uh, she's closing." Tom looked over at a schedule that was hanging on the wall next to a sign that gave a warning from someone known as a Surgeon General, but Morgan did not feel the need to ask about that now. "Should be here until two tonight."

"Good," Morgan nodded. "Because I need to speak to her when we finish our set. Alright?"

"Sure, uh, whatever you say," Tom answered. "Anything in particular?"

"Where she got her injuries that she's trying to hide," Morgan said, her eyes never leaving Jess.

"Ah damn it," Tom spat, throwing a rag over his shoulder. "That would probably be that no good rat bastard Colin."

Morgan looked to where Timm had been sitting, but saw he had already moved back towards the stage and was checking his violin was in tune. She was glad he wasn't standing there. She'd seen his temper in action and did not want him hunting this Colin down without knowing who he was. Odds are he'd knock the first man named Colin he found to the ground and beat him bloody. Not that she thought ill of Timm, but he did lack the subtlety that such a situation required.

"Who is Colin?" Morgan asked.

"If I tell you, why do I get the feeling something awfully violent will become the lad?" Tom asked her.

"Do we really look like the kind of people who would do such a thing to a person?" Morgan asked in return.

"I can only hope so," Tom said. There was something bestial in the way he said that. Like a bear giving a warning to something getting too close to his cub. "Colin is Jess' boyfriend. The two of them have been together for a couple years now. Never liked the guy, but seemed to treat Jess alright. Then came dialogue that came right out of the battered woman's handbook. She'd be saying shit like 'Colin wouldn't like me doing this' or 'oh, Colin said I can't do that.' And recently it's been getting worse. She's been calling out of work, saying Colin doesn't approve of her working here. I don't know why the sudden shift, but if he's started beating her I got two barrels under this bar with his name on them."

Morgan did not quite get his final reference about barrels. Perhaps getting him drunk and leaving him out in the cold for the elements to take care of, which seemed a brutal form of punishment, but not one Morgan felt above using on someone who acted in such a way. However, so far she only had Tom's speculation on the situation, and that was not enough to set them on such a path. She would have to speak with Jess before the night was through.

The next couple hours did not fly by in the same fashion as before. Morgan did not feel herself getting pulled into the music and transported away from this stagnant bar in the land of Boston, but rather quite anchored to it. Her eyes roved the crowd, watching Jess' every move and studying the face of every man she interacted with for clues to see if he was the infamous Colin.

There were a few moments when Timm would nudge her with his foot, forcing her back into the music and the realization that she was shifting her tempo too drastically or playing too forcefully, changing the mood of the music into a war march rather than a drinking song. In these moments she would close her eyes and attempt to meditate on the mood she was supposed to be setting and bring herself back into that headspace.

Morgan was all too happy when their final song of the evening came to a close, and without even looking in their tip jar, she rushed off the stage to find Jess, gingerly cleaning the now emptying tables.

"Jess," Morgan said, breathlessly. "I am very glad I found you before you left."

"I'll still be here a while yet," Jess said with a smile.

Her dark, curly hair shifted slightly and Morgan caught a glance at the deep purple bruise forming under one light grey eye. Jess quickly went to adjust her hair back in place, but Morgan reached out and gently took the young woman's hand.

"Colin did that to you," Morgan said, no question in her voice.

"How did you..." Jess' voice trailed off before shooting a look over at the bar. "Tom said something, didn't he?"

"Don't be angry with him," Morgan said. "I noticed your injuries. Heavy bruising on your legs, face, and I'm guessing arms. Plus cracked ribs on your left side. That was a heavy beating you took, and you still came in to work."

"No good health care," Jess shrugged. "Tom can only do so much."

"This isn't about Tom," Morgan said, gently steering the conversation back to where Jess was so desperate to avoid. "He hurt you, Jess. We can help you."

"I don't need help," Jess said quickly. Then she stopped, and Morgan could tell she was on the brink of tears. "Okay, maybe I do need help. But what can I do? I can't move out, not with... not with the baby coming."

"Baby?" Morgan's eyes flashed down to Jess' stomach. She wasn't showing, but reaching out with her senses, Morgan could tell there was another life force coming from Jess. She was pregnant. "Is the baby Colin's?"

"Yes," Jess sniffed out, fighting hard to hold back tears. "And he'll never let me go because of it. He'll fight for custody and then my baby will have to deal with what he does to me instead. I can't let that happen, I have to protect..."

A sob choked Jess' words and Morgan swiftly moved her into the private room where they had talked their first night free in Boston. She shot Tom a look and he nodded at her. Tom began clearing the tables and closed off the area Morgan was taking Jess so they could have privacy.

The young woman cried, but silently, as if not wishing to burden others with her sufferings. Morgan sat with her, clasping her hands to show support, but trying not to stifle the woman's mourning.

She saw herself as the only shield against brutality her baby had, and was willing to take the blows in hopes of giving that baby a chance at something better. It was noble, but foolish. Morgan knew that such passivity would only get her eaten alive by the beast she was trying to endure. You cannot endure the monsters in the night. Your only hope was to drive them away, or flee.

"Come with us," Morgan said softly. "We're staying at the Cathedral of the Holy Cross."

"I'm..." Jess started to say, but her voice broke. She took a moment, pausing to collect herself. In a stronger voice she tried again. "I'm not really a religious person, Morgan."

"Neither are many of us, and those that are, follow different gods," Morgan told her. "But Father Mitchell is a good man, and he has granted us a safe place to stay while we figure out our new place in this world. Even if you do not stay long, he may know what to do."

Jess laughed a little. "How very Quasimodo. I suppose running to the church for sanctuary is a possibility. But what if Colin comes there? What if by going there I bring trouble down on this Father Mitchell or the rest of you?"

"Don't worry," Morgan said with a wolfish grin. "We're good at handling trouble."

~ 16 ~

LUIS

Luis stood by the door leading out of their sleeping quarters. He was on high alert considering the information Morgan had given them regarding this Colin character and his involvement with Jess, the barmaid. He chastised himself repeatedly on the drive back to the church for not having noticed the girl's injuries sooner. Thankfully Morgan's eyes had been keener than his.

Perhaps it was that strange brew he had been drinking at O'Malley's. Tom had called it a microbrew and said that it was a craft beer of sorts. Other men around him had been suggesting that he try several different types and judge them based on the merit of their flavor. Luis seemed to have lost face in front of them after stating that all the beers were equally unpleasant in their bitterness, and a few more so for their fruitiness. He ordered a simple red wine and was quite content with that, in spite of the scruffy herd referring to him as 'basic'.

Once Morgan had approached him with the plight of the barmaid, Luis had pressed his hand to his chest and prayed to Nike to remove the haze from his mind. Cleared of drunkenness, Luis aided her in helping Jess to their van. After he had cleared the haze from Smithers mind as well, eliciting a few swears for having 'killed a perfectly good buzz,' they were on their way back to the church.

Father Mitchell asked few questions and spent less time getting Jess a cot and sitting comfortably. That is, as comfortably as he could possibly manage. The girl had several deep colored bruises and what Morgan had initially diagnosed as a cracked rib turned out to be a complete fracture. Luis was amazed the girl had been able to move around the way she did, let alone work through the night.

"There's not much we can do for her," Father Mitchell said as he passed Luis at the door. "I'm afraid she's going to need to go to the hospital. But that puts her at risk of this boyfriend of hers finding her."

Luis smiled at Father Mitchell.

"I'm afraid you forgot a few very important things, my friend," Luis said, nodding back at the cot where Jess slowly drifted off into a pained sleep.

Lee stepped over, one hand clutching his holy symbol around his neck, the other gently touching Jess' forehead. With a murmured prayer, a soft radiant glow exuded from Lee and washed over the barmaid's body. The deep purple of the bruises yellowed and faded slightly, and a soft sigh of relief issued forth from the girl. Lee stood up and walked over to where Luis and Father Mitchell were standing.

"I knitted the bones back together, and eased the bruising. I could cast the spell a few more times, however I do not believe it will do anything more to give her further relief," Lee told them, his voice neutral. The priest did not seem to notice the look of awe and shock on Father Mitchell's face. If he did, he made no indication, but Luis smugly enjoyed every second of it. To think that such amazement still existed in the world, it was a small victory.

"The rest will have to be natural healing," Lee finished, giving them both a nod. "Now if no one else needs me, I feel that I should get some rest."

"Uh... of course," Father Mitchell stuttered out in his amazement. He turned back to Luis as Lee made himself comfortable on his cot. "I suppose the hospital is no longer a necessity. I keep forgetting what you all are capable of."

"Never hurts to get those gentle reminders," Luis said, smiling.

"You're enjoying this, aren't you?" Father Mitchell asked.

"Watching your reaction to our abilities? Yes. It brings me pleasure to see one react to the miracle of the power we wield rather than just the raw violence of it. Wonder at the miracle of healing is pleasant," Luis turned his attention back to the barmaid laying in a far more peaceful sleep than he anticipated for the evening. "The violence that brought that joy to me, I am enjoying less so."

"Be wary of that temper," Father Mitchell warned Luis. "Do not repay a wrongful act with a wrongful act. Strive to do what is good for each other and good for everyone else."

"I feel smiting that cretin into paste would be quite a good thing for Jess," Luis growled. "And quite good for the rest of the world."

"But not good for Colin," Father Mitchell replied. His tone was gentle and Luis knew that he was not trying to draw anger, but it took a great deal of effort on his part to keep his temper in check.

"Why should anyone care what is good for a man who harms another in such a way?" Luis said. His fingers twitched as if to reach for his sword, but instead he shoved them in his pocket.

"It is not ours to avenge," Father Mitchell said. "For one day Colin's foot will slip, and on his day of disaster his doom will rush upon him."

"Who is to say that I am not his doom?" Luis asked.

"God does," Father Mitchell stated plainly. "He will meet his punishment upon his death. He will be judged. It is not for you or I to do so. We are healers, you of the flesh, me of the soul. Our duty is to Jess and all the others in the world who have been hurt. God will deal out the punishment for those who do the hurting."

"Your god takes too long to do so," Luis responded, his voice gaining heat as he spoke. "I am the sword of my goddess, and I wield it in her name. Your god has allowed too many evils to run rampant in the streets of your home. Perhaps mine has brought me here to clean up the messes yours refuses to tackle. Heal their souls, Father. I shall break their chains."

Luis strode away from the father, who did not pursue the conversation further. Falling into his cot, Luis stared at the ceiling lamenting his foreknowledge at how the night's rest would go unfruitful. He watched as Timm took up a post at the door, seemingly to block the entrance from Colin should he arrive. Quietly, Luis positioned his friction lock close at hand. While Timm may be rash and headstrong, occasionally he has good ideas.

Fading into a fitful sleep, Luis managed some rest, but still woke before the dawn. Donning the running gear he had acquired from the thrift shop downstairs, Luis slipped the friction lock into his pocket and made his way towards the door.

As he stepped over Timm, the young monk startled from his sleep and threw a wild punch in Luis' direction. The friction lock extended and caught Timm on his wrist, deflecting the blow. Timm yelped in pain and alarm, but Luis reached down and covered his mouth.

"Easy," he scolded in a hushed voice. "I'm going out for a run. Do not blindly attack someone coming down these steps. It could as easily be one of us or Father Mitchell as it could be this Colin."

Timm nodded at Luis before shifting back against the wall, nursing his wrist. Luis closed the friction lock and slipped it back into his pocket before climbing the stairs. He would have felt bad about causing Timm the minor harm, but felt it was a good lesson in responsibility for him. Brash action could cause others to get hurt, and Luis was in the business of very specific people getting hurt. The right people getting hurt.

The crisp air hit Luis' face and drew a fresh vigor from him. His muscles, stiff with sleep, soon warmed and were lubricated from the rhythmic motions of his run. The city was quiet in the early hours of the morning with very little traffic and fewer people to get in his way. Luis liked this time of day. It reminded him of the training grounds before the cadets could come in and churn up the mud. Even with the slight crunch of ice and snow beneath his feet, he found surer footing than he would have in those conditions.

As his heart beat harder against his chest, he soon found his rhythm breaking against the anger that still roiled in his mind. Father Mitchell was weak in his assumptions. A man like Colin needed to be put down, not coddled and forgiven like a spoiled child who'd kicked the family dog. No, this would require more than a stern talking to and wooden spoon to the rump. He was dangerous. Unfortunately for him, so was Luis.

As he thought this, his foot gave way underneath him as a patch of ice, black against the pavement snatched away his footing. Immediately his training kicked in and he threw his hands out to catch him, but knew that he could not do so in time. It seemed that Jess' were not the only bones that would need knitting together.

Then suddenly, something caught Luis mid-tumble. He hit the ground, but softer than he would have otherwise. A heavy form hit the ground next to him with a short exclamation of discomfort.

"Ack!" The voice cried, and Luis looked up to see a man dressed similarly to him fall back into a snowbank, his black coat and strange stretchy pants now coated white with fresh frost. He sat up gingerly and shook the snow from his now damp, moppish hair.

"You alright man?" he asked, brushing himself off with gloved hands. Luis was amazed to see how coordinated his clothing was. And though it was thin, the man was not bothered by the cold.

"Why yes, thank you," Luis said, getting to his feet and offering the other man aid in getting to his own.

He looked at Luis' hand, scoffed, and took it. With little effort, Luis helped haul the man back to his feet.

"I'm amazed to see you bounce back up like that," he said, brushing snow from his rear and looking Luis up and down. "That was quite the tumble. You must be made of stern stuff."

"I trained for years," Luis said, pride exuding from his voice. "It would take more than a paltry fall to hinder me."

"Right," the man said, giving him a strange look, though Luis was becoming accustomed to such responses by now. "Military man, I take it?"

"Of sorts, yes," Luis responded, attempting to do as Smithers had advised him earlier and give as little truth away as possible. Though he still could not bring himself to tell an outright lie.

"Well, how about you let a civilian give you a small piece of free advice if you don't mind it," the man said with a wry smile.

"Very well," Luis nodded. While not the direct method he had been hoping for, this was at least a chance for him to glean some insight on this world he'd found himself stumbling through. Any aid was welcome.

"Humans are pretty frail creatures," the man stated. "Oh sure, people have survived falling out of airplanes, getting stampeded, and there was even that one idiot who managed to cut off one of his own arms after getting pinned under a rock and came crawling home. But half those stories come from luck while the rest are mere stubbornness of will. Neither one will take you far in life. Hell, the average human can barely take the fall you just did without needing to go home and ice themselves for a week. Don't get overconfident, and don't overestimate the human body."

Luis mulled the words over in his mind for a moment. Perhaps it was true what he was saying. Luis' body had been tuned into that of a warrior's over the course of years, and imbued with the blessings of Nike that allowed him to push the boundaries of what it meant to be human. For a man like this, such a fall would have broken the bones, but in this world it was rare to have the ability to heal such damage in any form of timely manner. One could be bedridden for weeks, waiting for the slow march of time to heal their wounds rather than the blessings of divinity. For him to have made the effort to aid another at risk to himself was quite noble indeed.

"Then I thank you for your sacrifice," Luis said, bowing his head. "You put your own frail body at risk to aid me. And for that, I thank you."

"Hey, don't mention it," the man waved a hand at Luis, seemingly embarrassed by the display of thanks. "You get to my age and you risk your frail body just by sleeping wrong. And the only thing I really sacrificed was my hat... Where'd that thing go?"

The man turned from Luis and began digging through the snow bank he had fallen in, presumably searching for his hat. With ease, he lifted chunks of ice the size of his own head that must have weighted twenty or thirty pounds. Frail may not have been the word Luis should have used to describe him. His body seemed almost as well trained as Luis' own. To imagine he feared risk of injury, a man as strong as...

A man as strong as Colin must presumably be.

And a man as frail as Colin must be.

Realization began to dawn in Luis' mind. This had been what Father Mitchell was talking about the night before. Just as the Father had forgotten the power Lee and the others wielded, the blessings of their abilities, Luis had forgotten that the people of this world are not so blessed. It would be easy for Luis to take Colin and erase him from existence with a single blow, much as he had banished the ghost. However this was not a battle with supernatural forces. This was quite natural indeed. And it would be an insult to Nike to use her blessings to smite down someone as frail as Colin, for it would make Luis no better than the man he hunted. As Jess was frail beneath Colin's blows, Colin would be glass beneath his own.

"Ah!" the man called out, dusting off a worn knit hat. "Found it. All right mister, you have a good day now, and be safe out there. One slip could throw off your whole week."

He held out his hand for Luis to shake and the knight grasped it firmly.

"Thank you, sir," Luis said to him. "You provided me with more aid than you could have realized today."

"Hey, us runners got to look out for one another, right?" The man said with a smile, then put on his hat before turning to continue his run. Luis stood in shock as the man ran away, his black hat emblazoned with the symbol of Nike in vibrant orange.

For a moment he wanted to call out to the man, but instead paused and smiled. The knight looked up to the sky and touched his hand to where the pendent of Nike rested beneath his shirt.

"You sensed my weakness, my rage, and my error before I could make it," Luis said, in a quiet prayer. "Thank you for that holy messenger. I will raise myself to the challenge in the proper way, as not to shame your name. You are right, such a battle would have been a hollow victory."

Luis turned and continued his run, this time taking more time and care to where his feet were landing.

~ 17 ~

TIMM

Timm was unable to go back to sleep after Luis had woken him that morning. His wrist stung, but not badly enough to bother anyone about. Lee was the next to rise and willingly took over the position of guarding the room so Timm could go out and clear his head. Not thinking of running or training like Luis had done, Timm decided that the serenity of the night before was something he longed for.

Taking his violin, he found a street corner nearby where O'Malley's was sitting dark and closed for the morning. It seemed that taverns in this world did not keep the same hours as in his own, so setting up a ways down the street, Timm opened up his case and began to play.

He barely noticed the strange looks he was getting from passersby about his playing. A few coins found their way into the case but he didn't care. His mind was on the melodies that had come from Morgan's dulcimer the night before. Her music flowed through his head and his hands tried in vain to harmonize with them. There was something about the peace and beauty that came from her music that helped him relax. Or at least, from the first half of their playing that night.

She must have made her observations of Jess during their intermission because Timm noticed the change in her playing almost immediately. Most of the patrons had been too drunk by that point, but to him the slip was obvious. Her mind had become cluttered and distracted, and now he was suffering the same fate. Though it wasn't Jess' condition that had him so muddled.

This whole world had skewed his viewpoint on life so violently that peace was becoming harder and harder to come by. The violence and heartache of his home was still very present here, but there seemed to lack an outlet for the pain. People were forced to move about their daily lives and never truly get to address the wrongs being done to them because they lacked the time or the target. Where he came from if someone was doing to you what was being done to Jess, you hired mercenaries and the problem was solved. Or a hearty group of adventurers would take care of it for free, if just a bit of lodging or information.

Here it seemed people lived in a hive of isolation, darting from honeycomb to honeycomb without acknowledging that others even existed. In fact, people almost seemed surprised when others took an interest in their problems at all, let alone offer to help them carry the burden. He reflected on what Father Mitchell had said about bearing a cross, and how many hands make a burden lighter, but it almost seemed like these people on the street passing him would just as soon press down on your cross to make the burden heavier if it made their own lighter. It would have made him angry if it didn't leave him so very sad.

Hours must have passed before he'd even noticed. The sun was now standing high above him, melting the thin sheets of ice that coated the sidewalks, making it much easier for the average person to stride across them. Timm had barely noticed the issue when setting up. A small sum of money now sat in his case, though he did not deem it impressive enough to bring to Smithers as an addition to their funds. Perhaps he could get this coffee he'd heard so much about from Smithers with the amount he had.

Remembering the real reason he had come to this part of town so early in the day, Timm shot a glance down the street towards

O'Malley's in time to spy Tom unlocking the door and stepping inside. Making sure he had all his belongings, Timm started down the street to greet him.

The bitter cold that had been biting at him all morning was made known only by its sudden absence as he walked through the door to the bar. While nowhere near as sweltering as it had been last night, the old pipes that ran around the ceiling hissed with steam and radiated heat. Timm stared in wonder at how a simple trick could create such an inviting environment amidst the chill winter months.

"We ain't open yet," Tom called from behind the bar, not turning around to see who had entered. Timm walked forward in spite of his call.

"It's just me," Timm said, waving as Tom turned around. The bartender let out a sigh and did something below the counter that Timm could not see. He did hear a clicking noise however.

"Didn't take you for a heavy drinker," Tom said, removing a glass and polishing it. "Technically I'm not allowed to serve any alcohol for a few more hours, but if you don't tell Johnny Law, I won't."

"This Johnny Law must be quite busy if it's up to him to enforce that particular law alone," Timm said, waving off the alcohol. "I didn't come here to drink. Honestly I've been staking the place out all morning from down the street just in case you know who shows up."

"Colin?" Tom asked, setting the glass aside. "I doubt he'd show his face here, though he might be getting a bit more brazen lately. Though I've got to ask you one thing, if you don't mind."

Timm shrugged, "Go right ahead."

"What does Colin look like?" Tom asked.

Timm looked at him for a moment, realizing the mistake he had made. He had never seen the man and Jess was in no state the night before to give them any sort of description. With a sigh, Timm dropped his head onto the bar.

"That's what I thought," Tom said, a hint of laughter in his voice. "Though honestly, the sentiment is pretty damn noble. Didn't think Jess had such reliable friends. What more, they're also all strangers. Maybe this world ain't as fucked as I thought."

Timm picked his head up. "So you noticed it too, then."

"The state of the world going down the toilet? Yeah, I've picked up on a few hints about it," Tom said, laughing. "You'd have to have your head in the sand to have missed it. Or else shove it up your own ass."

"That seems rather impossible," Timm noted, but then added after a moment's thought, "Of course, a talented contortionist may be able to pull off such a feat."

"A contortionist," Tom snorted. "That actually sounds about right. They contort words to make money and stay in power. Rat bastards deserve to drown on the ship they sunk, but God knows they've made themselves lifeboats they can sit in while the rest of us sink."

Timm was unsure of who the old bartender was talking about, but he seemed to need to get this off his chest, so rather than interrupting the young man sat patiently and listened.

"Greed and corruption, that's all it is, and that's all it will ever be," Tom continued. "And where does that leave people like you and me? Where does that leave poor Jess? I mean, you look like you can handle yourself if some punk tries to get the better of you. And anyone messes with me or my bar and they'll be picking buckshot out of them down at the morgue. But people like Jess? Told by one side that the law is there for her, but seeing for a fact that she'd see more help from a group of strangers than the cops. Bah, it's a sad state we live in."

Timm nodded, understanding for the most part what Tom was talking about. His initial analysis of the world seemed to be quite correct. Most people were not willing or able to help, and those that were, appeared to be a rare breed indeed. Tom started to smile as he pulled the glass out again and filled it with ice. Then, he reached under the bar and pulled out a red can. With a flick of his finger a loud pop and crack filled the bar, followed by a subtle hiss. He began pouring the bubbling brown liquid into the ice filled glass and slid it to Timm.

"But then people like you come around, show me the world's not so bad," Tom nodded. "For that I'd like to thank you."

"Oh, no, that's okay," Timm raised his hands up, denying the beverage. "As I said, I'm not really in the mood for anything to drink."

"It ain't alcohol," Tom said, nodding at it. "It's a soda. A soft drink."

"Soft drink?" Timm asked, curious.

"You know," Tom said, gesturing at the bottles of liquor behind him. "The opposite of hard liquor. Soft drink. No alcohol, but tastes nice and sweet. Plus gives you a little kick of energy. The hard stuff knocks you on your ass, but the soft stuff picks you up."

"Hmm," Timm stared at the bubbling brown liquid with interest. "Such a potion could be greatly beneficial to our mission. Perhaps I should give this a try. How much do I owe you for it?"

Timm was reaching into his pocket for the change he had collected that morning when Tom raised his own hands.

"On the house, for helping Jess out," he said. "However, if you plan on spending your day here, I can keep them coming if you pitch in a little. Wasn't able to get the whole place cleaned up without Jess' help last night. Still got to wipe down tables, take out the trash, that sort of stuff. Feel like lending a hand?"

Timm picked up the glass and sniffed it. The bubbles seemed to escape the liquid and travel up into the air and right into his nose. They burned and tickled as they went, causing him to recoil slightly. Determination got the better of Timm and he sniffed hard to clear the sensation. In a swift motion, he downed the entire potion, leaving only a glass of ice behind.

It was sweet and syrupy, though not unpleasant. There was a slight burn that trailed his tingling tongue down to his now rumbling stomach. At first, something did not feel right. He shifted uncomfortably and felt a rise from his stomach. He opened his mouth to speak, or shout warning, but all that erupted was a mighty belch.

Tom looked at him with a smirk on his face.

"So…" he said, looking at Timm expectantly. "Is that a yes?"

A couple hours and several more of those amazing potions later, Timm had polished every table in O'Malley's twice, mopped the floor, cleared away the garbage into the dumpster out back, and cleaned every glass in the building. Tom had learned quickly to stay out of Timm's way while he was working and disappeared to the back for a while to catch up on what he called paperwork.

Around two in the afternoon, Timm heard the bell on the door ring. Knowing it was too early for a patron to be coming in, he rushed out from behind the bar to see who had entered.

"Notservingyet!" Timm shouted. "Tooearlyyouneedtocomeback-later!"

Luis stood in the doorway, a look of confusion and concern on his face. His hair was slightly tipped with frost and his clothes looked clean and fresh. Timm assumed he must have returned after his run and cleaned up in the indoor waterfall Smithers had called a shower.

"Uh," Luis said, seeming to recoil slightly from Timm. "Are you alright, Timm?"

"Neverbetterwhydoyouask?" Timm said.

"Because you're shaking slightly and your left eye is twitching," Luis pointed out.

"OhIthinkthat'sjustthesoda," Timm said, moving back behind the bar, taking out another red can and showing it to Luis. "TomsaysIcandrinkmyfillifI'mworking."

"Okay," Luis said, sitting down at the bar and reaching out gingerly to take the can from Timm's hand. For a moment, Timm did not want to let it go, but the stern look from Luis made it difficult to retain his grip. "Perhaps you should take a break from drinking these for a while."

"Buttheygiveyouenergy," Timm exclaimed, reaching out to take the drink back, but Luis was too swift for him. "AndI'mgoingtoneedenergytofightColin!"

"Perhaps, but you are going to also need to be in control of yourself during the confrontation," Luis said, holding the drink out of Timm's reach. "Remember, he is a basic human. No blessings or training like we've had. We cannot afford to lose control of ourselves."

Timm thought over the knight's words and nodded his head rapidly in agreement. "Okaythatmakessense."

He was just about to ask Luis why he had such a strange expression on his face when Tom came out from the back offices. "Well, it's looking mighty nice in here. Gave the place a decent spit shine I see."

"Spit shine?" Luis asked, a look of disgust on his face.

"Just an expression, no literal spit to be used," Tom said, then turned his attention to Timm. "Right, boy?"

"Ohnosir, nospitusedhere," Timm said.

Tom looked at Timm hesitantly, then at the bin filled with red cans behind the bar. "Uh, tell me now, son. How many of them sodas did you have?"

"Ilostcountafterseven," Timm answered. "ShouldItakeoutthetrash?"

"Nope, no I think we're good on that front," Tom nodded, concern in his voice, though Timm did not know for what. "This is going to be interesting later."

"What is?" Luis asked.

"He's on a sugar rush right now," Tom explained. "Next is the crash."

"What's the crash?" Luis asked, his voice now mirroring Tom's concern. However, before the bartender could offer a response, the phone behind the bar began to ring. Timm reached out to answer it, but Tom intercepted him and shooed him away.

Picking up the phone, Tom put it to his ear and said, "O'Malley's Pub, how can I help you?"

Tom's face darkened and his lips parted in a sneer that showed Timm an almost feral expression he had never seen the bartender's face make.

"No," his voice was practically a growl. "I gave her the night off. Come on down, though. I have a shotgun waiting here for you."

Without another word, Tom slammed the phone back down into its cradle, much harder than Timm assumed necessary.

"That was him?" Luis asked.

"That was him." Tom confirmed.

"So I suppose you just gave him an invitation," Luis stated, plainly. He twisted the can of soda on the bar, unopened and un-interested.

"I guess I did," Tom nodded. "And I suppose that means he'll be coming round later, looking for trouble."

"He'll find more than he bargained for," Luis stated.

"I think you're right," Tom smiled. "He's expecting just an old man with a shotgun. What he'll find is you guys."

"Let him come," Luis said, passing the soda to Tom who ex-changed it for a stem glass, uncorking the bottle of wine Luis had not finished the night before and poured him a glass.

"Yeah," Timm said, slamming his fist into his hand. "Lethim-come. Thenwe'lltakeouthetrash!"

Luis and Tom both turned to look at Timm, and the young monk noticed that their looks of determination were suddenly clouded with that concern again. He'd have to ask them why later.

~ 18 ~

LEE

Lee went about his business that morning with a simple drive. With all the chaos and strangeness that this world had to offer him, at the very least it was able to give him something he was used to handling. Jess was broken, and it was his duty to fix that which was broken.

As Timm made his leave that morning to go about whatever task he felt necessary to deal with, Lee also noted that Luis had left as well. The distinct possibility that he went for a run was there, however Lee felt it was irresponsible to go out on one's own knowing full well the dangers lurking outside the church's doors. He said nothing to Timm about this, however, as he also felt that it was not his place to scold others on their behavior. He was not their mother nor their keeper. He only had one ward to handle at the moment.

He was checking Jess' wounds and testing her rib when Smithers came down from the cantina with a cup of coffee in his hand. He looked around the room and saw that only Morgan was still in bed.

"Where is everybody?" Smithers asked, a slight note of panic in his voice.

Lee shrugged. "I assume Luis went for his morning run and Timm said he had business to attend to."

"Business?" Smithers asked, clearly irritated. Lee continued mopping the sweat off of Jess' face. "What business could that boy possibly have? He's been here what, like three days?"

"I don't know," Lee responded. "I was not inclined to ask."

"Why not?" Smithers asked in a tone that told Lee that the blame for others' actions was about to be shifted to him.

"Because I have but one charge to take care of," he answered plainly. "Unless you wish to work healing magic on the wounded girl. Everything else is immaterial right now."

Smithers growled a little, muttering darkly under his breath about crazy magic people and irresponsible children as he walked across the room and unrolled an oilcloth onto his cot. He took his shotgun out of his coat and began to break it apart. It seemed to Lee that he was cleaning each of the pieces he removed before putting it back together again.

During this time, both Morgan and Jess woke up. Jess gave a start seeing Lee standing over her, however the priest stood back as Morgan walked over and comforted the girl.

"Where am I?" Jess asked.

"You're at the Cathedral of the Holy Cross," Morgan said gently. "Remember? We agreed last night that you would come here. This is my friend Lee. He's been seeing to your wounds."

"You're a doctor?" Jess asked, turning her head to look at Lee.

He stepped forward, being sure to keep a comfortable distance between them and kept Morgan as a buffer. "Not exactly. I have had medical training and have some skill with healing practices that your doctors may call... unorthodox or alternative. However, as this was nothing major like disease or cancer, just a matter of setting and healing bones, I doubt those terms should give you much concern."

Jess looked at him for a moment, and Lee could see the concern was still very much alive in her, but a moment later she shook her head. "I suppose you're right. Is the baby okay?"

"Most of your wounds were localized in your ribs, legs, and arms," Lee said, keeping his voice level and tone neutral. "I take it you were thrown to the ground, curled up into a ball, and were kicked repeatedly?"

Tears began to well up in Jess' eyes, telling Lee that he was exactly right. Morgan reached out and took her hand, giving it a gentle squeeze. She turned to face Lee, making sure that Jess was unable to see the look of irritation directed at Lee.

Lee sighed. It seemed like it was going to be one of those days where he would be taking the blame for many other people's mistakes.

"Considering how the damage was directed, I would say that your baby was not in any immediate danger either during or after the attack," Lee continued. "Though, take this not-doctor's advice, and try to avoid putting yourself in that position again. For both your sakes."

Jess choked out a small laugh in between her tears and looked up at Lee, a slight sparkle appearing in her gaze that was not a part of the now freely flowing tears.

"You know," she said. "I might just take that advice."

"You should get more rest," Morgan said, softly. "We'll go get you something to eat, and then you should sleep a bit more. Just to speed along the healing."

She got up and started up the stairs. Lee followed after her, though he did not intend to make his way to the cantina.

As soon as they reached the top of the stairs, Morgan whirled around to face him.

"What was that about?" Morgan asked, her tone something between angry and upset, though Lee was unable to pinpoint which emotion was driving her most. "What kind of bedside manner were you going for?"

"The kind I am most used to," Lee stated, again keeping his tone neutral. "I try not to get too emotional when it comes to dealing with those under my care."

"Well it may not be emotional to you," Morgan said, the anger in her tone dying down more now. Lee was glad to see that her irrationalities were more under control than in the others. Though that itself presented a whole variety of questions in his mind. "But you just made her relive an exceptionally traumatic experience with a single, thoughtless sentence. How would you feel if you had to relive something that horrible while someone heartlessly evaluated you?"

Lee stared at her for a long moment, thinking about the people he'd lost in the place whose name he couldn't even pull from the depths of his memory. Their faces floated around hers, haunting him. For a moment, he felt the flickering of agony and rage kindling a flame of hatred and revenge in him. But it was not for this girl, and it would provide him with no benefit to his cause, and so the flames were smothered once again.

"I apologize if my approach seemed heartless," Lee said, choosing his words very carefully. He had been able to keep from betraying his thoughts and past so far, but Morgan was intuitive. He had to be careful around her. "However I ask you to keep in mind that during my time as a cleric at my temple, the gifts of healing I was granted were more to ease the suffering of those who were passing onto the next life rather than aiding them in clinging to this one. Emotional attachment is merely a kiln that turns one's heart to glass, allowing for it to shatter more readily."

"I'm... I'm sorry to hear that," Morgan said. Her eyes lost their fire and sadness flooded from them.

Lee breathed a silent sigh of relief. He had not lied to the girl, however he was adamant that neither she nor the others learned the whole truth. Giving them scraps and allowing them free reign to center their focus on themselves and whatever missions they took upon their shoulders would take him further in this gambit than lying. Morgan was different, however. Where Luis was a man on a mission, Smithers was focused on how he could deal with his world crashing down around him, and Timm was... well... Timm,

Morgan stood alone as another like him. One who watched and studied those she found herself surrounded by.

"No need to feel sorry," Lee stated, gesturing down the opposite hallway to the cantina. "I am going to pay Father Mitchell a visit to see what can be done about our friend downstairs."

"Oh!" Morgan said, her mood shifting. "That is a good idea. I'll join you."

Lee gritted his teeth slighting, having hoped that she would continue with her original plan to fetch food for Jess, but there was no helping that now. He turned and led the way to Father Mitchell's office, Morgan in tow.

The father was sitting at his desk as he was wont to do, and Lee knocked lightly on the open door. Father Mitchell looked up from the assortment of papers he was pouring over, rubbed his red eyes sleepily, and gestured at the two chairs opposite his desk.

"Sit down, sit down," he yawned, not getting up to greet them. Lee did not blame the man, considering he had been woken up very late to deal with more problems that they were dropping on his doorstep. "What can I do for you both this morning?"

He looked over at a clock on his desk as if to confirm. "Yes, morning."

"We wanted to speak to you about Jess," Lee stated.

"That's the young girl you brought in last night?" Father Mitchell asked.

"Yes," Morgan said. "Her boyfriend is abusive, and she's afraid that she'll get hurt, or worse, their child will. She's not far along, so there's a long time left where something could go wrong."

Father Mitchell sighed. "I'll be honest with you, the older members of the parish don't take too kindly to the unwed mother thing."

"Doesn't your holy book have the physical incarnation of your god come into being through an unwed mother?" Lee asked.

"Yes," Father Mitchell said, pursing his lips. "And I must say that it is impressive how much of a theologian you've become over the course of a weekend."

"I take my studies seriously," Lee stated.

"I see that," Father Mitchell nodded. "But far be it from me to say that there is no hypocrisy in the Catholic Church, and I in no way look down on the poor girl for her life decisions. Each of us has made a choice in our life, or had one made for us, that we regret."

Lee felt that familiar twinge in his stomach as Father Mitchell said those words. He hoped that he managed to keep his face a mask. It seemed like the father was another individual to be careful speaking around as well.

"That being said," the father continued. "I only meant to say that we may not be able to get much help from the higher ups in the organization. I may be able to set her up with a friend of mine in New York or California, but flying would be too expensive for me to arrange, so she'd either be taking the train or a bus."

"Will either of those options be safe?" Morgan asked.

"Oh, both are safe," Father Mitchell responded. "And difficult to track. But they're slower, so more time for this Colin fellow to sniff out her trail and go after her. If he can afford the plane ticket, he could be waiting for her on the other side."

"That would both be awful and terrifying for her," Lee noted, turning to read Morgan's expression. She seemed angry and scared all at once, though none of it was directed towards him, so it seemed he could put his full attention on the task at hand. "So if we did manage to slip her out of the city, we would need to be sure that she was being sent so secretively that no one knew. Is that possible?"

"Hide her face from the cameras, pay for the tickets in cash, and we all keep our mouths shut about it," Father Mitchell said, listing off the items on his fingers as he went. "Yeah, I suppose it could be done, but we'd have to be exceptionally careful as we did. Plus, she would have to give up everything about her life here in Boston. Usually that's the hardest part. People who go off and vanish for their own protection end up homesick, or missing friends, they get in contact and once loose lipped conversation later they're found again and back in the same trouble they were in before. Or worse trouble."

Lee noted that Morgan's hands were clenched so tightly into fists that her knuckles were turning white. Even he had to admit that there was too much with this plan that could go wrong. The simplest, and most logical plan was the one that Luis had stated the night before. If Colin were eliminated then Jess could go about her life freely and without fear.

He shook his head slightly at the thought. No, not even here could he advocate for such a plan. Even if it was logical. Or rather, even if it seemed to be the most logical plan. Sometimes the easy solution parades itself around as logic. A tempting offer that solves all your problems and makes perfect sense, who could resist? Lee knew better, that such offers were not the miracle solutions that were promised. There would have to be another plan. One that assured Jess' safety without compromising whatever ambiguous morality existed among these people Lee had found himself with.

"Thank you, Father Mitchell," Morgan said, standing. Lee mirrored her and stood to say goodbye to the father. "I wish there was something more we could do to help her, but it seems our options are not quite what we were hoping they would be."

"Seek, and you will find," Father Mitchell said, smiling at her. "Or, as some of my less pious friends may say, 'if you can't find a door, open a window.'"

Lee furrowed his brow at the father. "What kind of friends do you have that say that?"

Father Mitchell smiled. "Old friends, from when I was young."

"One of your regrets?" Lee asked.

"I wouldn't call them a regret," Father Mitchell said, speaking almost as evasively as Lee had earlier. "More like a learning experience that was desperately needed to get me where I am today."

Lee nodded as he and Morgan left the priest's office. That man was most definitely one he would have to speak very carefully around. Not for fear of exposure, but for fear of understanding.

"So what do we do now?" Morgan asked Lee.

He pondered on this for a while, looking at the options laid out before them. If they risked moving Jess to a place they deemed safe for her, there were many options for Colin to find her, and no guarantee that she would willingly stay in the place of their choosing. The other option risked putting a stain on their souls in exchange for the freedom of another, though it may also risk their physical freedom in this world's law came after them.

"I know the answer," Lee stated. "We need a window."

"But what's our window?" Morgan asked.

"She's resting downstairs," Lee stated. "Our window is Jess' insight on the situation. This is her life. We should not be the ones deciding for her. There is nothing worse than having the path of your own life chosen for you."

With that, Lee walked off to the cantina to get sustenance for Jess. The decision had been a difficult pondering for him, one with no emotional investment in the situation. This was going to be a terrible curse they were to place on her soul, and she would need all the strength she could muster to take it.

~ 19 ~

SMITHERS

Smithers sat fuming at the audacity of the children he found himself surrounded by. Morgan was a bit naïve, but she was young and he couldn't blame her too much. Especially seeing as she reminded him of one of his granddaughters, so he was able to admit his own bias on that. Lee seemed to have a decent head on his shoulders, but then his dismissive attitude and 'logical' way of thinking allowed the others to parade about willy-nilly. Luis can handle himself, of that Smithers was sure, but to go off into a city you don't know, alone, wasn't bravery, it was stupidity. And thinking of stupid, what in the hell was that boy Timm thinking? Luis had a schedule he stuck to, but Timm?

Sliding the last piece into place, his shotgun made a satisfying click that gave Smithers a flooding sense of serenity. The irritation he was feeling at the others hadn't faded exactly, but the monotony of familiar machinery coming back together in his hands was almost meditative to the old man. Whatever nonsense these kids dragged him into, at least these parts and pieces fit together in a puzzle that made sense to him.

Luis came bounding down the stairs, still high off the exertion of his run and greeted Smithers with a curt nod as he walked over to his cot to collect his street clothes. Smithers called out to him,

"

hoping to catch the knight before he disappeared into the bathroom to hose off.

"Enjoy your run?" Smithers asked, his tone harsh and irritated, though Luis did not seem to note this.

"Yes," Luis said, nodding again. "Quite invigorating, for both the body and soul."

"Yeah, I don't know about all that," Smither said, standing and holstering the weapon. There was nothing that set the tone of a conversation worse than a loaded gun in one person's hand. "But did you think that maybe it wasn't such a good idea to go?"

"Training cannot be put off," Luis said, walking towards the showers. "If you slip in your training, you will die sooner than if you hadn't. Victory cannot be achieved through inaction."

"Except when it can," Smithers said, drawing a quizzical look from Luis. Sighing deeply, Smithers explained. "We are being hunted. And how do predators work? They wait for one of their prey to be separated from the herd."

"I am no prey," Luis said, coldly. "Should they try to prey on me they will find themselves at the end of my sword."

"Baton," Smithers corrected. "How bout this, then? What if they saw you, decided you were too much to handle, but figured they'd follow you back here and burn this church to the ground, killing all inside?"

He threw his thumb over to where Jess was dozing off.

"Including the injured woman?"

Luis seemed to ponder this for a moment before responding.

"You make a good point, Wizard Smithers," Luis conceded. "Again, your wisdom should be taken into account. I will be sure to bring an extra pair of eyes with me on my runs from now on."

Smithers sighed at the nickname but decided to take the win where he could get it. "That's all I ask... I guess."

Morgan and Lee made their way down the stairs, saving Smithers from further conversation with the obstinate knight. Lee set a tray of food down next to Jess, who jerked awake with a start, but seemed to remember where she was quicker than the last time. Lee gave her the barest of smiles before joining the conversation away from his patient.

"I am glad you're back safe, Luis," Lee said to the knight. "Smithers expressed some concern about that earlier."

"We have just finished discussing that," Luis nodded. "I believe we've reached an acceptable compromise."

"Where the hell did you people learn to talk, some fancy boarding school or something?" Smithers asked. Seeing they were about to answer, he cut them off. "Never mind, not important to the situation. Morgan? Come here please."

Morgan was idly chatting with Jess but cut it short with a simple touch to the girl's shoulder before walking over. Smithers was amazed with the ease that Morgan could smooth over a situation. It was like watching one of those social media videos where the people reign in a wounded animal and make it a pet.

"Yes?" She asked, joining the circle they were forming.

Trying to throw off the feeling like he'd just joined one of those circles teenagers stand in at the mall, Smithers decided it was time to address the elephant in the room.

"We gotta figure out what we're going to do about the girl," Smithers said, trying to keep his voice low so Jess would not overhear.

"We must protect her," Luis said, without hesitation or room for discussion.

"For the rest of her life?" Smithers asked.

"Her wounds are healing well," Lee said to Luis. "We've done what we can for her. Father Mitchell said we could get her a ticket for a train or bus, whatever those are, and she can start her life anew somewhere else."

"While that abusive filth gets to walk free?" Luis asked both incredulously and a bit louder than Smithers would have liked. "What if he hunts her down, or decides to perform the same treatment on another?"

"It's hard to track that means of travel," Morgan said. "Though Father Mitchell warned that it only really works if the person going doesn't try to contact any part of their former life, or Colin could find her easily again."

"See," Luis said, pointing to Morgan. "This man is too dangerous to be left alive."

"Now hold on," Smither interjected. "That's two really bold statements being said at once."

"Two?" Lee asked, cocking his eyebrow at Smithers.

"Yeah," Smithers nodded. "One that we kill this man. And two, that he's a man at all."

"You think he could be some kind of fiend?" Luis asked, excitement tinging his voice.

"What?" Smithers asked, taken aback. "N-no! I was just insulting his manhood... Wait, when you mean fiends do you mean..."

"Demons and devils," Lee explained, and while not religious himself, Smithers felt an almost overwhelming urge to cross himself. Though that was probably just a side effect of sleeping in a church's basement.

"Yeah," Smithers said, nervously. "I don't think that's the case here."

"Besides," Morgan said, quietly, her voice so low that the three men stopped arguing to listen. "If she needs to really believe in the plan for it to work, then she's the one that needs to make the decision of where to go. Or if she should stay."

Smithers pursed his lips but couldn't fault the girl her logic. "Alright, that makes sense. Let the girl choose."

He walked over with Morgan but held a hand up as Luis and Lee tried to follow. "Let's not crowd the girl now. Besides, Luis, you smell awful. Go shower."

With a shrug, the knight went to the showers and Lee muttered something about getting himself something to eat before walking upstairs. Smithers went over to where Morgan was explaining the situation to Jess.

"So, he'll buy me a ticket?" Jess was asking. "Just like that?"

Morgan smiled at her. "Yes, just like that."

"Well, except for the one catch," Smithers said, sitting down at the foot of Jess' bed. "If you take it, you have to stay gone. You call anyone from around here, send a letter, or even an email, and this Colin jerk could find you again."

The light of hope died in Jess' eyes and Smithers felt the slightest twinge of guilt. But he knew that if this girl made the slightest slip up, it wasn't just her life on the line anymore. She touched her hand to her belly, mirroring Smithers' thoughts.

"My mother," she said softly. "And my friends. My job."

"I'm hearing a lot of 'my' in those sentences," Smithers said.

"I know," Jess said, biting her lip. "I need to think in terms of 'our' now. But I don't know if I can support us without them all. To go off, halfway across the country, no support system, no anything... I feel like I'll be more likely to fail. More likely to reach out for help. To put us at risk."

"You know what would come of that," Morgan said.

"I know," Jess said, gripping the sides of her head in her hands. For a moment, Smithers thought the girl may have broken down into tears, but she took a deep breath in and sat up to look at them. "Tell the Father that I am very grateful for his offer, but no thank you. I'll figure this out on my own. I'll go to my mother's or I'll move in with a friend..."

Smithers reached out and put one of his hands over hers, giving it two soft pats before pulling away and standing up.

"No you won't," he said, walking over to his cot and grabbing his bag. The comfortable weight of the shotgun fell against his back as he slung the bag over his shoulder. "Morgan, gather the boys when they're done primping. I need to go borrow the Father's van again."

"Uh..." Morgan said, turning to watch him climb the stairs. "Sure, but what's the plan?"

"Tell ya on the way," Smither said, without turning back.

***

Smithers stood in the doorway of O'Malley's just staring at the flurry of activity that was Timm. The boy was moving through the bar washing, wiping, and organizing at the speed of a cony with a bee on its ass. Tom stood off to one side, wiping down a glass Timm hadn't managed to poach from him yet, watching in similar confusion, though his expression was far more amused.

As the group came to sit down, Tom looked at Smithers and nodded at the boy. "He always like this?"

"Not usually," Smithers said, shaking his head. "What did you give him? Cocaine?"

Tom reached below the bar and took out a red can of cola and set it on the bar without a word.

"Ah, I see," Smithers said. "From here on out, you're not to serve them anything but water or alcohol. I don't think they're mature enough for soft drinks."

"You realize how backwards what you just was, right?" Tom asked with a smirk.

"At least liquor will put him under. Not, that," Smithers said, hooking his thumb at Timm, who had just bustled into the kitchen, kicked open the oven, and began scrubbing furiously.

"What is that?" Morgan asked, pointing at the can.

"It's a soda, miss," Tom said. "Would you like to try it."

Smithers shot him a look of irritation, which was met by one of sheer amusement on Tom's part.

"Sure," Morgan said, accepting the beverage, which Tom popped open for her. Morgan sipped at the drink gingerly. Her face screwed up as she pulled back from the can. "I don't know what that fizz is, but it hurts going up your nose. Otherwise, it's nice and sweet, but I don't think I can have more than this."

"Good to see a girl who knows her limits," Tom said, wincing as a crash came from the kitchen. "Try to teach the boys a little restraint when you get the chance. I think he's worked his way through half a case already."

"Heyboss, isthereanythingelseIcandoforyou?" Timm asked rapidly, coming into the room, breathing heavily through a large goofy grin on his face.

"Uh, yeah," Tom said. "Take that garbage around back?"

"Surethingboss, yougotit!" Timm said, the words barely out of his mouth before he was out the door. Thankfully, he remembered to come back and grab the garbage bags.

"You let him drink half a case?" Smithers asked, incredulously.

"I figured it would be worth it," Tom said, smiling.

"What would be worth it?" Lee asked, taking a seat at the bar next to Morgan and politely declining her offer of a sip.

"The crash that's coming," Tom's grin widened. "That boy's never had a drop of caffeine in his life, has he?"

Smithers barked out laughing.

"Okay, that makes it worth everything," he said, then turned to note the confused faces of the others. "We'll explain later, first things first, the plan."

"Right," Luis said, looking around. "You said if we came to the tavern that we'd find Colin and be able to settle Jess' problem once and for all."

"Not in my bar," Tom said, sternly, all mirth vanishing from his voice.

"No, not in your bar," Smithers said. "But he'll be coming here. So we need to be on the look out for him. I figure a guy like him is a coward. Maybe you threaten him a little, he backs down. Hell, maybe we'll get real lucky and he'll hit one of us. Press charges and off to jail he goes."

"And if those methods do not work?" Lee asked.

"I don't know," Smithers said, shaking his head. "All I know is the girl won't leave town and the asshat won't leave peaceably. We have a few hours before the place opens officially, right Tom?"

Tom nodded at him. "Close to six hours."

"Well then, serve me a coffee and I'll mull over our options," Smithers said, watching as Timm came back in and began frantically scrubbing a pot to the point he was convinced the boy was going to have a heart attack. "Until then, you lot make sure he don't kill himself."

Hours passed and coffee turned to whiskey in Smithers' cup, but still no revelation dawned on him. This boy Colin had gotten himself into one hell of a mess. Trying to work out his misplaced aggression from youth on his girlfriend was bad enough, but it had drawn the eye of some truly terrifying people, and Smithers was not sure that he could get the boy out of the hole he dug before Father Mitchell would have to start saying words over it. No proof meant no police, and if he didn't back down the knight or Brogue Lee would probably beat him to death without realizing he was just a guy.

Smithers turned to look at Timm, who was currently sitting in the stool next to him, face down on the bar, snoring and drooling from the sugar crash that was currently ravaging his body. The old man laughed, feeling like this was the first time he'd ever seen the boy at peace, and all it had taken was enough chemicals to give an elephant diabetes. Turning in his stool, Smithers looked at the rest of them. Lee sipping his water while listening to one of the regulars, Carl, tell him some dirty story that the priest either didn't understand or didn't care for, but was too polite to say anything. Luis had taken up a game of darts, seeming to prefer power over finesse in his throws, but still out classing the group that had turned up to play. Morgan was helping Tom deal with the aftermath of Timm's 'cleaning' and was pleasantly chatting with customers who all assumed she was 'the new girl' who was just 'filling in for Jess.'

Such a normal scene met Smithers' eyes, and if he hadn't known any better, he would have assumed that these were just ordinary young people going about their lives in a perfectly normal world. In spite of himself, he smiled slightly and tried to let the feeling linger. Alas, it was not to be, as the sight of a tricked out sports car with amenities that were never meant to be put on a model as high class as this one rolled up, playing music at the perfect volume to be both annoying and impossible to understand.

This level of douche-baggery could only mean that Colin had finally arrived on scene. Smithers hoped desperately that Plan A was going to work, because Plan B was most definitely going to be the death of someone.

~ 20 ~

MORGAN

Morgan was speaking with one of the regulars, a woman who had very many opinions on the topic of men, and not very many of them were good, when she saw a shift in Smithers' posture from across the bar. His body tensed and he seemed exceptionally interested in something happening outside the window. She looked out and saw several men exiting a vehicle and approaching the bar. Excusing herself, rudely from the reaction of the woman, Morgan made her way over to Smithers.

"Is that them?" Morgan asked, quickly.

"Looks like," Smithers said, reaching over and smacking Timm's shoulder with the back of his hand. "Hey boy, get up and get your game face on."

"Huh... what?" Timm asked, groggily sitting up at the bar.

"You get him together," Smithers told Morgan. "I'll grab the others."

"Okay," Morgan nodded as Smithers walked over to the dart board where Luis was chatting with some of the other players. "Come on Timm, Colin's here."

Immediately Timm's demeanor changed. His face hardened and he stood so quickly that Morgan had to reach out and catch the stool before it tipped over completely. As she was setting it back on all four legs, she looked up to see Timm walking purposefully towards the door.

"Timm!" Morgan said, her voice strained with urgency against the need for discretion. She looked over and saw that Smithers hadn't noticed the abrupt change in Timm's behavior yet and she didn't want to cause a scene. As Timm stepped through the door, she made her decision and followed him through it.

Timm stood in front of the door, arms crossed, his face twisted in a scowl that Morgan had never seen him wear before. He stared at the men who approached with nothing short of pure, unadulterated rage in his eyes. Morgan's stomach twitched and an overwhelming need to turn into something fast and run washed over her. It was at that moment that she realized she was afraid. Not of the men approaching, not of the situation, but of Timm.

One of the men, a cocky looking individual probably in his mid-twenties, approached Timm while laughing at something another had said. He briefly looked at Timm before barking, "Move."

"No," Timm said, eyes burning. The man staggered in his steps, having not slowed his gait at all. It seemed to Morgan that this person was not used to being told no. More than likely, this was Colin.

"What do you mean, 'no?'" he asked, irritation in his voice.

"Hey Colin, you gonna let this guy talk to you like that?" one of the other men said, confirming Morgan's thoughts.

"Shhh!" Colin hissed in irritation, waving off the man before turning to face Timm again. "Do you know who you're talking to?"

Timm looked him up and down. "No one of importance. Now piss off."

Colin looked like he'd been slapped, and Morgan couldn't help but smile at the face he made. A sense of righteous justice filled her, and the desire to run faded slightly. She found herself setting her feet and standing her ground.

"I don't know what made O'Malley think some two bit bouncer would keep me out, but I'm going in there, and I'm dragging that lousy bitch out of this dive," Colin snarled, puffing out his chest and trying to look impressive. Compared to Timm's stoic glare, he failed miserably.

"I hope ye got yerself some strong friends," Timm said, blinking slowly. Morgan noted his breathing pattern slowing down. He had mentioned something like this to her before, where he could alter his heart rate, calm his nerves, and keep himself from hyperventilating in a fight by doing simple breathing techniques. Her eyes shot over to where Colin was standing, breathing heavily with anger through clenched teeth. Apparently he never trained the way Timm had.

"Strong enough to beat your ass if you don't move," Colin said, drawing back a fist to throw a punch.

It came straight in on Timm, aimed directly for his nose, but Timm didn't even bother uncrossing his arms. A slight twist of his shoulders and turn of his head, and it looked like Colin had thrown his punch a foot and a half off the mark. Having not balanced himself properly, Colin staggered a step towards Morgan, who backed up swiftly to avoid being rammed by his flailing form. Catching himself, the angry man turned to face Timm, who wore the slightest of smiles now.

"I was more concerned if they'd be able to carry your sorry carcass out of here once I beat yours," Timm said, voice openly mocking. He seemed to be enjoying himself, but Colin decided to use that against him.

Morgan saw the flash of steel as a blade appeared in Colin's hand. Before she knew what she was doing, she leapt forward to tackle him before he could strike. With a twist of his hips and a sharp blow from his elbow, Colin evaded her attack and sent her driving down into the concrete ground. The taste of iron flooded her mouth and stars flew across her vision. She tried to call out a warning, but Colin was already driving the blade towards Timm, who moved too slowly to avoid the blade. It opened up his arm at the bicep, sending a spray of blood against the door.

A moment later, the door flew open and Lee stepped out, peering around. He saw Morgan laying on the ground and moved to help her, but she pointed frantically at Colin. Lee turned to see the bloody weapon in his hand and Timm clutching his arm in pain.

"Oh, so that's how it is," Lee said, dark energy gathering at the edges of his fingertips. He stepped forward, and Colin tried to block him, but had been expecting a blow or strike. Lee only needed to press his fingertips to Colin's chest, and an eruption of magic flooded him. Morgan watched as Colin writhed in pain, blood flowing from his eyes and nostrils. He staggered backward, coughing violently.

"What the fuck was that?" Colin gasped, his eyes were wide with shock and fear. Morgan looked at Lee, expecting that her expression was quite similar. She barely heard Colin crying out behind her. "I need some back up, boys!"

"Y'ain't getting it," Timm snarled, swinging at Colin with a bloody fist. Colin barely managed to duck out of the way of the blow, falling for Timm's feint and turning directly into the path of the uppercut. Morgan watched a tooth fly in a perfect arch through the air as Colin fell back, slamming into the ground without any attempt at bracing himself. He must have been unconscious before he even hit the ground.

"Now," Timm sniffed, wiping the side of his nose with his thumb. "Who's up next?"

Morgan grinned, thinking that after watching what had just happened, the others would just run, but apparently, they were dumber than she thought. Two moved in on Timm while one backed Lee into a corner. They completely ignored her on the ground, so she took the opportunity to scoot back a bit and clamber to her feet.

Timm was ducking blows from the two but was soon overwhelmed and outnumbered as Lee took a strike to his stomach, blowing out a harsh breath as the blow landed. A punch caught Timm across the jaw and Morgan saw him stumble for a moment. She had a plan, but was about to toss it away to jump in and protect

Timm's flank. Thankfully, the door to the tavern slammed open and Smithers' voice came calling out.

"The hell's wrong with you boys!" He cried out.

"Fuck off, old man!" One of the ones trying to hit Timm called out.

"Old man?" Smithers stepped out onto the street, brisling with irritation. "You rude little..."

Smithers swung at the man who had insulted him, who made no effort to avoid the strike from someone he expected was barely a threat, even laughing as he did.

Unfortunately for him, Smithers had been holding his taser when he threw the strike and it clicked to life as soon as they made contact. Morgan thought she saw the man's pants darken at the front as he jerked wildly, flying back a few feet from Smithers and Timm. He looked up at Smithers, shocked in more than one way.

"Old man my foot!" Smithers snarled.

These three seemed to be a lot tougher than Colin, leading Morgan to question why they would follow him in the first place. There wasn't enough time to ponder this, however, as she saw them attempting to regroup and assail her friends again. Ducking back behind the bar, Morgan hid herself in an alley. Pressing herself between two of the dumpsters, Morgan closed her eyes and focused on the form she wished to take.

Her nose pushed forward, darkening as bristles of grey and black fur rippled from its tip, across her face, and down the rest of her body. The sound of bones cracking, twisting, and reforming sent a shiver down Morgan's spine as it rearranged itself, throwing her off balance and down onto all fours. Thankfully, her hands had morphed, toughened into pads and claws that barely felt the chill in the pavement. Ruffling her fur, Morgan turned her eyes toward the mouth of the alley as the darkness dissolved away. The eyes of the wolf pierced through it.

She moved her shaggy form forward with grace and power like she never knew. Coming around the corner, she saw one of the men moving forward to retaliate against Smithers for using the taser, and Morgan had found her prey. With a snarl, she lunged forward, taking more delight than she probably should have as the man turned to see her and his face twisted up in terror. He turned as if to flee, but Morgan's fangs found the back of his leg and clamped tight around his hamstrings, dragging him unceremoniously to the ground, screaming the whole way.

A sudden flash of light caught Morgan's attention as she turned to see Luis bringing down his baton against the man on Lee. She could hear the snap of bone as Luis' blow made contact, but she knew it wasn't just the force of the knight's arm that staggered his enemy, but the strength of his faith. The man tried to back away, but looked down at his arm in horror and seemed too stunned to move.

Timm stepped forward and drove his fist down at the man Morgan held down against the ground, cutting off his screaming as he dropped unconscious. He turned to face the last two who were standing there dumbfounded, blood dripping from his fists and a snarling wolf at his back. Morgan played up the moment just a bit, letting a deep growl resonate from her chest.

"Yo man, we out!" the one with two good arms said, holding up his hands and backing up towards the car. When he had backed away maybe ten feet, he broke into a run, dragging the whimpering one with the broken arm behind them. They dove into the car and sped off, leaving their two friends behind.

Smithers turned to see Morgan standing there in her wolf form. She turned to look at him, her tail wagging in excitement at their victory. He stared at her for a moment, shock in his eyes.

"Uh," Smithers said, looking around at the crowd of people who were gathering. He began violently waving his hands at Morgan, yelling "Shoo! Bad doggie! Git!"

Morgan was confused for a moment, but turned and ran off towards the alley, shifting her form once she was out of sight of the people on the street. Smithers must have been trying to get her to change back, though he could have been more polite about it. Morgan looked back over her shoulder. If he didn't want people associating her with the animal attack, it would probably be better if she went in through the back door rather than come from where the wild beast just went.

She walked through the back of the bar, passing O'Malley's office, and entering the main room just in time to see Timm step in from outside. In the lights of the bar, he looked far worse off than he had outside. He was bleeding profusely from the cut on his arm and his lip had been split open. In spite of the injuries, he seemed to be in high spirits.

"Hey Tom," he called out across the bar of dead silent patrons. "Do you happen to have any rope?"

"Wh-why would you need rope?" Tom asked him.

"So we can tie these guys up," Timm answered, as though the answer was obvious. "We don't want them getting away."

"Right," Tom said, drawing out the word as he picked up a phone. He dialed it, and a moment later started speaking to someone on the other side. "Yeah, hello, my name is Thomas O'Malley, the owner of O'Malley's Bar by the river. Yeah, I was calling to report a stabbing that happened outside my establishment. The victim is fine, think the mugger bit off more than he could chew. Send an ambulance and maybe a couple officers, please? He'll be waiting for you outside. Thanks."

"Oh," Timm said, as O'Malley hung up the phone. "I suppose that works too."

"It does," O'Malley said. "Now get outside, you're bleeding on my floor."

As they stepped outside, Morgan reached out to touch Timm's arm.

"Here, let me heal that for you," she said as her fingertips hummed with the power of nature's healing magic.

Smithers' hand shot out and grabbed her by the wrist, pulling her hand away from Timm. Morgan saw Timm tense up, tightening his hands back into fists. For just a moment, she thought she saw a spark of light flicker from his palm, but turned her attention towards Smithers.

"Oh no, no," Smithers said, shaking his head. "What's gonna happen when the cops show up and Timm here is fit as a whistle and these two look like they just got hit by a truck?"

"If I were these 'cops,' I would assume that Timm was the assailant," Luis chimed in from where he was checking Lee for wounds.

"Exactly," Smithers said, "Then nothing happens to them and we're in a world of trouble."

"Oh," Timm said, visibly relaxing. "That's... a good point."

"Think you can handle the pain, boy?" Smithers asked, concern in his voice.

Timm nodded. "I'll be fine, better than that guy at least."

He gestured over to the man Morgan had bitten. He wasn't bleeding heavily, but the fang marks were quite visible through his torn pants. Smithers grimaced a bit as he looked at it.

"Any chance you can do something about that?" He turned and asked Morgan. "I mean, cops showing up to find a guy mauled by an animal may be hard to explain."

Morgan nodded. "I can do that."

She stepped over and felt the warm hum of the healing magic dance at the edge of her fingertips again. Reaching out, she felt it flicker from her to the wounds on the man's leg, slowly knitting closed the punctures she had caused only moments ago. The man, face down, groaned and propped himself up on his elbows.

"Uh... what the hell happened?" he asked, looking around with bleary eyes.

"That's a good question," Smithers said, before swiftly bringing his own baton around in a low arc, cracking the man across the jaw and knocking him out once more. "Okay, we need a plan and we need one now."

Morgan looked around at the mess they had made. She fully agreed with Smithers on needing a plan, and that little voice in the back of her head was screaming that running would probably be the best one.

~ 21 ~

LUIS

Luis surveyed the scene in front of him. Lee was fine and on his feet, two of their enemies had fled, and Timm sustained only minor injuries. While the outcome was not as ideal as he would have hoped, they had not lost any of their number and, according to Morgan, it was Colin who was lying unconscious at their feet. All in all, the situation was well at hand

"So, what are these 'cops' exactly?" Luis asked Smithers.

"Huh, well, I suppose you guys would understand it best as them being like the city watch," Smithers said, scratching at his beard. "They arrest people and can be quite dangerous to anyone who finds themselves on the wrong side of things."

"Ah, so they are trustworthy men and women of honor," Luis nodded. He did not know these individuals well enough to simply believe they should be trusted on merit. However, with all he had seen of this world, it was good to know that he'd be working with proper legal authorities in the aftermath of the attack. He nodded at Smithers, finally feeling as though he were standing on familiar ground.

"If that is the case, I shall like to speak with them in regard to what has transpired here tonight," Luis said.

"No to both of those things," Smithers said, shaking his head. "Y'all need to get out of here. Timm stays with me, doesn't talk to the cops. I talk to the cops while Timm gets medical attention while not speaking to the cops. And you guys head back to the church while none of y'all talk to the cops."

"I get the strangest feeling you do not want us talking to these cops, Smithers," Lee said, brushing himself off.

"Did ya get that impression?" Smithers asked.

Luis pursed his lips angrily. "I do not see why. We were involved in the incident; it is only just and legal that we speak to these cops. Tell our side of things."

"Your side of things involves being a magical holy knight from another dimension," Smithers shot back. "That will land you in St. Augustine again and the rest of us with you. You need to git!"

"You do not trust that we would know what information to omit and what information to provide?" Luis shot back.

"No," Smithers said, shaking his head. "Not in the slightest."

Luis felt his temper rising. He had hoped to be more involved with the fight, but Timm's impulsiveness had robbed him of even getting to confront Colin about his behavior towards Jess. Now Smithers was trying to rob him of the opportunity to ensure that the cretin was even punished! Without realizing it, Luis had taken two steps towards Smithers when he felt a hand lightly grip his arm. He turned to see Lee standing calmly behind him.

"I think it is best that we take Smithers' counsel on this one, Luis." Lee brushed one of the locks of long silver hair that had come loose during the fight from his face, pointedly releasing Luis' arm to do so. "He knows this world better. Besides, fewer stories means fewer conflictions on the one we need these cops to believe, if we want the best possible outcome for Jess."

Luis wanted to argue further, but Lee's calming demeanor and logical argument convinced him to bite his tongue and go along with Smithers' plan.

"Just know," Luis said, turning to Smithers. "I don't like this, and I don't approve of it."

"The plan don't need your approval," Smithers said, nodding at Luis. "But believe me when I say I don't like it much either."

In spite of himself, Luis found himself believing the old man when he said this. There was something about the way he held himself, the same way a soldier would, one who has seen many battles and would prefer not to again. But more than that, Luis saw in this man the same demeanor and authority he remembered his father carrying himself with. It was the confidence in purpose and wisdom of age, mixed with the slightest tinge of arrogance that made Luis both angry and proud that made him bite his tongue.

While he did not like skirting the law without getting the opportunity to ensure the justice will be done, nor did he like these underhanded tactics to ensure victory, Luis trusted Smithers' understanding of the world and those that inhabit it more than his own, and he respected the old man's authority on the matter. In this world, Luis had very little knowledge of the way things worked and had less authority when trying to act within it. He did have to accept it as the current reality, though that did not mean reality couldn't eventually change.

"Come on then," Luis said, starting down the street towards the church. "We'll need to get out of here before the cops show up."

He felt more than heard Morgan and Lee fall in behind him as they started down the icy streets. The warm feeling he had gotten from his morning run was fading. He knew that Nike was telling him that he needed to have faith, and he was sure that these people were part of his personal test of faith, but that did not mean he needed to like it.

Flickering red and blue lights began to converge on the scene as they left it behind them. A horrid shrieking siren cut through the still winter air, grating Luis' nerves as he ground down on his teeth.

"Must be some kind of alert," Morgan said.

"It is strange that they added those dancing lights," Lee noted. "They seem more of a means of disorienting others than warning them."

"Whatever the reason, they're obnoxious," Luis spat, feeling a headache beginning to encroach his thinking. "Let's just go."

Fuming in his thoughts, Luis continued to lead the way back to the church. He spent the next quarter of an hour marching through the snowy streets, reciting a prayer to himself over and over, calling upon Nike's power to clear his mind to the true path to victory. He felt his anger cool and his focus crystalize. Timm had done exactly what he himself wanted to do, charge into battle to defend the helpless and to secure victory. Luis couldn't bring himself to blame him for that. As for Smithers, the older man knew the ways of this world and was doing all he could through different channels to protect Jess, and that was the goal of the entire night, just as Lee had told him. Luis realized his anger came from having no part in the major victory, and such selfishness was not becoming to one who worked within a unit to secure the overall victory for his Goddess.

With a deep breath of chilled winter air, Luis felt the last of his anger and shame evaporate into cool, logical realization. When he opened his eyes, his mind was as sharp and clear and the night sky. Though looking around, he pursed his lips again, realizing that the neighborhood that he had led them into was not one that he recognized.

"Does anyone know where we are?" he asked, turning to Morgan and Lee.

Morgan looked around, peering at street signs and landmarks, but when she turned back to face him, Luis could see that her expression was just as confused as his.

"We're in the right area," she said with a shrug. "It has to be around here somewhere."

"Over there," Lee said, pointing off in the distance. "You can see the steeple, and at the top their holy symbol, I believe Father Mitchell referred to it as a cross, that makes it even taller, allowing you to find it when you are lost."

Luis and Morgan both turned to see what he was pointing at, and sure enough, Luis noticed the steeple of the church, though he was unsure what Lee meant by it being so tall you could find it when you were lost. Perhaps that had once been the point of such a device, however this temple to the Christian god was nowhere near as tall as the buildings that surrounded it, nor even as tall as many of the structures he had seen around the city. In fact, many of those dwarfed the church by a great margin. Though, in spite of this, stepping near where Lee was standing, Luis was just able to make out the tip of the steeple as it peeked between two of the nearby apartment buildings.

"Ah yes," Luis said. "I see it now."

"It would be easiest for us to reach the church by crossing the road here and coming around from that side street across the way," Lee said, pointing as he stepped out into the street. The roads were clear of vehicles at this hour, and a thin layer of frost had formed on the blackened roads, crunching as Lee's boots sank in.

Luis was about to follow him when the sound of crunching was drowned out by the roar of some horrendous beast. It was like nothing Luis had ever heard before, tearing through the night, as though a dragon had decided to tear the heavens asunder. His eyes snapped up to the sky, seeking the source of the roar, when he felt Morgan's hands grip his arm and turn him bodily towards the street where they had just come from.

Hurling down the road at speeds that Luis thought unimaginable without the aid of some kind of sorcery, came a man dressed in black leathers similar to those Luis had wrapped around his own shoulders, his face hidden behind a helm that encased his entire head. He rode on the back of a creature that reminded Luis of a horse, if such a beast were made of twisted, screaming metal that galloped across the snowy earth on a pair of wheels that threw the fine white powder into a mist of fog behind it. One single eye adorned its head, placed square between the horns atop its head that the rider clung to for support. The eye glowed with a ferocious yellow light that illuminated the path before it.

And in its sights was the brilliantly lit image of Lee.

Luis tried to shout, to somehow call warning to Lee before the creature and rider collided with him, but at the speed they were traveling, he could barely cry out his friend's name.

"Lee!"

The priest turned, his eyes wide and reflecting the light of the oncoming beast, sure that there was no hope in escape.

At the last moment, the beast swerved violently on its tail, whipping up a spray of snow and ice as it passed within inches of Lee. The rider's hand stretched out and violently shoved Lee to one side, sending him sprawling out of the street and into a tumble. His landing was broken by a snow drift that echoed with a loud splat, proving that it was more wet than frozen.

Thrown off balance, the rider twisted his body, hauling hard on the beast's horns trying to right it before he was thrown from its back. Spinning, the front wheel of his mount rearing up as he settled it pointing away from the street that would lead them to the church, the rider began waving his arms violently.

"Down!" came his muffled voice from under the helm. "Get down!"

It was then a similar roar came from the direction where the rider appeared from. Luis turned to see a van much like the one Father Mitchell had parked in the back of the church, only painted completely black, turn around the corner at a speed that did not compare to that of the black rider, but was far more than such a vehicle should be forced to withstand. For a moment, he thought it might tip over as two of the side wheels came up off the ground, only to settle again a moment later as the full weight of the vehicle came crashing down. It swerved drunkenly, as the driver attempted to correct his course.

The door panel on the side slid open, revealing two male forms clinging to the inside while simultaneously attempting to lean precariously out. One had a tousled mop of red hair, while the other wore his brown and cropped short, but both held in their hands a long black box with a nozzle at the end. Luis stared for a moment, pondering the design, and finding them eerily similar to the guns that Smithers carried, though these were much larger. The men lined up the boxes with the black rider, who responded, by twisting one of the horns of his beast, eliciting a loud, almost defiant roar.

Instinct took over and Luis threw himself at Morgan, dragging her bodily to the ground and covering her form with his own. Not a moment too soon, apparently, as the still air of the winter's night was broken by a stream of explosions. Sparks flew as the bullets sailed through the air, buzzing like angry hornets, sinking deep into the bodies of cars that lined the streets and showering Luis in dust as the brick exteriors of surrounding buildings exploded into powder, falling like ashen snow.

Luis chanced a look at the rider, who was the main target of the onslaught, only to see his beast reared up and roaring. The moment the front wheel of the beast touched the ground, he sped away, drawing the attack of the oncoming van. Using his superior mobility, the black rider led his pursuers away from the scene, and soon the sound of explosions dimmed and vanished in the night.

Carefully getting to his feet, Luis surveyed the situation. The street where they were about to cross was a mess of tracks from the vehicles and sported evidence of damage from the weapons the two had fired at the rider. Had any of them been in the street when such an attack had occurred, there was no magic or act of Gods that would have been able to piece them together again. The black rider had, whether it was his intention or not, saved all of them from a vicious and violent death.

"Were... were those guns?" Luis heard Lee sputter from the snow drift. He turned to see Morgan helping the priest to his feet.

"Not like the one that Smithers carries on his person," Luis said, thinking of the shotgun that the old man had been cleaning this morning. He had told Luis that it only held two shots per load, and he would have to be a foolish man indeed to not be able to tell those men had fired nearly one hundred times as many as that. The danger they posed should not be underestimated.

"But they were still guns," Morgan said, her voice slightly shaken.

Luis simply nodded, listening closely to hear if any more sirens were coming their way. In this moment, he fully understood the wisdom Smithers had shared with them of not speaking to the cops. There was no way that getting involved in whatever had just occurred would not unnecessarily put their lives at risk.

"Come on," Luis said, driving the others into action. "This is no place to stay. We'll be safe back at the church."

"Mighty bold statement," Lee said, cautiously following Luis across the street with Morgan by his side. "Assuming any place in this world is safe with weapons like that."

The knight did not want to say it aloud, but he feared the same thing. Their own world had held so many dangers, but it seemed that this world, through its lack of magic and divinity had made monsters of its own people, and armed them accordingly.

~ 22 ~

TIMM

Timm sat reclined on a gurney as people who called themselves "paramedics" were looking him over and shining lights in his eyes. The first time they had done this, he went to smack the device out of their hands, and was only stopped when Smithers grabbed his wrist and shot him a look that clearly said, "Boy, be on your best behavior." After that he sat still and tried to answer the questions the paramedic named Emit asked him while Smithers was over to one side talking to the cops.

"Okay, so we're going to ask you a few questions," he was saying to Timm. "You just try to answer to the best of your ability, do you understand?"

"Yes," Timm said, nodding.

"First, an easy one," Emit said, wrapping something around his arm, stifling the trickle of blood that came from the wound in his arm. "What's your name?"

"Thola Igerk Mue Moonflayer," Timm answered. He looked up to see the quizzical look he was being given. "Uh... but most people call me Timm."

"I can see why," Emit answered. "That one is supposed to be the easy one. Okay, let's go with number two: who's the President of the United States?"

Timm thought back on the conversation they had with Smithers a couple days ago about kings and presidents, and figured that he would know how best to answer it.

"Uh... an asshole," Timm answered, trying to remember Smithers' exact phrasing, though he felt he may just be falling back on the old man's favorite word to describe people instead. He looked up to see Emit peering back at him in surprise before turning to look at the other paramedic with him, a woman with dark skin and large brown eyes that were currently sparkling with laughter she seemed to be fighting to keep down.

"He's not wrong," she said to Emit. "I suggest you just keep going."

Emit shook his head and sighed. "Alright, how about to-day's date? Can you tell me what the date is?"

"February twenty-sixth," Timm responded confidently.

"You're a bit early, but not far off," Emit said, writing down something on his clipboard. "How about your birth date?"

"Midsummer," Timm answered, with the same level of confidence.

Emit's pen froze. The man sighed again, "Alright, I'll write down 'Midsummer' and let the nurses deal with it at the hospital."

"You think he has a concussion?" the female paramedic asked Emit.

"Honestly, I don't know if he's got a concussion, is a little loopy from getting stabbed, or if he's just some kind of whack-job..."

"What does 'whack-job' mean?" Timm asked, curious about the term, but he was fairly sure it was insulting. He wanted to be sure that they knew that he wasn't trying to waste their time.

"It's... well..." Emit said, turning to his partner for help, but she just smiled and came around the other side of the gurney.

"You ready to get to the hospital, sweetie?" She asked him kindly. Timm nodded at her, feeling that the hospital would be a lot better than being out on the street where everybody who passed by the scene would stop and stare at him for a little while. The group had been saying how important it was to keep a low profile for now.

"That would be nice, yes," Timm answered her, smiling. Between her and Emit, they quickly loaded him into the back of a large, boxy vehicle they had called an ambulance, and Emit stepped over to talk to Smithers.

Closing his eyes, Timm slipped his mind into a meditative trance. The bustling of the world around him began to fade, shouts became little more than whispers and the flashing lights were mere pulses against his eyelids. Pushing the distractions away as his master taught him, he limited his focus to the conversation between Emit, Smithers, and the cop he was talking to.

"Sir, we're taking your friend to the hospital now if you'd like to ride along with him," Emit was saying to Smithers.

"Thank you, I'll come along," Smither's answered.

"Hold on," another voice cut in, and Timm assumed it was the cop. The authoritative tone reminded Timm of Luis a bit, but something about it grated him and he grit his teeth. "I need a statement from him before you go."

"You've been talking to him for ten minutes," Emit said. "You haven't gotten a statement by now?"

"Not the old man," the cop snapped.

"Hey!" Smithers said, indignantly.

"The victim," the cop said, ignoring Smithers completely. "I need a statement from the victim."

"Get it at the hospital if you need it so badly," Emit said, coolly. "He's got a knife wound and I'm not risking his life because of your bureaucracy."

"Come on, I get off shift in thirty minutes, that will keep me on for another two hours at least," the cop said, irritation in his voice.

"Inconvenience you or lose my patient," Emit said, his voice getting closer as he walked away from the cop. "Such a difficult decision for me. Sir, if you're coming, please come now. I have no qualms leaving you behind either."

"Coming!" Smithers called out, then turned to the cop. "If you can't get to the hospital tonight, I'll bring the boy down to the station later on when he's feeling better."

Before the cop could answer, Smithers rushed over and Timm opened his eyes in time to see the old man clambering into the back of the ambulance before Emit closed the doors. With a couple bangs on the side of the interior wall, Emit signaled his partner it was time to go, and the annoying wail of sirens filled the air, making Timm's head twinge with minute pain. The ambulance rolled away from the scene and a very annoyed looking cop that Timm could see through the back window.

"He did not seem pleased," Timm nodded at the back door.

Emit looked over and regarded the cop disappearing in the distance and made some kind of grunt in the affirmative.

"Police have their jobs to do, as well as many other peoples' jobs to do, I don't blame him for being annoyed," Emit said. "But I do take issue with them interfering with my job."

Timm turned to face Smithers. "Police?"

"Another word for them," Smithers explained. "Cop, police, officer, po-po, the fuzz, 5-oh, pigs... Though the last few are insulting, so I wouldn't use them in polite conversation."

"Or any," Emit said, no inflection to his voice. "Now if you don't mind, we need to go over allergies and medical history. You're not bleeding badly, but we've called into the hospital that we're bringing in a knife wound victim and they take that stuff rather seriously."

Over the next fifteen minutes or so, Emit quizzed Timm on things he didn't particularly understand or know. Family history was a complete blank for Timm as he never really knew a biological family, and Smithers helped him fill in a few blanks regarding what particular medications and allergens were. By the time they had gotten to the hospital, Timm's head was hurting more from the interrogation than any other part of him was from battle.

There was a flurry of activity that even Timm's own sharp eyes and monastic training did not allow him to fully track. At some point, a nurse told Smithers that he was going to have to wait outside while Timm was tended to. The old man had not been overly happy about that, stating something about guardianship, though the nurse seemed to throw that idea aside based on Timm's apparent age. After a few tense and confusing minutes, several people had moved Timm off of the gurney, gotten his clothes off, put him in some kind of robe made of paper that closed the wrong way, and began asking him a multitude of questions.

"Okay, on a scale of one to ten, how would you rate your pain if ten is the worst?" one woman asked him as people moved rapidly through a room filled with similar beds, wounded people, and paper curtains. His were still open so he was able to see the activity around him. Seemed there were many people injured tonight besides himself, and many who he deemed to be in far worse shape than he.

"I'm not sure I understand what you mean," Timm said to her while his eyes continued to scan the room.

The woman stood and closed the curtain, blocking off his line of sight to the rest of the infirmary. "I just want to know how much pain you are in, gives me a better idea of what kind of medicine and pain killers you need."

"Oh, well," Timm thought about it for a moment. "I mean, now that the adrenaline has worn off, I suppose I'm in a bit more pain than I was before... So, I suppose a three?"

The woman looked at him, confused. "You are aware that three is pretty low on the scale, right? Ten means more pain. So, are you sure you don't mean seven?"

Timm pursed his lips for a moment as he thought. "No, I think a three is pretty accurate. It was only a small knife that stabbed me, and I've been hit by worse blades in training, so I'll stick with three."

"Oh... okay," the woman said, wide eyed at Timm. "In that case we'll only give you a light sedative."

"For what?" Timm asked.

"Well, we need to give you stitches," the woman was explaining. She had finally gotten close enough for Timm to read the badge that hung on her white coat. It read Doctor Anne Madison.

"Oh! You're the doctor!" Timm said, excitedly.

Doctor Madison cocked her eyebrow at him. "Does that surprise you?"

"No," Timm said. "It's just that no one really introduced themselves."

"Ah," Doctor Madison smiled, tension Timm hadn't noticed building seemed to relax from her shoulders. "My apologies, it's just been a busy night tonight. Big drain on resources."

"Then don't waste unnecessary ones on me," Timm said, waving his hand.

"We're still going to be stitching you up," Doctor Madison said, eyeing him curiously.

"Oh no, I appreciate that," Timm said, nodding. "But you can skip the pain killers, I'm fine without."

The doctor gave Timm an overly concerned look, and seeing that she was getting no reaction from him, she turned to the nurse standing by. He shrugged at her.

"I mean, normally people would do anything to get their hands on these drugs," the nurse said. "Are we going to complain that he *doesn't* want narcotics?"

"I suppose not," Doctor Madison resigned.

She took out a collection of items that Timm was only vaguely aware of, threaded a hooked needle, and began to stitch the wound closed.

It was odd returning to this older form of medicine that his master had used on the multiple occasions he'd received a laceration during training now that he'd become accustomed to Morgan, Lee, or Luis being able to simply touch him and immediately seal the wound. Timm smiled, actually reminiscing about the many times he would sit with his master chiding him over being foolish or rash and receiving the wound in the first place. The nostalgia overtook him and he began to hum a ditty to keep his mind off the rhythmic sting of the needle. The words, like much of his memories of home, were lost on him, but the tune remained.

The rhythm of the needle faltered for a moment, and as he looked up, Timm saw both the doctor and the nurse exchange a strange look.

"Are you sure you're okay, man?" the nurse asked him. Timm noticed that the man was surprisingly tense considering he wasn't currently the person having a long, hooked needle being jabbed through his arm.

"Oh yeah," Timm said. "Just thinking about home. Not my first time being stitched up like this, just reminded me of some good times."

"Heh," the nurse laughed. "A thrill seeker in your youth?"

"You could say that," Timm nodded, and gave him a wink. "But who's to say those days are behind me? I'm still young, and life is full of thrills."

Doctor Madison took out a gleaming pair of sheers and cut the cord that she had been winding through his skin for the past few minutes and gave him a sharp look.

"Now listen," she said, her voice stern. "Regardless of the reason, putting yourself in harms way for the sake of thrills is stupid. You come in here and take up my time when there are people who were in real trouble that need my attention not getting it."

Timm tried to speak, but she cut him off.

"That's not to say what you did tonight wasn't brave," she said, her voice softening. "You did a good thing protecting that girl, and I'll never fault anyone for that. But don't let your confidence be your undoing. And don't let it be the reason you let others get hurt. You aren't immortal and you're not a human shield. Just be careful out there and don't go looking for trouble."

Timm smiled at her, almost feeling a sense of matronly affection. He hadn't had that growing up, as it had always been just him and his master, but it was nice to feel. There was no venom in her words, only concern for the people under her care, and he could respect that.

"I promise you, ma'am," Timm said, holding up his uninjured arm solemnly. "I will not go looking for trouble. However, if it happens to find me, I make no promises that I won't do what needs to be done for the people I take care of."

Doctor Madison looked him up and down before sighing outwardly, though it lacked any actual disappointment.

"I suppose that's all I can ever ask of a patient like yourself," she said, holding back a light smile. "Now, Nurse Monroe is going to take you to your room. You'll be staying with us overnight for observation just to be sure there weren't any underlying issues."

"But I feel fine..." Timm started to say, but Doctor Madison cut him off again.

"And also, to keep the police from bothering you for a statement until after you've been given proper time to heal and get a good night's rest."

"Ah," Timm said, settling back into the bed and getting as comfortable as he could. "When you put it that way."

"I think you're really going to like your roommate," Nurse Monroe said as he pushed the bed away from the wall and began wheeling it down a hallway.

Timm tried very hard to control his breathing. He knew that Smithers would not have allowed him to be brought anywhere that would risk his life or freedom, but the parallels he was drawing between this hospital and St. Augustine were nearly impossible to ignore. The white lights passing overhead, illuminating the sterile white walls and the strange pockmarked ceiling began making his heart rate rise. Nurse Monroe turned into an open door that led to a room cut in half with a single curtain.

"Andy!" a croaking voice called out. "Andy, is that you?"

"Yes, Mrs. Goldstein," Nurse Monroe said, as he turned Timm's bed so that he was facing the doorway, giving him a good view of possible escape routes. "I'm just bringing in your new roommate."

"Well then get rid of this blasted curtain," the voice called out again. "If I'm going to have someone to talk to, I don't want to be shouting through a piece of cheap cloth!"

Nurse Monroe laughed and shook his head. Turning to Timm, he said quietly. "That's Ester, your roommate. She's a real pistol. I think you two will get along."

Timm was confused, but as Nurse Monroe pulled back the curtain, he saw the kindly face of an elderly woman who could be none other than Ester Goldstein. She had tubes connected to her face and arms that could in no way be considered comfortable, but still was smiling and greeted Timm warmly.

"Oh, what a handsome young man you are," she said, smiling. "My name is Ester, what are you in for?"

"I'm Timm," Timm answered, finding that he was indeed getting fewer looks when giving that response than his whole name. "And I got stabbed."

"Well then, that's exciting," Ester answered. "I'm only here for kidney stones."

"I didn't know kidneys had stones," Timm mused,

"They're not supposed to!" Ester said, with exaggeration. "Now then, how would you like to watch my favorite program with me?"

"Sure," Timm responded, not quite sure what she was talking about. He watched as she pulled out a small box covered in buttons and pointed it at a larger box on the wall in front of them. As if by magic, the box lit up with color and sound, filling the room with upbeat music and images of four older women seeming to have an array of mundane but hilarious adventures. Judging by the lyrics of the song, they were friends and thanking each other for such relationships.

"They're having a marathon tonight," Ester said, excitedly. Again, Timm was not sure what that meant exactly, but he settled in and decided to allow Ester and her four magical friends to help him follow the doctor's orders and heal.

<h1 style="text-align:center">~ 23 ~</h1>

<h2 style="text-align:center">SMITHERS</h2>

Smithers ground his teeth in irritation at Officer David Lynch. The man was as persistent as he was irritating. It was about the fifth or sixth time the man had him answer the same questions, after following the ambulance to the hospital in his squad car. So much for wanting to get off shift and go home. It was almost as though the man had a personal bone to pick with this Emit the EMT.

Smithers risked cracking a smile at that thought. Boy should have thought about his professional choices a bit harder with a name like that.

"Something funny, sir?" Lynch asked him, though the use of the word 'sir' was fully a formality judging by the lack of anything resembling respect in his voice.

"Gotta keep smiling these days," Smithers responded, snappishly. "Especially when someone is trying your patience by asking you the same damned questions over and over, that you've answered truthfully, while waiting to hear how your friend is doing in the Emergency Room."

Smithers saw Lynch's body tighten up. He looked like a man capable of incredible violence, and one not used to having his authority questioned. However, in the past few days, Smithers had seen things that made this boy look like no more than a posturing puppy.

"I served in Iraq and now on the streets of Boston," he said, expecting to garner some kind of respect from Smithers. "You will treat me with respect!"

"Boy, Uncle Sam had me sign a forest's worth of documents saying that I'm not allowed to tell you where I've served," Smithers barked back in an authoritative tone that made Lynch quell. He never raised his voice, knowing full well he didn't have to. "I've been on most continents, seen things that would make you piss yourself or vomit, and half those things I've seen because I've done them. Now if you want to start a dick measuring competition on tour of service to gain respect, I hope you've come to the table with something more impressive than a compliment from a Hooters waitress."

Lynch blanched slightly at the look Smithers was giving him. The old man couldn't be sure, but he was probably wearing an expression that held too many memories of his times outside the states. It probably wasn't in his best interest to be flashing that background around here, especially trying to keep a low profile, but he was tired and worried and had about had enough of this boy trying to impress him like he was a pretty girl rather than an old man.

The cop stumbled over a few words, trying to somehow salvage the situation, when a female officer walked up beside him and put her hand on his arm. Lynch jumped slightly, as though he thought he were being attacked, but looked down to see the woman standing there, about a head shorter than he was.

"Hey, Lynch," she said, calmly. "Why don't you grab a cup of coffee, it's late."

"But I..." Lynch started, but the woman took the pad of paper out of his hand and shooed him away.

"Go on," she said. "I've got this."

Lynch looked at Smithers with a mixture of annoyance and fear that gave Smithers an odd sense of satisfaction. Taking the cue from the female officer, Lynch muttered something under his breath that Smithers was sure was only him trying to make himself feel better before wandering off to wherever it was someone could get a decent cup of coffee in a hospital. Wherever that mystical fairytale land was, Smithers was slightly jealous he couldn't go too.

"I'm sorry about that, mister..." the woman's voice trailed off, not looking at the papers in front of her that Smithers knew contained his name. She was waiting for him to give it, either out of a polite gesture or because she was taking over the interrogation.

"Smithers," the old man answered. "Just Smithers, no need for that mister stuff. Just creates a false front of respect for people who ain't got none."

The woman clearly caught his meaning, though it didn't show on her face. She was Lynch's polar opposite in every way, barely breaking five foot even with long dark hair tied into an immaculate braid that only had a few frizzy defectors trying to escape after what Smithers was sure was a long night for her. Only a fool would think her dark brown eyes were as doe-like as she played them up to be. Smithers saw a sharp intelligence behind them as they flicked and scanned the room, constantly searching for danger or information.

"Well you may not go in for the formalities," she said, nodding slightly as she did. "But my name is Officer Carla Rivera. Would you mind terribly helping me understand what Officer Lynch was trying to figure out? I can barely read his notes."

Smithers sighed slightly. "Good cop it is, then."

"Preferable to bad cop, I would think," Rivera said, a small smile playing on her face.

"You would think," Smithers said, biting his tongue. "Listen, same story for the tenth time, I was at O'Malley's with the kid..."

"Kid?" Rivera asked, her eyebrow cocked up.

"He's in his twenties," Smithers said, waving his hand. "To me, at that age, they're all kids."

"Valid," Rivera said, flipping to a new page in the book, scratching down notes. Smithers' eyes flicked over the page and saw she was writing in Spanish. He grinned slightly as she looked up from her notes at him. "Then what happened?"

"Well, Timm went outside with a girl," he held up his hand, cutting off Rivera's next question. "Before you ask, I do not pay attention to that boy's love life."

Which wasn't exactly a lie, he didn't care about such frivolities. No need for Rivera to know that he went outside with Morgan for reasons other than making out in an alley. In fact, even better if she never heard the name.

"Next thing I know, he's yelling. I go out to see what's wrong, and they attack me too," Smithers said, still not exactly lying. "So, I do what any old man would do in that situation. I take out my stun gun and give that whippersnapper a zap!"

For a second, Smithers thought he may have gone too far using a term like 'whippersnapper,' but Rivera's keen eyes only paused on that word for a moment before finishing her notes. Perhaps it didn't translate well, but eventually he saw her scratch down the word 'mequetrefe' before moving on and he huffed out a laugh.

Rivera looked up at him to see he was reading her notes.

"Do you understand what I'm writing, sir?" she asked, and it took only a moment for Smithers to translate her Spanish in his head.

"For the most part," Smithers said, in a far more formal Spanish. "I learned in Spain, so the dialect is a bit different for me."

Rivera cracked a smile at him, but continued in Spanish. "You know, it was not polite how you were talking to my partner over there."

"It was not polite the way he was talking to me," Smithers responded, eyeing her. "There is a reason that your profession gets a bad reputation, and he's it."

"He's not usually that bad," Rivera said, with a sigh. "It's just late and he's under a lot of stress."

"You're his partner," Smithers said. "But you are talking like a wife trying to make excuses for bruises."

Smithers saw Rivera's eyes flash with anger.

"Don't take that the wrong way," Smithers said, holding his hands up in a pacifying manner. "I just believe that we should be holding people to a higher standard. Wouldn't you agree?"

It seemed as though Rivera was mulling over several responses in her mind before she finally came up with one she liked. Smithers could respect a person who thought before they spoke. Perhaps one day he'd be that person too.

"Perhaps you're right," Rivera said. "Uncouth, but right. I apologize for my partner's behavior and will discuss it with him after he's managed to get some rest."

"I appreciate that," Smithers said, nodding.

"However," Rivera said, switching back to English. "As it was a weapon used in a crime, I am going to need to confiscate your stun gun."

Smithers' heart sank.

"You can pick it up when you bring your friend by to give his statement at the station," Rivera continued. "Once it's been processed for fingerprints and cleared that this particular serial number was not used in any previous crimes, then you may collect it from evidence."

Reluctantly, Smithers reached into his pocket and pulled out the device, careful to just use his forefinger and thumb to pull it out, and dropped it into a plastic evidence bag that Rivera held out for him.

"Thank you very much for your cooperation," Rivera said, sealing the bag and placing it under her arm for transport. "Now then, if you don't mind, I just have one more question."

"What is it?" Smithers asked, dejectedly.

"Your friend who's getting stitched up, how is it that he's speaking with an Irish brogue and has a name from a Native American reservation?" Rivera asked, and Smithers could tell that she was genuinely curious about it.

In spite of himself, the question caught him so off guard that he just started laughing.

~ 24 ~

LEE

Lee did all he could to calm his heart and his mind. After the experience in the street between the black rider, as Luis called him, and his pursuers with their guns, he was finding it difficult to get a hold of his thoughts. With each crack and whiz of a bullet, he felt his thoughts scatter like birds fleeing the cry of a hawk. By the time they had returned to the Cathedral of the Holy Cross, he managed to gain enough control, limiting his biological reaction to a mere tremble of his hands. Luis, being the man of action that he was, thankfully got the door.

"We must go talk to Father Mitchell," Luis said, his tone carrying authority, though far calmer than he had been when speaking to Smithers earlier. Either the walk or the explosive encounter had helped the knight find clarity, though he hoped it was the former.

"You're right," Lee said, grateful to hear his voice was not following the suit of his hands. "Though I am unsure if he will still be up."

"Worth a shot," Morgan said, with a shrug as she started walking down the hallway towards the Father's room. "Right?"

"I suppose so," Lee said, begrudgingly following. He had hoped to be able to take to his bed and finish recovering from the evening's events before reliving them, but it seemed there was no stopping his compatriots now. Besides, stepping away would only

214

arouse concern in them, and with people like these, concern may well grow to suspicion.

That is how he found himself sitting before Father Mitchell in his office. His door had been left open and the light spilled from inside, a glowing beacon to any who needed to find him. He had told them he was up late working on a sermon, but given that it was only Thursday, Lee saw no reason for his fellow priest to still be awake at this hour. Though with the ease it was to locate him, Lee assumed that Mitchell had left his own door open and obvious in case Jess needed to seek comfort. It was something Lee appreciated in the man. He was not heavy handed in his offerings of faith, but left them easily accessible to any who wanted them.

Luis had just finished explaining what had happened at the bar, with Morgan filling in blanks for moments the knight had not been present for. Father Mitchell nodded along politely, only interrupting when asking for clarification. His eyes had grown a bit wide when Morgan mentioned the bit about becoming a wolf and bringing down the one man.

"But don't worry," she had reassured him. "I healed the leg with my magic so that the cops didn't realize he'd been attacked by an animal."

"Well, that's good then," Father Mitchell said, his voice slow and measured. "Though for future reference, you may want to refer to them as police."

"Who?" Luis asked.

"Cops," Father Mitchell explained. "The term is seen as somewhat derogatory for the police. Though to be fair, many incorrectly attribute that name to the phrase 'Citizen on Patrol,' but it actually gets its base from the Latin word 'capere,' meaning to take, seize, or capture. 'Capere' became 'caper' in French, amusing since a caper in modern times is an illegal activity. When the word made its way over to English is when it became 'cap,'' eventually becoming 'copper,' which in the 18th century was shortened to 'cop.' So you can see why they probably wouldn't like the term, and it would be best to stick with 'police.'"

Lee noted the information, though noticed Luis' eyes glazing over at the explanation. Morgan seemed to be nodding along politely, but was also less than enthused at the impromptu lesson in linguistic history. He, however, found it to be quite useful information and made a mental note to be sure to look up more about this Latin language.

"So, will it be safe for Jess to go home now?" Morgan asked, seeing the etymology portion of the conversation was over.

"That's still up in the air," Father Mitchell explained to a now somewhat deflated Morgan. Quickly, he added, "She is in a pretty tight spot as far as her living situation goes. Colin is guilty of assault with a deadly weapon, so at the very least he could see a sentence of five years in prison. And that's after a trial, which could take months to years to actually procure."

"So he could be put away for a good long while," Luis said. "Then I don't understand the issue."

"He could be bailed out," Father Mitchell explained. "He could be let go by the police for lack of evidence."

"Timm stayed behind," Lee explained. "Allowed himself to gain the substandard benefits of your medical system as opposed to our aid in order to provide evidence."

"This is true," Father Mitchell said. "However, I am explaining the difficulties facing Jess at their worst possible scenario. Besides that, she may not want to return to the home where such atrocities took place. That is one reason why I'm working with local women's shelters and social workers to help her find new housing in a safer environment."

"Oh," Morgan said, breathing a sigh of relief. "So, there is help coming."

"In a sense," Father Mitchell said, smiling. "Maybe not the help you were hoping for or anticipating, but I'm doing all I can, just as you are. Have faith. Much like your friend Timm, God so loved the world that he was willing to sacrifice himself for it. And that is the love we must all have for each other."

"I don't understand that," Luis mused. "If he loves the world so much, why is it so terrible out there? Why are people like Colin allowed to behave in such a manner?"

Father Mitchell sighed, and Lee noted he wore an expression that clearly said that he has had to answer this exact question many times before. Though Lee did agree with Luis' sentiment. In their world, there were many different gods with competing viewpoints, but it seemed that there were far fewer being worshiped here. One would think that the champions of these gods could easily step in and carve a path for good to tread in this world.

"God does not work like that in our world," Father Mitchell said, almost answering the very concerns in Lee's mind. "He has given us a guide, with very few commands. In fact, there are really only eleven that come to mind. The Ten Commandments and the greatest lesson Jesus ever taught, to love your neighbor as yourself."

"What are the tenets of your religion," Luis asked. "These ten commandments?"

Father Mitchell walked over to a box resting against the side of his bookshelf. He dug inside for a moment and came out with a pile of books. Lee saw that they were all the same book, a simple black cover with gold leafing on the sides and an inlaid title that said, "The Holy Bible."

"Usually, these are for our young parishioners who are going through their confirmation," Father Mitchell said as he placed the books on the desk in front of them, specifically not putting the books in any of their hands. Lee smiled in his mind, again impressed at the man's ability to lead without forcing. "If you wish, you may take a copy and read the roots of our religion. I have no wish to convert those who already have zeal for their own religion, but offer this as a token of knowledge to help us get to know each other a bit better."

"Thank you," Lee said, standing and taking one of the books. "I look forward to seeing just what your Christianity is all about."

Luis took one as well, as did Morgan, though she seemed to Lee to only be taking the book because she assumed it would be rude not to.

"The others can come get one for themselves as well, if they like. Though as I recall, Timm already has one," Father Mitchell said, sitting back down behind his desk. "Or you can share, it is up to you. I just hope that we can continue to work together on things like this. United, it's amazing what humanity is capable of. With faith and unity, we could all be a powerful force for good."

"With all the suffering out there, it's sometimes hard to believe that," Luis said, mournfully.

"Not to rely too heavily on the nihilist philosophy, but Kierkegaard was also once quoted as saying that 'all life is suffering.' And that it is on us to 'find the things in life worth suffering for.' Though to be fair I may be paraphrasing that quote a bit. It is quite late after all."

"Then we shall not keep you," Luis said, standing. "If there is anything else we can do to help you, please let us know."

"Just keep doing what you're doing, I suppose," Father Mitchell said, standing as well, offering his hand to each of them in turn. "Have a good night, and get your rest. I feel that with the lives you choose to lead you don't get much time for it."

He bid them good night and the three began to make their way back to their lodging downstairs. Lee was pondering the book in his hand and the philosopher the Father had mentioned. That was another author that he may need to look up in his studies on this world. It was a moment before he realized that Luis had stopped at the top of the stairs and had to cut himself short to keep from bowling into the knight.

"I am concerned about how much we tell Father Mitchell," Luis said, not mincing his words.

"What do you mean?" Lee asked him.

"I was specifically leaving out information," Luis said, then turned to Morgan. "Such as you turning into an animal to fight."

Morgan looked a little sheepish. "Sorry."

"It was not done out of malice," Luis said, clearly not angry with the girl. "However, this world does not seem to have our ilk among them. I feel certain things are best left unsaid. There are few people we can trust."

"I trust Father Mitchell," Lee stated, surprising himself as he did. But it was the truth. Father Mitchell was everything he presented himself to be; a kind and generous shepherd who led a flock towards what he felt was a good death through means of a good life. While their religions may differ vastly, Lee felt that Father Mitchell's valued the same things Lee himself valued.

"I trust the man as well," Luis said, lowering his voice. "It is the institution that I do not trust."

"The church?" Morgan asked.

"The Religion," Luis said, nodding. "Note how he always states that he is the one helping, that he needs to be careful about what he says or does because of others in the church?"

"Others like Pearson?" Lee asked, starting to understand Luis' suspicions. The knight nodded at him.

"It seems that Mitchell is a good man trapped among an old guard," Luis continued. "I feel it would be best for us and for him if we limit the amount of information given to him in order to keep him in the dark enough that the shadows may protect him from our actions, should they ever conflict with his religion."

Lee pondered this for a moment. "A lot of what you're saying makes sense, though it seems oddly reflective of what Smithers was saying to you earlier about the police."

Luis pursed his lips thoughtfully before he spoke. "I spent the walk back thinking on the wisdom of Smithers' decision on how to handle the police and found that there may be times when I need to set my ego aside in favor of the greater good. A small victory is not worth throwing the greater away."

Lee was satisfied with this answer. It seemed that he had been right about what Luis needed, and that the knight was quite wise in his actions and thoughts, given the time to properly process them. Swift to battle was the man of action, but clear of mind is the true warrior.

"Very well," Lee said. "We shall be selective with the information we provide Father Mitchell, if only for his own good."

Morgan looked between the two holy men, and Lee could see she was trying to figure out exactly what was going on, but was coming to a loss. She sighed, walked past them, and began going down the stairs.

"Just be sure you're quiet," she said as she descended. "Jess may be asleep, and we don't want to wake her."

Luis followed her next leaving Lee upon the landing above the stairs alone. He looked around at the dramatic art and symbolism that plastered the walls. There were many styles, though one kept popping up more than others. The image of a man sacrificed upon the very cross this religion used as its symbol was a powerful image indeed, and for almost a moment the man wearing a crown of thorns upon his head with a spear in his belly looked almost like Father Mitchell.

He too was a man who would be willing to be nailed to a cross in order to take the pain and suffering away from others. That was what a man like him was willing to suffer for. However, Lee could not help but feel that such suffering did nothing but take, because it could not save. He reached up and clutched his own holy symbol in his hand, holding it so tightly that he could practically feel the heat of the forge searing his flesh.

This was not what the hammer and nail were meant for. Sacrifice and torture were not worthy of reverence. The job of the nail was to build, and the purpose of a hammer was to forge. Items of creation should not be used for destruction. They would all have to be sure that this organization did not taint these items further in their pursuits, nor allow Father Mitchell to be strung up on that cross along with his savior.

With this declaration as his evening prayer, Lee descended the steps, deciding to use the bible given to him by Father Mitchell as research material. Though that could wait until morning.

~ 25 ~

TIMM

It was around episode three or four that Ester fell asleep, but Timm decided to keep on watching. A nurse came in every hour on the hour to be sure that his vitals were good, whatever that meant, and on one of the visits in, he decided that he'd been there quite long enough.

"When will my friend be able to take me home?" Timm asked the nurse, this one a middle aged woman who carried the added weight of a comfortable life.

"That older gentleman waiting down at the ER?" she asked, thoughtfully. "I'm pretty sure we sent him home. No sense having him stick around all night for you. The man needs his rest just as much as you do, sweetie. Now we'll see how you're holding up in the morning and hopefully send you on your way then."

Timm pursed his lips, feeling agitated by the answer, but not wanting to take it out on this kind woman just nodded and settled in for a night of watching more of this wondrous box.

It was a good plan, though unfortunately it only lasted about another five minutes or so. Timm was feeling well enough to move, to train, and to test just what his body could handle in its current state. At one point, he had tried to do some calisthenics, however the machine by his bed started beeping furiously, causing a team of nurses to rush in and chide him for exerting himself too much. This time he had a better plan.

Slowly, Timm began to peel back the stickers the nurses had put on his chest. He saw that they were connected to the machine.

"Don't do that," Ester's voice said, taking Timm so off guard he nearly jumped. He turned to see the old woman peeking one eye open. "If you take the nodes off, it just thinks you're flatlining."

"Flatlining?" Timm asked.

"Your heart stopped," Ester explained, pointing one finger weakly at the wire attached to the machine that ran up to the wall. "Unplug it first. Just stops sending a signal. Blips clear off the screen. They'll notice if they look, but otherwise it doesn't alert them like ripping those puppies off will."

Timm nodded at her and followed the wire from the machine attached to him to where it stopped at the wall. There was another wire there that seemed to connect to the machine Ester was hooked up to. He looked at her and pointed to the wire.

"Leave mine," she said, waving her hand. "I'm not going any-where, and I'd like a crash cart if I start flatlining."

Timm nodded at her, not really understanding what she meant by a 'crash cart,' but respected her wishes and only pulled the wire attached to his machine. To his surprise, it came out easily from the wall, only being connected by three metal prongs about an inch long. He was curious about what was inside the three little holes left behind, but felt it was a poor time to start investigating some-thing so mundane when the whole of the hospital was still waiting for him.

Stepping outside the room in only a paper frock, having removed the uncomfortably warm foot coverings the nurses kept insisting he needed to prevent a fall, Timm looked around to be sure that he was indeed alone. The hall was quiet, aside from the occasional beeping of machines from within the rooms that lined the hallway.

Making his way down towards what was called a 'nurse's station,' Timm found the area deserted. The nurses in question must either be helping other patients or stepped away for personal reasons, and Timm couldn't help but smile at his luck at finding the place deserted. Checking the hallway again and finding it clear, he slipped behind the counter and began looking over what he could find.

Along the walls of the station were impressive looking paintings of children that, if Timm didn't know any better, seemed like moments miraculously captured via magic into a small square. He assumed that these were the children of the nurses themselves. The desks were less impressive, merely having file upon file filled with boring documents that told Timm little more than the name of patients and useless information about their physicalities. Perhaps this meant something to the doctors and nurses, but to Timm, it was worthless information.

One thing caught Timm's attention as he turned to leave, however. Folded up on the nurse's station counter was a collection of greyish, almost oily feeling paper printed in black and white. The image at the top of the open page was of a small, fragile, and familiar figure. Patrice, the young girl they had visited with Father Mitchell just a few days prior was sitting in her hospital bed, happily smiling at him. He smiled back and turned the papers to get a better look. As it turned out, the writing on the paper was about her as well.

Miracle Child Expected to Die Now Shows No Signs of Cancer the bold print at the top read. *Young Patrice Garret, age six, has been battling with cancer nearly half her life. Her mother, Latoya Garret, who works multiple jobs to afford treatment, had been told that her daughter had merely months to live. Any parent would face that news as unbelievably grim, and possibly give up hope. Latoya, however, never gave up her faith, and had ongoing meetings with local clergy who would visit Patrice in the hospital. Recently, during one of those visits, Patrice's cancer vanished, as though by an act of God. Patrice herself describes the priest who visited her as 'an angel sent by Jesus.' While the Vatican could not be reached for comment, local church authorities have been quoted as saying that "All thanks should go to God, but we can spare a few for the doctors and nurses who so tirelessly work to end suffering."*

Timm could not be sure who the writer was talking about when they mentioned "church authorities," but he grinned thinking that the quote sounded a lot like something Father Mitchell would say. He put the papers back the way he found them, or as close as he could remember, and thought how it was a shame he never really got to talk to Patrice when they had first visited. He and Morgan had walked away to allow for the holy men to do their work, and only got to be part of the tail end of things. It would be nice to see the girl, and perhaps tell her a little more about the warrior 'angel' who had saved her life.

Remembering that her room had been a few floors up, and shuddering at the thought of another claustrophobic elevator ride, Timm made his way to the stairs. He managed to slip through before a nurse coming out of another patient's room could spot him and made a mad dash up the stairs, paper frock flying wildly as he went. The skin where Doctor Madison had stitched him up stretched and pulled against the cords embedded in it uncomfortably, but Timm relished in the light stinging of his wounds. Pain was the body's way of telling you that you were growing stronger, at least that's what his master had always said. Besides, any real damage done could be fixed by Lee or Morgan later.

Reaching the floor where he believed Patrice's room to be, Timm stepped out and began searching the numbers to direct him. There were a few times he needed to turn around and reorient himself, almost as though the building were designed to confuse people trying to navigate it, but soon the walls were once again lined with drawings of sponges with human faces and oddly proportioned animals. He knew that he was in the right area.

There were no nurses at this station either, leading Timm to believe that perhaps they had all been called away for one reason or another. He shrugged it off and decided it was best to just be thankful that his path was easily cleared for him. Smiling to himself again, he thought that perhaps it was divine intervention.

Ahead of him, and at the end of the hall, Timm saw the room he was looking for. Grinning, he picked up his pace, but then something odd occurred to him. He looked back at the hallway and saw that each room had at least a dim light pouring out from under the door, even at night when the patients slept. That had been one reason he was having such difficulties falling asleep himself. Turning back to Patrice's room, Timm saw that it was completely dark.

Perhaps the nurses turned them off to help the child sleep better, but Timm was unsure if such a thing would be done considering how strongly they normally held to the rules. The hairs on the back of his neck rose and he felt every muscle in his body scream with silent tension. He focused his senses to see if he could hear any danger and suddenly realized what was wrong.

It was the silence.

Not a single machine was beeping.

The tension in his muscles snapped and before he knew what his body was doing, he had cleared the last forty or so feet to Patrice's door, throwing it open to bear witness to the gruesome scene within. A man stood over the small girl's bed, holding one of her pillows pressed down hard over the girl's face. She was violently struggling against his weight, but being so small and so frail her attempts did little more than tire herself out. Timm could see her limbs begin to move more sluggishly with every attempt.

Timm screamed something wordlessly at the man, who seemed to start in surprise as the young man threw himself into the room to aid the girl. His instincts suddenly screamed at Timm, forcing him to drop at the knee, sliding forward and taking a layer of skin off his leg as it ran against the ground, but managed to drop below the swinging arm of another man standing off to one side of the room. Timm assumed this was either back up or a look out who was absolutely terrible at his job. Either way, he was immaterial. Saving the girl was priority number one.

Seeing Patrice's body failing, Timm used his momentum to get back up to his feet and charge at the man trying to kill her. The familiar clacking noise of an extending baton behind him gave Timm enough notice that his attacker was not done with him yet. Half turning, Timm managed to get his arm up in time to intercept a blow directed for his head with the meaty part of his forearm. There was a sickening crack as metal met bone, but his training and years of pain told Timm that his arm hadn't broken, at least not yet.

The blow caused him to stumble back a few steps, putting him directly in line with the man smothering Patrice. Timm stepped forward, taking his stance, and sent an attack driving towards the head. Sensing the strike, the pillow-man ducked out of the way, causing Timm's fist to crack against the machine attached to Patrice that was no longer beeping. Timm saw the wire attached to this one had been removed from the wall as well. Fury took him as he whipped around, sending his right fist in an uppercut between the man's arms, hoping to force him to drop the pillow and deal with him.

The strike connected, and Timm was met with the satisfying sound of teeth breaking with the force of being clamped together with such devastating speed. Though the pillow-man seemed to be made of sterner stuff than Timm anticipated, taking the blow and keeping the pillow against his quarry. Anger welled inside Timm, but his master's voice rang out in the back of his mind:

"Don't focus on the head! A wise man will keep it guarded. Focus on a variety of strikes that target the many weak points of the human body!"

Swiftly switching strategies, Timm turned at the hips, drawing his fist flat so that his palm would strike his opponent in the chest, right under the ribcage to strike the pillow-man's diaphragm. With a whuff of pain, the pillow-man staggered backwards, his hands clutching at his chest as though trying desperately to grab the air that had been forced from his lungs. The pillow fell to the floor and Patrice rolled after it, gasping for air herself.

Timm smiled as he watched Patrice get herself to safety, and at the same time provided Timm with all the excuse he needed to start going all out against these guys. The one with the baton came up from behind and attempted another swing on Timm, who deflected the blow downward, sending it into the side of the bed, cracking the flimsy material of the guard rail. He turned his attention toward the pillow-man who he was sure would take advantage of the distraction to strike at Timm with his own baton.

There was a glint of metal as the moonlight from the window reflected off of the blade the pillow-man had drawn from a sheath at his side. A weapon Timm had not seen since leaving his own world whistled through the air towards him. Reflexes took over as Timm felt the edge of the blade barely miss the side of his head as he twisted his body in an attempt to create space between him and his opponents. However, in a tight room like this one, space was the one thing he would most definitely get.

Electric pain pulsed through Timm's body as the baton made direct contact with his spine. The shock rushed through him and practically turned his legs to jelly. Reaching out, Timm gripped the rough fabric of the hanging curtains, nearly ripping them off the wall as he used them to steady himself. He knew that if he fell to the ground, it would not take long for these two to take him apart, the only question would be if he died from being hacked to pieces or bludgeoned into paste.

Regaining his footing, Timm measured his threats. Fighting two on one was sure to get him killed. He needed to take out one of his attackers completely so that he could focus on defending himself against only one. The one with the sword was most dangerous. He could block a baton with his arm, but try that with a sword and you'll lose the limb. He had to disable the swordsman first, and his master was very specific about how to disable an enemy.

Timm moved in on the swordsman, feinting an attack to the man's head, causing the sword to be brought up in a defensive stance. Taking advantage of the raised blade, Timm quickly got within his reach, making the sword nothing more than a useless hunk of metal. Stepping in, Timm drove his bare heel down the front of the man's shin. Had he been wearing boots, this technique would have ripped the flesh down to the bone, but as it was, the attack did little more than cause the swordsman to yelp in pain. That was all Timm needed him to do, as the distraction created an opening to the man's chin.

Striking up with his palm, Timm connected with the pillow-turned-swordsman's chin, driving it forcefully backward. The strike itself was not overly powerful, as Timm had not had the proper footing or distance to drive with full force, but that did not matter much when the corner of the annoying, beeping, boxy machine was directly behind him. Between his natural born reflexes to get away from the strike, and Timm's own strength helping him along, the man thrust his head back into the metal point with enough force to impale his skull. He dropped to the ground, red blood mixing with grey ooze as he slumped over.

Not having the time to contemplate the ferocity of the attack, Timm turned to face off with his remaining attacker. Baton still raised, Timm saw the slightest of tremor in the weapon as the man looked down at his now dead companion. There was weakness in hesitation, and Timm was not willing to share this weakness with the man. Lunging forward, Timm threw a punch across the man's jaw, which swung open with the strike, and seemed to not quite line up properly anymore. Pressing the advantage, Timm threw a second punch at his gut, hoping to wind this one like he'd done the first.

Silvery pain rang through his hand as though he'd just driven his fist into a pile of loose metal. The ringing sound of mail met his ears and Timm looked up at the man in shock that he would be wearing chainmail under his clothing.

"*Deus vult*," the man uttered, at Timm, though what the language was, the young monk could not have guessed. Nor did he have time, because it soon became clear that the words were not for mercy or surrender as the baton came down at Timms head.

Ducking to one side, Timm managed to take the hit on his shoulder, but his worn out body would not be able to take much more of a beating. Heat was rolling down his arm and Timm was very aware that he had ripped his stitches. He needed help, but there was no one to call. Smithers had left, and even if he'd been in the building he might as well be miles away for all the good it would do.

The gleam of metal caught Timm's eye, reflecting the moon with the brightness of a burning sun and reinvigorating Timm. *No, Timm thought to himself. Like the rising sun, hope will come. Help will come. Even if you have to help yourself.*

Scooping up the sword, Timm called out in a hoarse voice, "Nurse!"

He swung the blade violently, but not being used to the weapon, the wide arch only caused the man to jump back and out of the way of the strike.

"Nurse!" Timm cried out again, this time louder. "Doctor! Anyone!"

The man was moving in again, and off balance from the swing, Timm knew that his upper body was open. Leaning into it, he twisted his body backwards, extended his leg, and drove his heel into the oncoming attacker's chest. There was the sound of snapping ribs as the baton flew across the room and the man staggered backwards to the ground.

"Who are you!" Timm screamed at the man, barely making a question of it. "Why are you here!"

Lying broken on the ground, the man coughed blood up onto his shirt, and looked up at Timm with a grin belonging only to a madman.

"*Ad maiorem Dei gloriam,*" the man sputtered out between coughs, and faster than Timm could react, he pulled something small from his waistband and pointed it at his companion. There was the sound of an explosion and flash of light that made Timm jump back in surprise, bringing up the sword to defend himself.

As he turned, he saw the man pressing the mechanism he held to his own chin, the manic grin even wider than before.

"*Gloria in excelsis,*" he said, and Timm was too slow to stop him. The flash of light came again and the wall behind the crazed man was painted in reds and greys.

The sword clattered to the ground and Timm felt his stomach churn. It took all he had in him to keep from vomiting at the sheer horror of the scene before him. These men were sent to kill a child, and when overwhelmed, they chose to take their own lives rather than be apprehended. The only sound in the room was weeping. Timm was unsure if it was him or Patrice who was making it. A few moments later, he got up and found the young girl and took her up in his arms. They stood that way for a long minute, just taking comfort in each other's presence.

"Who were they?" Patrice asked.

"I don't know," Timm said, hardening his resolve and putting Patrice gingerly on the bed, careful to face her away from the two bodies. "But I'm going to find out."

Timm went over to the bodies of the two men and began searching through their belongings meticulously and worked very hard to keep from looking at the bloody messes that had been their heads and harder to think of how none of the sounds of combat had alerted anyone to the need for help in this room.

Each of them had been carrying the same book, titled the Holy Bible. He set one aside to show the others. Around their necks, and over the ring mail they had been wearing, he found they were both wearing a simple silver cross. He recognized the holy symbol as the same one Father Mitchell wore, though his had been made of a much simpler wood. The one who had been trying to kill Patrice had a scabbard on his belt, and Timm chose to take both it and the belt he wore to carry the weapon back, as well as keep the robe around him closed.

Timm, realizing he didn't have a bag or pockets to carry this stuff in, grabbed the pillow off the floor, ripped the case off of it, and threw his collection inside, using the other attacker's belt to tie it off. It was then that something caught his eye. Tattooed on the man's inner arm, at the bicep, was a circle with twelve short curving lines arcing out in different directions. He went over to the other man and checked his arm. Sure enough, in the same place, he had a matching tattoo.

Grabbing a pen off the side table, Timm flipped open one of the bibles to a blank page and sketched the symbol inside. Closing it up, and taking the pen for good measure, Timm went over to Patrice and picked her up.

"Come on," Timm said, "I don't think it's safe here for you anymore."

"Are they going to try to kill me again?" the girl asked, tears in her eyes.

"I don't know, but do you know that angel who took your cancer away?" Timm asked her, trying to keep his voice calm and smooth while simultaneously on edge trying to keep a look out for the next attack. The little girl nodded at him. "Well I know where he is. We're friends, so I'm going to take you to him. And you know an angel won't let anything happen to you."

He walked over to the doorway and looked outside. The hallway seemed clear, which just made him more nervous about what was going on. The fact that no one heard anything or was coming to help meant that either these men had killed everyone between them and the girl or that the people who did hear didn't care.

"Okay," he whispered, half to the girl. "You need to be very quiet; we don't know who else is up here."

Patrice nodded at him, and steeling his resolve, Timm stepped out quietly into the hallway. Slowly and carefully he retraced his steps to the staircase, still not trusting the elevator. The last thing he wanted was to be trapped in a box if more of those guys came at him. The patter of his feet and blood as it fell from his arm were the only things he heard. As he passed the nurse's station, he looked over the edge and saw a pair of legs sticking out from under the desk and a pool of blood turning brown with age and exposure to air. She had been dead a while.

Shielding Patrice's eyes, Timm got to the stairs and began slowly making his way down. As he did, he spoke to Patrice.

"When we get downstairs, hold tight to me, we're going to walk out of here like we own the place," he explained.

"But you're bleeding," she said, her little voice clearly concerned.

"Yes, I am," Timm agreed. "But I've done that plenty of times before. And my friends can patch me up when we get there."

"Where?" Patrice asked.

"You know the church Father Mitchell is from?" he asked her. She nodded. "Good, that's where we're going. I'm very fast, and I can get us there, but if something happens to me, I want you to just keep going. Get yourself to that church, do you understand?"

Her grip tightened slightly, but she nodded at him. Timm reached the bottom step and looked out the little window into the lobby. This was not where they had brought him in tonight, but he did remember it from when they had visited before. If he remembered correctly, the doors opened automatically. If he moved quickly enough, they would be through before anyone could catch him.

"Good," Timm said, pushing the handle down and giving the girl one last big smile. "Then away we go."

Pushing the door open, Timm walked briskly towards the door, his eyes locked on his target and his stride quick and confident. They were halfway to the door before the bizarre scene drew any attention.

"Sir?" a voice called out to him. "Uh, sir?"

Not wanting to risk any kind of confrontation, Timm ignored the voice and kept walking. A flurry of movement in the corner of his eye told him that someone was coming to grab him, and he knew that it was time to just move.

"Hold tight," Timm whispered silently to Patrice before breaking out into a run.

No one expects an injured man to be as spry or fast as Timm was. Hell, most people were surprised to see how fast Timm was in general. The man in a uniform similar to that of the cop who had been harassing him earlier, though not quite as menacing, reached out and grabbed empty air that had held Timm less than a second ago. By then, Timm had already crossed the threshold of the first set of doors and was well on his way out the second before a voice called after him. He was unsure of what it said, but he was willing to bet that it was something along the lines of a demand for him to stop.

That demand was not to be met, and soon he found himself dashing down the dark icy streets of Boston with Patrice in his arms. There may have been sirens and lights at some point in his run, but he was putting everything he had into this escape. Any person could be another one of them, any car could be housing them. It was not worth the risk of stopping.

Taking to the streets themselves, Timm passed several cars at the speed he was running, drawing a few strange looks. But just as his feet were growing numb with the cold, the spire of the church appeared on the horizon, spurring him on further. Rounding the corner, he saw the wooden door where they had first met Father Mitchell and ran headlong toward it.

As he banged against the door, calling for anyone inside to come answer it, he was realizing that he could not feel the impact of his arm against the door and the gnawing fear of frostbite began to work its way through his brain. He banged harder, hoping to be heard, or at least to feel the impact. Either would be good news.

Just as his strength was giving out, the door opened, and before him stood Father Mitchell. The priest looked at Timm as though the monk was nothing more than a walking corpse. He supposed that's exactly what he looked like, dripping blood and skin probably turning blue.

"Please," Timm said, nearly collapsing. Father Mitchell reached out, supporting both Timm and the child, pulling them into the merciful warm. "Please. She was attacked."

Timm felt the warmth flood him and it seemed a shame to not embrace it. He let it wash over him, and soon the darkness followed.

~ 26 ~

LUIS

Luis snapped to attention as soon as Father Mitchell began descending the stairs. The knight was a light sleeper due to necessity and was out of his bed before the priest had even called for help. He was up the stairs and beside Father Mitchell in moments. Seeing Timm dripping with blood, Luis got his shoulder under the man, easing the weight from the priest who seemed to also be carrying a small girl. He gave her a strange look, suddenly recognizing her as Patrice, the child he'd removed the cancer from just a few days earlier.

"What happened?" Luis asked.

"I'm not sure," Father Mitchell replied. "Timm was pounding on the door, half frozen to death, saying how someone had come to the hospital and attacked Patrice."

Luis pursed his lips in thought as they reached the bottom of the stairs. After lowering Timm into the closest bed, which happened to be his own, Luis crossed the room to where Smithers snored and gave the old man a shake. Luis was surprised to see his eyes open almost as quickly.

"Huh?" Smithers asked. "What is it?"

"Timm's back," Luis reported. "He brought the girl we healed the other day with him."

"That boy did what?" Smithers bellowed, causing everyone else in the room to awaken as well, including an old homeless man who had stumbled in the day before. Father Mitchell went over to reassure the man that everything was fine, and he could go back to sleep.

"Lee," Luis turned to the priest and gestured at Timm. "Heal him, if you'd please."

Lee nodded and crossed the room, and Luis noted that much like himself the priest slept fully dressed, and even managed to get his shoes on in case there had been need for a quick escape. He stood over Timm for a short minute, seemingly identifying the beaten man's wounds before muttering a prayer to his god and laying his hands. Color returned to Timm's cheeks and the bruises went from deep purple to a sickly yellow color, but Luis, having had his own share of such bruises, knew that meant they were on their way to being fully healed.

"Best I can do for now," Lee said. "I'd rather not spend more energy when there seems to be danger about and the rest can heal on its own."

"Mix magic and natural healing," Luis nodded. "Wise."

"Here, give her to me," he heard Morgan say as she took the child from Father Mitchell's grasp. Smithers turned down his bed and the two tucked the small child into the folds of the blankets.

Morgan's hands moved over the girl in a similar way to Lee's, but no prayer was offered. For a moment, Luis thought he caught the scent of wild mint and lemongrass.

"She's not wounded," Morgan reported, looking over at Timm, who was now breathing steadily. "Is he going to be alright?"

"He is," Lee said, plainly. "He's probably just exhausted at this point. Needs his sleep."

"He'll get it in a moment," Luis said, giving Timm's shoulder a gentle shake. The monk groaned slightly and tried to go back to sleep, but Luis shook harder.

"Luis," Lee said, "I must ask that you don't disturb my patient."

"We need to know if he was followed here," Luis said, bluntly. "Won't do your patient any good to be murdered in his sleep."

Lee chewed his lip for a moment before answering, "I can see the wisdom in your decision."

Timm's eyes fluttered open with a groan, and he tried to sit up. Lee stepped forward to push him back down, but Luis instead helped Timm sit up. It would be better for him to be upright when reporting his findings. The world was clearer when you were on your feet, or at least close to it. Timm held his head in his hand for a moment before looking up at those who stood around him.

"Well good morning, everyone," he said with a weak smile.

"Not quite," Luis said. "Tell us what happened."

Timm began regaling them with the tale of his escape from his hospital room, to which Luis ground his teeth slightly at how he endangered them by being bored, but instantly forgave the man upon hearing that had he not, the girl would have been killed. When Timm got to his explanation of the fight, he began pantomiming his attacks, Lee had to step in and physically restrain his arms to keep him from flailing about during the retelling. By the time Timm got to when he ran out into the frozen night, Smithers walked over to join them.

"What did I miss?" he asked.

"Oh, well you see, Ester and I were watching a marathon of her favorite show, and I got bored so..." Timm started retelling the story again.

Smithers held up his hand. "Short version, please."

"Patrice was attacked, but Timm was there to stop them," Luis reported, concisely. "Two bodies left behind and now we have the child."

"Oh, for fuck's sake," Smithers breathed out in irritation. What he was irritated at specifically was difficult for Luis to tell, but the knight shared the sentiment. This was not something they needed right now.

"Hey," Timm said. "There's a child present. Language."

"She's asleep," Smithers said. "Took two stories and a song, but she's asleep."

"You seem good with children," Lee said, his eyes studying Smithers in a way that told Luis it was not merely an observation.

"Spend enough time with them and you either have to be or you have to be gone," Smithers said gruffly. "Problem at hand?"

Timm reached down and pulled a tied up pillowcase off his belt and spilled its contents out on the bed in front of him.

"This is all the stuff I pulled off of them," Timm explained. "I also got a sword."

"They were carrying swords?" Smithers asked, surprised.

"Well, one was," Timm said.

"Do you intend on using it?" Luis asked Timm, his voice not particularly hiding the desire he felt for the weapon. It had been too long since he held a sword in his hands, and while he did not think the weapon of a hit squad would be as elegant as the sword he lost coming to this world, beggars could not be choosers in this instance.

"I mean, I can use it, I know how," Timm said, slightly deflating Luis as he spoke. "But it's never really been my style."

"If I may then?" Luis asked, holding out his hand.

"Sure," Timm shrugged, undoing the scabbard on his belt, and handed the short sword over to Luis. The knight examined the weapon, feeling its balance and weight. It was a different make, and the metal was strangely forged, but it would definitely do for now. He lay it across his lap, taking comfort in the weight as Timm continued sorting through the contents of the pillowcase.

Smithers was examining the small gun Timm had taken from the one assailant with great interest, though Luis noted that he wasn't taking as much care as he'd seen the old man use on his own weapons. He was looking over every inch of the gun, not quite looking down the barrel, but holding it much more precariously than he'd ever seen Smithers handle a weapon before.

"Is it not real?" Luis asked, thinking that was the only explanation for Smithers' haphazard handling of such a thing.

"Oh, it's real alright," Smithers said, tossing it onto the cot, unceremoniously. "It's also FUBAR."

Luis cocked his eyebrow at the old man, prompting him to explain.

"Busted," Smithers said, barely explaining anything. "I'm surprised the damn thing isn't in pieces on the hospital floor. It's a ceramic gun, and a piss poorly made one at that. Though even at that level of quality, probably cost a pretty penny to make. Hell, I'd even bet that they hoped it would shatter after a couple shots."

"Why would anyone make a weapon out of ceramics," Luis asked, bewildered. "What possible use could something so fragile be?"

"Well, good for getting by security," Smithers explained. "Guns are usually made of metal; most weapons nowadays are. So, they have these things called metal detectors that make a real loud and annoying noise when they detect metal."

"Thus, having a weapon made of ceramics would not set off the detectors," Lee concluded, prompting Smithers to tap his finger against his own nose.

"Exactly," the old man smiled. "Granted, the damn things can barely take the force of the bullet flying out of them. Combustion isn't good on the frame. That's why mine are made of metal, holds up better, and is easier to clean. This thing was only supposed to be a one time use."

"Then why did they not use it on the girl?" Luis asked, and noted Lee, Timm, and Morgan all shifted uncomfortably at the question.

"Probably because a pillow is quieter," Smithers said, undaunted by this line of thought. "Less suspicious too. A bullet in the head prompts an investigation by police. A girl stopped breathing after she'd had cancer for a long while doesn't really get a lot of attention."

"So, the gun was the last resort," Luis said, nodding.

"It was," Timm said, his eyes growing distant. "The second guy used it on himself right in front of me rather than get caught. After he said something really strange."

"A zealot sent to kill a child, failed, so he killed himself," Smithers said. "Great. Okay, I'll bite, what did he say?"

"A few things," Timm shrugged. "But they weren't in a language I understood. But they both did have the same tattoo. I figured that may be a clue, so I sketched it out in the book they were carrying and brought it back."

Luis looked at the book Timm was pointing at and recognized it as the same book Father Mitchell had given to them earlier that evening, though the cover was red and made of smooth leather. The gold inlay was exactly the same though.

"You defaced a bible," Smithers said, and Luis was unsure if there was pride or irritation in the old man's voice. "Well, might as well see it."

Timm flipped the book open to the inside cover. Inside Luis saw the image of a circle with twelve hooked lines jutting out from the outside of the circle. At the bottom of the page, in a scrawling handwriting were the words *Oderint Dum Metuant*.

"Was that what he said to you?" Luis asked, thinking maybe Timm had written it down as well.

Timm peered closely at the writing. "No, I didn't even see that there before."

"Lemme see that," Smithers said, reaching over and looking at the words at the bottom of the page. "Damn, I need to brush up on my Latin."

"Wait," Luis said, excitedly. "You know what language it is?"

"Well, yeah," Smithers shrugged. "Took it in high school, but it's been a while. This seems like a phrase I learned at some point. Maybe the Father will know. He said he was going back upstairs to call Patrice's mother..."

"Why would he know?" Morgan asked, curiously.

"He's Catholic," Smithers said, as though that explained every-thing. The blank looks Luis and the others gave him must have told him that they needed more information than that to fully under-stand, so he sighed and continued. "The main language of the Holy Roman Catholic Church is Latin. The priests have to study it and even be able to perform church services in Latin in order to become fully ordained in the church."

"So, he can translate for us," Timm said excitedly, grabbing the book and throwing off the covers. As he was still in the paper gown that the hospital had given him, Luis looked away from the extensive amounts of Timm he had no interest in seeing. When he looked back up, Timm was running excitedly for the stairs.

"Wait!" Smithers hissed out, getting to his feet.

"I'll watch him," Luis said, vaulting over the cot and making his way for the stairs. "You keep watch over the girl."

Smithers relented and sat back down in a huff. Luis shot up the stairs after Timm, sword at his side, and felt a little guilty about having Smithers stay behind on false pretenses. Sure, he wanted there to be protection for Patrice should these individuals show up again, however he wanted to be sure that he was in the forefront of any action that may come up. Timm had found himself at the center of the conflict with Colin and now with this new shadowy organization. Luis was not letting the monk out of his sight in hope of being able to get a chance to finally stretch his muscles out.

Luis finally caught up with Timm at Father Mitchell's bedroom door. In spite of being injured, Timm was able to outrun pretty much anyone on the team, though that was in no small thanks to Lee's healing. The monk was already banging on the Father's door.

"Father Mitchell!" he cried out, pounding his fist on the door. "Father Mitchell, we found something!"

Luis saw that in his excitement, Timm wasn't exactly measuring his strength, and before the knight could call out for Timm to calm down, the sound of cracking wood filled the hallway. Luis inwardly sighed as he approached the door. He saw the knob turn and the door rattle slightly, but other than that it did not move.

"You warped the door," Luis said to Timm, keeping his voice flat.

"What?" Timm asked, looking at Luis then pushing on the door. It didn't move.

"It's stuck in the frame," Luis explained. "You need to calm down and think, sometimes Timm. Not just react. Now we need to force the door open. Hopefully without breaking it further..."

"Father Mitchell!" Timm called out, cutting Luis off. "Stand back from the door!"

"What?" Luis could hear Father Mitchell's muffled voice call from inside. "Why?"

Before Luis could stop him, Timm reared up on his front leg, and with the force of his entire body, kicked forward with his rear leg. Such a kick would easily have broken open any heavy wooden door. Unfortunately, it seemed that Father Mitchell's office door was not built of the same stuff that the older parts of the church were made of. This door crumpled under Timm's attack, breaking clear of its own hinges, and sliding in a full two feet before coming crashing down longways on the floor.

Father Mitchell stood to the side of the door, phone held to his ear as he stared in surprise at the sudden open portal between his bedroom and the hallway. There was a stunned silence for a moment as Timm processed the sight before him.

Father Mitchell stood in the middle of a simple bedroom furnished only with a small bed and writing desk. On the wall was the cradle to a phone which the priest was currently holding to his ear. The Father was wearing a pair of pajama bottoms and slippers, but seemed to have been in the middle of changing as he was not fully dressed. Timm noted the man's build and determined that he must undergo a similar training routine as Luis or himself in order to have the musculature he did. He was on the verge of asking Father Mitchell if he'd had any form of warrior's training when the priest cut him off by speaking into the phone.

"No, Latoya, everything is fine here. Patrice is safe, and you should get some sleep. Come by in the morning and we'll discuss the next few steps. Don't worry, I'll handle this."

He walked over to the wall and hung up the phone. Luis heard the priest take a deep breath before turning around to face them. His face was strained, but he seemed to be holding his temperament in check.

"How can I help you, Timm?" Father Mitchell asked.

"We need you to look at this bible," Timm explained, rushing in. Luis noted that he had not heard a single word said to him about slowing down and thinking before acting, or reading the situation at all that Father Mitchell was currently annoyed, but followed in anyway.

"What about the bible?" Father Mitchell asked, as Timm opened the cover to the drawing of the tattoo and the Latin phrase at the bottom, explaining how he'd gotten them. His expression grew dark as Timm explained, to the point where Luis noted the priest's mouth had become nothing more than a thin line.

"The tattoo I don't recognize," Father Mitchell said. "But this phrase, I've heard it before. Several times in books and histories."

"What does it mean?" Luis asked.

"It means, 'Let them hate me so long as they fear me,'" Father Mitchell translated. "And I can tell you, that it has never been used by anyone on the path of righteousness. You said you got this off of the men who tried to harm Patrice?"

"I did, as well as the same holy symbol you wear. I figured you may know something about them," Timm said.

Father Mitchell shook his head. "While these individuals may have something to do with Catholicism, it is not any sect that I know about. The problem with religions becoming as large as they have is that some will interpret the Word how they wish to justify their actions rather than how God wishes us to be. The Word was never meant to be used for violence, though too often it has been."

"So, what do we do now?" Luis asked.

"You? Go to bed," Father Mitchell said, tiredly. "I do not have such a luxury, but you should go to bed. I feel He will be calling on your services soon enough, and you will need your strength. Mine, on the other hand, are being summoned now."

Luis nodded at the priest. "Come on Timm."

"But..." Timm started to say, but instantly cut himself short when he saw the look Luis was giving him.

"You need to heal," Luis said, his arms folded across his chest. Timm begrudgingly nodded and walked out the now wide open doorway. He paused for a moment, stepped back in the room, and picked up the splintered door. As they made their exit, he propped the door against the empty frame, examined his work, then walked away towards the basement.

Luis shook his head. Where brash action had brought victory, it had also garnered frustration from an ally. The knight's hand rested comfortably on the sword at his hip as he walked down the dimly lit hallway after Timm, not even bothering to try to keep up any further. He would go at his own pace, being sure to keep his eyes open. Whoever these men worked for, they had declared war on him and his people. And wars were not won by speed, but by stamina. Luis needed to be sure to save his strength so he could save those he fought with.

~ 27 ~

MORGAN

Morgan waved her hand over the sleeping child, creating a plume of lavender scented air. The small girl muttered momentarily in her sleep, but soon settled peacefully into her bed, a small smile tugging at the sides of her mouth. Morgan smiled back at the child, happy to see that she was finally resting and not just worn down from fear and pain. The sound of boots on the stairs turned her attention away from Patrice, and the crackling of flame appeared in her hand.

Luis eyed her as he descended behind Timm, who's bare feet had not made a sound on the carpet. Sheepishly, she closed her hand and relaxed the magic she had drawn instinctively away. Timm plopped himself back onto his bed and stared silently at the floor. Luis began unlacing his boots and sat down on his own cot.

"How was Father Mitchell?" Morgan asked. "Is he okay? We heard a bang."

"Physically, yes, he's fine." Luis answered, placing the sword, sheathed, under his pillow. "However, emotionally may be a different story."

"Did something happen?" Morgan asked, but Luis simply settled back in his bed, slipping one hand under the pillow where the hilt of the sword would be. For a moment, he caught Morgan's eye and looked over at Timm, before settling back down and returning to his shallow sleep.

Morgan looked over at Timm, who had curled his feet up under the paper gown and stared silently at the floor so hard that she feared he may well burn a hole in it. He looked worn and tired, and was definitely going to need new clothes before he could leave the church. She made a mental note to stop by the thrift store to pick up a new outfit for him in the morning. For now, it seemed to her that Timm needed a different kind of support.

She walked over and sat down next to him on the cot. He kept staring at the floor, not seeming to notice she had even approached him at all. Gently, she lowered herself onto the bed, and sat watching him quietly for a moment. His features were drawn and tense, and his somber expression aged his normally exuberant face to reveal pain she had never seen him wear before. Carefully, she reached out and placed her hand on his shoulder. Slowly he looked up to meet her gaze, though his eyes seemed unfocused and cloudy.

"We're really far from home, aren't we?" he asked her, not fully looking at her. His eyes looked past her, as though looking at someone off in the distance.

Morgan's eyes slipped as well, the blank white wall behind Timm suddenly a lush, green forest. The sound of children laughing and calling out to one another echoed in her ears as the scent of rich petrichor threatened to overwhelm and brought tears to her eyes. Tears she could not afford right now, and she blinked them back with a smile.

"We are," she said, a slight sigh of longing in her voice. Morgan reached up and attempted to smooth Timm's hair, still damp with snow and sweat. A good hot shower would certainly do him well, but he needed rest.

"I don't understand this world," Timm said, swallowing hard after he spoke. Morgan pretended not to notice him fighting back the tears. Instead, she busied herself turning down his bed before gently pushing him back and pulling the covers over him.

"I don't either," Morgan said, reassuringly, continuing to stroke his hair. Timm's eyes began to flutter as exhaustion finally took him. "But we'll figure it out together. Get some rest."

She stayed there for a few moments more, watching his breathing slow and his tension relax. At least in sleep he could finally put down the weight he forced himself to carry on a daily basis. Envious of the kind of sleep both Timm and Patrice were enjoying, Morgan stood up and returned to her cot.

The dim light from the staircase cast a soft orange glow on the room, but even that amount of light was enough to keep Morgan from being able to fully fall asleep. With a wave of her hand she willed her magic to form into the scents of her forest home again. Though the name of the woods was beyond her mind's ability to grasp, whatever foul curse blocked the words could not block the memories completely, and with the scent of fresh mountain air and river water, Morgan finally fell asleep.

* * *

Morgan woke to find that she was not the last to rise today, a fairly uncommon occurrence. Luis must have already gone for his morning run, Lee was not in his bed, but Morgan could hear the shower running, and Smithers' cot was made and his bag missing. Looking over to Patrice's bed, she saw that sometime during the night, Latoya had joined her daughter in the bed, and now lay with her arms wrapped around her daughter protectively. Smiling at the pair, Morgan made her way upstairs to see if she could find Smithers and breakfast.

Predictably, Smithers was standing at the counter sipping at a mug of coffee. Judging by the genial nod he gave her as she entered, Morgan assumed it was at least his second cup. She went over and poured herself a bowl of cereal, grimacing slightly at the box of flakey corn that had been horrifically sweet the previous attempt she made at eating it, and instead elected for one that seemed to be a far blander o-shaped style. This one had a bee on it, and was only slightly sweet. Morgan crunched merrily on her bowl.

"You know, that tastes better with milk on it," Smithers said, sliding a red and white carton at her. "Pour it on and give it a go."

Morgan shrugged and did as he instructed, giving the milk a moment to sink into the bowl. She scooped some up in her spoon and took another bite. The flavor had changed very little, but the milk kept the cereal from drying out her mouth as she ate and cut back more on the sweetness of the food.

"That is better, thank you Smithers," she said, looking over at the old man, who's attention was fixed on a small box in the corner. Turning to see what it was, Morgan noticed that it was a television much like the one they had hanging over the bar at O'Malley's. "What are you watching?"

"Currently," Smithers said, a note of irritation in his voice. "I'm watching a dumb person show another dumb person how to make a basket out of a damned garden hose."

"Uh..." Morgan said, understanding that this idea was clearly a dumb one but not really understanding why. "Why are you watching that, exactly?"

"Because heaven forbid the news actually report news," he said, sneering as he took a sip of his coffee. "Seriously, you want a placid, easily manipulated people? Keep 'em stupid and keep 'em content. Bread and circuses, Morgan. They always go for the bread and circuses."

Before Morgan could ask Smithers to explain exactly what 'bread and circuses' meant, Father Mitchell walked into the room. He was not wearing his normal priestly attire, but rather a pair of blue denim jeans like Luis wore, a black button down shirt like Lee's, and rather than wearing it, he carried his white collar in his hand.

"Has it come on yet?" he asked Smithers as he briskly walked over, snatching up a mug of his own and began pouring coffee. It was only when he reached for the milk that he seemed to even notice Morgan was standing in the room. "Oh, good morning, Morgan. Did you sleep well?"

"As well as I could," she said, with a shrug. As she looked closer at his face, she saw the dark circles forming under his bloodshot eyes. "Did you sleep at all?"

"Not a wink," he said, smiling. "Thankfully, I don't have any services today so I can more easily relax, so long as the crisis is averted."

"You mean the hospital," Morgan said.

"I do," Father Mitchell said, sipping at his coffee and turning to the television. "Why on earth are they making a basket out of a garden hose? That hose has to cost at least twenty dollars! They could go to a dollar store and pick up a pre-made basket for a fraction of the cost with fewer wasted materials."

"That's what I was saying!" Smithers cried out in agreement.

Morgan stood there in confusion as the two men discussed the decline of modern entertainment and common sense, when suddenly the story on the news shifted and they both abruptly ceased speaking. The screen showed the image of a hospital, Morgan thought it may have been the one they had gone to when they visited Patrice, but since the image was from the air she could not be sure. Dozens of police cars were surrounding the building, their lights flashing against the darkness of the surrounding buildings, though the hospital itself was bathed in light. Morgan could not see her on the screen, but a woman was talking, apparently describing what had happened.

"On a sadder note, hospitals are no strangers to disaster and death, however most of us expect them to be the place where we are able to cope with the aftermath of such things. Late last night at Mass General Hospital, this was not the case," the disembodied woman was saying. *"It seems that two men broke into a child's room in an attempt to kill her. Nurse Emilio Cortez was murdered in an attempt to protect his young patient, and the men who attempted the heinous crime were determined dead on arrival by police. Witnesses say a third man, who may have been involved,*

was seen fleeing the hospital with the child in his arms, however he is still at large. Police state the child in question has been recovered and is currently with their mother in a secure location."

"There," Father Mitchell said, a sigh of relief in his voice. "All tied up in a neat little bow."

"Yeah, yeah it is," Smithers said, sipping at his coffee. Father Mitchell turned to look at him, a weary look of worry on his face.

"Why do you say that as though I missed something?" the priest asked, his body suddenly getting tense.

"Because you did," Smithers replied as he took another sip of coffee. Father Mitchell grit his teeth as he waited for Smithers to continue, but the old man took his time with his coffee. Morgan had never considered Father Mitchell as a man capable of violence, but saw the battle going on in the priest's mind. Finally, Smithers set his mug down and turned to Father Mitchell.

"A third man who may have been involved is still at large," Smithers said, gesturing at the television. "They're talking about Timm."

"Yes, but what of it?" Father Mitchell asked.

"That means people are going to be looking for him," Morgan said, biting her lip in worry.

Smithers clicked his tongue and pointed at her, not looking away from Father Mitchell. "Girl from a crazy magic dimension got it that quick."

"Pretend I had my door broken down after being woken ridiculously early to be told I have a massive legal problem to deal with and am working on a pitiful amount of sleep," Father Mitchell said, crossing his arms.

"Fair point," Smithers relented. "Problem is, even though no description was given on the news, bound to be one floating around out there. Which means people are going to be looking for him and asking all manner of irritating questions."

"So, keep him inside for a few days," Father Mitchell shrugged. "I'm a priest, not a magician. I did all I could, even getting his discharge papers put together, and let me tell you that cost me a lot of favors."

"Favors I'm not going to question how a priest has coming to him," Smithers said, waving his hand dismissively. "My problem is that the cops have been waiting for Timm to be discharged so they can get his statement. They're going to know he's out, and if he doesn't go to them..."

"They're going to come for him," Father Mitchell sighed heavily and sat down on a stool. "Damn, I knew I would miss a thread."

"Happens to us all," Smithers said. "I'm going to go get him. Maybe if we go early enough, we'll get them while they're tired and not paying attention as closely."

"You think that will work?" Father Mitchell asked, a wry smile on his face.

"Nope," Smithers said, leaving the room. "But it's the best shot we've got."

With that, Smithers left Father Mitchell and Morgan in the canteen, the silence only broken by a man talking about the superiority of red socks over white, but Morgan didn't bother to pay attention to what he was saying.

"I'm sorry," she said to Father Mitchell.

He looked up at her, confused. "What?"

"I said that I'm sorry," Morgan said, placing her bowl down and sitting on the stool opposite him. "It seems we've brought a lot of trouble down on you."

Father Mitchel laughed. "While my life was never this complicated before I met all of you, I don't think you've done anything that requires an apology. Though to be fair, I don't know all you've done since you've gotten here."

Morgan took a breath, but Father Mitchell cut her off.

"And that is not an invitation to tell me," he said, sternly yet smiling. "It is better if I have plausible deniability should anything less than legal happen."

"Plausible deniability?" Morgan asked.

"The less I know, the less I have to lie, the less trouble I can get in," Father Mitchell explained simply.

"Oh," Morgan said, nodding.

"But do not think that you and your friends are a burden upon me," Father Mitchell went on. "I mean, if anything, you're a blessing!"

"Hard to believe that, all things considered," Morgan replied, gesturing at the television. "You're dealing with all of this because of us."

"Yes," Father Mitchell nodded, looking over at the television. "Yes, I am, but do you know what I'm not dealing with right now because of you all?"

"What?" Morgan asked.

"A child's funeral," he said. His voice was quiet but clear. There was anger there, but it was righteous fury that was so palpable that Morgan could feel a shift in the air. "You stopped her death, twice. First when Luis ripped that horrible disease from her, and again last night when Timm risked his own life and freedom to pull her from those who wished her harm."

He turned to face Morgan, and she could see that he was smiling warmly again, the anger quelled enough that it slipped back below the surface. Morgan knew it was still there. Father Mitchell was the kind of man who would hold on to the anger, but she trusted that he would use it as a force to motivate him towards good, not lash out needlessly at others.

"I would happily go without sleep to save my friends if it means fewer funerals," he said, and Morgan could see the exhaustion seeming to evaporate from him. Then he laughed, "And it's not because I'm lazy in my duties, believe me."

Morgan laughed as well, happy to see that they had found someone in this world who was willing to do so much for them, and so much for those around him. They quietly stood and took care of their dishes while the television continued to speak in the background of the horrible and wretched things of the world that she had found herself in. But as she worked, she still smiled, because she knew that in spite of all the terrible things that existed in this strange new world, there were people like Father Mitchell who would work tirelessly to see evil defeated.

~ 28 ~

SMITHERS

After the night he had, Timm slept soundly in his cot, his body in a state of complete relaxation. He neither stirred nor moved a muscle besides the steady, calm breaths that made his chest rise and fall. Had no one in the room known he was there, his silent sleep would have gone completely undisturbed.

Unfortunately for him, Smithers knew exactly where to find him.

"Up you get!" Smithers shouted, pulling the blanket off of Timm with enough force to send it flying unceremoniously across the room.

Timm yelped, jumped to his feet in an attempt to defend himself from the unknown wakeup call. In his fervor to get to his feet, they ended up tangled in the paper gown he was still wearing from the hospital, tearing it, and Timm ended up flat on his ass looking up at Smithers.

"Glad to see you're an early riser," Smithers told him, moving away from the cot and packing up supplies. "You're gonna need to keep being quick on your feet if we're going to keep ahead of the news."

"What news?" Timm asked, and Smithers heard the creak of wood and metal as the boy was probably using the cot to help himself up. He recovered quickly, Smithers gave him that, plus it helped that Lee tended to the boy after he fell asleep. But the old man didn't want him getting too comfortable all things considered.

"The news of your little escapade last night," Smithers explained. "Pretty soon you're gonna have every cop in the city looking for you, and I want us to be laying low before that happens. So, get your scrawny ass in that shower, clean off the blood, and put some real clothes on yerself."

"The only clothes I had are still at the hospital," Timm said.

"Then I'll send Morgan to pick out some new ones from the thrift shop," Smithers said, patting himself down to find his keys. He hadn't been driving his truck too much with their escape from the hospital a few days ago, but he wanted to be sure that Father Mitchell's van wouldn't get tied in with Timm if things went wrong. "Now go get yourself cleaned up!"

Timm muttered something as he walked away towards the bathroom, and for a moment Smithers felt he may be being too hard on the boy. After all, he had gotten the girl to safety, and was smart enough to bring her to Father Mitchell for safekeeping. Had he tried to go anywhere else there may well be a man hunt and an amber alert they'd be dealing with right now. Shows the boy had something rattling between his ears besides a concussion.

But Smithers recognized that kind of cockiness and arrogance, having seen it in enough young men during his time, and it lingered in a few of the old ones too. Though very few of those. And if Timm wanted to reach a ripe old age like he had, Smithers was going to have to make sure that the boy had a damn hard time keeping his balance too.

"Never get comfortable with arrogance," Smithers muttered under his breath.

"What's that Smithers?" Luis said, still ruddy and covered in sweat from his run. Boy was barely breathing hard for what he earned, but Smithers tried not to be jealous of youth. There were parts to miss, but there was a hell of a lot more that Smithers was happy to leave in the past.

"Oh, just something someone taught me once," Smithers said. "Never get comfortable with arrogance, think you're the smartest guy, or the fastest guy, or the toughest guy, and you're bound to be caught off guard when you meet the actual smartest, fastest, or toughest guy. Worse yet, when they're all the same guy, and it ain't you."

Luis pondered on this thought for a moment. "That is good wisdom. It pairs well with the wisdom of my sword master. She would always tell us to never stop training to be the best, because the best never stop training."

"A wise woman it sounds," Smithers nodded. "Got a favor to ask you, by the way."

"What is it?" Luis asked, collecting a towel to dry his face of sweat and melted snow.

"A polite request for services rendered, but that's not important right now," Smithers said, referencing a movie he was sure that at his age, Luis wouldn't get even if he had been born in this world. Before the knight could ask anything further, Smithers continued. "I need to take Timm to the police station to give his statement on the stabbing yesterday. Without it, Colin could walk free and all this mess would be for nothing. Just keep an eye on things here in case more of those assholes from the hospital show up?"

"Hold down the fort while you take Timm to secure our victory," Luis said, nodding. "I can accept these terms. Especially now that I am armed properly."

Luis reached under his pillow and pulled out the short sword Timm had confiscated from his attackers the night before. Smithers felt his jaw tighten seeing it.

"You know," Smithers started, trying to be delicate with his words. "Normal people don't really go walking around with those things on their hips anymore. Not unless it's at a Faire or something, and then usually they're fake. And peace bound."

Luis furrowed his brow. "Then what is the point of carrying them?"

"Uh... ever go see a play?" Smithers asked, hoping that would explain things.

Apparently it did, as Luis' expression softened.

"Ah, I see, they're only decorative at that point," Luis commented. "It would be a shame to waste a true blade for such a purpose."

Before he was forced to agree and start discussing the finer points of bladed weaponry, Morgan came down with the clothes she had picked out for Timm at the behest of Father Mitchell who seemed to be on the same wavelength as Smithers. Luis offered to take them into the bathroom and drop them off for Timm to change into while going in for his own shower.

Timm came out of the bathroom a few minutes later, mostly dry, and dressed in an odd assemblage of clothing. Morgan had outfitted him with a neon pink pair of running sneakers that clashed horribly with the bright blue and incredibly stretchy workout pants. He wore a green tee shirt with a white shamrock surrounded by the phrase 'let's get sham-rocked' and Smithers was sure that he neither understood what the shirt meant, or caught the irony of the statement considering his accent. Finally, slung over his shoulder, Smithers was amazed to see another peacoat, which Morgan must have spent most of her time finding for him considering the state of the rest of the outfit.

"Feeling refreshed and ready to go?" Smithers asked him.

"Yeah," Timm said, though the effect was stifled a bit by him yawning midway through the word. "Let's get going."

As he passed, Smithers reached out and grabbed the boy's arm to stop him.

"Whoa there," he said, letting go as he felt Timm's muscles tense up. He needed to remind himself that these people aren't normal folk. They've grown up in a world that seems like violence is the only language they've been taught in. "Slow down there, we gotta practice."

"Slow down or hurry up, Smithers?" Timm asked, a note of irritation in his voice.

"A little of both," Smithers said, jingling the keys before walking up the stairs. "I'll drive, you practice what you're going to say to the cops. We don't want you slipping up, because that's exactly what they want."

"What do you mean?" Timm asked, following Smithers up the stairs.

"See, cops do this thing where they ask you to repeat the story you tell them a few times, hoping to catch you in a lie," Smithers explained on their way out to his truck, which took a few tries to get started between the cold and it being so old. Smithers could relate to the old girl as he tried to get his engine going in this cold. "Thing is, it works. And it works well. Making you repeat a story will eventually get you to mess up."

"But since we're telling the truth, won't we be fine?" Timm asked.

"Thing is, we're not really telling the truth are we?" Smithers asked, as the engine finally turned over. "We set Colin up to attack us in order to save Jess, we tell them that they get us for entrapment and Colin walks."

"What's entrapment?" Timm asked.

"What we did, and it's illegal," Smithers explained. "Secondly, I told you they get you to tell the story a bunch of times until you mess up. I never said that a liar specifically messes up. Cops want one thing and one thing only, to close cases. If it's easiest for them to throw Colin away for this, we're in the clear. If there's hang ups and it's easier to put you in prison for it, and you give them a reason, they'll do that too."

"That seems exceptionally lazy," Timm said.

"Eh, sometimes it's lazy," Smithers said, feeling his anger at how the police function ebb slightly. "Actually, a lot of times it's laziness. Or bias. Or ego. Hell, you'll rarely hear me say good things about these people, look up the Stanford Prison Experiment and

Perceived Power if you wanna really understand my feelings on the matter."

"I think that's more Lee's thing," Timm said.

"You may be right," Smithers nodded in agreement as they pulled out of the parking lot and Smithers carefully navigated his truck on the still icy roads. "Suffice to say, there's a whole lot of shit wrong that needs fixing and is getting ignored like a water heater in summer. But with so many problems in the world, the ones that actually do give a damn about shit are over worked. Sometimes it's just more cost effective or less demanding to go with the easy solution to the problem. They're using Occam's Razor and we're the ones that end up getting cut."

"Ooh," Timm's eyes brightened with excitement. "Is Occam's Razor a powerful magic blade? A sword that slew a dragon? Or felled an army?"

"Uh..." Smithers shot the boy a look, seeing the child like wonder on his face. "It's more like an economical concept adapted to psychology dictating that the simplest solution is more often than not the correct one."

Timm looked at him blankly.

"Basically, don't complicate crap," Smithers said, brow furrowing. "Now tell me what you're going to say to the cops."

Smithers had Timm tell him, fix the details, and tell him again. By the end of the drive, Timm had recited the story at least a dozen times. As the old man put the car in park, he had Timm tell it to him one more time.

"Come on, Smithers," Timm complained. "I have it!"

"Prove it, tell me again," Smithers said, crossing his arms. "Because that cop in there who's getting your statement is going to take any excuse, and screw up, and use it against you. And if you go down, I go down. That will eventually lead them to Luis, Lee, and Morgan. Worse yet, it will eventually lead them to Patrice and Latoya. Not to mention Father Mitchell."

Smithers turned and jammed his forefinger into Timm's chest, forcing the young man to look him in the eye.

"Be sure you get this right," Smithers said, with as much intensity as he could muster.

Must have been enough, considering Timm recited his story again to Smithers perfectly. Finally satisfied with the result, Smithers opened the door and got out of the truck with Timm following suit. They made their way down the block to the station, and Smithers led Timm inside.

The inside of this particular precinct looked the same as every other precinct Smithers had ever been in. Even this early in the morning, it was bustling with activity probably spilling over from the night before. The cops either looked bored and tired or harried and tired, there were none in between. Above them glowed long fluorescent lights, most of which were actually working, and the air was filled with the annoying hum that came with them. Some people referred to it as a white noise, but Smithers could always hear it, regardless of how long he spent in a place, he always heard that hum in the background if it was present.

He took Timm by the elbow and led him up to the counter where one of the bored and tired cops was leaning on the counter, sitting a good three feet higher than they were. Smithers knew the explanation for this was because they wanted a clear view of what was going on in the waiting area, but he also knew that explanation was pure bullshit. The real reason was if you have to look up at someone then you're most likely going to be intimidated by them.

Smithers, not one to be easily intimidated, especially after all he'd seen and experienced the past couple days, walked right up to the counter and spoke to the bored cop on duty.

"Name's Smithers," he said, directly and clearly. "I was told by Carla Rivera to report here as soon as possible with my friend here so he could make his statement after being stabbed last night."

The bored cop stirred slightly, turning to look at Smithers, clearly confused.

"Your friend here was stabbed last night?" he asked, as though that was the only bit he'd heard clearly.

"Yes, outside of O'Malley's pub last night," Smithers nodded. "I spoke with Officer Lynch, but he was such a schmuck that Rivera stepped in and took over. Now we're coming in to finish the statement. Thought it would be best to get it out of the way as quickly as possible."

"Right..." the bored cop said, pulling out a binder in front of him and reading over its contents painstakingly slowly. "Says here Lynch and Rivera are off duty. Won't be back until later tonight. But we've got a detective you can speak to if you don't mind waiting fifteen minutes or so. He's on a call."

"We'll wait," Smithers nodded in agreement and took Timm to go sit down. In hushed tones, he made Timm go over his statement a few more times before the detective called him in.

"Doesn't this look kind of..." Timm paused and looked around. "Suspicious?"

Smithers looked up at a woman wearing a skirt way too short to be comfortable in this weather and a tube top made in no natural color found on this earth shouting a stream of expletives at a rate that would make any rapper past, present, or future feel utterly inadequate.

"I think we're good," Smither said, dryly. "Just one more time before..."

"Smithers?" A stern voice called out, shushing even the colorful in every way prostitute who had been yelling.

The man standing at the door was built like a block of stone, all sharp edges and solid muscle. He wore a suit and had his badge hanging around his neck by a beaded chain, but Smithers could tell at a glance that this man would have no trouble acting in the field. Either he had only been recently promoted to detective, or he was the kind of man who could never leave the street behind.

"My name is Detective Cardozo," he said, in the same stern voice. "Come with me."

Without further prompting, Smithers found himself reflexively getting to his feet and approaching the man. A glance to his right told him that Timm had done the same, and the two of them followed the broad man through the twists and turns of the inside of the police station. After a few minutes, they were sitting in a pair of uncomfortable wooden chairs overlooking a mountain of paperwork piled up on Cardozo's desk. He had a computer sitting to his right, its screen black, and a yellow legal pad in front of him that he was currently tapping his pencil on.

"So, you're the one who got stabbed outside of O'Malley's last night?" Cardozo asked.

"Yes, I am," Timm responded, smiling uncomfortably. Smithers got the impression the boy was starting to see what he had meant.

"You seem to have recuperated quite quickly," Cardozo pointed out.

"It was only the arm," Smithers interjected. "Stitches and a night's rest. Can't afford to keep that bed occupied too long."

Cardozo gave Smithers a wilting look, and the old man felt anger well up inside of him. No one had dared give him a look like that since he was in boot camp. Clenching his fist under the table to the point he felt his fingernails cutting into his palm, Smithers forced himself to keep his emotions in check.

"I know how expensive a stay in the hospital can be," Cardozo continued. "Been shot a few times. But I'm glad to see you're feeling better."

"Much," Timm said. "The healers here are quite skilled."

"Healers," Cardozo repeated, jotting something down on the paper in front of him.

Smithers looked down and saw he was writing in shorthand. He remembered a little of how that worked from what they taught him in school, but it was a dying skill. Between not being able to remember it overly well and trying to read upside down, Smithers was unable to make heads nor tails of what Cardozo was making note of.

"Mr. Smithers," Cardozo said, cutting off his train of thought. "Why don't you step outside, grab yourself a cup of coffee across the way while your friend and I finish up here."

Smithers wanted to object, but could think of no reasonable excuse as to why he would. Cardozo was cutting off support, forcing Timm to do this on his own. Smithers was going to have to trust the boy. Silently he stood up, nodded at Cardozo, then gave Timm a look that he hoped said 'you can do this' more than it did 'don't fuck this up' and walked out the door.

He paced over to the coffee table and began fixing himself a cup. Normally he would take it black, but the kind of coffee you get at police stations was not the kind that anyone should have to suffer through without some sugar. Smithers set to work creating a drink-able concoction and realized after he had been stirring and sipping for five minutes trying to get the taste right, that he was just trying to occupy himself with something besides panic.

"Yeah, it was the weirdest thing," Smithers overheard an officer standing nearby saying to another. "It was like Google Earth or one of those documentaries. The face was just completely blurred out."

"Couldn't the tech guys fix it up?" The other responded. "I mean, it's footage from a hospital security system. How hard could that be?"

Smithers' ears perked up. They had to be talking about Timm's escape last night. Maybe the faces were the guys who Timm had fought? Or maybe, and this was asking way too much of the uni-verse he was sure, maybe it had been Timm's face that had been blurred out.

"Nah, see they told us that the footage they got was already scrubbed," the first officer explained. "Basically, someone had taken it, edited it, and then ran that through some kind of screen recorder."

"What?" the second asked. "What does that even mean?"

"IT guy said it was like rubbing dirt on a page then photocopying it," the first explained with, what Smithers clearly recognized as, a sense of self-importance granted by being the first person something was explained to explaining it to the second. "Basically, what we got was the photocopied version."

"So basically, there's no way to clean it up and figure out who that guy who took the girl out of the hospital was?" the second asked.

"Well, we can go by the witness descriptions," the first suggested, eliciting a laugh from the second.

"Fat chance," he said. "If the idiots describing the guy don't screw it up, then the media will. We'd have a better chance of the asshole just walking into the precinct today."

Smithers smiled slightly at that comment. Basically, the cops had no idea that it was Timm they were looking for, and there was no way of connecting him to anything. At least they had that going for them. One crisis averted.

He looked up at the door to Cardozo's office, chewing on his lip nervously. Now it was on Timm to keep the second crisis at bay. Sipping at the still bitter and slightly burnt brew, Smithers waited for close to forty-five minutes for Timm to come out.

When the door finally opened, Smithers' heart both rose and sank with such fervor that he was afraid he'd go into cardiac arrest right there at Cardozo's feet while the detective approached.

"Well, we're just about finished here," Cardozo explained. "I sent a write up to the boys downstairs, and they'll send up a printed copy that your friend there will have to sign to make it all official and clean, but I think we have enough to put that shit-stain away for a while."

"That's good to hear," Smithers said, then eyed the detective. "You've been after this guy for a while?"

"Oh yeah," Cardozo nodded. "I really can't go into details here, especially considering on-going investigation and all that, but this guy, who shall remain nameless as per this conversation..."

He eyed Smithers back, making the confidentiality of their conversation exceptionally clear. Smithers nodded to communicate his understanding before Cardozo went on.

"Well he's been a frequent abuser," Cardozo said, cracking his knuckles. "But if the woman doesn't come forward and report the assault... hell even if she does, very little ever gets done. Makes it hard for those of us that want to see justice done."

"Those of us?" Smithers asked.

"Yeah," Cardozo nodded in acknowledgement to Smithers' comment as a man approached him with a manila envelope. "And we rank too few."

He accepted the envelope and took the papers back into his office for Timm to sign. In less than another quarter of an hour, Smithers and Timm were walking back into the crisp morning air.

"That wasn't so bad," Timm said, stepping down the stairs that led up to the police station.

"Maybe for you it wasn't," Smithers said, still feeling exceptionally tense. "But for some of us, the sitting and waiting to see what would happen was more nerve wracking than facing off with a ghost in a public park."

"Hey," Timm said, turning to face Smithers. "That was way more fun."

Smithers rolled his eyes at Timm, and continued carefully down the icy steps. One would think that these would get a bit more attention and salt, and Smithers had plenty of salt for the police department to use.

The roar of an engine caught Smithers' attention as he took the last step. His foot caught a patch of ice and he felt his foot go out from under him. Timm shot in, catching Smithers under his arms and kept the old man from tumbling down. They both looked for the source of the roar. Tearing down the street at a speed that would make one question the sanity of the rider for reasons including, but not limited to, the condition of the road and proximity to a police station, came a black motorcycle. The rider of the bike was wearing all black, leather jacket and denim jeans, complete with boots that went halfway up his calf, and a helmet that covered his entire face.

As the rider passed the two of them, he slowed down and turned to look in their direction. Time slowed with the motorcycle and Smithers felt the familiar sense of impending cardiac arrest as he was sure the rider met his eyes in spite of not being able to see them. Catching up with itself, time resumed its normal passage, and the engine revved up again, sending the rider careening down the street. Smithers barely remembered to get the license plate in time. It was clearly a Massachusetts plate, but considering the lettering, he was sure it was a fake. There was no way anyone at the DMV would allow "FCK YU" as a legal plate.

"Are you okay, Smithers?" he heard Timm ask, based on his tone, not for the first time.

"Yeah," Smithers said, finding his footing again with Timm's help. "Yeah, I'm fine."

"What's wrong?" Timm asked him, and Smithers didn't bother hiding the fact that what had just happened perturbed him.

"Oh, nothing," Smithers said, casually. "Same as always since I've met you people. We're probably going to die. Let's go."

Smithers walked back towards where he'd parked the truck. He had every good reason to go back to the church and tell the others about what happened, but he could think of twice as many reasons to go to O'Malley's. Putting the truck in gear, he made his choice.

~ 29 ~

TIMM

"I can catch him," Timm said as Smithers put on what he called 'the blinker' and stared distantly at the red light.

"No," he replied, his voice a monotone.

"But I'm fast!" Timm implored, reaching his hand towards the door handle. "I'll figure out who he is and we can…"

There was a loud clicking noise in the cab of the truck, and Timm found the door suddenly locked. He looked over to see Smithers pull his hand away from a button on his door and put it back on the wheel, beginning his turn in the opposite direction of where the black rider had gone.

"What are you doing?" Timm asked him.

"What does it look like?" Smither's answered. "I need a drink."

Timm cocked an eyebrow at the old man. "It's eight in the morning."

"A wise ol' hippy once said that it was always five o'clock somewhere," Smithers answered, turning his truck in the direction Timm realized was the way to O'Malley's pub. "And I intend to take full advantage of the Tao of Buffet today."

"Tao of Buffet?" Timm asked, settling in and accepting that he was not going to get to chase the black rider.

"Jimmy, not Warren," Smithers explained. "Both are billionaire asshats, but one makes good drinking songs, so he gets a bit of a pass from me."

Timm pursed his lips and listened to Smithers go on and on about margaritas and a place called the Caribbean. He was explaining how he would much rather be there than freezing his ass off in Boston, and Timm could relate. He too would rather be somewhere else rather than here at the moment. Mostly, he would like to be trailing that black rider.

Timm was unsure of the intentions of the rider, but he was exceptionally suspicious. During his retelling the night before, Luis had mentioned an attack that had almost gotten Lee killed. The priest had only been saved by the actions of a black rider. Timm suspected that they may have been the same rider, and wanted to catch him to determine if this was a friend looking out for them, sheer happenstance that they were in the same place at the same time, or if this person had a more malevolent reason for suddenly appearing in their lives.

Smithers put the truck in park outside of O'Malley's. He got out and went right up to the door, which Timm assumed was locked, and thus didn't bother getting out of the vehicle only to have Smithers return a moment later. To his surprise, the door flew open without any resistance and Smithers disappeared inside.

Surprised by this, Timm decided it was better to follow the old coot and make sure he didn't do anything that would leave Timm walking the whole way back to the church on his own. The police could very well be looking for the man who escaped with Patrice from the hospital. Or worse yet, more of those people he found in her hospital room could be hunting them down. Leaving Smithers alone and inebriated would be a death sentence at that point.

Hopping down from the cab of the truck, Timm made his way to the front of the bar, noting that the sidewalk in front of the establishment had been washed away. As Timm opened the door, however, he noticed that a few spatters of blood had managed to escape the cleansing and stood drying in the cold morning sun. He grit his teeth at the memory and went inside.

As he entered, Timm realized that Smithers and O'Malley were not the only ones at the bar. He walked over and recognized one of the regulars who had been there almost every time they had. Now that he thought of it, the chubby man had been here pretty much every day, except outside of business hours. It took Timm a moment of intense thought, but the name finally came to him: Carl Newman.

Smithers settled into a bar stool next to Carl and pointed at a bottle of whiskey on the wall. "What are you doing here so early, Carl?"

"You're implying he ever left," Tom said as he began scooping ice into Smithers' glass. Timm sat down at the bar, but didn't order anything.

"Neat, Tom," Smithers said, stopping Tom in his tracks. The bartender looked up at Smithers, who returned his gaze with a steady one of his own. Tom shrugged and dumped the ice back into the bucket and set the empty glass on the table before reaching around to the bottle Smithers pointed to and poured it out.

"What do you mean, never left?" Timm asked.

"He's been like that since last night," Tom said, sliding a glass of water to Timm. Timm sipped at it politely. "Doesn't seem like he's slept in a while. Hasn't talked either. Dunno if he's in there or not. All I know is, he's not drunk. That was the first and only drink he ordered all night, and that was at about nine."

Timm looked over at the glass that Carl had clutched in his sausage fingers. The whiskey had a very pale color in comparison to the one Smithers was drinking, though it too did not have any ice in it. Upon closer inspection, it seemed filled nearly to the brim and a ring of water pooled at the base of the glass. Timm assumed that the drink had been ordered with ice, but not so much as sipped, leaving the ice to melt, dilute the drink, and create condensation at the base. Tom was right, whatever condition afflicted Carl, it was not drunkenness.

Had Timm not realized the evidence of this, he may well have thought that Carl was deeply under the influence of the drink. His shirt was rumpled and tie half hanging around his neck like a noose not yet tightened. His hair was matted and a mess, and his eyes were red and puffy as though he'd spent the night silently crying at the bar while no one was the wiser. Though, Timm thought, with the events that had been happening right outside, who would have noticed the man?

"Carl!" Smithers all but shouted at the man. "Carl! Are you okay in there?"

Carl started, and turned to face Smithers as though he only just realized the old man was sitting next to him. Slowly, a look of horrible understanding crawled across his face. With an agonized wail, Carl slammed his arms and head onto the bar, sending the undrunk whiskies spilling across the bar top. The wailing turned to a heavy sob as the man bellowed his misery.

"I fucked up!" Carl managed to choke out between sobs. "I fucked up so bad!"

Smithers looked between Timm and Tom, both of whom seemed completely thrown off by the sudden turn of events. Smithers put his hand on the man's shoulders and tried to comfort him, though all any of them could do was wait for the sobbing to die down. When it finally had, about ten minutes later, Smithers was finally able to start asking Carl questions.

"What do you mean, Carl?" Smithers asked. "What did you do?"

"I did something stupid," Carl sobbed. "I got involved with Nathan O'Brian."

Smithers froze and the sound of glass shattering filled the air as Tom dropped the whiskey glass he had been trying to recover.

Timm had only seen a few exceptionally talented hunters manage the stillness that overcame the old man, and for a moment he was quite impressed. It was only after he noticed the minor trembling that had wracked through Smithers' entire body did he realize that the old man was not enacting some hidden talent, but was stricken with a level of fear Timm had never seen before.

"Fuck."

Both Smithers and Tom said the word at the same time, with the same inflection, letting Timm know just what had caused Smithers' fear.

"Who's Nathan O'Brian?" he asked, wondering what kind of man could create such fear in the man who had faced down a ghost not two days before. He turned to look at Tom when Smithers wouldn't answer him. "Who is this guy?"

Smithers finally broke his silence.

By screaming at Carl.

"The *fuck* did you do, Carl?"

"I was dumb!" Carl managed to choke out from a wave of fresh sobs. "You know how it is, the wife was nagging, the girls are teenagers now, everything is all about them. I was looking for a little excitement in my life..."

"So you get in bed with Nathan O'Brian?" Tom asked.

Timm wondered if there hadn't been some kind of misunderstanding and this was all about Carl getting caught cheating on his wife with this Nathan person, but it seemed to be a stretch considering the reaction of the other two.

"It's not like that," Carl said. "I figured I could run a few small jobs for him. Little stuff, like a few drug drops or something. You know, get the blood flowing, feel alive again, and get a little extra money for the girls' college fund."

"It is like that, Carl!" Smithers said, the pitch of his voice growing increasingly higher. "It is exactly like that!"

"Smithers," Tom said, passing the old man a bottle of whiskey. "Have a drink and let the man talk."

Smithers accepted the bottle but didn't bother with a glass as Carl went on with his story.

"So everything was going great, I got what I needed out of it, so I figured I'd retire from the game, no harm, no foul," he explained, his face growing tight. "But O'Brian, he wanted more from me. A 'going away present' he called it."

"Oh god, Carl," Tom said, taking the bottle from Smithers, though rather than cleaning the top off and putting it back, he took a swig from it before passing it back. "What is he having you do?"

"He... he wants me to kill someone," Carl said. Smithers and Tom both nodded as though they had expected as much. "They want me to kill Vincent D'Angelino."

Smithers and Tom stopped nodding.

"Oh god," Smithers said.

"You know," Timm broke in. "None of these names mean anything to me, so I'm feeling a lot like the Rose of this situation."

All three men turned to look at him.

"What," Smithers asked, closing his eyes, and pressing his fingers to the bridge of his nose. "Are you talking about, boy?"

"Rose," Timm said, gesturing to the other men in the room. "You are all like Dorothy, Blanche, and Sophia having a conversation. And I'm sitting here not understanding a word of it, like Rose."

"Boy, I neither know nor want to know how you know these things," Smithers said. "I also do not want to know which one of us is who in that conversation."

"You're definitely Sophia," Tom said, with a wry smile before turning to Timm. "But you've got a point. Okay, so the first thing you need to understand is that Nathan O'Brian is the head of the Irish mob in town. Basically, he's a brutal and terrible crime lord."

Timm looked over at Carl. "You got involved with a crime lord because you were bored?"

"I feel like I'm kind of getting enough judgment here," Carl said.

"I disagree," Smithers piped in.

"I wasn't trying to be judgmental," Timm explained. "I was just asking for clarification. I've done dumber things out of boredom."

"For fear of knowing what those things are, let's move on," Tom said. "Well, Carl here now has been tasked by one brutal crime lord to kill the son of another brutal crime lord, Don Anthony D'Angelino, head of the local Italian Mafia."

"Smithers has already expressed his distaste for the authorities," Timm said. "But wouldn't this be exactly the situation they should be called in on?"

Tom turned to Carl. "Who'd he take as collateral?"

"My family," Carl said, sobbing beginning anew. "They grabbed the girls on the way to school, and had my wife call me to tell me they were alive, for now."

"Classic mob playbook," Smithers said, taking another swig of whiskey. "Call the cops on them, they off the family."

"And if I try to kill D'Angelino, I'm going to die!" Carl cried out. "They gave me a gun, told me to follow the kid, and try to get the shot off before his bodyguards kill me. If I don't do it, O'Brian will kill my family, if I somehow succeed D'Angelino will kill my family, and no matter what, I end up dead or wishing I were."

Timm pondered this for a few quiet moments. These rival factions were criminals, he sincerely doubted that either one of them disappearing would upset anyone. However, Vincent D'Angelino had, as far as Timm knew, done nothing wrong. Nathan O'Brian was taking advantage of Carl's stupidity and using his family as a means of forcing him to do O'Brian's dirty work. Timm saw clearly who the worst person in the situation was.

"So," Timm said slowly, formulating a plan in his mind. "If this Irish mob were to be taken out, how deeply would the cops look into it?"

"They'd probably try to find out what happened," Tom shrugged. "But I can't imagine it would be with a fervor to arrest. Hell, I bet there are a few who would try to send the person who did it a god-damned fruit basket."

"Well, I do like fruit, but I wouldn't need a reward for it," Timm said.

Carl looked up at him, shocked.

"What are you saying?" he asked.

Smithers looked up too, only his expression was horrified. "Yeah, Timm. What *are* you saying?"

"I'm saying that you don't need to worry about it, Carl," Timm said, standing from his stool. "Smithers and I are going to collect our friends, and we're going to take care of this Nathan O'Brian person."

"We are?" Smithers asked, his voice trembling.

"We are," Timm nodded. "Carl, get in the truck, we're going to our safehouse to gather the others and plan. Smithers, you're driving."

Smithers cackled madly as he and Carl made their way out of the bar.

"I'm going to die!" the old man wheezed, but Timm ignored him as he tightened his peacoat around him.

Suddenly a thought occurred to him.

"Hey Tom," Timm said, turning around to see the bartender absentmindedly cleaning the spilled whiskey before pouring himself a large glass.

"Yeah?" Tom asked, without looking up.

"Would this mob be willing to attack a church?"

Tom thought about it for a moment before answering. "Well, both the Irish and Italians are Catholic, so I'd say so long as it was a Catholic church you were looking to protect, then you should be fine. Though I don't see any reason they wouldn't go after an Episcopal or Baptist place. People like this are very much 'I don't care what horrors are unleashed so long as it doesn't hurt the things I care about' kind of people."

Timm nodded at him. "Thank you, Tom."

"No problem," Tom said, as Timm walked through the door. "And good luck."

Timm walked towards the truck trying very hard not to think about how his sharp ears had caught what Tom muttered under his breath as the door closed.

"You're gonna fucking need it."

~ 30 ~

LEE

Lee began his day by making rounds with both Patrice and Jess. The young girl was bouncing back magnificently. In spite of having had a disease that ravaged her body maliciously only recently removed, and being attacked in the dead of night by assassins, Patrice seemed to be in good spirits, if not a bit exhausted. Her body was healing well, and the time spent with her mother here had given them both the spiritual healing needed to truly allow their wounds to close.

As for Jess, the woman's body was doing well, but it seemed the years of fear had taken their toll on her. There was a nervous energy about her, and a desire to be doing something other than laying in a bed, but Lee would not allow her to get up. Enough damage had been done to put her and the baby at risk, and knowing that doing nothing was the best thing she could do for her baby finally convinced her to stay put, if begrudgingly.

Once their physical and spiritual needs were taken care of, Lee took to tending to his own. Cleaned up and fed, he had settled into his prayers when Father Mitchell descended the stairs in full ceremonial robes.

"Good morning, all," he addressed the room. "Do you have plans for the day?"

"Mostly just planning on coming up with a plan of what to do next," Lee answered. "I feel the best course of action for us would be to learn as much as we can about this world before we interact any further with it."

"Not sure how successful you'll be in that venture," Father Mitchell smiled.

"Why do you say that?" Luis asked, seeming a bit on edge. Lee was noting that the knight quite often seemed suspicious of others' intentions. Whether he realized giving this air or not, it definitely affected those around him. Father Mitchell's guard went up almost immediately.

"I'm not saying anything about your abilities," the priest said, holding up his hands placatingly. "Just that you cannot study anything without interacting with it."

"That does make sense," Lee said, throwing a glance in Luis' direction in hopes of settling the knight down. "Then we wish to interact as little as possible to avoid further issues with the people of this world."

"Then we shouldn't expect to learn much," Morgan offered, causing Lee to purse his lips. The young girl lacked a lot in experience, however Lee felt it would be a mistake to discount her wisdom. She had a knack for insightfulness, especially when it came to other people.

"Might I make a suggestion?" Father Mitchell asked. "You and Luis are both holy men, back in your world?"

"That is correct," Lee nodded.

"Well, today is Sunday, our day of worship," Father Mitchell explained. "Would you all be interested in joining us for service this morning? It should only take about an hour or so."

Lee looked over to Luis. He was leaning against the wall, body tense and arms crossed over his chest in a defensive stance. For a moment, Lee thought he might be hesitant to attend the service due to religious reasons, however then he noted where Luis was standing. He had positioned himself so that he was standing between Jess and Patrice's beds and suddenly his hesitation made sense.

"Would it be safe to leave them unattended?" Lee asked, gesturing at his resting patients.

"I believe they will be," Father Mitchell said. "However, if you feel safer staying with them I will not ask you to leave them unattended."

Luis considered for a moment before nodding. "I trust your order well enough to attend in good faith of their protection."

Father Mitchell smiled. "Very well, I look forward to seeing all of you in the main part of the church. We will be beginning shortly."

Father Mitchell went upstairs, leaving the three alone with their sleeping wards. They looked at each other curiously.

"What do you think this service will be like?" Morgan asked.

"My goddess never asks for prayer and worship," Luis explained. "Nike only wishes we seek out victory in all we do. By doing so, we honor her. What about you Lee?"

Lee pondered on this thought for a moment. His religion never really asked for worship, and it was always difficult to explain to outsiders. However, he'd been traveling with these people long enough to know they were willing to listen, and if they did not truly understand, they were not ones to judge harshly.

"Goibniu is a god of the forge, however his realm does not end there, as he is also the god of hospitality," Lee explained. "To honor him is to be honorable to others and work to create rather than to destroy. Much like Luis, my church does not demand worship, but service. I do not know what we can expect by going to this 'service' as Father Mitchell calls it, but to do so would be to repay his hospitality towards us. I feel it is the proper thing to do."

Luis nodded in agreement and Morgan got to her feet.

"Then let's head over there," she said, leading the way

* * *

Lee found himself sitting in a pew about halfway through the service feeling a headache coming on. While the music was lovely, and the church itself had been finely constructed with beautiful stone work and stained glass images of meaningful moments within the Biblical Lore, for some reason this religion felt the need to perfume the entirety of the church with plumes of incense that both dried the eyes and throat while choking the air around him with a dull haze. Apparently this was not even a special occasion or feast day when it was used, but something that was regularly utilized within worship. The crowd that had gathered seemed quite used to the effect of the cloud, though by the looks of who made up the gathering, they had decades to adjust.

Thankfully, it seemed that all people attending the service were given a guide to how the entire thing would be laid out. The service seemed to be broken into three distinct pieces: an opening prayer and welcome, a selection of readings from their holy book, and a means of communion before recession. Lee was also interested to see that there would be a sermon given by Father Mitchell about halfway through. If nothing else, it would be quite interesting to hear him speak to a crowd on his religion rather than just in respect to whatever foolishness he and his companions were getting involved in.

The first twenty minutes or so passed in a blur to Lee. Stories and letters were told and spoken of, songs were sung, and prayers were recited in one voice by the mass of people who attended. At one point he looked over at Luis and Morgan. The knight was standing at attention, though it was unclear to Lee just how much he was actually absorbing. Morgan shifted a bit uncomfortably from time to time, as though doing her best to be polite, but not fully enjoying her time spent within the church. Lee looked around and saw the enclosure of wood and stone and realized it made sense for Morgan, who was tied to nature to not feel overly comfortable within. This place seemed as cut off from the natural world as one could get.

Finally, they got to the story Father Mitchell would be speaking on that day. Lee gave this one his full attention. Their god had taken the form of a man to walk among the people and went out in fishing vessels with the workers who had not been able to catch any fish at all that night, however when the god decreed they throw their nets overboard they caught so many that their nets tore. Lee listened and considered the story, feeling it was nothing more than a god wishing to brag about his power to those he was trying to lure into his service.

Feeling disappointed and underwhelmed, Lee sat back in the pew as Father Mitchell took to the pulpit. He felt it was best to at least finish out the service. It was the hospitable thing to do.

"Be not afraid," Father Mitchell's voice rang out, clear and strong, pulling Lee's attention immediately back.

"Be not afraid," Father Mitchell repeated his voice softer than it had been a moment before. Lee was impressed with the Father's ability to command a crowd and listened intently. "These were the words Jesus said to Peter when he fell to his knees feeling he was too sinful a man to be given such an impossible task. The work that was being asked of him was too much, so much so that his nets would rip, his tools would shatter, and he would be left overwhelmed."

It began to dawn on Lee, the story was not just a brag, but a metaphor. Idly he thumbed at the copy of the bible that Father Mitchell had given him the previous night. He had read part of it and was unimpressed. However, he realized his folly. He had been reading the book and taking the stories literally. Now it seemed that there was interpretation required.

"Peter, as many know, was the first Pope of the Catholic church," Father Mitchell continued. "He had been called upon to build a church; not construct a building, but build a community in a time where such community was punishable by death under the Roman rule. An impossible task. Be not afraid. You will be called upon to perform impossible tasks in your life, whether it be in your faith, in your community, in your work, or in your family. And when you are, remember these words. Remember that you are Peter here, an imperfect person set before a herculean feat..."

The sudden booming voice of Smithers cut through the pregnant air of the church.

"We who are about to die, salute you!"

Lee snapped around, seeing the old man, being pulled back unsuccessfully by Timm as he entered the church. As quickly as he could, Lee got to his feet, only to see that Luis had already made it halfway down the aisle with Morgan hot on his heels. Aiding Timm, Luis managed to drag Smithers back out of the church. Turning to face Father Mitchell, Lee gave him a small bow of apology and rushed to follow the others. As he left, he could hear the Father clear his throat and attempt to regain the flow of his sermon once again.

Back in the basement, Smithers had been laid out on a cot and was cackling wildly.

"Is he afflicted by something?" Lee asked, rushing towards the old man to check him for curses or poison.

"Not unless you count being drunk," Timm said, with a shrug.

"He got drunk this early in the morning?" Lee asked.

"At a police station?" Luis inquired as well, to which Lee had to concede was an even more illogical point.

"Hold on," Morgan said, calming the room. "Let Timm explain what's going on. First, Timm, who's this?"

Lee turned and noticed, for the first time, another man was standing in the room with them. He was slightly overweight and was wearing a sweat-stained button down shirt, loose tie, and rumpled pants. His hair was unkempt, his face and eyes were ruddy, and tears had drawn streams in the dirt that discolored his cheeks. Furthermore, Lee recognized this man from their trips to O'Malley's Pub.

Timm began to explain to the group about the trouble Carl had gotten himself into and Smithers' reaction to the knowledge that in order to help the man they would need to face off with the Irish Mob and its enforcers.

"Then it seems that we're to go on a crusade against them," Luis said, and Lee could not help but notice the gleeful gleam in his eye.

"Luis, we're looking to rescue these people," Morgan said. "Not start a war."

"They started the war when they took those people," Luis argued back.

"No, they didn't," Lee said thoughtfully. Luis looked like he was ready to argue further, but Lee cut him off. "This war started long before that. Long before we got here. It seems we're walking into a fight that has been being waged for decades."

At those words, Luis relaxed his shoulders and scratched at his short beard. "Then what are we supposed to do? Let these people die?"

"No," Lee said, half a beat faster than Morgan and Timm. "But we need to keep in mind that we're not starting a war, we're jumping into someone else's. If we think of this as taking on the whole mob, we're going to be dragged into an unwinnable situation."

"What do you suggest then, Lee?" Morgan asked, cocking her head to one side, and Lee could not help but be reminded of a curious dog.

"Keep focus," Lee said.

"We are focused," Timm said.

"No, I mean on the task," Lee clarified. "Our goal is to find Carl's family, rescue them, and get out. We don't need to hunt down this Nathan person, we don't need to wipe out the Irish Mob. We treat this as any crime family from our world. Get in, perform the task without being identified, and get out."

"So less of a crusade and more of an extraction," Luis said.

"Correct," Lee nodded, recognizing now that Luis understood things more clearly when laid out tactically and militaristically. He would have to file that away and use it in the future to avoid confusion when dealing with the knight. "If we are able to extract these women, we can find a way to smuggle them out of the city without giving Nathan access to them or have him find out who we are."

"Meaning we just have to win one battle, not a whole war," Timm said.

"Precisely," Lee said, smiling.

"Oh, so fucking easy!" Smithers called out, sitting up in the cot, cackling wildly. "We'll just go in, beat up the mob, then get away Scott-free! Except that won't happen! Do you have any idea who you're all messing with?"

"A crime family," Lee said. "Nothing more."

"Way more!" Smithers shouted, the mirth gone from his voice. "They're way more than that! The mob is organized crime! They own cops, they own people, if they want you, they will find you! They'll go after people you care about to get to you, they'll kill women and children indiscriminately. Hell, they'll do worse than kill them. These assholes are not above torturing children if they think it will get them what they want."

Lee looked steadily at Smithers and waited for him to finish. As the old man spoke, Lee focused very hard on his words and not on the images of memory that flashed through his mind. He began counting backwards from one hundred, splitting his attention as much as possible to be sure that his brain did not have room to maneuver past what was happening in the present, and when Smithers had finally stopped talking, Lee took a deep breath.

"They are a crime family, nothing more," he repeated. "If you think that we've never dealt with people who work in such ways in the past, you are horribly mistaken. People like that exist regardless of what plane of the multiverse you are from. There will always be those who are cruel and competent enough to build an empire on the backs of others, fueling their war machines with the blood of the innocent. None of us here would stand for it in our world, so I ask you one simple question now, Smithers: do you think we'll stand for it here?"

Smithers looked at Lee for a moment. Their eyes were locked in a battle of will. Lee hoped his exuded determination to counteract the fear he saw emanating from Smithers'. Silence penetrated the room, and Lee could scarcely hear anyone breathing, until Smithers let out a breath and laughed silently to himself.

"We're all going to die," he said again, shaking his head.

Lee smiled at the old man.

"Come now, Smithers. Have a little faith," Lee said, grinning to himself. "And be not afraid."

~ 31 ~

LUIS

Heading up the stairs to find Father Mitchell, Luis almost bumped into the priest who was descending down to meet them.

"Ah, Luis," the priest said, seemingly frazzled. "I was coming to find you."

"I was doing the same," Luis nodded, and led the way back down. "It seems we've found another mission that we may need your help on."

Lee and Timm filled the Father in on the issue at hand and the further need they would have of the priest in order to protect more innocents in his church.

"It seems you have a habit of finding those in need," Father Mitchell sighed, pulling off his stole and revealing the simple priests' clothes underneath.

"I apologize for the inconvenience," Lee started to say, but Father Mitchell cut him off.

"You've brought me another person in mortal peril," Father Mitchell said, his voice tired, but resolved. "And I will never turn such people away. I just worry about the frequency you seem to find these individuals."

"Apparently we're focusing on a single target right now," Smithers said, an edge of sarcasm in his voice. Luis bit his tongue. He understood the old man's concerns, but felt that this was not the best way to be behaving at the moment.

"And you're targeting Nathan O'Brian?" Father Mitchell asked.

"Yes," Luis said curtly, cutting off any further quips. "We heard that he may be Catholic and were wondering if you knew anything about him."

Father Mitchell shook his head. "He does not attend my Church, or at least he does not attend my services. There are several throughout the day, though he may well just not be a practicing Catholic. But as for knowing *of* him, there I can help you a bit. He's quite infamous, especially among law enforcement."

"The police know of his crimes?" Lee asked.

"Yes," Father Mitchell nodded. "They probably have quite the file on him."

"Then why does he still walk free?" Luis asked.

"There's a difference between knowing something and being able to prove it," Father Mitchell said, smiling. "Take it from one in my profession, that is quite a notable distinction."

"And you can count getting any help from the cops out completely," Smithers said, sourly. "Odds are they'd try to make a sting out of the operation, get these women killed, and then call it an 'unfortunate incident' before shunting us out the door."

"So, the only chance of saving these women would be to do so ourselves," Luis said with a nod. He felt that would be the case regardless, and rested his hand on the hilt of the sword that hung with a familiar and comfortable weight on his hip. "I'm fully prepared and willing to do so. Let's go."

"Go where?" Smithers asked. "We don't know where they're being held. We don't know how many men are guarding them. We don't know crap."

It was hard to argue with Smithers' logic here. Luis pursed his lips and pondered the situation. Perhaps Smithers' initial concerns were not so unfounded as the rest of the group had thought, though the representation of them may have been somewhat irksome. In order to find the women they had taken captive, they would need to locate either Nathan O'Brian himself, or glean the information from his subordinates. It was infrequent for the two to constantly be together, and with an organization this size there were probably several places where low ranking members would gather.

"Father Mitchell," Luis said, connecting his thoughts together. "Where might members of this organization gather?"

"Well," Father Mitchell said, thinking. "It's a Sunday morning, so I'd assume church with their families if they've got one. The younger ones may end up at a bar or something to watch a game or hang out with friends if they don't have a job."

"I don't suppose O'Malley's would be such a bar," Lee said, cocking an eyebrow.

"As if Tom would allow that kind of riff-raff in his bar," Smithers said, scornfully, and Luis found himself agreeing. Tom did not seem the type of man to allow those of ill-repute to frequent his establishment.

"More likely you're going to find them in the waterfront district," Father Mitchell said. "There are a few bars out that way where people who work the docks or shipping yards would frequent. There's no work today, but people involved in mob business tend to be creatures of habit, going where they know is safe, or at least where they know there will be back up."

"Pack hunters tend to stick to familiar territories," Morgan piped in. "But that means where we find one we're going to find a lot. I doubt they'll just tell us what we want to know and let us go."

"They won't do either of those things," Smithers said, checking over his shotgun and making sure that there were shells loaded into the barrels.

Luis was starting to understand the function of the weapon from the times he'd ask Smithers questions while the old man tended to the weapon. Having seen the destructive force of firearms, Luis had garnered some interest in them, but wished to learn more about them before seeking any personal training.

"Then we go in there and we make them tell us," Timm said, driving his right fist into the opposite palm. Thanks to Lee's aid, he seemed recuperated and ready to go.

"I agree," Luis said, patting the sword on his hip. "We go in, get the information we need, and we go save those in danger."

"You realize we do that, and these guys will try to kill us, right?" Smithers asked.

"Yes," Luis nodded. "But that makes them no different than any other threat I've ever faced in my life. I fail to see why that should matter now."

With that, Smithers relented and soon Luis found himself with the others walking from bar to bar along the waterfront. The first couple were busts, either closed or filled with sports fans who were simply there to watch some kind of game that Luis neither paid any attention to nor cared to learn about. When asked his affiliation by one of the so called "super fans" as Smithers defined him, Luis simply answered that he was aligned with Nike.

"Yeah man!" the super fan responded. "Just do it! Am I right?"

"I have no idea," Luis responded, before leaving the drunk and dumbfounded man standing confused as he walked out the door.

"This is taking too long," Luis said, going to put his hand on the hilt that was no longer there. Smithers had forced him to carry the sword in a duffle bag rather than walk around with it on his hip as would be logical. However, the old man had been insistent that the police would frown upon him carrying such a weapon, so in the bag it was.

"There are just a few more bars to check," Smithers said. "If we don't find anything in those, we can come up with another plan, but for now we've gotta stay the course."

Grumbling, Luis followed, accepting Smithers' logic and following him to the next bar on the list, a place called Micky's. Stepping inside, Luis instantly noticed the major difference between this bar and the others they had been to so far. There was no jovial atmosphere here, no sports fans drinking and rowdily screaming at television screens. Several men sat in the back, drinking and quietly talking while the game that all the others had been watching played silently over the bar where the bartender stood polishing a glass. He finished his work and moved about, giving the new arrivals a pointed look before continuing about his business, polishing the bar, but needing to work around a man's head as he lay passed out in his stool.

"Think this is the place?" Luis asked, slowly slipping his hand into the duffle bag at his side, eyeing the bar patrons around them.

"Possible," Smithers responded. "But no way to be sure without asking around a bit. Just be careful what you say here…"

"Oh barkeep!" Timm said loudly, stepping out of reach before either Luis or Smithers could grab him. "I was wondering if you could tell me if we could find a Mister Nathan O'Brian at this establishment."

The entire bar went dead silent.

Luis tried to trade a look with Smithers, but saw that the old man was staring hard at Timm, his face turning a shade of red that was nearing purple. In spite of this, Luis also noticed that he had started sweating profusely. Looking over, he saw the men at the back table were also staring at Timm, and their hands were reaching below the table. Luis felt the cold steel of his sword against his hand, and took the grip lightly, attempting not to draw any attention.

"Who's asking," the bartender said, leaning against the bar and bringing himself down to Timm's eye level.

"Oh, you know," Smithers muttered under his breath. "Just some people who will be dead tomorrow."

"Thola Igerk Mue Moonflayer," Timm responded, confidently.

"Alright then," the bartender said with a nod, though Luis could see the confusion on his face. "Why ya asking?"

"I want a meeting with him," Timm said. "For business."

"Do you now," the bartender asked, eyeing Timm up and down. "You from the homeland?

"Of course," Timm said, gesturing at himself and the ridiculous outfit he was wearing. "Can't you tell."

"Wrong answer," the bartender grinned. There was a click from under the bar and Luis heard the door lock behind him.

"Magic!" Luis breathed.

"Automatic locks," Smithers muttered back before calling out. "Hey! I ain't from the homeland, can you let me live?"

"Nathan is none too happy when someone from the homeland comes over trying to muscle in after he's done all the hard work to take over Boston," the bartender said, ignoring Smithers. "So it seems we're going to have to send a message to your retainer."

"You might not want to do that," Timm said, and Luis could hear the grin in his voice. In spite of himself, Luis felt one of his own tugging at the corners of his mouth.

Time seemed to slow for a moment as a flurry of activity happened all at once. Several of the men in the back got to their feet. A couple in the back pulled out their guns and aimed at the group, while another charged forward, brandishing a knife at Lee, who had stepped too far forward as they had entered. Smithers grabbed the edge of a nearby table and flipped it forward, creating cover between him and the gunmen. The old man grabbed Morgan's arm and dragged her to the ground as the air filled with the sound of small explosions and bullets ripped at the heavy wood.

Off to the right, the bartender grabbed a nearly empty bottle off the bar, smashed it, and used the broken glass to take a swipe at Timm's throat. The monk nimbly bent backwards at his hips, using the bar as a counterbalance to keep from hyperextending, barely creating enough space between him and the bartender's reach to avoid having his throat opened in a gory spray.

Luis smoothly drew the sword from inside his duffle bag and stepped in between the approaching enemy and Lee. His blade was four times as long as this man's, but he was taking no chances with the sheer number of enemies they had to fight. He sent up a prayer to Nike and a holy light began to glow around his blade.

"I'll show you bastards how to fight!" Luis cried out, striking the man with such force that the knife he held went spiraling from his grasp. A gout of blood shot into the air and the man looked down at the bloodied stump that had been his forearm a moment before, wound seared closed by the holy light of Nike. Dumbly, he looked between the stump and Luis, completely oblivious to Lee, who stepped in and threw a punch across the man's jaw, dropping him to the ground.

Luis turned to congratulate Lee on the strike, only to see the gunmen change focus, turning their weapons on him. Grabbing the priest, Luis took a note from Smithers' play and tipped a table over to create cover.

Over by the bar, Luis could hear Timm combating the bartender.

"If you tell me now, I don't have to knock you out," he heard the monk saying.

"Fuck you!" was all the retort he seemed to be getting from the bartender.

Luis looked over and saw Timm vault the bar top, using the bar as a shield from the other assailants. He threw a pair of blows at the bartender landing each with a meaty sound. The first caught him in the gut, forcing the large man to bend over slightly. Taking the opportunity, Timm drove his other fist directly into the large man's nose. Luis heard bones crunch as his head rocked backwards. To his surprise, the large man straightened up and grinned down at Timm, blood pouring from his nostrils.

"Oh," Timm said. "You're tougher than you look."

"Yeah," the bartender said, swinging the bottle at Timm again, cutting deep into the muscle of the monk's forearm, causing him to cry out in pain.

Luis stood to go to Timm's aid, but a burning pain caught him in the shoulder, forcing him to his knees again. Blackness tugged at the edges of his vision as the pain threatened to overwhelm him.

"That's what you get for hurting my brother, ya son of a bitch!" Luis heard someone cry out before a fresh volley of gunshots rang out. He looked up to see Morgan and Smithers taking cover behind a table six feet away from them.

"Morgan!" Luis cried out. "We need cover!"

Morgan looked at him and nodded. She rolled her neck and bared her teeth as her bones cracked, shifted, and reformed. Fur exploded from her skin, covering her in a shaggy grey coat that rippled down her body. Her knees snapped and reversed directions as her jaw extended and teeth drew out into points. A moment later, Morgan the girl was gone, replaced by Morgan the massive wolf. Before any of them could react, her furry form darted out from behind the table and charged the gunmen in the back.

Luis grinned at the sight. No training in the world can prepare someone for a massive form of fur and fang to come charging out from behind a table where you thought just an old man and girl were hiding a moment before. The gunmen paused for a moment to try and process what they were seeing, but by the time they had realized they should be screaming, it was too late. Morgan hit one full on and sent him crashing to the floor under her massive bulk. He was shrieking as her fangs dug into the arm he threw up in an attempt to protect himself.

"Shoot it!" the bloodied man shrieked. "Shoot the fucking dog!"

The other two shook themselves out of their shock and turned their guns on Morgan. One found his mark, eliciting a yelp of pain from the wolf, but the other was so shaken that he could not possibly shoot straight. A bottle of booze behind the bartender exploded in a spray of glass and liquor, causing the large man to curse out loud.

"Watch what you're doing with that thing!" he snarled, taking another swing at Timm with the broken bottle.

"Why are you people doing this?" Smithers cried out, though Luis wasn't sure if he was talking to the bar patrons or to the rest of them. The old man grit his teeth and stood, leveling the shotgun above Morgan's wolfish head and unloaded both barrels at once.

The wall behind the gunmen was instantly peppered with thousands of tiny holes and sprays of red. They staggered backwards into the wall and slumped to the floor in twin pools of blood. With brutal efficiency, Smithers broke the stock and ejected the two shells he had just spent and loaded two more in with a single movement before turning the gun on the gunman who was approaching Luis and Lee from the side and released a single barrel blast at that one. In spite of diving for cover, the man was hit and sent spiraling back into another table, which broke under his weight and they both crashed into the ground.

Luis took the opportunity to go to Timm's aid. Using his good arm, Luis mimicked Timm's actions and vaulted over the bar as well, but took up the bartender's other side in order to flank him. Swinging his sword laterally at the man, Luis attempted to drive his pommel into the back of his head and knock him out. The pommel made contact, but the bartender rolled with the hit, swinging wildly with the broken bottle. Luis intercepted the attack with the blade, causing the glass to shatter completely in the large man's grip.

He stared down dumbly at it for a moment before looking up at Luis, still standing in his parrying stance. Luis gave the man a grin before Timm reached up and tapped him on the shoulder.

"Excuse me," Timm said, causing the confused bartender to turn. As he did, the monk drove his elbow across his jaw with the precision of Luis' sword. Bones crunched and Luis had to jump back as the large man fell so that he wasn't pinned beneath him.

Luis stood and surveyed the room. Lee was moving from body to body, pressing his hands to wounds as a divine light shone out from him. Morgan was dragging bodies across the ground towards him in order to make his work easier. Smithers walked over to the bar, reached over, and grabbed a bottle. He retired to a table and pulled out the cork, not bothering to retrieve a glass.

"I think that handles this front," Luis said to Timm. "A bit brash, but no less effective."

Luis pressed his hand to his shoulder and closed his eyes. With a flash of light, the pain subsided, and he pulled his hand away from a healed, if still bloodied, arm. In his hand was the bullet that had hit him in the shoulder during the fight. Luis was about to toss it to the side, but changed his mind, placing it in his pocket instead.

"Hey, think you could..." Timm said, gesturing to his arm.

Luis nodded and pressed his hand against the monk's arm and with another flash of divine light closed the gash.

"Thanks," Timm said, rubbing his arm slightly at the phantom pain. Luis knew the feeling all too well. "What's the plan now?"

Luis shrugged. "We did our best to leave at least a few alive, right?"

"What do you think I'm doing?" Lee called out from across the room. He didn't even bother to look up from his work. "I'm not able to heal all these men, but I can at least stabilize their wounds so they won't bleed out."

"Good," Luis nodded. "Then we can rouse one to answer our questions. If that one doesn't, we'll dispatch him and try another."

Luis looked up to see Lee giving him a dirty look.

"Dispatch him non-lethally," Luis clarified. "I'm not advocating for pointless murder."

Seemingly satisfied with the response, Lee returned to his work. Luis heard a low, throaty growl coming from Morgan and turned to face the girl. She was well over nine feet long before you got to the tail in this form, far bigger than any true wolf that Luis had ever seen. He assumed this was the kind of beast that could only exist in the hidden forests and groves that druids tended to. Her head alone was as big as his torso.

Under her weight, Luis saw the squirming form of a wounded, but still conscious man. He was whimpering as he looked up at the massive beast that had him pinned to the ground. Luis smiled and walked over to the man, pointing his sword at him.

"Well then," he said. "It looks like we have our first volunteer."

~ 32 ~

TIMM

"We need information," Timm said, glowering at the man on the ground.

He looked to his right and saw the point of a sword near his throat. To his left there was a slavering wolf snarling, head pitched low in an aggressive stance. Above him, Timm stood, arms crossed.

"Yeah, alright," the man said, lifting his hands in a whimpering surrender. "I'll tell ya whatever you need to know."

Timm smiled slightly, pleased with the response he was getting. Seemed all these men needed in order to see reason was a simple demonstration of skill.

"We want to know where Nathan is keeping the girls," Timm said, firmly.

"Uh," the man stuttered, looking around. "What girls?"

Morgan snarled and snapped her fangs at the man, who winced back and shrieked.

"Don't play games!" Timm growled.

"Not playing any games!" the man whimpered. "But you have to be more specific! Big operation and what not! Do you mean the hookers? Do you mean one of our girls? What do you mean by girls? Please! I wanna tell you, honest I do!"

Timm bit his lip and thought for a moment. This guy didn't seem to have much fight left in him if any. He could be wasting their time, waiting for backup, but considering how he was crying in a pool of his own blood and now a little urine, Timm didn't think that was the case. Maybe playing tough with this guy wasn't going to work well. He decided to take a different approach.

"The Newman girls," Timm said, softening his voice. "Should be a mother and her two daughters. Nathan O'Brian took them as a means to manipulate Carl Newman. Do you know where they are being held?"

"Oh, those girls," the man nodded, smiling with understanding. "Yeah, yeah, I know where they're being kept. They're down on the waterfront, warehouse district. You're looking for Warehouse seventeen. They're being kept in there."

"Any guards," Luis asked, not taking Timm's cue to use a softer tone.

"Ah, yeah," the man said, wincing away from the sword. "There should be a few, but I don't know the number."

"Anything else you want to tell us about this warehouse?" Timm asked.

"Uh, I don't think Nate will be down there," the guy said, thoughtfully. "He does like to check on operations, but there's no telling where he is right now. Odds are, considering they shouldn't have more than pistols and rifles."

He looked around at the bloodied mess around them.

"And it doesn't look like you're going to have much problem with the pistols," he said.

"Thank you for your time," Timm said, still smiling. With a quick jab to the jaw, Timm watched the man's eyes cross as his head slumped back and slammed against the floor.

"We got a location," he called out to Smithers, who was taking another swig from the stolen whiskey bottle.

"Fantastic," Smithers said. "By the way, did I hear him say the word 'rifles'?"

"Yup," Timm responded. "What are those?"

"Guns," Smithers said, pulling himself from the table and shuffling over to where the slumped over gunmen were. "Really big guns."

He began rifling through the gunmen's pockets and pulling out ammunition and set to work checking over the guns they had, collecting them in a bag. Luis went over to talk to Smithers as Timm began dragging the unconscious bodies over to the bar as Lee tied them up. It took about fifteen minutes or so, but Timm had managed to create a pile of them behind the bar. If someone were to come in, no one would be visible. Also, he had been sure to leave the bartender at the bottom of the pile. He smiled in his victorious pettiness and walked away.

"No," Smithers said emphatically. "No, no, for the hundredth time, no!"

"It makes the most sense," Luis said. He was holding one of the guns taken from their attackers. Timm noticed that he was holding it from the end the bullets came from with his finger a good distance away from the trigger. He was also being sure to keep it a good distance from Smithers as the old man kept reaching for it.

"It makes zero sense!" Smithers said, practically frothing at the mouth. "Now hand it over before you hurt someone, boy!"

"I will not!" Luis said, taking a step back to position himself in a way that made it impossible for Smithers to make another grab for the weapon. "These people are using weapons that are way more advanced than our own against us, we need to be armed with the same weapons if we have any hope of taking them out."

"You've got no damn clue how to use it!" Smithers said, angrily. "None of you do!"

"How hard can it be?" Luis asked. "You point and pull. Even an idiot can use one."

"And a shit-ton of them do, every day!" Smithers snarled. "That's how you get such a high mortality rate from the damn things! People who don't know how to use them feel they have a right to, and most of those people don't have a pair of brain cells to rub together. Guns ain't toys."

"Smithers, no one is saying they are," Morgan said, having reverted back to her normal form. She was hugging herself tightly around her middle, looking nervously between the two. "But Luis does have a point. He's a trained warrior, and knows how and when to use a weapon."

Smithers was breathing deeply, and Timm could tell that the man wanted nothing more than to turn his anger against Morgan. For a moment, Timm thought he might. But rather than do so, Smithers took a deep breath and turned to face Morgan.

"You lot may be warriors, you may be superhuman, you may even be 'magic,' whatever that means," Smithers said, his voice strained. "But that don't mean you know a damned thing about *that* weapon. Every year, folk who think they know something about how to use them end up blowing away some innocent person. You're just as likely to kill the people we're going in to save as you are the asshole keeping them prisoner."

"Honestly," Lee said, stepping forward. "I have no interest in such a weapon. I don't feel safe around them. In spite of your knowledge and training with them, Smithers, I don't even feel safe when you're the one holding it."

Smithers nodded at the priest. "Yeah, I don't blame you for that one. They're dangerous, unruly weapons, even when professionals have them..."

"That being said," Lee continued, cutting Smithers off. "I have put my life in Luis' hands before and don't feel any less safe with him holding it than you holding it. If he wishes to keep the weapon on his person, I have no objections."

Smithers grit his teeth angrily, but did not argue with Lee's assessment of the situation. Timm looked down at the weapon in Luis' hand and decided that in spite of the need to arm themselves properly to deal with this world, he had to agree with Lee. Guns made him uncomfortable. He looked up and met Morgan's eye.

Silently they both seemed to agree that neither of them wanted the weapon either.

A sound caught Timm's ear and he cocked his head to one side. It sounded familiar, like from the scene the previous night at the bar.

"Hey Smithers," Timm said, eyes still closed as he listened. "I hear sirens coming, probably a mile or so off, but it's hard to tell with so many tall buildings around."

"Time to go," Smithers said, corking the bottle he'd been drinking from and shoving it in his bag before grabbing a cloth off the bar and wiping down parts of the bar and table. "Cops are on their way, and we don't want to be here when they get here."

They left through the front, to Smithers' dismay, due to the fact that there was no back exit. Smithers was muttering about poor architectural design as they piled into his truck and made their way down towards the warehouses. Smithers was sure to park a few blocks away from where the warehouses were located and kept looking in his rearview mirror. Timm kept his eye out as well, watching for any sign of flashing lights or approaching police, but none appeared.

"Why did you wipe down parts of the bar?" Morgan asked him as they walked. Timm fell into step behind her, also curious about the reason, though considering the mood Smithers was in did not want to ask. It seemed Morgan, for whatever reason, got a pass.

"Fingerprints," Smithers said, curtly. He turned to see Morgan looking curiously at him and sighed. "Okay, so fingerprints are largely unique between people. It's not a perfect system, and modern forensic science does show that people can share a fingerprint pattern, but for the most part, they're used to identify people."

"So are people's fingerprints used to identify them normally?" Morgan asked. "It seems they'd need to know what yours looked like to worry about leaving them behind like that. And you didn't ask us to wipe ours away."

Smithers and Timm both blinked at Morgan.

"Uh, that's pretty insightful there, Morgan," Smithers said, scratching at the scruff growing in around his chin. "Yeah, they keep fingerprint records for various reasons. Either you committed a crime, or you needed to be cleared of one, or you worked in a field where they needed to be able to check that you weren't a criminal..."

"Seems a lot of focus on criminality," Morgan said.

"Uh, yeah," Smithers nodded. "There's a lot of that in this world. Lots of security, not a lot of trust."

"Why is there a record of your fingerprints?" Timm asked.

"Oh, uh," Smithers said, taken a bit off guard. "Because of a job I worked. I don't really want to get into it, but if you worked for them, then you got it done. That was that."

"What job?" Timm asked, narrowing his eyes in suspicion.

"Government job, pretty standard stuff," Smithers said. "We're coming up on the warehouses, come on, this way."

Smithers led them across the street to a darkened area near a large building. There was a tall fence made of interconnected metal strands that were far stronger than their thin design made them appear. At the top of the fence were coils of wire that stuck out about a foot in either direction, covered in what Timm thought may be serrated barbs.

"What's that at the top?" Timm asked.

"That's barbed wire," Smithers explained, and Timm rolled his eyes at this world's uncanny ability to name things in the most obvious way. "Gonna make climbing over a pain, but maybe we can throw a leather coat or something over the point we climb up and we can lessen any injuries."

"Or we can do this," Luis said, stepping forward and drawing his sword. With one quick slice, he severed a collection of the interconnected wires in such a way that they could be parted like a tent flap.

"Or we could do that," Smithers said, pulling open the fence to allow everyone to pass.

Once they were inside, Smithers began to lead them through the maze like structures of the warehouses. Or perhaps it would be more accurate to say that they were labyrinthian. The path was fairly clear, but it was impossible to know what building was important or how they were laid out without having some kind of intricate knowledge on the system the builders used. Timm decided his energy would be best spent on memorizing the way back than trying to determine what the way forward was. That was best left to Smithers.

After about ten minutes of walking, Smithers held up his hand to halt their movement. He pointed ahead of them and Timm peeked around him to see why he had paused. Ahead, there was a large warehouse building that looked exactly like the others they had been walking past this entire time, however Timm did note that there was a giant '17' painted on the doors, outside of which, two men stood as though keeping watch.

Both men were dressed fairly similarly, with warm looking hats that Luis called a beanie, sunglasses to ward off the brightness of the day that was all the more suspicious as the sun crested below the edge of the horizon, and heavy looking coats that were not closed against the coming night's chill. Timm looked closer and determined why. Under each of their left arms was a bulge that would have been impossible to reach for had the coats been closed. It seemed that they were the armed guards they had been warned about.

"We have the guns," Luis said, quietly. "We could take them out from here."

"Guns are loud," Smithers said, irritation at the edge of his voice. "You might take those two out, but if they have an army inside, all you've done is killed us and probably those women along with us."

"Isn't there a way to silence them?" Luis asked.

"This ain't a goddamned movie!" Smithers snarled in a harsh whisper. "That ain't how a silencer works! This is why I didn't want to let you have one in the first place."

Timm could see Luis and Smithers were about to start rehashing the same argument again and did not feel like wasting the time on it. He caught Morgan and Lee's eyes and jerked his head around the long way of the warehouse, pressing a finger to his lips for them to be quiet. Morgan nodded and Lee looked over at Luis and Smithers, grimacing. He turned back to Timm and nodded as well. Silently, they left the two to their disagreement and slipped around the edge of the warehouse until they were able to position themselves behind the guards.

"We need to do this as quickly and quietly as we can," Timm said.

"And try not to kill," Lee added, though he seemed to be looking more at Morgan than Timm. She smiled up at him sheepishly, then started rooting around for a weapon. She found a plank of wood cut into a perfect rectangle that looked to be four inches wide, two thick, and about the length of her arm.

"Is that going to be enough?" Timm asked her.

Morgan grinned wolfishly at him and brought the wood to her lips. Whispering a word, tendrils of vines and sprouts grew out from the wood, wrapping it firmly in greenery. As the plants finished growing, the vines erupted in thorns around the edge she was not holding.

"I think that should do it," Morgan said.

"Perfect," Timm nodded. "We hit them fast, and hard. On my mark."

"Go," Lee said, his eyes turning dark as he reached out a hand and sent black mist erupting from their hiding spot at the man on the right. The mist wrapped around the man's head and he grabbed at the sides of his head as if a loud, painful noise started ringing in his ears.

Taking her cue from Lee, Morgan burst forward from the darkness, her club held high. Hoping to gain the advantage, she swung at the one Lee had already injured, bringing the thorny mass down at the back of his shoulders and driving him forward. Ducking in swiftly to cut off the man's cry, Timm drove his fist across his jaw, sending the smoldering remains of a cigarette scattering across the ground, dancing like a firefly in the dying light.

He turned to throw a punch at the other man, standing there, mouth agape, but had overstepped his reach and swung wide. Timm saw the man recover and begin reaching for the weapon under his coat, knowing that as soon as the shot went off their whole plan was going to go up in smoke. However, before the man's hand could find his weapon, it shot up to cover his ears, as the black mist that had formed around his fellow's head wrapped around his own. Blood poured from between his fingers, and he slumped to the ground.

Timm looked up to see Lee, his eyes fading back to their normal light hue as the spell dissipated from his lips.

"Good catch," Timm said, nodding.

"Thank you," Lee said, his expression sick. "Unfortunately, I'm not able to do anything less than lethal with magic."

Timm looked down at the dead man at his feet and felt a little ill himself. He had to remind himself that this man had, if nothing else, resigned himself to evil deeds if he was not an evil man himself. His death meant they had a chance to save the lives of three others, not counting their own. Timm tried to see it as an acceptable loss.

"Okay, I'll hide the two of them," Timm said, picking up the dead body and slinging it over his shoulder. "Maybe that will buy us a little more time."

Lee nodded and looked over as Smithers and Luis moved briskly up to meet them.

"You were supposed to wait!" Smithers whispered hoarsely.

"We didn't have time," Timm argued, then turned to Luis. "Grab the other one, we'll hide them in the alley."

Luis nodded and threw the other man over his shoulder in a similar fashion to Timm.

"Just don't go running off again," Smithers said. "You'll get yourself killed."

"You want to take the lead?" Timm asked. "Then take the lead. But do it now."

He stormed off and found a dark area near where they had been hiding. Timm and Luis placed the bodies in a corner and leaned a pair of wooden palettes in front of them. Looking down, Timm saw a few tools that had been abandoned. A length of chain no more than five feet long and a crowbar had been dumped next to the wall and forgotten, though the palettes seemed to have offered protection from too much rusting. Timm picked them both up and walked back to the group.

"Hey, Lee," Timm said, offering the chain and crowbar out to him. "Something a little less than lethal?"

Lee smiled at him and nodded.

"Thank you," Lee said, reaching out to take the length of chain. "The chain will do nicely."

Timm nodded at him and gripped the crowbar tightly before turning to face Smithers.

"Okay," Timm said. "So what's our next move?"

~ 33 ~

SMITHERS

Smithers was fuming.

Between Luis' damn insistence on getting to use a weapon he had no business holding let alone firing and the trio of loose cannons who just went off against a couple of mobsters in the middle of their own territory, he wasn't seeing how they were going to get through this clusterfuck alive, let alone get these women out safely.

He took a deep breath. This wasn't the first time he'd been in what felt like a hopeless situation, but he'd been a lot younger then, and had people he could rely on by his side. These were not those people. These people were insane, dysfunctional, and not the kind of people you should ask to pick you up a cup of coffee. And here they were, working on what would have been a year long sting operation by the FBI thrown together on the walk over.

Smithers felt his breathing getting erratic again and kept trying those breathing exercises they taught him at the clinic. Part of him wished he hadn't been such a pig headed young man and actually listened to the doctors back then. But pride will get you, every time.

He looked at the group he was stuck with and considered the task at hand. He could spend all night wishing he had the old band back together, wishing he were younger and stronger, but these were the people and body he had. And as his grandfather used to say, "put all your wishes in one hand and shit in the other then tell me which one fills up first."

"Alright," Smithers said to the group, hoping that his voice wasn't shaking as much out loud as it was in his own ears. "Timm, you're the fastest we got. I want you to peek your head in, see what's to be seen, and report. We'll figure out what we're doing once we know what we're working with."

"Okay," Timm said, as he opened the door a crack and looked inside. Smithers barely felt like he'd had time to blink before the boy pulled his head back out again and started drawing in the dirt.

"It's a wide open space," Timm was explaining as he drew. "There's a few guys sitting at a table playing cards, but they're about a hundred feet away from the door. Not far from here, there are metal stairs that lead up to a narrow hallway that snakes around the outside of the building looking down."

"A catwalk," Smithers said, nodding. "Best place to start, gives us a good look around the whole building, a bird's eye view, if you will."

Timm nodded. "There are also rooms up there. Worth checking those out."

Smithers cocked his eyebrow at the boy as he sketched out about five different doorways and marked their locations. He'd gone from complete goofball and reckless fighter to tactician in the span of a breath. Looking up at the others, Smithers saw them each evaluating the crude map that Timm was drawing as well, seemingly enthralled, as though memorizing every point.

Smithers shook his head, clearing away the thoughts.

"Okay, so we go in quiet," he said, voice low and growing with confidence. "We don't engage if we don't have to. And if we do have to, take them out quietly if possible. We don't want this breaking out into a firefight."

"Right," Timm nodded. "If they burn down the building, it could hurt the women."

Smithers opened his mouth to correct Timm on what the term "fire fight" meant, but closed it again and figured the boy was technically correct.

The others got into position by the door, and Smithers gave Timm a nod to enter. The boy led the line towards the stairs that led up to a catwalk. They were metal and wire, and Smithers was nervous that their weight on the stairs may alert the guards, but Timm and Morgan were light steppers, while Lee and Luis followed carefully behind him.

Smithers noticed that both groups had subconsciously flanked him, keeping him in the middle where he would be protected from oncoming attacks by two individuals on either side. The old man chewed his lip thoughtfully, unsure if this was because he was old and frail, and needed protecting, or if it was to allow those who went up into melee clear paths towards the enemy. Considering their newfound strategic maneuvers, Smithers decided to give them the benefit of the doubt and say they were being tactical, not condescending.

Timm approached the first door and Smithers held his breath. Quickly and practically silently, the boy opened the door, peeked his head in and pulled it out again.

"Just a desk and some chairs," he whispered, shaking his head and moving towards the next one, doing the same thing. This time, however, Timm pulled back quicker and took extra caution in closing the door. He turned back to look at the group, eyes wide, and held up two fingers.

Smithers pursed his lips, then grinned. He waved Timm forward and approached the door, digging through his pocket as quietly as he could, pulling out a single penny. Deciding it was best not to question the design plans of the warehouse, and rather just thank his lucky stars they probably went with the cheapest possible contractor, Smithers carefully worked the penny into the door jam.

"What are you doing?" Morgan whispered to him, her eyes wide with concern.

"Pennying the door," Smithers explained without explaining.

Morgan looked as though she wanted to press the issue, but Smithers finished his work and waved Timm forward again. To his credit, the boy just nodded and moved towards the next door. Morgan, seeing that they were moving on, dropped the issue and kept going.

Timm approached the next door, opened it, and stood squinting at the darkness longer than he had at every other door. Before Smithers could stop him, Timm slipped inside.

"So much for tactical," he muttered darkly under his breath.

"Should we follow him?" Morgan asked.

"Hold on," Smithers said, turning to Lee and Luis behind him. "Stand watch and be ready to back us up."

Luis nodded and quietly drew his shortsword from its sheath while Lee seemed to look down in prayer, but, Smithers realized, he was in fact actually watching the men playing cards below them with great interest. Turning back to Morgan, Smithers nodded for her to follow.

The room was pitch black. Either there were no windows, or some dumbass had painted over them. Either way, he was pretty sure there was nothing OSHA compliant with this place. He saw Timm moving slowly through the mostly empty room towards three humanoid looking forms tied up on the floor. As he got close, the forms squirmed in almost panicked gestures.

"Don't worry," Timm said, softly. "Your husband sent us."

Morgan turned on the little keychain flashlight she must have still been carrying from that job fair they had crashed and illuminated the room slightly. The cheap little toy did enough to let Smithers see the image of three women. One was obviously a good deal older than the other two, probably in her forties, had squirmed in just the right way to position herself in between Timm and the other girls. Smithers was impressed. Even in such a dire situation, she was doing everything she could to protect her babies.

When she heard mention of her husband, the woman froze. Morgan took the opportunity to slip forward and remove the woman's gag.

"We're here to help," she said, her voice so soothing and gentle that even Smithers felt his wired mind relax a hair.

"You're Norah, right?" Smithers asked, recalling from the conversations he'd had with Carl about his family life.

"Y-yes," the woman sputtered, her voice so low Smithers had to strain to hear it.

"Good," Smithers nodded, turning to Timm and Morgan. "Get them untied, with any luck we can slip past the guards with them in tow and never even have to fight."

"Why do it?" Timm asked, untying the women with Morgan's help. "Why tempt the gods like that?"

"I'm the eternal optimist," Smithers answered, the sarcasm lobe of his brain going off before the one that could control that impulse could stop it.

"It seems they've been hurt," Morgan said, her soothing voice growing hard. "There are marks on their skin like they've been beaten."

"They didn't do more than just smack us around a little," Norah explained, unbinding her daughters' hands and pulling them in closely, shushing their crying. "They wanted to assert dominance or something. I don't know. I just knew we needed to listen or things could get a lot worse."

Smithers felt a rage bursting up in his chest, not just for the fact of what these women went through, but because of the rational way Norah explained the beating she had undergone. She knew the safest way to deal with monsters like the men downstairs. And now, thanks to their father's stupidity, her daughters did too. Why was it that innocent people needed to learn how to survive in a world of monsters rather than the monsters be taken down? Where was the justice for these people? For all people?

He looked over at the girl with healing hands gently brushing the hair from one of the crying girl's eyes, reassuring her that everything was going to be alright. Just a few hours before, he'd seen her turn into a wolf and rip a gunman's leg out from under him, sending the thug sprawling across the floor only to be beaten down by the man that stood to the side, shaking with the same rage Smithers was feeling. The man who'd jumped a bar, dodging bullets to beat the information needed to find these women and bring them home to safety.

His eyes wandered toward the doorway, outside of which he knew there was an honest to god knight whose conviction had him charge into battle against a known titan of death with fearless disregard for his own safety because innocents were in danger, and he refused to stand by and do nothing to stop it. Where a priest of a god Smithers had never heard of, held his faith so strongly that he was willing to accept the faith of others and be the first real Good Samaritan Smithers had seen in a good long time.

Realization struck him like a lightning bolt. These people were absolutely insane, they knew nothing of this world, and they did not belong here in the slightest. They were completely and utterly beyond the prejudices and poisons that had seeped so deep into the society and the culture that they walked into it pure and untainted. They weren't playing hero. They weren't just a bunch of reckless assholes. They actually cared, and they believed, fully and with conviction, that monsters needed to be slayed, innocents needed to be protected, and that they were equipped better than anyone to do the job.

This mentality could be extremely dangerous in the wrong hands. Smithers had seen despots believe they had divine right to rule. He'd seen fanatics believe that their skin color made them better than anyone else around them. Even people who'd believed that they were born better because they were more skilled at exploiting others for money. But these people were actually equipped better than anyone else to take whatever they wanted from whomever they wanted, and they were here, in the middle of a mob hideout, risking their lives for strangers.

Smithers realized they weren't just stupid assholes.

They were brave, heroic, stupid assholes.

"Smithers," Morgan said, nodding at the door where Timm had the women lined up to go through. "You want to take the lead?"

"Yeah," Smithers said, his voice tight. He drew his gun and took a defensive position opposite Timm.

Yeah, he thought, *why not? About time I fought for a cause I actually believed in.*

~ 34 ~

LEE

The men at the table below Lee were so engrossed in their game that he thought there was very little chance any of them would have heard a full holy service being performed, much less a conversation between himself and Luis. Lee had many questions he wanted to ask the knight, such as his feelings on the world they had found themselves in, if he was concerned about their inability to remember the fine details of their home, or even if, in spite of all the flaws of the land around them, he even wanted to return to that home.

Lee had been questioning all these things so deeply that it had even seeped into his prayers. Now, finding himself in this den of monsters and thieves, Lee was wondering if returning home would make any difference. Were people here really any different than people there? Evil reigned regardless of what soil he stood upon.

"Psst," Lee heard to his right. Looking back at the doorway, he saw Timm's bright features smiling broadly.

"Found them?" Lee asked.

Timm looked puzzled for a moment, then nodded vigorously.

Lee turned to Luis, placing the back of his fore and middle finger against the knight's arm to get his attention without startling him. With the slightest movement of his head, Luis looked back at Lee.

"Lead the way," Lee said with a nod. "They're found, and we're leaving."

The nod given was barely perceptible. Luis began to move across the catwalk with a singular purpose, and Lee followed behind him, eyes never leaving the men below who were playing cards.

From behind Lee, there was a clicking noise and the sound of rushing water. Looking over his shoulder, he saw a man with a large gun strapped over his shoulder stepping out of a doorway at the end of the catwalk. He was wiping his wet hands on the front of his pants as he turned and looked up, eyes meeting Lee's.

There was a pregnant moment as they stared at one another. Lee stood rigid, breath held in his tight throat, not wanting to look at the gun hanging from his side for fear of actualizing it. This one was much larger and much more terrifying than the one that had been fired at him the previous night, and Lee was concerned with the kind of power the monstrosity could possibly hold.

And so, the moment held, frozen in time. Until Smithers stepped out from the doorway and saw Lee staring behind him in fear.

Lee gave the old man credit. He didn't turn to look, ask for confirmation, or waste a single second. Smithers spun on his heel, dropping to one knee, and pointed his gun at the man behind him, letting off a shot before the other man had untangled his gun.

Smithers' shot sent a spray of blood across the back of the warehouse wall, though it was not a mortal blow. He went sprawling away, ducking back into the room he'd come from to gain cover from Smithers' follow up shot.

Lee turned and saw the first of the young girls standing frozen in the frame of the doorway. His eyes shot down towards the men at the table. They were in motion, hands going for their weapons and a line of targets on the catwalk above them. Without thinking, Lee charged forward, tackling the girl out of the doorway as a shower of sparks exploded above him.

They fell bodily to the ground as the girl shrieked in terror. Lee tried to shield her body with his own, but she squirmed out of his grasp and tried to rise. Knowing this would only make her easier to hit, Lee grabbed her wrist and pulled her to the ground, shouting as he did.

"Get down!" Lee called out, to both the girl and anyone listening. An older woman grabbed the girl, aiding Lee in getting her to the ground. He assumed this was the mother, and hunched up on his shoulder to be sure to guard her too.

"Looks like optimism failed us," Lee heard Timm shout, "Morgan get your game face on!"

Lee looked up and saw Timm duck out the door. However, rather than turning left or right on the catwalk, the monk grabbed the railing with one hand and vaulted over the side, presumably dropping the thirty feet down to the stone floor below him.

Morgan shot a glance over her shoulder at Lee.

"Get them out!" she yelled, her voice turning gravelly and harsh as her nose and mouth began to protrude outward, growing into a snout. Bristling grey and white fur spread out from her blackened nose and her eyes turned a predatory yellow.

Lee had seen her take this form before, and knew that she would be too large to fit through the door if she transformed here, but before she lost her bipedal standing, Morgan stepped through the door and fell onto newly formed paws, turning and charging to her right. A bloodcurdling scream filled the air as one of their enemies surely just died a painful death, horrified by the werewolf that had just emerged from the prisoners' room.

The sound of gunshots rang constantly, some Lee was sure were coming from Smithers as a means to aid them, but the fear gripped his heart with icy fingers. The sound disoriented him, the flashes of light began to blind him, and there was so much screaming all around him that he wasn't even sure he could say that they weren't coming from him. He had handled the clash of steel against steel, he'd thought he'd seen Hell before, but this was different. This was worse.

Heat flashed across his face and the light blinded him so that his eyes screwed shut against his will. The rhythm of the bullets was a cacophony of chaos that mirrored his own erratic heart.

Slowly, the beating of the bullets turned into a metronome beat he could follow. They slowed, and as they did, so did his heart. The heat grew in intensity, but the light faded. Lee opened his eyes and found that he was lying on the hot stone floor of a glowing, torchlit cavern. An explosive hiss of steam drew his attention away from the rocky walls to the large forge that was being worked by an enormous man in a cloak. His back was turned toward Lee, but the priest could see that he was hammering away at a piece of steel the size of Lee's entire body.

"Would you care for a drink?" the man asked, not turning around as he continued to work the steel.

"Uh..." Lee answered, looking around at the forge. Everything around him was scaled so large that he felt no bigger than a child. "No thank you, though I appreciate the offer."

"Hmm, polite, I like that," the man said as he turned, and Lee saw that the man working the forge was wearing nothing more than the cloak on his back and belt around his waist. A bold choice for a man working with such hot materials. The man caught Lee staring.

"Is this not how I'm depicted?" the giant of a man asked, spreading his arms wide.

"It is," Lee said, bowing low at the waist. "It is an honor to be in your presence, great Goibniu."

"And in yours, Lee Eraple," the god Goibniu responded, bowing, though not quite as low as Lee had. "So, what brings you to me this day. It is rare I get such crises brought my way."

"I..." Lee started to say, then looked around. "I'm not sure. I'm not even sure how I got here."

"You got here the same way everyone gets here," Goibniu said, placing down his hammer. "Your mind is built to withstand any puzzle or inhospitable company put before it, but trauma was never something you learned to handle well."

"I feel I've been handling it just fine," Lee stated firmly.

"No," Goibniu said. "You're ignoring it, which is not the same thing. But this conversation is not to discuss that matter, but rather to hammer out the imperfections that need work now before we place you back into the fire through which you'll be forged."

"I don't understand," Lee said, looking up at the god.

"Few do," Goibniu said, his voice somewhat sad. "I have very few worshippers, Lee. Very few indeed. And because of this, my power wanes. My few are faithful, however, so this allows me plenty of time to be sure what I craft is pure, well balanced, and sharp. Not all gods get such fine material to work with."

"I wouldn't go so far to say that I am a fine material," Lee said, shifting uncomfortably in the god's gaze.

"I would," Goibniu said, cutting him off. "And that's what matters. I do not work with brittle iron or subpar silver. However, it is in every crafter's best interest to remember that unworked or ignored, iron will rust and silver will tarnish. Once forged, it must be cared for."

Lee stood for a moment, waiting for the great craftsman to continue, but he simply returned to his work, pulling the blade out of the water and examining the tempered steel.

"Is that all?" Lee asked, curiosity getting the better of him.

"Hmm, maybe the manners still need some work," Goibniu muttered before turning his attention towards Lee. "What more could you need?"

"The people I'm with, the people we're saving, they're going to die," Lee said, his voice emphatic. "I was hoping that you'd be able to grant me some wisdom on how to deal with these weapons that our enemies wield."

"Weapons are weapons," Goibniu shrugged. "Well crafted and forged, or cheaply made, they are a tool with a task. You are no different. I just hope you function better than their tools function."

He turned and began to beat the steel with the hammer, causing every word Lee attempted to shout to him to be drowned out in the ringing of steel. The hammer falls became more wild and rapid and Lee found himself shouting incoherently, more out of frustration than fear as the explosion of sparks from the anvil blinded him.

Opening his eyes, he saw the three women huddled together in front of him, screaming against the hail of bullets flying around them. Lee found his own throat raw, as though he'd been screaming through his whole conversation with Goibinu. Heat pressed against his chest, and Lee looked down to see the pendent he wore of a hammer striking a sword glowed with the same intensity of the blade worked at the forge he had just visited.

"A tool with a purpose," Lee whispered, his jaw tight. He looked up to see the screaming women had dissolved into sobs. Lee got to his knees and looked at the battle through the door.

Timm was ducking shots on the floor below as one of the men kept trying to shoot him at close range. The hail of gunfire was making it nearly impossible for Timm to land a clear punch on his opponent. The snarls of a wolf could be heard, though Morgan was out of Lee's sight. He had no idea what was happening with Luis or Smithers, but every now and then the men below would duck behind cover as gunfire was returned their way.

Lee pressed his hand against the mother, who looked up at him, eyes filled with fear.

"Stay here," he said to her, a newfound calmness emanating from his voice. "We'll come for you as soon as this is over."

Without waiting for her reply, Lee stood and stepped brazenly through the door. A bullet whizzed by his head like an angry hornet, but he did not flinch. He was a tool, and he had a job to do. To his right, Morgan had her fangs wrapped around the arm of a gunman who had climbed the stairs to get a better shot on Smithers, whom she was now protecting from this new assailant's attacks. Smithers was letting off shots, but seemed unable to get a clear line of sight as the men below had cover and he did not.

To his right, Lee saw Luis fallen back on the ground, blood leaking through the leather of his coat, his left arm hanging limply at his side. A man with a gun was rushing up the stairs at him, and Lee recognized what he needed to do. With a flick of his arm, Lee sent the chain flying at the man running up the stairs. The throw was weak, and the man merely lost his footing for a moment.

"Is that the best you've got?" the gunman snarled up at Lee who was now kneeling by Luis. "You throw like my sister!"

"That's not my purpose," Lee said, his hand pressed against Luis' shoulder. There was a flash of brilliant white light and the man on the stairs held up his hand to shield his eyes.

"It's mine," Luis said, raising his now healed left arm to reveal the pistol Smithers had tried to take away from him. There was an explosion of light and sound from the knight's hand as the man he had aimed it at jerked back and tumbled down the stairs.

"Stairs are clear!" Luis called back to Smithers and Morgan, gripping both Lee and the railing to help himself back to his feet. He let go of the railing, but held on to Lee's arm for a moment longer. "Thank you, brother."

Before Lee could respond, Luis charged down the stairs to aid Timm.

Lee looked back over his shoulder in time to see Morgan jerk her head and send the man she was gripping to tumble over the side. He was not as graceful as Timm, and Lee heard a sickening crack as his head made contact with the stone below before any other part of his body. Smithers charged down the stairs on the opposite side as Morgan followed hot on his heels.

Not wanting to remain the target on the catwalk, Lee dashed down the stairs behind Luis, doing all he could to ignore the body at the bottom.

Smithers was walking forward, gun raised, letting off shot after shot. Lee noted that his shots were not panicked or rapid, but cool and measured, and always on his exhale. He also saw the man coming up from behind him. Before he could shout a warning, Timm ran towards Smithers, leapt up onto the side of the crate the hidden assailant was using as cover, and ricocheted himself down on the man with a powerful punch, dropping him to the ground.

"Gotta pay attention to your surroundings," Timm said, giving Smithers a wink, not noticing the man on the ground beginning to raise his gun.

Lee flicked out a hand and the man Timm had knocked down grabbed the sides of his head and screamed in pain before passing out. The gun clattered harmlessly to the ground. Smithers looked at the man, then over to Lee, giving him a nod. Lee returned it and went over to where Luis was finishing dispatching an individual that Morgan had pinned to the ground. He didn't feel the knight needed any help, but he did want to hide his smirk from Timm.

"Well then," the monk said, brushing his hands off. "That was a lot easier than I expected it to be."

"Why do you need to tempt the gods," Smithers asked as he walked over to each of the downed men and collected their weapons and ammunition.

"What are you doing that for, Smithers?" Lee asked.

"These men are going to use these weapons to do the same thing to other people as they did to those women," Smithers said, pointing up at the catwalk where Carl's family was still waiting. "I'll use them to stop people like them from doing just that."

"I thought we were fools off to die," Luis said, sheathing his sword and looking sternly at Smithers.

"You are," Smithers said, shrugging. "But hey, better to go out in a blaze of glory then waste away in some nursing home, am I right?"

Lee was unsure of what a nursing home was, but he smiled regardless. It seemed the task they were drawn here for was getting more likely to succeed with every tool that was properly utilized. He looked down at his hands. He was not a combatant like Luis or Timm, and had no taste for weapons like Smithers. Though she utilized the power of the earth around her much like how Lee called upon the power of his god, he was also nothing like Morgan. Different tools for different jobs making the overall task successful.

"Great," Timm said, starting for the stairs. "I'll go get the girls."

"Uh," Lee stepped forward, putting his hand on Timm's arm. "I think it's best that I do that."

"Why?" Timm asked.

Lee looked Timm over and made note of the now ruined, bloody clothing. There was even a possibility that some of the blood on Timm's clothes was his own. Lee made a note that they would need to start carrying spare clothing with them on these types of missions.

"The right tool for the right job," Lee said, patting Timm's shoulder, and immediately regretting it. He wiped it dry on a piece of thick cloth handing over one of the nearby crates as he walked towards the stairs.

"The right tool for the right job," he repeated to himself with a smile.

~ 35 ~

MORGAN

Lee brought the women downstairs while Smithers and Luis collected the remaining weapons that the guards had dropped. Timm was busy trying to wipe as much blood off of himself as possible. Morgan, not wanting to drop the wolf form just yet, stood guard and listened.

Upstairs, behind the door that Smithers had "pennied" she could hear two voices yelling at one another.

"There was shooting out there! Open the damned door!" One voice was yelling.

"It's stuck!" Another responded. "How many times I gotta tell you?"

"Shoot out the handle!"

"It's reinforced steel, you want to die? Just eat your own barrel in that case."

Morgan whimpered slightly, trying to get Smithers' attention. The old man looked up at her and grinned.

"What is it, girl?" he asked. "Timmy fell down the well again?"

Morgan cocked her head to one side in confusion.

"Sorry," Smithers said, laughing. "Never thought I'd be able to make that joke in the proper context. Not dead and perfect jokes. It's a good day."

Morgan pawed at the ground, growling.

"Oh fine," Smithers said, sounding disappointed. He turned to the top of the catwalk just as Lee was exiting the room where the women had been held, all three in tow. Smithers let out a sharp whistle to get Lee's attention. "Cujo says it's time to go!"

Morgan decided to assume that was another reference she didn't get, and padded her way over to the edge of the stairs Lee was descending with the three women. She was unsure how all of them would fit in Smithers' truck, but figured that would be a problem they could solve once they'd gotten out of the area.

"Where did that girl go, mommy?" one of the girls asked, clinging tight to her mother. Morgan gave her a nudge with her muzzle and the girl drew back at first, whimpering slightly.

Morgan couldn't blame her. She'd forgotten the battle they had just waged left her looking like quite a mess. Her muzzle was covered in blood and she was sure her teeth were stained with it. She took a step back, sat, and started wagging her tail. The girl watched her warily for a moment before a small smile broke across her face. She reached out and started scratching Morgan behind the ears.

"Honey, that's a wolf," Norah said, her voice fearful. "And a big one at that, you shouldn't pet it."

"Don't worry," Smithers said, walking over with a rifle now in place of the shotgun he usually carried. "She's well trained."

Morgan shot him a look.

"I believe it is imperative that we get out of here," Lee said. "As quickly as possible before reinforcements arrive."

"Or cops," Timm added.

Morgan pricked up her ears, listening intently. Timm was right, off in the distance she could hear the high pitched wail of sirens. They were still a long way off, but it would probably be best to not still be here when they arrived. In an attempt to get them started, Morgan began following their trail from when they entered earlier that evening.

It was fairly easy to do as a wolf. Even with the scents she was following being confused with the ones wafting around her from them standing right next to her, Morgan was able to follow her human scent back to the tear in the fence. Lee helped Norah and her children through, quickly followed by Timm, Luis, and finally Smithers, who turned to her as he passed through.

"I don't think you're fitting through like that," he whispered to her. "And a giant wolf is going to cause a stir on the street. Probably a good time to drop it before those girls turn around."

Morgan turned to see Lee had the girls and their mother distracted, and from the way they'd reacted to seeing her in this form in the first place, she assumed they were too distracted through the fight to see her original transformation. Taking the moment Lee had given her, Morgan shifted back into her human shape and slipped through the links of the fence.

"Which way back to the truck?" Morgan asked as she stood up.

"You're back!" the girl who had pet Morgan as a wolf said, excitedly. Then she looked around in confusion. "Where's the puppy?"

"Patrolling," Morgan said, cutting off any further hilarious references Smithers may have been cooking up. "Pack animals are good with that."

The explanation seemed to satisfy the girl, who looked to be younger than her sister, though probably not by much. In fact, looking at the older of the two girls, Morgan didn't feel she was far off from her own age. Maybe four or five years. Both of them clung tightly to their mother and Morgan felt a small wave of jealousy wash over her as she thought of the lavender scent of home being carried on a warm breeze.

"Truck is this way," Smithers said, interrupting her thoughts.

He began trudging through the dark, icy streets as a light dusting of snow began to fall. Morgan shivered slightly, wishing she'd gotten more than a sweatshirt to keep her warm and found herself missing the furs she'd have during the winters back home.

The sounds of sirens were now apparent even to her human ears, and she could tell the others were getting nervous too. With the way the city was built, all stone and tall buildings, it was nearly impossible to tell what direction the sirens were coming from. At any moment one of the cop cars could come bounding around the corner and spy them, a large group of people wandering where they shouldn't be while covered in wounds and blood.

Morgan heard the blood roaring in her ears as her heart began to beat faster. She hadn't been this nervous fighting against the mob in the warehouse where there had been bullets flying past her, but then she had the strength of the wolf on her side. She currently felt drained and feared that she had pushed herself too hard in that last fight, drawing too much on the power of the earth. Exhaustion was beginning to set in. If they were attacked now, she would be of little to no help.

The roar of blood was replaced by another familiar roar. Morgan turned in time to see the flaring light of a single yellow eye come tearing around the corner of the street behind them. The beast roared as it sped towards them, the rider on its back donned all in black leather, helm completely obscuring his face.

"The Black Rider," Luis hissed, hand going for his weapon, but not drawing it immediately.

"Go that way and you'll get picked up by the cops," the black rider said, his voice somewhat muffled from within the helm. "You want to head left, down that alley. Loop around to where your truck is parked. You'll get home safely."

"Who are you," Timm asked, his voice accusatory.

"Not a friend," the black rider said, twisting the head of the beast he rode upon. "But not your enemy either."

For a moment, Morgan thought he looked directly at her. She looked back, where she thought his eyes might be, but saw nothing besides her own reflection in the helm. The beast beneath him roared to life and the moment ended with him disappearing into the night, the sound of his mount piercing the night with its screams.

"Nice guy," Smithers said.

"He's the one that saved my life," Lee said. "Got me out of the way of those gunmen."

"He's the one we saw leaving the police station," Timm added. "Did you see the writing on the back of the bike."

"Not very appropriate," Norah said, watching as the rider vanished.

"No," Morgan agreed. "But I think we should trust him."

Smithers looked at her and seemed to be weighing something in his mind. The sound of sirens got louder and the old man shook his head.

"Every instinct I have is screaming not to trust him," Smithers said. "But I'm going to trust Morgan on this one."

Smithers nodded at the alley. "Let's listen to biker-boy."

Morgan smiled as Smithers hurried them down the alley. She had been standing in the back by him and only ducked down just as the flashing red and blue lights of the police car that had been down the street Smithers had originally been leading them towards sprang to life and took off down the road to the warehouse they had just come from.

"Well," Smithers said. "I'll be damned."

"Seems he was trustworthy after all," Morgan said, smirking.

The sound of gunshots rang out in the distance. Morgan turned toward them, the bottom of her stomach falling out as she realized it was the direction the black rider had gone.

"All things considered," Smithers said nervously, "How about we just put that in the maybe pile and file it away for later."

Morgan nodded, not fully understanding the nuance of what Smithers said, but getting his meaning. Hurrying, they all made their way back to the truck. Smithers put the women in the cab with him, and threw a tarp over the rest of them in the bed of the truck to not attract attention from any police about 'why he was hauling bloodied youths in the back of his truck.'

The trip back to the church was longer and less comfortable than it had ever been. She found herself sandwiched between

Timm and a lump of metal that housed a spare tire according to its label. Under the blue tarp, everything was tinged with its hue, and neither water nor scent could escape its bind. Morgan felt sick with the remnants of blood and sweat that emanated around her, but managed to control her stomach in a desperate attempt to avoid adding the scent of vomit to the mix.

When Smithers pulled the tarp away, Morgan was the first to vault over the side of the truck and breathe the piercing cold air in deeply. It was so cold it burned the inside of her lungs, but Morgan didn't care. The fresh air was all she needed.

"Okay," Smithers said. "Let's get them inside and comfortable."

"Good idea," Timm said, starting for the door.

"Wait," Smithers said, grabbing Timm's arm. "Not you, you go take a shower. Lee, go get him some new clothes."

Lee nodded. "I'll check and see if the thrift shop is still open."

With that Lee led Timm inside, ignoring any and all protests that he was fine and just wanted to talk to Father Mitchell.

"Someone should talk to him," Luis said, once Timm was out of earshot.

"Yeah," Smithers said with a sigh. He looked exhausted. Morgan felt for him.

"Do you want us to do it?" Morgan asked.

"I really should handle it," Smithers said, straightening up. Morgan could hear his bones cracking as he did.

"You should get some rest," Luis said. "Take Norah and the children to Carl and lay down. Morgan and I are more than capable of reporting our success to Father Mitchell."

Smithers looked for a moment like he was going to argue, but his glassy eyes looked over the two of them and finally he just nodded.

"Just report and come to bed," Smithers said, shuffling off towards the church, gesturing for Norah to follow with her girls. "We can figure out our next step in the morning."

Morgan and Luis watched them disappear into the church. They stood there for a moment and did not speak. The wind was cold, and though Morgan felt the urge to shiver, she looked over at the stoic Luis and saw that the cold could not seem to touch him.

"You're thinking about him, aren't you?" Morgan asked.

"The Black Rider," Luis said, his voice cold.

"Do you think he is our enemy?" Morgan asked. "He saved us. Twice."

"Where I come from, there was a knight who wore all black armor," Luis explained. "He had been in a holy order and was revered across the land. Then one day, he turned his back on his god, his shield brothers and sisters, and donned the black armor. He had broken his oath."

"You think it's the same man," Morgan asked.

"No," Luis said, and Morgan did not doubt that the knight knew for sure. "I fear that this man has broken his oath. Some words may be true, but caution is needed."

Morgan nodded, and as she did, Luis began to walk across the snow covered ground towards the church. She followed him into the warmth and light of the building. They made their way across the tile floor. Morgan noted the squeak of their shoes as they walked. By the time they made it to the curtain that Father Mitchell was using to block off his bedroom, the light was on and Father Mitchell called from inside.

"Come in," the priest called. "Door's unlocked."

Luis and Morgan stepped through the curtain to find the Father sitting at a small desk next to his bed. He was dressed simply, though lacked the white collar Morgan had grown so accustomed to seeing him in. He turned around in his chair and looked them over before standing up.

"Shall I ask why it's only two of you coming to see me?" he asked playfully, though Morgan could hear the note of fear in his voice.

"Timm needed a shower," Morgan explained. "And new clothes."

"Lee went to procure some," Luis added. "And we sent Smithers downstairs to deliver Carl's family to him and rest."

Father Mitchell breathed out a sigh of relief. "Good, I believe that means everyone is accounted for."

He paused for a moment, thinking.

"Why does Timm need new clothes again?" he asked.

"They are..." Morgan searched her mind for a word.

"Unsalvageable," Luis supplied.

"Ah," Father Mitchell said, presumably deciding he did not want to know exactly what Luis meant from the word choice.

"We just thought you'd want to know that everyone is safe and accounted for," Morgan said, smiling. "Now we'll let you get back to resting."

"Not much of that being done, I'm afraid," Father Mitchell said, smiling through his tired expression. "What with all the good works being done."

"You are a man who does good work," Luis agreed.

Father Mitchell shook his head. "I did not mean my own work; I meant your good works. The number of people you've helped since arriving on my doorstep in the middle of the night. It is staggering."

"You helped us," Luis said. "It is only fair."

"You've done more than balance the scales," Father Mitchell said with a laugh. "You walked into the lions' den and came out without a drop of blood on you."

"You should see Timm," Morgan said, suppressing a giggle.

Father Mitchell held up his hand. "Again, not something I'm overly interested in learning more about. Plausible deniability, remember."

"Right," Morgan said.

"But as I've said, you've been doing a lot of good work around here. You know what they say about work well done, right?" Father Mitchell asked them.

"No," Morgan said, cocking her head curiously. "What do they say?"

"It begets more work," Luis said, his tone was flat, but Morgan could see a smile creeping in on the edge of his mouth. "I assume that you have a task for us, Father?"

"I do, if you don't mind," Father Mitchell said, sighing. "I'm afraid I have no one else I can turn to on this matter."

"Don't worry," Morgan said, smiling brightly. "We'll always be around to help. Especially those in need."

"I'm glad to hear it," Father Mitchell said. "Go get some rest, you're going to need it for what's to come."

Morgan and Luis bid Father Mitchell good night and began walking down towards the basement. Luis wandered over to his cot, slipping the sword under the pillow where it would be within easy reach should he need it. Smithers lay snoring in his bed, still in the clothes he'd worn during the battle. Lee had returned with clothes for Timm and left them folded on his cot while he sat in the corner in prayer. The sound of the shower running complimented the curls of steam escaping from under the bathroom door told her Timm was relishing the hot water.

And in the corner, curled in an exhausted embrace, was Carl, Norah, and their two girls, asleep in each other's arms, holding themselves so close that nothing could ever tear them apart again.

Morgan smiled as she went over to her cot and laid down. She pulled the covers up around her, and thought for a moment of lavender and warm breezes. Then she thought of cold air and smiling faces, of jokes and references she couldn't possibly get, of fearlessness and faith, and of passion and good work. She fell asleep, happy to know that no matter what her future held, these things would continue to be present, whatever world she found herself in.

**Listen to more on the podcast
Reliably Chaotic! Available wherever
podcasts are sold.**

*Visit us at: www.reliablychaotic.com/ or
www.patreon.com/ReliablyChaotic*